HEXED IN HAWES

A DI ADAMS MYSTERY

KIM M. WATT

For further information contact www.kmwatt.com

Cover design: Monika McFarland, www.ampersandbookcovers.com

Editor: Lynda Dietz, www.easyreaderediting.com

ISBN ebook: 978-1-991381-01-9

ISBN paperback: 978-1-991381-02-6

First Edition October 2025

10 9 8 7 6 5 4 3 2 1

CONTENTS

To you, lovely reader,
who has followed the adventures of snarky cats and crime-solving
dragons, and embraced invisible dogs and inexplicable ducks.
Thank you, always.
You are truly magical.

A NOTE BEFORE WE BEGIN

Lovely people, thank you for joining me for another wild romp through the Dales.

Well, less *romp*, more *increasingly frantic chase with ever-higher stakes*. I mean, it wouldn't be an Adams book if it wasn't, would it?

I will firstly offer an apology to the lovely people of Hawes, and assure them that I don't really think their village is rife with aggressive sheep and lurking Fae, but is instead very delightful and a lovely place for a family holiday (and the creamery is definitely worth a visit). I'm also sorry for taking certain liberties with the landscape, but, you know. Writer's license and all that.

Honestly, the Dales is one of my favourite places in the world, and Hawes is a beautiful part of it. It'd be worth risking the sheep for a visit even if they *were* a problem. Which they're not. Promise.

With that disclaimer taken care of, I am going to assume you, lovely reader, have arrived here after a meander through the previous books in DI Adams' series. If not, I shall reiterate my usual assurance that you won't be *too* lost if you haven't read the others (although questions about invisible dogs and safe caffeine levels may persist).

I shall also let Beaufort Scales readers know where this book fits into the series: between *Coming Up Roses* and *Beast-Laid Plans* for those of you keeping track. The full reading order can be found on the website, should you be interested.

Everyone caught up? No one from the Hawes tourist board still eyeing me suspiciously? Good.

Grab your duck and your very big stick.

You're going to need them …

Happy reading!
Kim

1

———

FINE & DANDY

THE DAY WASN'T MEANT TO START LIKE THIS.

No day was meant to start like this.

Although, Adams had to admit as she leaned out of her gate and stared down the path toward the woods, it was a less unlikely start than she might've imagined just a couple of years back, and a *whole* lot less unlikely than she'd have chosen, given the chance.

Somewhere a night bird screeched, and something pale flitted through the trees, and her breath caught, her hands tightening on the baton and her rubber duck–shaped brass keyring. To the left, fields washed up to the houses on the edge of town, while on her right the last of those houses gave way to farmland. The streetlights were distant, the paths were empty, and the moon cast a thin, pale glow over the fading night. No cars rumbled in the distance, no insomniac looked out of a window to see her daring the night. She could've been the last person in an empty world.

She bloody well wasn't, though. There was *someone* in those woods. And they'd been in her house.

Detective Inspector Adams stepped out into the silence of

the long pre-dawn, her pale blue pyjama bottoms near luminous in the dark, and whistled again for Dandy.

There was still no sign of him, and the shadows seemed a
little deeper for it.

Not that it was going to stop her.

SHE'D WOKEN with her heart already going too fast, breath
tight in her chest and a light sweat clinging to her shoulders
despite the open window. She resisted the urge to roll
straight to her feet, holding herself in place with one hand
clutching the bottom sheet. She couldn't recall what she'd
been dreaming of – monsters over rivers or under cities,
stalking automatons or swift-footed wolves, faeries or
goblins or sodding toothy hamsters. Or possibly geese. Geese
were always an issue.

She checked her watch. Two a.m. A thoroughly useless
time. Too early to get up, but already so late it almost guaranteed she wasn't getting any more decent sleep. She rolled
over, automatically making room for Dandy, who, despite
her being fully aware dogs on beds – even invisible dogs –
were generally frowned upon, always slept on about eighty
per cent of hers. She stretched, frowned, then reached out
with one hand, followed by a foot.

"Dandy?" She sat up, scanning the dim bedroom. The
glow of the one light on the road outside seeped through her
gauzy curtains, barely bright enough to sketch the room in
indeterminate lines and shapes, but Adams could see enough
to tell it was empty. No LED-red eyes glowing in the darkness, or shaggy, Labrador-sized form blotting the carpet. Not
that she'd ever seen him sleep on the carpet when there was
furniture not designed for him available, but Dandy was as
variable in his habits as he was in his size.

She started to reach for the bedside light, then stopped. The whole night felt *off*, uneasy and strange, like lightning glimpsed on the horizon, silent and full of threat. She reached for the bedside drawer instead, easing it open and dipping her hand inside. Her collapsible baton was there, instantly reassuring, and next to it a keyring holding her car keys, a mini multi-tool, and, more importantly, a small rubber duckie worked in brass. Technically the duck was a torch, but she didn't squeeze its wings to activate the LED bulb, just closed her hand over it carefully.

Only once she had both the baton and the duck securely in hand did she sit up. She didn't take her time, didn't try to be sneaky about it, simply rolled straight off the bed and put her back to the wall, eyes on the bedroom door. No movement on the small landing beyond, and she could see a window of moonlight lying across the rented house's worn carpet, thrown from the bathroom.

Still no Dandy.

She crossed the room and stepped softly out onto the landing, then checked the bathroom and the tiny second bedroom, which still contained half a dozen boxes she hadn't quite got around to unpacking. Nothing to explain her unease, other than the persistent lack of an invisible dog. She wondered vaguely if he'd suddenly become invisible to her as well as everyone else, but she was fairly certain he'd have tripped her over by now if that was the case.

Movement, and her breath caught in her throat, her hand tightening on the baton.

No, not movement *exactly*. A shifting, an unfamiliarity in the old house's air. The feeling of her space containing someone else, the awareness she wasn't alone. She tried to peer downstairs without leaning too far into the stairwell itself, but it was impossible. All she could see was the last tread, and the light coming through the glass in the front door. No shadows painted in it, no dirty footprints on the rug, but someone was here, or had been. The hairs on her neck and the twist of her belly were sure of it.

The stairs were as old as the rest of the terraced house, but she'd been here long enough to know their quirks and creaks. She took her time, bare feet silent on the carpet, and once she arrived on the tiny patch of entrance hall below, she went straight to the door and checked it. Locked. Not that it necessarily meant anything around here. Dandy didn't need a door, locked or unlocked. He simply passed through dimensions by his own mysterious methods, just like cats did.

Straight into the front room, with its rarely used TV and comfily sagging sofa, the curtains still open over the big window that looked over the street. She kept close to the wall as she slipped across to it, peering out from the cover of the room's shadows. Across the road, the houses were chunky semi-detached numbers with small front gardens that held patches of lawn and bins and flowerpots and shrubbery, but there was no movement in any of them. The houses themselves were dark, the street still, no unfamiliar cars or suspiciously late-night pedestrians to be seen. It looked perfectly civilised and peaceful, any quiet Yorkshire neighbourhood slumbering its way toward the early summer dawn. The back of her neck was still chilled under her head wrap, though, and her arms prickled with the tension of the hairs standing to attention. Something was definitely off, and maybe it was just Dandy being missing, but she didn't think so.

The kitchen was at the back of the house, and opened directly off the front room. It was a compact, tidy space equipped with a tiny table holding two chairs, the worktop clear and the whole place still smelling warmly of coffee and last night's cheese on toast dinner. It was as empty as the rest of the house, nowhere to hide anyone bigger than a stray cat (and while Dandy was no fan, and cats were more of an issue than Adams had previously imagined, a cat wouldn't have chased him out). Whoever had been here was gone.

Adams whistled, then called, "Dandy?"

No response, not that she'd expected one, and that uneasy feeling in her stomach tightened into something hard and ugly. Someone *had* been here. She could feel it, like finger-prints smudged on a glass, shadows of a stranger. So where was the bloody dog? Had they *done* something to him? Surely he'd have woken her otherwise.

"Dammit," she whispered to the night, and pulled on her trainers from the rack by the back door before snapping the baton out to full length, the noise hard and angry in the empty house.

She didn't open the door straight away, taking a moment to examine her little back garden through the window over the sink. Unsurprisingly, it was empty, and even the low light couldn't disguise the fact it was in need of some care, her half-hearted attempts at a handful of flowerpots mostly reduced to scraggly, half-dead things. The flagstones that formed a small patio area below the concrete step to the door needed a good pressure washing, too, but the light was kinder to that. Tall wooden panelling divided her garden from her neighbours', and at the bottom a gate led out to a dirt path, and beyond that the fields, racing to meet the countryside that encircled the town. It was darker on this side of the house, away from the streetlight, the stars pinholes to brighter planes, and the fell that rose in the distance was a deeper shadow in the night, blank and near featureless under a thin moon.

Adams stepped out onto the worn mat at the back door and shivered, considering going back inside for a hoody and a sports bra. Dandy's absence and the sense she'd felt *some-*

thing when she was upstairs made things feel urgent, though. If something – some*one* – was out here, she was already playing catch-up.

She pulled the door closed and locked it, just in case anyone got past her, gaze shifting warily over the night. She checked both neighbours' gardens, pulling herself up to peer over the fences, but they were as empty as her own, other than a startled rabbit who froze among some carefully caged lettuces.

"You're not going to be popular, mate," she murmured, and dropped back down, turning to the gate.

Out on the path, she looked each way uncertainly. Left led back toward town, while right led to a small woodland and more fields, farmland and greenery reasserting itself. Both directions looked equally empty, although the shadows were deep and there were plenty of hiding places – even assuming her intruder was human-sized, and that, she'd discovered, was a *large* assumption. She sighed. Somewhere cattle lowed, and a motorbike growled on a distant road, but otherwise all was stillness, expectant or watchful, or both.

The last time she'd been out here in the middle of the night it had been winter, everything ice and frozen earth, and she'd had a very unpleasant tussle with small, unseen assailants. She didn't fancy a repeat, especially not without Dandy. Nor did she want to meet any other non-humans, now she thought about it. The more Folk she encountered, the less she fancied running into them on a dark night. Although she had to be fair. There were plenty of humans she wouldn't want to meet either. But she could arrest them, at least.

She whistled again, the sound high and carrying in the crisp air. It might be summer, but the Dales only gave so much credence to the season. She waited a moment, then whistled again. Still nothing.

And maybe it *was* nothing. She no more understood what Dandy did with his time than she understood his curious relationship with the laws of physics as she knew them. He could be off on his own Dandy jollies, with no idea she was even looking for him. He was, in actual fact, quite probably fine and dandy.

Adams sighed even more deeply. She was evidently spending too much time around DI Colin Collins. If she wasn't careful she'd be collecting cheese and cooing over trains.

But the danger of bad jokes was hardly the important thing right now. What was, was the fact it wasn't just a missing Dandy or a nightmare that had her out here in the pre-dawn chill. Her skin was still crawling, the hair standing to attention like she was a cat with its hackles showing. Even when she'd been a regular copper, blissfully ignorant of things like invisible dogs and mystery ducks and hidden dimensions, she'd known this feeling, and never disregarded it. It had seen her safe when logic would've left her felled in a London backstreet.

She tapped her baton lightly against her leg, the duck held loosely in her other hand, and waited. Sometimes that was the best tactic. If one waited long enough, something would show itself. Although she felt more like *she* was the one showing herself, exposed on the open path despite the low light, and when a cat leaped to the fence of the house next door she started, lifting her baton automatically as she turned. The cat hissed, baring its teeth, and she frowned.

"Where did you come from? You don't live here." There were cats on the street, of course – bloody things were everywhere – and she'd found herself cataloguing them the way she did humans, a reflexive listing of presence and characteristics. Skinny one-eyed tabby two doors down. Alarmingly large ginger tom across the road, with a belly that brushed the grass when he walked. An assortment of half a dozen (at least) variously coloured cats living with a cranky older woman at the end of the street, who yelled at them all indiscriminately, mostly to accuse them of stealing her dinner, her sherry, and her socks. Two sleek black cats living diagonally opposite Adams, with a couple who pretty clearly couldn't tell them apart.

So yes, plenty of cats. She was aware of their scrutiny, even though she didn't acknowledge them. That was risky, according to the one cat she did speak to. It'd draw attention to her, and apparently that could bring undefined but severe consequences. She felt having an invisible dog probably drew enough attention, but she wasn't about to start talking to the neighbourhood cats anyway. She didn't need that on her reputation. It was bad enough being from Down South. Also, cats were so bloody annoying, even when they didn't talk.

But there wasn't anyone else around to ask, so she said, "Seen anyone unusual out?"

The cat – a lean brown tabby-ish thing with distinctive, cheetah-like markings, who gave off a distinctly feminine air – lifted her lip slightly, showing a tooth, but didn't answer. She remained balanced on the top of the fence, moonlight reflected in her eyes, and they stared at each other.

"Helpful sort, aren't you?" Adams asked.

The cat narrowed her eyes, and seemed to be on the verge of saying something, then movement down the path, toward the woods, caught both their attention. For a moment Adams thought it must be Dandy, but the shape was wrong, the dimensions uneasy. It was four-legged, or seemed to be, but it was hard to be sure in the distance and the dark. All she could make out was a pale form fading in and out on the edges of the trees, too heavy to be a deer, too slight to be a cow, and too tall to be either, unless her sense of proportion was way off. Which didn't seem impossible – the thing was ill-defined and *unsettling,* and she couldn't say why. Just some old instinct sitting up and screaming at the unknown, perhaps.

Then it turned toward them and her breath caught. The goosebumps on her arms violently recruited more on her neck and back, and she drew toward the fence, for whatever scrap of cover it might offer. She could feel the thing's regard, ancient and alien, and her hand tightened on the duck, not enough to turn the light on, but enough to feel the comforting bite of its wings. Her heart was so loud in her ears it drowned out the night, and she swallowed hard, shouting down the part of her mind that seemed to have decided flight was the best option. She was a copper. If there were any instincts calling the shots around here it was going to be *fight.*

She, the cat, and the thing in the woods stared at each other, and another figure appeared next to the creature. This one had a more human shape, tall and slim, and while Adams couldn't see their face, she was as aware of their regard as she was of the beast's. They raised their hands, and for one confused moment she thought they were waving for her attention, then the cat hissed by her head, and she realised she was looking at some unknown, creepy-spooky Folk of a kind she'd never encountered before, and they were quite likely about to hurl some sort of curse at her.

"*Bollocks,*" she hissed, and dived for the nearest gate, trying to fumble it open as the night thrummed with sudden heat and power, that imagined, distantly glimpsed lightning feeling like it was gathering overhead.

"Get off!" the cat squawked as the fence wobbled with Adams' attack on the gate. "Get your own spot!"

Adams ignored her, scrabbling one hand through a round gap in the wooden panel and trying to find the latch. The hair on her arms was making an active attempt to detach itself as static gathered around them, and the cat hissed again, directing it at the woods rather than Adams. She glanced over her shoulder, and the figure seemed closer, or larger, still indistinct, both hands raised and held out to their sides, and that pale, glimmering form still lurking behind them, some vast and ghostly stag perhaps, horned and fragmented and impossible. Her chest was tight with the fright of it, the sheer impossibility of what she was seeing, and static snapped at her fingertips, making her jerk back from the gate. The whole night was alive with creeping electricity, sparks arching and dancing on the fence and among the trees, and Adams gave up on trying to escape, raising the duck instead and aiming it at the advancing figure.

"Detective Inspector Adams, North Yorkshire Police," she announced, her voice firm and clear. "Stop right there."

"Genius," the cat said. "You really think that's going to work?"

"I don't see you doing anything," she snapped back.

"That's because I'm smart enough to know you can't arrest the Old Folk, Detective Inspector Adams," the cat said, her voice smooth and authoritative. "You're out of your depth."

"Oh? So I should just sit on a fence and be snotty about it?"

"If you know what's good for you," the cat said, and they stared at each other until a snap of particularly vicious static spat from the fence to the cat's nose, and she yowled, jerking backward and almost falling off.

"Good for you, was it?" Adams asked, then her attention was pulled back to the approaching creature, which had swept forward in a wash of pressure, setting her eardrums popping and her skin crackling. She tried to step forward, to speak up again, but found herself frozen in place, mired in fright and dismay while the looming, pale beast from the woods swelled over the shoulder of the oncoming figure – the Old Folk, whatever that was when it was at home – and the night grew darker and deeper, the human world more distant, and as much as she tried to tighten her hand on the duck, to use its light, she couldn't seem to manage it.

And she might've stood there until the Old Folk plucked her from the earth, helpless and unresisting, except movement surged in the field, and she, the cat, and the two creatures swung toward it, Adams suddenly able to move as the suffocating grip on her slipped. A great, hairy beast bounded through the short-cropped grass, dreadlocks flying and red eyes glowing, looking like a black sheep gone huge and feral and a little grey.

"Old Ones' *sake*," the cat muttered, and vanished into the garden.

Adams ignored her, clamping her hand down on the duck and sending a pale, somewhat uncertain beam of light down the path. "Hold it right there," she ordered the intruders. Or tried to – in the moment her attention had been captured by the oncoming Dandy, both the pale stag-like form and the upright one had vanished. She frowned, peering toward the woods, but there was no sign of them. They were just *gone*. There was only Dandy, flying toward her with his LED-red eyes alight in the dark.

He hurdled the drystone wall at the edge of the field effortlessly and slid to a stop so close she had to step back to avoid him trampling over her feet. He was bigger than usual, and she put a hand on his head, examining him.

"What's happening?"

He just panted up at her, tail wagging gently, and she pointed at the woods.

"What was that? Was it to do with the cat?"

His mouth snapped shut, tail drooping as he looked over

his shoulder at the woods, then up at the fence, nose twitching.

"No—" she started, but he was already leaping for the top of the wooden wall. He barely tapped it with his paws as he went over, setting it wobbling again, then vanished into the garden to the accompaniment of snapping bamboo stakes and tumbling pots.

"*Dandy!*" She pulled herself up on the fence so she could peer over the top. "Get out of there!"

He looked up at her, then crashed through a few more tomato plants on his way to the other side of the garden, where he leaped over the next fence and disappeared again, presumably in pursuit of the unknown cat.

"More worried about the forest monsters," she hissed after him, but he didn't reappear. She dropped back to the path and scanned the field and the path to the woods. The landscape looked empty and innocuous, and she shivered as the cool air made itself felt. That sense of a lowering storm had dissipated entirely, and somewhere a normal, non-dandy dog barked. Further off, a truck changed gears, the sound muted and commonplace, a landmark in a world tilting at the edges.

She could almost believe she'd imagined the whole thing.

Not quite, though.

But whatever it had been – whatever *they* had been – it was gone, and she wasn't poking into the woods looking for footprints in the dark. The night might feel more familiar now, but everything could change once she was under the cover of the trees. She turned away from them and went back to her own gate, letting herself in and already vaguely calculating if it was worth trying to sleep before she had to get up again.

She was halfway to the door when Dandy came plunging over the fence, took a stand between her and the house, and started barking, a flat, hard, warning sound. She stopped short, staring at him.

"What?"

He just kept barking, and she looked from him to her house, that creeping dread back in her belly.

She had an idea she wasn't getting any more sleep tonight.

2

CAFFEINE, HEXES, & CAT-SIGNALS

"*Shh*," Adams said, holding one hand out to Dandy.
"Come on, enough."

He kept barking, regular and flat, a hard-edged warning.

"*Stop*," she snapped. "I get it."

He did stop, finally, his floppy ears back. With his heavy, dreadlocked coat it was impossible to see if his hackles were up, but she was sure they were. It was in the stiffness of his legs as well as the tension in her own shoulders. They stood there in the sudden, empty silence left in the wake of his barking, and she waited for lights to come on and the neighbours to start shouting at her from the windows, telling her to keep it down, but of course that didn't happen. Most people could no more hear Dandy than they could see him (although she'd noticed that he was apparently easier to hear than see, for those who were a little more open to such things, resulting in some very confused walkers when he was chasing squirrels *in* the trees), so all they'd notice was her out here in the dark in her pyjamas, waving her baton, shouting at nothing, and talking to cats. Great optics. Just what she needed to turn up on bloody TikTok or something. That'd definitely land her a serious chat with her DCI.

She straightened up, adjusting the front of her T-shirt, and looked around as casually as she could. No one seemed to be peering out from behind the curtains of the houses to either side of her in the row. It didn't mean they weren't, of course, but it made her feel slightly better.

Dandy hadn't moved, his shaggy paws planted wide and his head low. He was back to his favourite golden retriever size, which seemed to suggest there was no immediate threat, but he definitely wasn't relaxing.

"What is it?" she asked, her voice low. Behind him, the kitchen door was still shut, as she'd left it, and she couldn't see anything immediately wrong.

He shifted, pointing his nose at the heavy mat which lived directly outside the door, theoretically to stop him dragging every dead leaf in the woods inside with him. She squinted at it. It was out of alignment, and her stomach twisted, although there was no reason why that should worry her. It wasn't like she kept a key under there or anything, unlike a bewilderingly large proportion of the population. But it did indicate *something* had happened. The mat was hefty and rubber-backed, and she'd never had to adjust it since she'd put it down. Plus, she was almost certain it had been straight when she left the house.

She stepped up to join Dandy on the flagstones of the small patio, and they looked at the mat, taking up most of the one big step that led from the door to the patio. Adams started to crouch for a closer look, and Dandy growled.

"Easy," she said, and he subsided but still watched closely, panting on her shoulder as she eased the tip of her baton under the mat, trying to flip it over. The rubber-backed hessian was too bulky, though, so after a few fumbled attempts she simply slid it sideways, hoping she wasn't destroying any evidence in the process.

The mat made a scraping sound as it moved, feeling too loud and toothy in the silence, but flopped off the step easily enough. Dandy growled again, and Adams put a hand on his back, as much to reassure herself as to quiet him.

On the slightly grimy stone someone had left some marks. She couldn't call them drawings, or even a design. They weren't much to look at, no skulls and crossbones or poison bottles. They didn't glow with threat, or look like they'd been scorched into the flags with magical flames. In fact, they looked like they'd been etched there using the time-honoured teenage technique of rough scratching using any handy sharp thing, like a stone or an old nail, which was pretty unimpressive.

She frowned at the marks. There was no language she could recognise, and the sharp-angled cross-hatchings and twisted spines that linked the marks made no real sense, but she was certain they weren't random. They meant *something*, and she didn't need Dandy's deep, steady growling to tell her not to touch them. Something about the proportions and how they met was *wrong*, as if they pressed into some impossible dimension, whispering of teeth and terror, cold nights and high skies and screaming silence. Or shining, horned beasts in shadowed woods, and electrical storms on the horizon.

Adams shivered, fishing her phone out of her pocket with stiff fingers, and snapped a couple of photos before gingerly retrieving the mat and dropping it back into place. The night felt immediately warmer with the marks covered.

She straightened up, looking around the little yard as if the mystery sketcher might've left a calling card, some sign as to who they were and what they wanted. She couldn't see anything else out of place, though, and looked back at Dandy instead. "Any ideas?"

He tipped his head. He'd stopped growling now the marks were covered again, but his tail was still down, and the thin moonlight made him shadowy and strange, his luminous red eyes still unsettling after all this time.

Adams pointed at the door, but before she could even ask, Dandy growled again, deeper and more pointed than before.

"Right. Clear enough." She turned and went back down the garden, Dandy loping past her and vanishing through the gate before she could open it, not that she saw him do it. It just sort of *happened*, and all her brain could offer up in explanation was the suggestion that maybe he'd never been on this side of the gate to start with. She didn't argue with it. That way lay migraines. And at least it suggested there was nothing to worry about out there. Whatever had been in the woods – and had presumably left the marks, since she doubted she'd had two sets of creepy nocturnal visitors, or she hoped she hadn't – must be gone.

Even so, she kept her baton at the ready as she joined Dandy on the path, checking both ways before heading right, away from town and toward the shadow of the waiting trees. Still no movement, and no sense of that gathering, unseen tempest, and soon after, they skirted the last house in the row and turned right again, hurrying down a little snicket to end up back out on the road, still as empty and silent as it had appeared from the house.

Her car was pulled up to the kerb outside her house, and she clicked it unlocked as they approached, then opened the boot to dig inside. It held a bag of gym gear, the ubiquitous wellington boots, a high-vis jacket, a kit bag of various work equipment (some police-specific, others rather more her-specific), and a large wooden stick that could probably be called a staff. It hadn't come out of the boot since she'd needed it to deal with a sorcerer's book, but it always made her feel vaguely reassured to see it there, even if she always opted for her collapsible baton as a much more manageable option.

She dug a workout hoody out of her gym bag and pulled it on, giving a little shiver of appreciation at the extra layer, then approached her front door warily. The terraced row had no front gardens as such, just a couple of shallow steps leading from the pavement up to the door, and through the bay window she could see the kitchen light spilling softly across the lounge floor. For one moment she felt like a voyeur, peering in at her own life, the walls she hadn't hung pictures on yet, the empty sofa with a throw on the back, the coffee table devoid of any welcoming clutter. The place looked like one of the sparser sort of Airbnbs, or perhaps the aftermath of a split, someone run off with half the contents.

She grimaced slightly, and stopped before she reached the steps, looking at Dandy. He looked from her to the mat and back again, and gave a considered growl.

"Really?" She poked the mat with her baton, ignoring his escalating growls as she fumbled it aside. Sure enough, another set of marks lurked beneath, twins to the one out the back, or near enough. Not that she was an expert, but they certainly set her teeth on edge just the same as the others. She tucked her baton under one arm so she could take a photo, then replaced the mat and stepped back, looking longingly at the kitchen light. Her coffee machine was in there.

But even if she'd wanted to brave the strange marks with their deep undertow of threat, Dandy was watching her with stiff legs and his ears back. When she tried to step to the window, to get a closer look inside and see if there were any signs of an intruder, he slipped in front of her, so she bumped into him before she could get close enough to touch the glass.

"Not even a peek?" she asked him, and he leaned against her legs, impossibly solid for a creature who walked through walls. "Okay." She scuffed him behind the ears and stepped back. Dandy might be as inconsistently helpful as he was variably sized, but when he *was* helpful, he tended to know what he was doing.

"Alright, then," she said aloud, and turned back to the car. At least she still had that.

SHE LASTED in the car until the early Yorkshire dawn bloomed bright enough to steal the shadows from the street and the rich pinks and golds from the sky, sitting slouched down in the driver's seat with her eyes shifting from the mirrors to the house to the road in front of her, wishing she had some coffee, toast, chocolate, or basically anything at all to make the waiting more tolerable. Dandy, on the other hand, sprawled out on the back seat with all four paws in the air and snored contentedly.

His was evidently the correct approach. No one twitched the curtains of her house, or passed the upstairs windows, or crept down the snicket from the path to the woods. No ghostly stag-thing stalked along the street. No nefarious step-scratcher appeared to scratch more steps in a nefarious manner, which, now she thought about, wasn't an activity she was even sure how to define officially. Threatening graffiti, perhaps? She certainly couldn't arrest anyone for it, but she'd be having strong words.

There was no chance of it, though. The street remained steadfastly empty. Not even the unfamiliar cat came back, although she spotted the one-eyed tabby marching down the road with a struggling bird in its mouth and a determined set to its stride that made Adams think someone was about to get a very rude wake-up call.

She shifted in her seat, bracing her forearms on the wheel and taking a final look at her house. Nothing had changed, and the odds were nothing would now it was light. Although, how did she know? Maybe the strange cat had done it, and cats could turn up any bloody time or place they wanted without anyone questioning it. Or maybe it had been some other creature as invisible to her as Dandy was to everyone else. Or there was no reason for anyone to come back at all, because the marks didn't need minding. She didn't know enough about it, and she needed to fix that.

She checked her watch. It was after six, and she was desperate for both a coffee and the loo. She started the engine, setting Dandy scrabbling upright with a startled *whuff*.

"Great company, you are," she said, pulling away from the kerb.

He licked her ear, which she took to be an apology. And to be fair, she'd had worse stake-out partners.

At the station she let herself in the back door, having swapped her pyjama bottoms for her gym leggings while still in the car, and went straight to the staff room to put the coffee machine on. The place was empty, smelling faintly of window cleaner and old printer pages, and she took the coffee with her into the little office she shared with DI Colin Collins, wondering how long Dandy would keep her out of her house. She could only wander about in her gym gear for so long. At least she wasn't turning up to work in her pyjamas. Just because she had an invisible dog and talked to cats was no reason to let all her standards slide.

She took a grateful gulp of coffee and unlocked her phone, quickly tapping out a message and hitting send before shoving it back in the pocket of her leggings. Nothing would be open in town for her to get breakfast yet, so she checked Collins' desk drawers, finding a half-eaten packet of digestive biscuits lurking in the bottom one.

"Plain?" she muttered. "Standards are slipping."

But they were food, and she had caffeine. Everything else could wait.

THE REPLY to her message blipped in while she was still waiting for her next cup of coffee to dribble through the station machine.

Ooh, hexes! So cool! I'm on my way.

So cool was not a term Adams had considered applying to creepy hieroglyphs turning up at her front door, and she definitely hadn't invited anyone to come up and start poking around them. She hit dial.

The call was answered almost immediately, and an impossibly perky voice said, "DI Adams! You have *hexes!*"

"Morning, Chloe."

"Yes, morning. I'm just getting my stuff together and I'll be right there. You haven't moved anything, have you?"

"I didn't ask you to come up. I asked if you'd seen anything like them before," Adams pointed out.

"As if I *wouldn't* come up! Do you know how rare it is to see an *actual hex* in the wild? This is fantastic!"

"They're not in the wild. They're on my doorstep. Steps, even."

"You're not still at home, are you?" Chloe asked, her voice suddenly serious. "You shouldn't be in the house if you've got hexes on it. We don't know what they do yet."

"No, Dandy wouldn't let me go back in."

"You were out? Wild night in Skipton, was it?" Something

clattered, followed by a distinctly final-sounding smash. "Oops. Well, we probably don't need any distilled fell water gathered on the full moon in April, anyway. Regular tap water'll do just fine."

Adams pinched the bridge of her nose, closing her eyes briefly. They were gritty with sleeplessness, and she forced them open again before it could feel too comfortable, tucking her phone between her ear and her shoulder so she could put a second capsule in the coffee machine. "I wasn't out. I woke up and thought …" What had she thought, really? Now, with the caffeine kicking in, she wasn't sure anymore. "I must've heard something. When I got back Dandy wouldn't let me into the house."

"He's a good doglike creature. *Hmm.* I'm out of freeze-dried holly berries. I mean, we don't *need* them, but with a hex I'd rather be sure—"

"*Chloe.* I only asked you if you'd seen anything like those marks before. I don't want you rushing out here with your witchy emergency kit, or whatever you're thinking."

"Oh? And who else are you going to call?"

Adams could hear the smile in Chloe's voice, and she swallowed a sigh. It was true. She didn't exactly have some sort of supernatural helpline she could turn to. There was Thompson, who, as with all cats, came and went as he wanted, or there was Rory, but not only was he disconcertingly posh, all he really had was a library of semi-helpful books and a high tolerance for weirdness. And nice shoulders, but that was beside the point.

Chloe – whether she was a witch or not, and whatever that even meant – was the only person Adams knew who was likely to jump at the chance to help out, and didn't seem to have any sort of ulterior motive going on. The young woman ran an esoteric store called The Occult Onion in Leeds Market, and despite that, Adams had yet to see her in anything tie-dyed, or wearing crystals, or offering to realign anyone's chakras, which gave her at least a little credibility in Adams' eyes.

"*Fine,*" she said aloud. "But you're just having a look, right?"

"So you'd like them left in place, then? Cursed house your sort of aesthetic, is it?"

"Just … call me when you're close. I'll send you the address."

"Catch ya soon." Chloe disconnected, and Adams took her mug from the machine, rubbing her face wearily with her free hand. No crystals, true, but the perkiness was just about unbearable. No one who favoured that much black should be that perky.

ADAMS WAS WOKEN by the creak of the office door and Dandy's *whuff* of greeting. She looked up from where she'd had her face pillowed on her arms, squinting at Collins.

"Morning," he said, pausing in the doorway to examine her. He mostly filled it, a big man with short-cropped hair and a round, pink face. "Going for overtime, are you?"

"No," she said, yawning. "I've been hexed."

Collins nodded and headed for his desk, setting a large mug of tea down so he could pull his coat off. "It worries me that this doesn't seem *that* surprising. Who hexed you?"

"No idea, but Dandy won't let me into my own house. Chloe's on the way to take a look at them."

"The hexes?"

"Yes." She straightened up, stretching. "I wasn't inside when it happened, I don't think. I woke up and Dandy was gone, so I went out to find him and …" She stopped. She didn't want to think about the shape in the woods, antlered and monstrous, or what the cat had called the *Old Folk* and their creeping storm. It seemed faintly unreal now, the threat drained by daylight and caffeine, and she already felt ridiculous, talking about hexes. She needed more information before she started prattling on about monsters in the dark. "Anyway, Dandy finally turned up, but then when we went back to the house there were these marks under the doormats. Chloe says they're hexes."

Collins lowered himself into his chair, which gave a comfortable creak. "And Dandy won't let you past them?"

"No."

He looked around vaguely, evidently meaning to give Dandy an interrogatory glance. "I suppose he knows what he's looking at."

"Better than I do, anyway," Adams said with a sigh. "I spent the night in the car, but I didn't see anyone about. Just one strange cat."

"Do we need Thompson?"

"Yes. Can you charm him out with some smoked salmon or something?"

"I can try. We need to get a cat-signal."

Adams grimaced. "That's terrible."

"I know," Collins said cheerfully, and took a sip of his tea. "Do you need a toothbrush or something? Not meaning anything by it, but ..."

"Yeah, yeah." Adams pushed herself out of her chair and headed for the door. Chloe wouldn't be far off. She may as well get herself feeling at least slightly human.

3

MYSTICAL AT A PRICE

Adams was leaning against her car, trying to persuade the morning sun to join forces with the coffee and wake her up properly, when Chloe pulled up in a compact and well-worn pink Ford Ka with large eyelashes fitted to the headlights. She swung out, a slight young woman clad in black skinny jeans and a purple sports bra under an oversized black singlet that showed off her pale arms. It had a large tree printed on the front which was in the process of eating a terrified lumberjack.

"Ay-up," she said, grinning.

"Hadn't pictured you as an eyelashes person," Adams said, nodding at the car, and Chloe glanced at it.

"It's my mum's. Insurance took *ages* to pay out on the one that went into the tarn, and then they gave me such a tiny amount that I can currently just about afford a fifth-hand moped, if I get lucky. So I'm using Mum's until I decide what to do."

Adams grimaced. It wasn't *exactly* her fault that Chloe's car had ended up in the tarn, but it had been she who got

Chloe tangled up with werewolves – weres – which then led to the whole tarn situation. "Sorry," she said aloud.

"Don't be. Better for the planet," Chloe said, taking an ancient canvas satchel from the passenger seat. "And if this one gets nicked by weres it'll be no great loss."

"This is nothing to do with weres."

"How do you know? These could be revenge hexes for shutting down their magic beer scheme."

Adams could hardly argue, considering she had no idea who last night's intruder was, what they wanted, who they might be working with, or even if they were definitely responsible, so she just said, "What now?"

"Let's take a look," Chloe said, rubbing her hands together. "This is *amazing*."

"On second thoughts, the car does suit you," Adams said, and Chloe made a rude gesture at her. "Mostly, anyway."

They headed for the front door, Dandy pressing closer and closer to Adams, until he finally stopped dead in front of her, wedged obstinately against her legs. "We're just taking a look," she told him. He looked up at her, eyes mostly hidden by the dreadlocks, his stance stiff and unmoving. "I can't do anything to sort this out if I can't get near them, can I?"

"Is that your invisible pup?" Chloe asked.

"He doesn't want us any closer."

"Smart," Chloe said. Like every other non-Folk person Adams had come across (with the exception of one irritating journalist), Chloe couldn't see Dandy. She seemed more aware of his presence than most people, though, and she waved a hand vaguely in the air toward him. "We're going to figure this out," she told the pavement. "Look, I've got witch hazel."

Dandy looked from her back to Adams, not budging.

"He seems unimpressed."

Chloe gave her a sideways look. "He gets that from you."

Adams had a final sip of coffee, took the lid off her travel mug, and held it out just in front of Dandy. He leaned forward, but before he could take hold of the scarred plastic handle she held the mug away to the side. He hesitated. "Go on," she said. "We're not going in. Have your coffee and let us get on."

"I'm not sure even invisible dogs should have coffee," Chloe said.

"He just steals it if I don't give it to him."

"That's poor training, then." She grinned when Adams scowled at her, then added, "*Ooh*, the cup vanished!"

"That's what happens when he picks something up," Adams said, and stepped around Dandy.

They crouched in front of the step, both of them regarding the mat dubiously. Adams thought she could feel something greasy and unfriendly, hooks sunk into meat like the cruellest trap, and next to her Chloe shivered, her hands tightening into fists on her knees.

"Alright?" Adams asked.

"Sure." All the humour was gone from her voice, though, and she opened the top of the satchel, taking a pair of latex gloves out. "Want some?" she asked Adams.

Adams was about to refuse, since she usually had her own, then realised she was still in her gym gear. "Please," she said, and pulled on the pair Chloe handed her as the young woman found a small cloth pouch and shook a handful of stones and animal bones out of it. She placed them evenly around three sides of the mat, leaving the side pressed to the door clear, then took a piece of chalk from the bag. She sketched runes between the bones, while Adams watched curiously.

"What do they do?"

"Stop anything sucking us in," Chloe said.

"I don't think there's a black hole under there. I looked earlier."

"It could be a faery trap of some sort," Chloe said, still drawing. "Even if they don't suck you in, they can get into your head and before you know it you'll be spending every full moon running over the hills in your nightie, searching for another."

"Oh. Great."

She glanced at Adams. "Do you know anything else about it? Did you see anything?"

Adams hesitated. Even here, with the presence of the hexes looming in front of her, the midnight encounter with the Old Folk and its steed or familiar or lap-monster or whatever the hell it had been seemed faint and unreal. And it made no *sense*.

"I can't help you unless you tell me," Chloe said, and Adams gave her an appraising look. In the sunlight Chloe had a smattering of pale freckles across her nose, and her skinny frame made her seem even younger than she probably was, but her tone was no different to one Adams had used herself innumerable times, on any number of unhelpful individuals.

"There was a … thing."

"Right, *well*. A *thing*. That changes everything."

Adams scowled at her, and she grinned. Adams huffed. "A cat said it was an Old Folk?"

"An Old Folk? Really?"

"Yeah. What is that? I mean, it didn't look *physically* old, and the cat definitely said *an* Old Folk, as if it was a specific thing."

Chloe nodded. "It's another term for the Good Folk. The Gentry," she added, when Adams just gave her a puzzled look.

"It wasn't some posh sort in Hunter wellies."

"No, *the Gentry.* Fair Folk. Good People." Chloe shook her head when Adams still looked at her blankly. "Bloody hell, Adams. *Fae.*"

"Oh. Like faeries? I've met them. This one didn't look like that."

"A Gentry's a whole other cauldron of mischief. Technically a whole bunch of kinds are classed as fae, and *faeries* isn't even that specific, although if you want to get picky, they have to have wings to be a faerie. Loads of fae don't, and some of them are even decent sorts. But an Old Folk, or a Gentry, is very specific."

"Why do I feel that means specifically bad?"

"You know how sorcerers used to be near enough human, but became so powerful most of them are barely recognisable as that anymore?"

"Ah … yes?"

Chloe shook her head. "You really need to read some books."

"Give me the highlights."

"Well, a Gentry is to average fae what a sorcerer is to humans."

Adams rubbed the back of her neck. "That seems bad."

"It is. They're not even meant to be in the human world. They were banished, if I remember right."

"And do they hang out with … ghost stags?"

Chloe blinked. "Ghost stags?"

"Sort of?" Adams waved vaguely. "Big, horns, a bit glow-in-the-dark."

"That I need to look up," Chloe said, frowning, and looked back at the mat. "A Gentry being involved makes this even more likely to be a faery trap of some kind, though. Or a fae hex, but I have *no* idea how to deal with one of those."

Adams looked back at the mat, feeling that snarling electrical energy from the night before again, as if it had left echoes etched in her bones. "Do you mean someone's trying to suck me into faery land?"

"It's just Faery. But you'll be fine."

"Why? Because of Dandy?" She glanced around at him reflexively, but he was still occupied with trying to get the last dregs of coffee out of the mug.

"Well, that too. But mostly you'll be fine because, even if that happens, you know what faeries really are. You know they're not cutesy little sparkling wish-granters who can't wait to dress us up and send us to the ball, or super-sexy demi-gods with impossible abs come to ravage us in all sorts of delightful ways. So even if you get whisked off to Faery, you'll figure things out." She glanced at Adams. "Probably be the first person in history to arrest a Gentry, too."

Adams considered that for a moment, then said, "Thanks," and took her baton out, extending it without moving from her crouch. "Do you want me to lift the mat?"

"Not yet." Chloe went back to her runes, and Adams examined the street, waiting. It looked empty, but guaranteed someone would be curtain-twitching. Probably multiple someones. This was the problem with small places. London she could've had a full-on exorcism on her doorstep and all that would've happened was someone yelling at her to keep it down.

Eventually Chloe rocked back on her heels. "Alright. That should do it."

Adams peered at the markings on the stone, which circled the edge of the step. "What about the house side? There's none on there."

"I don't fancy reaching over to do it."

"Isn't that an issue?"

Chloe shrugged, then grinned. "We'll find out, won't we?"

"What sort of witch *are* you? Shouldn't you be all mystical about this?"

"I'm only mystical when I'm charging for it," Chloe replied, and got up. "Punters like the drama. Come on, one side each. Just flip the mat straight up against the door. I've put some herbs and stuff on it, so it should kind of close the circle itself."

Adams thought *kind of* seemed less than reassuring when they were talking about being sucked into Faery, and *herbs and stuff* was more like a recipe suggestion than a counter-hex, but she didn't say anything, just positioned herself at one corner of the mat and wriggled the tip of the baton under it. Chloe got ready on the other side, clutching a cheap-looking pen with a bank logo on the barrel. Adams considered pointing out it was a pretty rubbish magic wand, but decided not to. She preferred Chloe as she was rather than dressed for drama, after all.

"Ready? Flip," Chloe said, and they flicked the mat up, Adams pinning it against the door with the baton while Chloe rocked back on her heels, staring at the stone.

"What?" Adams asked. "How bad is it?"

"Um…"

Adams looked down at the hex. Or, rather, where the hex had been. The stone was blank, slightly greened with mossy growth, and not only didn't bear a single mark, there was no sign any had been there at all. She blinked at the step, then looked at Chloe. "Did your herbs get rid of it?"

"No."

"But it was there!"

Chloe poked the stone gingerly with the pen. "I can't feel anything."

"You did when we got here. You shivered." Adams could feel an accusatory tone sneaking into her voice, and she swallowed.

"True. I did feel something, but I tend to pick up on other

people's stuff. It might've just been a shadow of what you were feeling."

Adams looked at the step for a long moment, then turned and clicked her fingers at Dandy. He looked up, grabbed the mug, and trotted over to join them. "It was there," she said, pointing at the blank concrete, and he tried to sniff it with the mug still in his teeth, then whined. She wrestled it off him. "Check properly, you overgrown muppet."

He huffed, examined the step, then yawned and shook himself off before wandering back onto the street to stare at the two black cats, who were watching them from the low stone wall that enclosed the front garden of the house across the road.

"They *were* here."

Chloe looked up at the house. "You said there was one out the back, too?"

"Yes."

"Let's take a look." She headed back down the pavement, and Adams let the mat drop into place, frowning. It *had* been there. She was sure of it.

THE TWO BLACK cats watched them go, and Adams wondered if she should just ask the bloody creatures what they'd seen, but Thompson's warnings that not all cats were Watch, but any cat *could* be Watch still lingered. She'd never asked exactly how the Watch policed the divide between humans and Folk, or why they were the ones nominated to do so, or even just what made cats the best option for such a thing. She had learned over the last couple of years that many things made less sense than she'd like, and even more lacked explanation entirely. A duck wasn't just a duck, survival could hinge on chocolate, and physics was oddly pliable. Cats being some sort of secret police was hardly the revelation of the century. She'd always thought they looked like they were up to something, even before she'd known they actually were.

So talking to random cats was probably a good way to land herself with a whole lot of other troubles, and she had more than enough as it was between the ghost stag, the Gentry, and vanishing hexes. She caught up to Chloe, intending to ask her if there was some sort of invisible ink for hexes, when her phone rang. She fished it out of her pocket, glancing at the screen. *Mum,* it read, and Adams grimaced. This was not the moment at which she wanted to be fending off questions regarding her love life, workload, and eating habits. The family check-in would have to wait. She clicked the call to silent, and they rounded the corner of the little snicket that led to the path behind the row of houses, Adams looking warily for more cats as they went. She didn't see any, but that didn't mean they didn't see her. Cats were like that.

"Where did you see the ghost stag and the Gentry?" Chloe asked her.

"In the woods at first, then they – or the Gentry, at least, the other thing was kind of hard to make out – walked right toward me and this cat."

Chloe frowned. "So they put the runes down after?"

"I … don't think so? They seemed to take off when Dandy got back." Or maybe they had? Perhaps. Maybe the Gentry had already done the front door ones before she came out, and had somehow sneaked up behind her to do the back door while she was looking for Dandy. They'd have to have been fast, but she didn't know how fae worked.

"But they couldn't have put them there before," Chloe said. "You'd never have got out of the house."

"How do you know? Maybe they were one-way charms."

"That doesn't make any sense. What would the point be in shutting you *out* of your house? Anyone chucking hexes about would either be trying to drag you through a faery portal or trap you, maybe in like a time loop or something. Keep you out of the way for a while."

"Time loops are a thing?"

Chloe shrugged. "They're in the stories."

"Stories," Adams said, trying to keep her tone mild.

"All good stories have some truth in them," Chloe said, and Adams swallowed a sigh. She supposed they did, but it was hardly anything to be basing an investigation on. It wasn't *evidence,* wasn't anything one could photograph or bag up and file. It was *ephemeral,* and deeply annoying.

She took another glance at the woods, which stood green and innocuous along the path. An elderly man toddled toward the trees, accompanied by a stiff-legged, somewhat rotund golden Labrador, and Adams had to resist the urge to shout after him not to go into the shadows under the trees. They hid unseen things. But she could hardly explain that, so she just turned away and opened the gate into her garden, leading the way to the back door.

"Can you feel anything?" she asked Chloe, and the younger woman grimaced.

"Sort of? What do *you* feel?"

Adams looked at the mat, and shrugged somewhat help-lessly. She could still feel *something* clawing at her, but now she couldn't tell if it was memory or reality, or even remember exactly what she had felt last night. Everything felt uncertain and uneasy, the edges of the day crumpled by exhaustion and caffeine, so she just shook her head. "I don't know."

"Well, we'll figure it out."

Chloe treated this mat the same as she had the other, sketching out chalk runes and placing stones and bones and flower petals along three edges. Adams looked longingly up at her bedroom window as she waited, wishing she could at least go in and get some work clothes. It didn't seem worth risking being booted out of the timeline for, though.

"Alright," Chloe said, straightening up and wiping her hands on her jeans, leaving dusty white prints behind. "Let's have a look."

They took their positions at either side of the mat, and Adams said, "Ready? Lift."

The mat slapped against the door, and Adams kept it trapped there with her baton, looking at the bare stone beneath with a bleak sort of acceptance.

"*Huh*," Chloe said. She didn't move to touch the step, just stood up again.

"They were there."

"Oh, I believe you." Chloe looked directly at Adams as she spoke, and Adams found herself searching for the lie in her face, but she couldn't find it. "I mean, you sent me photos," the young woman added. "I can't see you faking them for a joke, or making up anything this detailed. You're neither that imaginative nor that fun."

"Thanks?"

"Sure," Chloe said cheerfully. "Look, *something* obviously happened. Maybe if we can find that cat they might have some answers."

"I don't trust cats."

"No one does. But they can be useful."

Adams couldn't disagree with that, and she sighed. "Alright, so what do I do? Can I go in, since the hexes are gone?" Or were never there, but she couldn't bring herself to believe that. She'd *felt* them, felt the raging hunger of them. Chloe was right. She wouldn't make that up.

"Do you want to go in?" Chloe asked. "Does that seem like a good idea?"

Adams looked at her door. There was nothing here now. She *wanted* to believe she could just step over the mat and go in, have a shower and get changed, make a coffee in her favourite mug and put on her comfortable, worn-in boots, then walk out into a world that might not make sense, but which she felt she still had a grip on, however tenuous at times. She sighed. That would be wonderful, until she discovered it was a hundred years later, or whatever happened in fairy tales. Or *faery tales* with an *e*, since apparently faeries could tell if someone was using *fairies*, and they were unpleasant enough that no one needed that.

"No," she admitted.

"There we go, then. For what it's worth, I wouldn't risk it either."

"Can you find out about vanishing hexes?"

"I can try," Chloe said agreeably. "How about your posh mate? He's got a fancy library, doesn't he?"

"Rory? Not fancy, but he's got some books." Adams had been spending some time trying to work her way through them, but what she really needed was someone to summarise them for her and present the highlights. The self-indulgent ramblings of a bunch of ancient rich old boys was hardly riveting reading. She always ended up drinking coffee in Rory's kitchen and arguing about the relative merits of chocolate brands instead.

"Try him," Chloe suggested.

"I can give you his number."

"I've got it. But you may as well do it."

Adams managed not to grimace. It was all the more reason to keep him out of it, just as she'd prefer to have kept Chloe's help to over the phone only, but increasingly she found herself needing the weird sort of expertise held by cats, witches, and impoverished human gentry. "Alright," she said aloud. "Well, thanks."

"Sure," Chloe said, following Adams as they headed out of the gate and onto the path. The fields beyond were luminous in the summer sun, the trees exuberant splashes of deeper green, and birds were rioting in the woods. Adams found herself eyeing the shadows distrustfully, looking for the old man and his dog to reappear, or for a flash of horned, glimmering movement. Then they were back down the snicket, the woodland lost to view and normality reasserting itself, such as that was.

"Do you need somewhere to stay?" Chloe asked, startling Adams.

"What?"

"My sofa's not super-comfortable, but if you need a place …"

"Oh. Right. Thank you. Um … I've got somewhere." She hadn't actually thought about it, but she could get a hotel for a night or so, she supposed.

Chloe nodded, stopping next to her car and frowning slightly. "Be careful, wherever you go. I've never even heard of vanishing hexes, so I'm going to guess it's some heavy magic. Someone's not messing around." She dug in her bag and found the chalk and the little pouch containing the remaining stones, handing them to Adams. "Take these. I'll send you a diagram of how to lay them for protection."

"Thanks," Adams said, staring at the bag. "Really."

"Sure," Chloe replied, and grinned. "I thought I wasn't going to get to play in any more of your cases after the weres. This is *awesome*."

Then she was gone, swinging into the pink car and waving cheerily as she pulled away, the eyelashes fluttering in the wind of her passage. Adams didn't move, listening to the birds singing and cars rumbling on the nearby road, and wondering what the hell she did now. Find last night's cat, perhaps. She could hardly get on the station's computer system and search for known hex casters in the area.

She looked at Dandy. "Can you find Thompson? Get him to come and see me?"

Dandy gave a whuff that she took to be acquiescence, because he bounded off down the road and then was gone, leaving her suddenly bereft. She swallowed, straightened her shoulders, and gave her house a mournful look, then frowned. A curl of paper stuck out of an empty flowerpot on the windowsill. She didn't remember seeing it last night, or even when she'd arrived with Chloe. It didn't look like rubbish. It was cream, heavy stock, and it sat there in the sunlight, offering up a threat or a promise.

She somehow doubted it was going to be the latter.

4

WELCOME TO THE DALES

ADAMS DIDN'T PICK UP THE PAPER STRAIGHT AWAY. SHE STOOD there for a while, looking at it, then checked the street each way, without much hope. The only sign of life was the fat ginger tom, sprawled on his back on one of the little lawns across the street with his tail twitching as he stared up at the birds in the trees. He didn't seem to be paying any attention to her, and she could hardly interrogate him.

She still didn't move from the pavement, scowling at the plant pot. She had no Chloe to ward any new hexes off, and no Dandy to check it for her. She couldn't *feel* anything, but no one had ever accused her of being over-sensitive.

The street stayed quiet, just birdsong and the sound of cars passing on a different road filling the air. Someone had been cutting the grass, and Adams could smell the damp green scent of it. She checked on the cat again, but his eyes were closed now, one paw twitching faintly. He definitely wasn't paying attention.

"Dammit," she muttered, and fished Chloe's gloves out of her pockets, pulling them on again before quickly taking the couple of paces to reach her steps. She didn't touch them, just leaned over to fish the paper out of the pot. It felt grainy and luxurious even through the latex, and as she lifted it out she discovered a pale lilac ribbon knotted elegantly around the roll, holding it closed. It looked like it should be a Valentine's note, or a wedding invite so fancy it was hand-delivered, then she caught a whiff of something overly sweet and floral from it, making her reconsider. It was something a great-aunt with too much time on their hands would make, she decided. Fussily elegant and pointless.

It didn't *feel* pointless, though. It didn't have the aching dread of the hexes, but its simple presence put her teeth on edge. She checked the street again, but there was no one to be seen, so she carried the note gingerly back to her car, wondering if she dared to read it inside. She didn't want anyone to see it, but what if she accidentally hexed her Golf? She was pretty sure her insurance wouldn't cover that.

After a moment of indecision, she opened the hatchback and sat on the edge of the boot, holding the little scroll. With any luck she could hurl it away if it exploded with curses or something. She had an idea Chloe would be judgemental at her again for her current choice of action, but she'd had enough waiting around for one day. She tugged the ribbon gently, catching it as it uncurled, the paper loosening but not opening entirely. She took a breath and unrolled it the rest of the way, feeling for a moment that she should be shouting *hear ye, hear ye* and wearing a tunic.

No hexes jumped out at her, and she wasn't suddenly sucked into a faery portal. There was just the textured, cream paper, and elegant handwriting in deep purple-blue ink, full of curls and flourishes, and a few too many dots, as if someone had got carried away with the accents.

Let this serve as a warning, it said. *Deliver unto me The Book, or next time the hexes shall bind thee and all those ~~you~~ thou lovest forever.*

Kind regards, Velmyr Duskthorn, Lord of the Fae.

Adams stared at it for a moment, then said aloud, "Kind regards?"

No one was around to answer, and she rolled the note up again. *The Book.* There was only one book she could think of that deserved capitalisation. It was a sorcerer's book, and she'd taken it from a dodgy cop last year and given it to dragons for safekeeping. It was an unpleasant thing, that book, full of power and false promises. She definitely wasn't giving it to someone calling themselves *Velmyr Duskthorn,* hexes or no hexes.

Plus she didn't like threats. That wasn't something she was going to simply let slide, fae lords or not. She wondered if she really could arrest a fae – or a Gentry, since she supposed that must be who the note was from.

She could certainly try.

Adams tucked the note into an evidence bag with a certain degree of satisfaction, stashed it in the glovebox, then moved her car a little further down the street to where a tree cast enough shade to fend off the strengthening sun. She'd stocked up on water and a haphazard supermarket haul of chopped fruit, some nuts, and a pack of egg sandwiches before meeting Chloe, and now she steadily worked her way through them as she kept watch on the house. But even with the fuel, the heat was soporific, and as the morning slipped into afternoon she found her head drooping toward the wheel more often than not.

Finally she got out and followed the snicket to the path behind the house again. She peered each way, feeling both obvious and ineffectual. Velmyr Duskthorn – or whoever had left the note and the hexes, if they hadn't – was evidently good at going unseen. Yet she didn't feel she could just *leave.* What if the hexes came back, or were still there, simply hidden somehow? It felt like leaving an unexploded mine on the street, just waiting for a cat or a kid to trip over it. Well, a kid. Probably not a cat. She went back to the street, looking for the local cats and wondering if she should risk talking to them after all, but even Ginger had made himself scarce. She sighed, feeling fractious and irritated. Sitting around was getting her nowhere. And she had some actual evidence now.

It was time to see if fae had fingerprints.

Twenty minutes later she pushed into the office armed with an inadvisably large coffee, and nodded at Collins, who was on the phone.

"I can't give you a restraining order on the journalist, Aunty Miriam," he was saying.

"Ervin?" Adams said. "I wouldn't mind a restraining order on him."

"Not that one," Collins said, looking up at her. "Apparently the cryptid ones are still creeping about."

"Good luck to them," Adams said. Anyone who thought they could be creeping around the Toot Hansell Women's Institute without getting a scone to the ear for their troubles was either vastly ill-informed or braver than she was.

Collins just said into the phone, "Are they trespassing? No? Then there's nothing I can do. I'm sure they'll get bored and leave soon. Alright. Call me if you get worried." He hit disconnect and looked at Adams. "Do you think Walter would really eat a journalist?"

Adams considered it. Walter was the oldest and grumpiest of the Toot Hansell dragons – and she hated how easily that came to her, *Toot Hansell dragons,* as if that was a perfectly normal thing and not the stuff of storybooks and fandoms – and while the dragons, as a whole, were more inclined to partake of baked goods and tea than engage in wholesale destruction, she had suspicions Walter would prefer a more traditional approach, given the option. He'd very nearly eaten her suspect in the last tangle she'd had with Toot Hansell and its W.I.

She took a sip of coffee. "I'd still be more worried about what the W.I. might do to them."

"Fair point." Collins examined her. "Still gym gear? I take it you can't get inside yet, then."

"No." She didn't elaborate, and he raised his eyebrows, waiting. Finally she sighed and said, "They were gone."

"The hexes?"

"Yes. Like they'd never been there. But we still agreed I probably shouldn't go inside. Just in case." She waited for Collins to say, *in case of what,* or to look at her *like that,* the way everyone had looked at her in London after the brush with the bridge monsters, even though she hadn't even talked about them. The fact mental health reasons had come up in both the leave she had taken before her transfer, and the transfer itself, had been enough to earn her that look.

But Collins just nodded and said, "*Huh.*" He picked up his mug, found it empty, and set it down again. "I sometimes think I understand why the bottom drawer bottle used to be a thing."

"I don't think that was to do with dodgy dimensions."

"Still. I almost fancy reinstating it. Is anything likely to eat me this time?"

"*This time.* You've not been eaten once."

"I never used to have to worry about being eaten at all," he pointed out. "It wasn't even a concern until you turned up."

"Well, no one's hexing *your* doorstep," Adams said, more shortly than she intended. She grimaced and pushed the coffee away. She'd had too much, but it wasn't just the sleeplessness driving the craving. She should be going for a run instead to try to shake off the creeping unease.

"Leads?" Collins asked.

"Well," she started, and her phone rang. She took it from her pocket, scowling at her mum's name on the display. *Again.* She couldn't talk to her now. Her mum would know instantly that something was off. She hit ignore and held up the evidence bag. "I found this. Chloe thinks there's some super-fae called a Gentry involved, and I've no idea if they do fingerprints, but it's worth checking. Plus Chloe's looking into the photos I took, and the whole vanishing hexes thing, and she suggested talking to Rory, too."

"Have you?"

"Not yet." She tapped her fingers on the desk. "I want to speak to Thompson first. Dragging a civilian into things—"

"Rory's hardly a civilian when it comes to this stuff," Collins pointed out. "He was pretty handy with the werewolves—"

"Weres," Adams said. "They get snotty if you call them werewolves, apparently."

"Well, we can't have that. Anyhow, he was handy with that, and with York."

"I know, but ..." But the more people poking around faery traps and hexes, the more likely someone was to bloody well fall in. "Let me see what Chloe and Thompson come back with first," she said. "I might be back home by tonight."

"How unusually optimistic of you," Collins said, getting up and taking his coat from the back of the chair. "I have a complaint about egg theft. Coming?"

"No, I'll take this down to Lucas," she said, tapping the bag.

"Suit yourself." Collins headed for the office door, but as he opened it he stepped back hurriedly. "Ah ... hello?"

Adams looked up as Rory and Chloe trailed in, Rory clutching a tray of coffees and flanked by his two border collies. Behind them was DCI Maud Taylor, her face unreadable.

She looked at Collins. "Sit."

Collins retreated to his chair and sat, and Maud waved Chloe and Rory to the two visitors' chairs, then closed the door firmly behind her and crossed her arms. Maud was compact, blonde, and given to floral blouses and a certain deceptive twinkliness, which wasn't much in evidence right now.

Rory set his tray of coffees on the desk and held one out to Adams wordlessly.

"Oh. Thanks." She took it, looking warily at Maud and feeling far more dishevelled and discombobulated than even her sleepless night warranted.

"Enabler," Collins said to Rory, and he grinned.

"I do what I have to."

Adams scuffed the ears of the dogs, who were looking around with an air of general disappointment at the lack of Dandy, and waited to see what happened next. She wasn't sure if she was about to be given a caffeine intervention or a dressing down.

There was a long, slightly uncomfortable pause, while Collins took one of coffees with an appreciative noise, and Chloe and Rory stared at their own drinks, looking increasingly ill at ease. Before either of them could break, though, Maud said, "What's going on?"

"How do you mean?" Adams asked.

Maud pointed at Chloe and Rory. "These two sneaking around the place again? Like Harrogate? It's more Toot Hansell rubbish, isn't it? I can't *move* for sodding Toot Hansell rubbish these days."

Adams supposed she should be glad Maud left off the *since you got here* bit, but she heard it anyway. *Toot Hansell rubbish* seemed to have become a byword for *magic,* which at least meant no one had to use *that* word. She couldn't stand it herself, so she didn't blame Maud for avoiding it.

"Hexes," Chloe piped up.

"I wasn't asking you," Maud said, not looking at her. "I'm asking my DI, who is apparently running unauthorised stakeouts and keeping information that impacts the security of the force from me."

"It doesn't affect anyone else," Adams said.

"I'm sorry, are you not part of this team?"

Rory cleared his throat slightly and said, "Should we—"

"Quiet," Maud said, and Rory stared at his coffee with great interest.

"It's only just happened," Adams said. "Plus my understanding was that *other* cases weren't to be common knowledge."

"Doesn't change the fact you were targeted, and at your home," Maud said. "According to your team of experts here, it's a bit more than a note through the door, too."

"Possibly," Adams said. "But it's that as well." She held up the evidence bag. "I was about to take this to Lucas."

"You got a *note?*" Chloe asked, and held her hand out. "Can I see it?"

"You may not," Maud snapped, and took the bag from Adams. "Gloves?"

Collins dug in his desk drawers, while Adams looked at Chloe and Rory, then said, "Should we catch up later?"

Maud took a pair of blue latex gloves from Collins. "They stay. They're apparently in possession of more facts than I am, which I discovered by the simple expedient of threatening to arrest them unless they told me what they were up to."

"You're spending too much time around our Adams," Collins said.

Maud sniffed, opening the bag and fishing the note out.

"I'd be threatening you two as well if there wasn't too much paperwork involved. You need to learn to communicate better."

"You always say you don't want to know anything about this sort of thing," Collins protested, and Adams couldn't help feeling faintly relieved that she didn't have to make that point.

"I do when it's coming after my officers," Maud said, frowning at the note. "Talk."

So Adams did, telling her as much as she knew – which was very little – and omitting the part about the Gentry and their antlered beast, as well as the suspicious cat and the *feel* of the hexes themselves. That just felt like a step too far, and she could already hear the impossibility of what she was saying. As accepting as Maud had been about *other* cases, this was too much. There would be *the look*, and there would be soft voices, and then there'd be a suggestion she took some leave, and she couldn't stand it. She *couldn't*. So she left out as much as she could, describing the hexes as simply a threat, the Folk version of a dead animal left on the doorstep. And not the good sort, like dragons sometimes went in for.

Maud listened, then looked at Chloe. "You have a lead on this?"

"Working on it," Chloe said. "Rory has some books I want to take a look at."

"Here," Rory said, nudging a carrier bag with his foot. "I dug out any that looked relevant."

Maud tucked the note back into its bag while Chloe craned her neck in an effort to see it. "So what's your plan, Adams?"

"Keep watching the house until I get a decent lead."

"You already look like you've been sleeping in a hedge," Maud said. "We can put someone else on it."

"It has to be me."

"No, it doesn't."

"But what's Harrison— I mean, Graham, or whoever going to do if a … a person who casts runes turns up?"

"Take photos. They'll be under orders not to engage." Maud handed the bagged note to Collins. "Take a look."

Collins found another pair of gloves and pulled them on, giving Adams an almost apologetic look. "It does seem risky, you being on it all the time."

"I can help," Rory offered.

"This is still police business," Maud said.

Rory looked at Adams, smiling slightly. "That sounds familiar."

"Well, we're right." Adams took her phone out as it rang, and silenced it. Her mum again. She really needed to call back, but now wasn't the time.

Collins had opened the note, and now he looked up. "Ah …"

Maud interrupted, looking at Adams. "Where are you staying?"

"I haven't thought about it."

"Well, you're off duty now. Your leave starts tomorrow anyway."

"What?" Adams said, a sudden swooping misgiving in her belly.

"Holiday? You took a week off because your parents are visiting?"

"Your *parents?*" Rory asked, his smile widening.

"Oh *bollocks.*" Adams scrabbled in her pocket, almost dropping the phone as she fumbled it out. She hit dial, knuckles tight on the case. The phone rang once, twice, and kept going until it hit voicemail. "Oh, sodding hell. They've been trying to call me all day. They're driving up." She checked the time. "They must be almost here." Or *here.* At her house. Stepping on damn invisible hexes. *The hexes shall bind thee and all those thou lovest forever.*

She jumped out of her chair, running for the door, and Maud snapped, *"Stop."*

Adams looked back at her. "They're going to the house. You saw the note."

"You're not driving." Maud took her car keys from her pocket. "Let's go."

They pulled out of the car park with a squeal of tyres, Maud driving with a sure, sharp confidence, barely touching the brakes as she slid through the streets, aiming straight for Adams' house. Adams ignored the route, trying her mum's phone again, then her dad's, swapping back and forth, her heart too fast and her breath harsh in her throat. Her hands were shaking too much to attribute it to the caffeine or the sleeplessness, and she swallowed hard as Maud swung smoothly around the final curve, accelerating along the line of parked cars and tiny front yards. Adams gave up on calling, hunting for her parents' car, suddenly realising she didn't even know if they'd changed it recently, her mind serving up images of the tatty green Volvo estate they'd had when she was a kid.

Maud came to a hard stop in front of Adams' step, and Adams scrambled out of the car, looking around a little wildly. No unfamiliar vehicles that she could see, but then why weren't they *answering?* Had they already got here, and the hexes had snatched away the car as well as them?

"Any sign?" Maud asked.

"No. *Dammit.* Where the hell are they?"

Even as she spoke, Collins' car slid around the corner and stopped just behind Maud's. He climbed out, his face serious. "Nothing?"

"Nothing. And they're not answering."

"You're sure they were on the way?"

Adams poked her phone, finding half a dozen unread text messages. One was from Rory, another from Chloe, and the rest were from her mum, cheerily chronicling a series of rest stops. The last one … she checked the time. "They should be here." She turned to look at the house, hating it with a sudden wave of such intense fury it made her stomach turn over. Who the hell was this *Velmyr?* What had he done, and why? And where the hell was Dandy? And Thompson? And, more to the point, her parents?

Even as her mind served up the worst possible scenarios, a nondescript silver Vauxhall Corsa turned into the street and pootled toward them. They turned to watch. The passenger side window slid down and an arm emerged, waving cheerily, gold bracelets clinking on the wrist, and Adams pressed her phone to her chest, knees suddenly weak with relief.

The Corsa slowed even further, looking for a spot to park, and Collins waved helpfully, pointing that they should double-park next to the car behind him. The Corsa stopped, and Adams' dad put his head out of the driver's window, the tight curls of his hair short-cropped and greying.

"Are you sure?" he asked. "I hear the police are awfully strict in these parts." His gaze shifted to Adams, and he grinned.

Adams returned the grin with a bit of a wobble, and took a deep breath, steadying herself before she started for her parents' car. Her mum was already climbing out, a solid, straight-backed woman with her braids gathered into a luminously floral scarf that somehow managed not to clash with her bright sundress.

"Hi," Adams called, and an ancient green Land Rover came roaring around the corner with a belch of exhaust, barely stopping before it ran into the tangle of cars.

Adams' dad paused half out of the Vauxhall, and looked at the Land Rover dubiously. "Are we in his spot?"

"No, it's fine—"

"We're not exactly parked well, though. Are we in the way?"

"Hugh, it's fine," Adams' mum said. "I'm sure we'll sort it out in a minute."

"But if they want to get past—"

"Hello, Adams' parents," Chloe called, opening the passenger door of the Land Rover as the border collies piled out over her. "*Ow!*"

"Adams?" her mum said, looking at her. "Really, Jeanette? *Still?*"

Adams sighed deeply, trying not to look at Rory, and that was the point at which Dandy came bowling out of nothing, ran straight into her legs, and sent her to the ground. He stumbled, recovered, and sprinted off without pausing, Thompson in close pursuit with his teeth bared and his ears back, yowling, *"Touch my scruff again, mutt, and I'll make sure you never have puppies!"*

Rory's border collies broke into a volley of barking and joined the chase, the one-eyed cat from across the road flung himself over the fence and into the fray, closely followed by the two interchangeable black cats, and (very slowly) by the chubby ginger tom, and Maud held her hand out to Adams' mum.

"Welcome to the Dales," she said, raising her voice to be heard over the barking. "DCI Maud Taylor."

"Gloria Adams," she said. "Such a pleasure."

5

MORE DEXTER THAN HANNIBAL

MIDGE AND PINTO CAUGHT UP WITH THE CAT JUST AS THE pursuit transitioned from a chase into a hostage situation. Dandy had chosen a handy tree and bolted up it, and Thompson took a leap after him, all ragged ears and fury, but Midge intercepted, bumping the cat mid-jump and sending him off course. Thompson tumbled sideways, landing lightly and skittering across the pavement, spitting curses as he went. A ripple of amusement went through the watching cats, which were multiplying rapidly, more appearing from the house down the lane to line the walls, and giving Adams the impression of a species-swapped edition of *The Birds*. Thompson took another run at the tree, but both Midge and Pinto blocked him, keeping him at bay no matter which way he turned. He backed off, stalking in a frustrated circle and resorting to some truly inventive cursing, all but incoherent with rage.

Rory whistled to the dogs, but they ignored him, intent on protecting Dandy from the furious cat. "Heel!" Rory called, and Hugh looked on with interest.

"Working dogs, are they?" he asked.

"In theory. Lazy, mostly." Rory headed over to call them away, and one of the cats on the wall spat at him as he went past, hissing something Adams couldn't quite make out, but which didn't sound like just cat noise. "Steady on," Rory said, and glanced at Adams as she got back to her feet, brushing her leggings off. Thompson was still cursing, and at some point even the least observant person was going to realise it wasn't all feline-based.

"Be right back. I just need to grab that cat," she said to her mum.

"You have a cat now?"

"No, just … don't want a fight."

"Of course." Gloria turned to watch Adams as she jogged after Rory. "Quite varied, this country policing."

"It keeps things interesting," Maud said.

Adams ran to catch up to Rory, avoiding eye contact with the watching cats. There were far too many of them, even given the often overrun nature of the garden at the end of the street, and their regard felt full of threat. She couldn't tell if there were strange cats among them, but she didn't see the curiously marked one from the previous night. Maybe she'd just never seen all the street's cats together in one place before. But it wasn't her primary concern right now, anyway.

"*Thompson*," she hissed as she got closer, but he ignored her. He kept trying to reach the tree, apparently too put-out to try a cat's teleportation trick (he insisted it was called shifting, but it looked like teleportation to Adams). Midge and Pinto were taking their guarding duties very seriously, though, and he couldn't get past. This was apparently just one insult too much for him to cope with, and he was spiralling into ever deeper paroxysms of rage.

"I will skin you *alive*, you *mutts!* You're nothing but the degenerate dregs of a corrupted and maggoty family tree with no relation whatsoever to—"

"*Thompson!*"

His gaze snapped around, and he glared at her, teeth bared. "And *you!* You set that joke of a walking mop—"

"Shut up," Adams said, and tipped her head at the watching cats. "Just *shut up*."

Thompson's eyes narrowed, green and furious, his tail whipping so hard it looked like it was about to knock him over. But he stayed silent, clearly with great effort, and Rory skirted him to grab Midge and Pinto. Thompson looked away from Adams to spit at the dogs, then turned back and ran straight at her. She stepped back hurriedly, thinking he was angry enough to attack her, and he leaped, snagging her arm with both paws, his claws ripping the skin.

"*Ow!*" She grabbed him with her other hand, meaning to pull him away, and he hissed, "Lift me up, you radish. Pretend I'm your cat."

"Why?" she whispered back, but cradled him against her anyway, while above them Dandy gave an outraged *whuff*.

"Because I don't know for sure who here's Watch, and if it's not clear I'm on you, they're going to put someone on you. Also, I'm injured." He raised one front paw to her, and she spotted a torn claw.

"Diddums."

He hissed. "It's *your* fault. But come on, move. Ignore your mutt. The less attention we draw to him, the better."

Adams thought that Dandy's whole being invisible thing was doing a good job of that on the human side, and for the cats, well. They could hardly miss the bloody great dandy perched in the tree like a misplaced sheep, but Thompson knew more about such things than she did. She turned back to the group by the cars, where Chloe was exclaiming over Gloria's earrings, and, judging from his gesticulating, her dad was explaining to Collins just what route they'd taken to get here. She looked at Rory.

"Alright?" he asked.

"No. That was too close."

He nodded. "We got here in time, though."

"Barely. And how the hell am I going to explain all this?"

He shrugged. "You'll think of something. You always do." He gave her an easy smile, and she looked at the other cats, who were all eyeing Thompson with varying degrees of suspicion. What was she meant to do about *them*, as well?

"What're you looking at?" Thompson hissed at the one-eyed tabby, who hissed back, looking from him to Adams. "Oh, you think you're keeping tabs on things? May as well lose that other eye, you're that blind."

"Oh, knot your tail and feed it to a pelican," the tabby said, her voice thin and smooth. "I see more with my one eye than you do with two." She looked from Adams to Rory, hissed at them both, then jumped off the wall and vanished into the garden.

"Knot your tail and what?" Rory asked.

"Feed it to a pelican," Adams said.

"Pathetic," Thompson muttered, then they were too close to the little group of humans for him to talk any more, and he just glared around with his whiskers trembling.

"Are you sure that's not yours?" Gloria asked. "She seems very comfortable."

"He. I'm … pet sitting."

"Right." She looked unconvinced. "Don't forget your dad's allergic."

"Yes, sorry."

"It's alright, I've got antihistamines," he said cheerfully. He was digging in the boot of the car. "Can we go in, then? I'm parched."

"No," everyone except Maud said. She just looked at the sky and sighed slightly.

"Why on earth not?" Gloria asked. "If it's a bit messy,

Jeanette, I remember your bedroom at home. I think I can handle it."

"No, it's not that. It's not safe."

"Not safe?" Both her parents looked at the house dubiously, as if expecting it to erupt into flames at any moment.

"Electrical issues? Gas leak?" Hugh asked. "I can take a look."

"I don't think calculus will help," Adams said. "But no, that's not it. It's a … Well, it's …"

"Bedbugs," Maud said, and everyone looked at her. "Utterly infested."

"*Ew*," Chloe said.

"Quite." Gloria looked at Adams. "Why didn't you tell us? Where are we going to stay now?"

"It's a bit embarrassing," Adams said, trying not to scowl at Maud.

"Not at all," Maud said briskly. "Big problem this year. Tourists bringing them up from London." There was a moment's silence, then she added, "Ah, not your sort of tourists, obviously. People who've been in hotels and whatnot."

Gloria still looked unconvinced. "And you can't just spray them?"

"Fumigation," Collins said, rocking on his heels. "Only option."

"And they're busy," Adams said. "The fumigators, I mean, not the bugs. With all the B&Bs that have them, you know."

"The bugs are probably busy too," Chloe said absently. She was watching the cats disperse.

Gloria gave her a dubious look, then said, "Well if the B&Bs have them and you have them, where do we stay?"

"Out of Skipton," Adams said. "Only option." As far from vanishing hexes and creeping Gentry as possible.

"You can stay at mine," Rory said. "The holiday cottages

are booked up, but there's room at the house. Hot water's a bit iffy at the moment, though. I think I went through a pipe. Or maybe some wiring. Hard to tell." He petted the dogs, frowning. "I mean, there are some puddles, but there's always puddles."

"You need to look at that," Hugh said. "Run some traces, that sort of thing."

"I'm mostly trying to stop the roof falling in," Rory replied, and found some dog biscuits in his pocket.

"My aunt's got a B&B," Chloe said. "In Leeds, though. Hardly a country break."

"No," Maud said. "Adams is using my cottage in Hawes, aren't you?"

"Yes?"

"Yes. Nice spot. Cheese factory not far off. Good walking. No infestations."

"That's nice of you," Hugh said, resettling the bags in the boot. "So no chance of a cuppa first, then?"

"It would've been nice to know ahead of time," Gloria said. "I hadn't planned for a holiday cottage. I don't think I brought enough food."

Adams thought that was unlikely. She'd never seen her mum go for so much as a weekend away without enough food for a month. "We'll figure it out," she said aloud. "But we can't go inside here. Don't want to take the things with us. Maybe if you head into town and grab a cuppa there? I just have a couple of things to finish up before I can leave."

"Or I'll just tell you where to find the key," Maud said to Gloria. "Head straight up to Hawes, and we'll pack Adams off as soon as she's done her last report."

Gloria looked at Hugh. "Will you make it, love?"

He shrugged. "I can wait a little longer. Still got some tea in the thermos. Always better than going to some caff, isn't it?"

"I suppose," Gloria said, and enveloped Adams in a hug as well as she could, given the cat. Adams lingered there for a moment, smelling the familiar, warm scent of her mother, soap and body butter layered over something deep and rich and enduring, then straightened up.

"I'll be right there," she said.

"Make sure you are. I brought curry."

Adams' stomach immediately forgot the egg sandwich and grumbled hopefully. "Promise."

THEY STOOD THERE A LITTLE AWKWARDLY, watching Hugh work the car around until he was pointed back into town, then trundle off with Gloria waving out the window again. They waved back dutifully, then Adams looked at Maud.

"Thanks."

"You should be safe enough out there."

"Wait – I'm not really going, am I?"

"Of course you are. You need the break."

"But I have to find out—"

Maud shook her head and turned away, beckoning Adams with her. Adams followed, frowning, with Thompson still held in her arms, and they walked a few steps away from the others before Maud stopped and examined her.

"What is it?" Adams asked.

Maud looked as if she was thinking something over, then said, "Sleeping alright?"

"Um … yes?"

"All this Toot Hansell stuff. Bit stressful, isn't it?"

"I suppose. What's this about?"

Maud didn't answer straight away, searching Adams' face with a cool, professional gaze, then said, "That note was blank."

Adams closed her eyes, rocking back on her heels. "Dammit."

"Your lass there said there were no marks on your house that she saw. She swears the photo you sent her was real, but when she showed them to me … well, could be any step, couldn't it?"

Adams opened her eyes, her stomach suddenly sick. She was aware she was holding Thompson too tight, but he didn't complain. "What do you mean?"

"I mean I know there *are* Toot Hansell things. But there are also mental health things, and I can't help but feel that there's some intersection, especially given your reason for leaving London."

Adams swallowed around a hard knot in her throat. "They put down mental health break because they couldn't put *Toot Hansell stuff.*"

"Sure," Maud said, but it wasn't a *sure* of agreement. "But what I want is for you to take this week with your parents, keep away from Skipton and your cases, and then we'll revisit this once you return."

"But—"

"*No.* No dragging Collins into things. No using station resources to trace fingerprints on bits of blank paper. Nothing. Go walking. Eat cheese. Drink wine. Clear your head." She glanced at Thompson. "Stop dragging stray cats about."

Thompson growled, but didn't say anything.

Adams took a deep breath. Maud's flat tones said this wasn't a suggestion, and she was better to agree than to argue and risk making her one-week holiday a month-long suspension. "Alright."

"Good." Maud turned and led the way back to the group. "We're done here. Collins, you can cover Adams' leave from today, yes?" She barely waited for him to nod before waving vaguely at Rory and Chloe. "Your ... *consultants* can head off, too."

"*Consultants*," Chloe said, raising her hand to Rory. "Sweet!"

He high-fived her, and looked at Adams. "You don't want a look at the books?"

"No," Maud said, before Adams could answer. "She's going to join her parents." She looked at Adams. "Do you want a lift back to the station?"

"I'll grab one with Collins."

"Alright. I'll text you the code for the key safe. Please don't go drawing runes on my cottage," she added, nodding at Adams' front door, where Chloe's protective runes were still visible on the step. "Or clean up if you do." She headed for her car without waiting for an answer, and Adams watched her go, still clutching Thompson, her arm stinging where he'd scratched her.

No one spoke until the DCI had pulled away, then Adams shifted Thompson so she could free a hand to rub her face.

"*Ew*," he said, examining his coat. "You bled on me."

She ignored him. "I need coffee."

"You don't," Collins said. "You need to go to Hawes and have your holiday."

She gave him a sharp look. He'd seen the note after Maud, so he must know it had been blank, too. "I'm not just walking away."

"You should," Chloe said. "I don't have an answer on the hexes, but nothing about this is good, especially not if there's a Gentry involved. You need to drop out of sight for a bit."

"A *Gentry?*" Thompson demanded.

"Apparently," Adams said.

The cat huffed. "Well, then, the witch has it. I've no idea what the hell's going on here, but if it involves bloody *Gentry* you don't want to sit around waiting for them to come back."

"But what if they find me there? With my parents?" As soon as she spoke she felt the weight of the words, and swallowed hard, her throat dry and rough with sleeplessness and caffeine. "They're safer up there without me."

No one spoke for a moment, then Rory said, "Even if you don't go, what's to say they won't be found there anyway? And then there's no one around to look after them."

"You think they might be targeted?" Adams asked, thinking of the note again. But how could they have *known?*

Rory grimaced. "I don't know. But the timing ..."

The timing. She might've forgotten in the muddle of sleeplessness and antlered night stalkers that her parents were on the way, but she'd had this booked for a long time. They'd been up once before, when she'd not long been in Yorkshire, coming to Leeds and trying to be enthusiastic about the thin cold wind snarling around the buildings, and the crumbling edges where the north had slid into cracks of neglect and forgetfulness. She'd fended off a second trip by visiting them last year, but this time they'd insisted they needed to see Skipton, and her dad was fixated on some bloody viaduct where he wanted to see a steam train.

So, yes. This trip had been planned, and her time off had been booked, and if she'd been in bed when the hexes were laid she'd presumably have been trapped inside, or sent off to Faery, and her parents would've walked straight into the house and fallen into the same trap when they came looking for her. It was hardly a stretch to imagine someone using them as leverage against her. Maybe they'd even been the target rather than her, since Chloe seemed to think Faery wouldn't have much hold on her.

She looked at Thompson. "The hexes are gone, but can you take a look anyway?"

"I don't know if I want to do anything after you set your beast on me."

"He's not a beast."

"The *scruff*, Adams. He had me by the *scruff*. And I've told you before, I don't approve of his methods of travel. Just tell him to come and bark politely at me next time, and I'll find you. I don't need to be *dragged*."

"We're doing a lot of talking to a cat on the side of the road," Collins said. "I thought that was against your whole ethos?"

"She hangs out with a hellhound. The cats around here know exactly who she is. And any humans just think you're talking among yourselves." Thompson wriggled. "Put me down, though. Let's look at these vanishing hexes."

Adams set him down, the unease thick and hungry at the back of her throat. It wasn't just about her parents, either. *The cats around here know exactly who she is.* "Am I under some sort of surveillance?"

"Sodding hell, I can whiff them from here," Thompson said, ignoring her as he trotted to the front door. "Have you tried sending the mutt over them? Just to see what happens?"

Dandy whined, looking up at Adams, and she gave him an unobtrusive pat. "He's joking."

"I'm not."

She sighed and watched Thompson pad up to the mat, followed by Chloe and Collins. Rory stayed with her, Midge and Pinto fussing over Dandy as if he'd been in dire peril, and not just being chased by a miffed feline.

"Are you alright?" Rory asked.

"Sure. Faery traps *and* a parental visit? Fab."

"They seem nice."

"They *are*. It's annoying as anything, because I can't really be upset at them poking their noses in." She nodded at the house. "You're not taking a look?"

"I suppose. I can feel it, though. I don't like it."

She looked up at him, lean and vaguely dishevelled in a

way that suggested he'd got dressed before he was quite awake, rather than it seeming like a style choice. "Even Chloe wasn't sure she could feel it earlier. Said she might just be picking up on my unease."

He shook his head. "I'm quite sure you've never made my hair stand up." He shot her a sideways look. "Not in a bad way, anyway."

She decided to ignore that. "Thanks for the offer of a place to stay."

"Purely selfish reasons," he said, his grin surfacing. "I'm angling for Adams childhood tales."

"Well, for that you can definitely take a closer look. Come on." She followed the others, feeling Rory's reluctance in a shadow of her own, but he came with her, hands in his pockets.

The dogs didn't, though. They stayed by the kerb, and Midge set up a wobbling howl that summoned a couple of cats to the top of next door's wall.

"What're you looking at?" Thompson demanded of them. "Never seen a bloody border collie before?"

"What is it?" a black and white cat asked. "I can smell it."

"Come take a look if you're so curious."

"Sod that." They stared at each other for a moment, then the black and white cat shrugged. "Whatever. Just keep it over there, can't you? Don't need any curses on the street. We just got rid of the Pekinese that lived down the end. It's been nice since." He vanished, leaving the other cat, which just stared at Dandy with wide orange eyes until Thompson hissed at him. He gave a little squawk of alarm and fell backward off the wall.

"Bully," Chloe said.

"Got to establish one's authority," Thompson replied, and watched her and Collins flip the mat up. His ears were already back, and he didn't move from his spot, paws planted wide and his whiskers twitching. Adams thought she saw a shiver pass through him, but she couldn't be sure.

Collins looked at the blank stone, then at her.

"They were there," she said, trying to damp down the defensiveness in her voice.

"I believe you," he said.

"I can show you the photos."

"No need." He looked at Chloe. "Is it like invisible ink?"

"Still working on it," she said, and scrabbled under her singlet. "Ugh, Mabel's in my bra and won't come out. I don't think she likes them."

"Mabel?"

"Snake."

"Leave her there," Thompson said, his voice flat. "Cover the step. Those your guarding marks around the edge, witch?"

"Yes."

"Not bad."

"Can you see the hexes?" Adams asked.

He looked at her, his eyes green and cool. "No. But I can sniff what was here, and it's not your basic faery trap, not that anyone's meant to be using them in public places these days anyway. They're meant to only be for bare hills and secret woods, where if people are silly enough to go into them they can't say the legends didn't warn them."

Adams wanted very much to ask why *any* faery traps were allowed, but instead just said, "So what was it?"

"*Is* it. They're still there, even if we can't see them. This thing ..." He trailed off, looking at the step, then said, "Hard to know for sure, but it's powerful. It could open a rift in dimensions. Turn the mat into a black hole the moment you stood on it. Throw you out of time and space. Or the house itself might be intended to fall out of this plane of reality, or the timeline. You'd be in there making a cuppa and thinking you were off to work in half an hour, and meanwhile civilisations have fallen and been born again outside."

No one spoke for a moment, then Adams said, "Who would do that?"

"You're the detective, figure it out," the cat said, without much heat.

"How do we counter it?" Chloe asked.

"We can't until we know what it is. Your protective charms'll hold it well enough, though."

Adams nodded, then said, "What about the postie? I don't want the postie being shunted into another dimension."

"They'll be fine if they don't cross them," Thompson said. "For now, get yourself away. Keep your head down, and your parents' as well. Don't talk to anyone. Get that beast away from you, too. The less he's around, the better."

"I can't just send him away," Adams said, touching Dandy's heavy coat. He whined.

"Hide him, then. You need to be as invisible as possible until we know where these came from." There was no humour in the cat's tone, no warmth, not even room for negotiation. He spoke in cut, final tones that made Adams unconsciously straighten up, and she saw Collins doing the same. "This isn't some robots in York or dodgy beer in Harrogate. This is a whole other level, and it's totally against Watch protocol. It's going to be drawing a lot of attention, so you're going to have to watch for any sort of fae – not just Gentry – *and* any cats sniffing around. No telling what they might decide to do to tidy up the situation."

"Got it," Adams said. Maybe she wouldn't have agreed so easily if her parents hadn't been here, but she wasn't taking any risks now.

"And us?" Chloe asked.

"Do your research," Thompson said. "Might help figure out a way to remove them. But I'm going to find who laid them." And just like that he was gone, the step empty but for a few drifting cat hairs.

There was silence, until Rory said, "Well. I didn't know a cat could creep me out."

"They always do me," Chloe said, finally extricating Mabel from her bra. "Have you seen what they do to mice? Serial killers, the lot of them."

Adams thought she was right, but also that the safety of her parents was resting on one of them now. She just had to hope he was more a Dexter than a Hannibal.

6

OFF ON HER HOLS

ADAMS POKED THE DOOR OF THE COFFEESHOP, BUT IT remained resolutely locked. She sighed, and looked down the street. It wasn't actually cobbled, but somehow gave the impression that it should be, lined with old stone buildings and half-timbered structures holding tea shops, pubs, foodie places, and an array of souvenir shops. In the two days they'd been in Hawes she'd been into three of them, and they all sold variations of the same ceramic mugs decorated with woodland creatures, tea towels with Yorkshire sayings, and an astonishingly large range of overpriced, overly twee greetings cards. There were also a couple of artier places selling tranquil watercolours and moody landscapes, a sweet shop her dad had already been into three times, a village hall with a second-hand bookshop attached, and another book-shop with an owner so spectacularly grumpy that even her mum had been impressed.

Other than that, Adams had spotted one interesting shop which looked like it contained a jumble sale's worth of old farm implements, writing desks and sideboards, lockets and pocket watches, moth-eaten hats and umbrella stands, but she hadn't ventured inside. Her mum had banned *anyone* from going in, as she insisted the car couldn't cope with her dad buying two coatracks, a taxidermied ferret, and a coal bucket for their non-existent fire, so no one was allowed near it in case that resulted in him somehow shopping via osmosis.

Not that Adams was exactly in a shopping mood. She was itchy and irritable, and the lack of progress reports from *anyone* would've made her wonder if her phone had lost all ability to receive messages or calls, except for the fact that Rory, Chloe, and Collins had all been in touch. They just hadn't had anything to tell her.

Right now, she needed coffee. Even more than usual, considering she hadn't exactly slept much since they got here. She'd sat up until her parents fell asleep the first night, so she could sneak out and lay Chloe's guarding runes on the doors and windows. She had no idea if she'd done them right, or what they were meant to guard against, and she couldn't feel any difference with having them in place, but at least it was *something*. Not anything that made her feel she could ease her vigilance long enough to sleep any more than in fitful dozes that night or the following one, though.

So coffee was called for. She could've had some at Maud's holiday cottage, of course, which was compact but comfortable, and surprisingly well-equipped, although the pod machine made strange noises when she turned it on, and disgorged only a pallid trickle of unpleasant-smelling water. Luckily she'd bought a cafetière before leaving Skipton (it made it easier for Dandy, too, as he considered pods to be a personal insult), and stocked up on coffee, so she had supplies. But her dad would be up soon, if he wasn't already, and a morning cuppa with her dad – or anyone – required having preloaded on caffeine first.

But in picturesque little villages in the depths of the Dales there didn't seem to be much call for early-opening coffeeshops. None of the cafes looked to even have kitchen lights on, and the hotel on the main street wasn't open to the public yet. She briefly considered abusing her authority and flashing her warrant card to get into it, but with her luck they'd serve her a mug of instant.

Adams sighed again and leaned against the wall next to the coffeeshop door. She'd had a decent cup here the day before, and she wondered if she could just wait until it opened. It wasn't unpleasant, the summer sun already well up, raising heavy, chunky shadows from the buildings and lifting the scent of warm earth and wild fields from somewhere out of sight. She rubbed the back of her neck and stretched, wondering what the hell she was doing. She should've just packed her parents straight off home again.

But. *But.* The timing. *Was* someone keeping that close an eye on her, and therefore her parents? It was impossible to be sure, one way or the other, and that meant she needed to keep them close until she knew they were safe. Even if things didn't always feel that safe in her vicinity these days.

Movement further down the street caught her eye and she turned toward it, hoping for a coffee van ambling in to the rescue, but it was only Dandy in hot pursuit of some pigeons, dreadlocks flopping wildly. There was her answer. If there had been coffee to be had, he would've sniffed it out by now. She was going to have to go back and brave the morning chitchat.

She pushed off the wall and set off at an easy jog along the street, Dandy racing to catch up to her. He had a feather stuck to his snout, and she paused to pluck it off him as unobtrusively as possible. That was just what she needed, pigeon feathers appearing mysteriously in the cottage. She was already spending an inordinate amount of time scuffing away paw prints and stray leaves before her mum could spot them.

Dandy huffed, apparently unimpressed with her grooming, and bounded off again. She followed, smiling slightly. At least one of them didn't seem to be suffering too much from caffeine withdrawal.

ADAMS LET herself back into the holiday cottage to the scent of lightly burnt toast and frying bacon, and grabbed a handful of Dandy's hair as he tried to rush past her.

"*Do not,*" she hissed, and he gave her a reproachful look, his eyes half-covered by dreadlocks. He didn't pull away, at least, but he had a definite lean in the direction of the kitchen going on. "I swear, there'll be no coffee for you for *a month.*"

He huffed, and straightened up.

"Good boy," she whispered, pulling off her trainers and putting them on the rack by the door.

"Is that you, Nettie?" her dad asked, leaning around the kitchen door. "Early run, was it?"

"Yes," she said, not entirely untruthfully. The route might've been dictated by the need for coffee, but she'd taken in some trails first.

"Nice morning for it," he said. "Go and get yourself a shower and I'll do you some scrambled eggs."

"You don't have to—"

"Need the protein after all that exercise." He pointed a butter knife at her. "Also if we start healthy we can make bad choices later."

"That is not how it works, Hugh," her mum called from the kitchen. "Is she running again? That's every day!"

"It's only been two days," Adams muttered.

"That's two days in a row!" her mum shouted, although she couldn't have heard her. "Hasn't she heard of rest days?"

Her dad reached behind the door and handed Adams a mug of coffee. "Dose up."

"Thanks." She took the mug, then looked at him. "It's got milk in it."

"Oh." He frowned. "Sorry, love. I don't know how I did that. I'll make you another."

"No, it's good. Back in a moment." She turned away and climbed the stairs, Dandy following her with his eyes on the mug. Two days. That left four at the *least*, and that was assuming she could let them go home at the end of the trip. That they were safe by then, not about to be snatched up by a fae trap as soon as they were out of sight, and right now she didn't see how that was going to happen. But no matter what, she was going to need more coffee.

Upstairs, she persuaded the ageing electric shower to disgorge a trickle of tepid water, frowning at the three flying ceramic ducks that were mounted on the wall by the bathroom cabinet. She had an idea Maud hadn't updated the decor since inheriting the cottage. She couldn't imagine the DCI going in for pink walls in the living room, flounced covers on the sofa, and the impressive variety of heavy floral curtains on all the windows. But the beds were comfortable and the doors had decent locks, plus the back garden was fully walled and the street was quiet enough that it was easy to spot anyone lurking about the place. She could hardly complain.

Before leaving Skipton she'd done a fast-paced whip through a couple of shops to pick up a pair of jeans and some T-shirts in addition to the cafetière. She'd have been more put out if high-speed visits to a very limited selection of shops hadn't been her preferred method of shopping anyway, and now she pulled a new hoody on over her top and wandered downstairs barefoot to find both her parents standing in the tidy little kitchen. They were staring at the rather modern oven mired amid the old wooden cabinets.

"What's going on?" Adams asked, heading straight to the cafetière and scooping more coffee into it. Her dad had already rinsed it out, and she hoped he'd put the grounds in the garden. Her mum had put it in the rubbish the first morning, and Adams had told her it was more environmentally conscious and good for the plants to just dump it in a pile under the apple tree. She'd been rewarded with a mystified look and an agreement to do so in the future, while she tried to unobtrusively hold Dandy back from attacking the bin.

"Your father's lost the bacon," Gloria said now, putting the kettle on.

"Maybe it was a fox?" her dad suggested, taking the grill pan out and putting it in the sink. "They've left it very clean, at least."

Adams looked around for Dandy and spotted him vanishing through the open door that led to the garden.

"It won't be a fox," her mum said. "They're not going to just come in off the street with people in here."

"Out of the garden," her dad pointed out. "But I see your point. Maybe it's the ghost army, then."

"The what?" Adams asked.

"There's a ghost army around here somewhere. Kingsdale, I think? Maybe they got peckish."

Gloria gave Adams a pained look, then said, "More likely cats. I spotted a tabby in the garden earlier. It looked rather like the one from the other day, but of course it can't be. Scooted off as soon as it saw me. Sneaky creatures, aren't they?"

She didn't know the half of it, Adams thought, and went to the door. "Where?"

Her mum topped up two mugs and the cafetière with hot water and gave her an amused look. "It's a cat, dear. You can't arrest it."

"No, obviously. But … well, we can't let him – it – just steal the bacon, can we?"

"No one can ever stop a cat doing what it wants. Sit down and try not arresting anyone for a few days. It'll be good for you."

"I'm not wanting to arrest anyone."

"I don't know. You have that look," Hugh said, taking more bacon from the fridge. "We best keep our noses clean, Gloria, love. She'll be after us next."

"A week is a long time without arresting anyone for our Jeanette," Gloria agreed.

"Regretting taking time off yet?" Hugh asked, tipping his head at Adams.

"No. This is great," she said, rinsing her mug out.

Her parents just looked at her.

"Okay, fine, I would *probably* have only taken a couple of days off, but I needed to take some holiday. Plus, you know, bedbugs."

Hugh gave the pan a somewhat cursory scrub, then put more bacon on it. "*Bedbugs.* I think our daughter just doesn't want us spending time around her friends. We might embarrass her."

"It's not that."

"I hoped she was hiding a secret boyfriend," Gloria said, handing Hugh a tea. "Or girlfriend." She considered it. "Or non-gender-conforming person of interest."

"A person of interest sounds like I'm considering arresting them, not dating them," Adams pointed out.

"None of our business what you get up to behind closed doors," Hugh said, checking the grill. "We've all got our thing."

"Person of your interest, then," Gloria said to Adams, ignoring him.

"No."

"Weren't you seeing someone called Isha in Leeds?"

"No. Well, maybe. Sort of. Not anymore." Adams wouldn't have called it a *breakup,* because she hadn't thought there was anything to break up *from,* but she had an idea Isha didn't agree with that assessment, given how their last dinner together had gone. People were so *complicated.* They needed to arrive with clear instructions, preferably in writing so it was easy to refer back to later.

"What about that Chloe?" Gloria asked. "She seemed very nice. Too skinny, but nice."

"No."

"Rory? Quite posh, but—"

"*No.*"

"Well, it's nice to see the local area," Hugh said, turning his attention to the toaster and frowning. "Hang about. I'm sure I already put some in. Am I going dotty, love?"

"Probably," Gloria said. "You were always going to be the first to go."

Adams had to push down a sudden surge of anxiety, even though she knew they were both joking. Or she hoped they were. "I'm going to check for that cat." She headed for the door to the garden before the conversation could swing back toward her lack of dating activity, although not quite quickly enough to miss her dad saying, "We should find her someone to arrest. It always makes her feel better."

He was right. Arresting someone *would* make her feel better, but until she figured out how to counter fae hexes, plus how to find and detain some kind of faery sorcerer with a ghost stag, there wasn't much she could do. So instead she just looked around the garden, ignoring Dandy panting bacon-scented breath at her with no sign of contrition. He had toast crumbs on his nose, too, which was no surprise.

The garden was a long wedge of somewhat patchy grass, hardy flowerbeds, and a few old fruit trees with a green-stained wooden bench sitting under one of them, all captured between tall stone walls. The cottage was terraced and in the middle of a row, so the only entry or exit to the garden was a high wooden gate fitted to an arch at its bottom, the gate's wood weathered and softly greened by the damp. On the far side of the wall was a public footpath and a chattery little stream, surrounded by greenery and blooming flowers, and almost small enough to jump over. She'd already tried to find a way to secure the gate, but there was no lock, nor any way to install one without drilling a hasp into both the gate and the wall, and she didn't like to think of the damage she'd do, or Maud's reaction, if she tried it. At least the cottage itself was secure enough, the old windows and wooden doors creaky but resilient. And now also protected by her inexpertly drawn protective runes, for all the good that might do.

Adams wandered toward the gate, the damp grass soothing on her bare feet, sipping her coffee as she went. Birds sang rowdily, but there was no sign of a cat, or anyone else for that matter. She glanced over her shoulder to make sure she wasn't going to be overheard. The outside table was already set for breakfast, her parents still fussing around in the kitchen. She took her phone from her pocket, held it up to her ear, and said, "Thompson?"

There was no answer at first, and she tried again, a little louder.

A flash of tabby movement, and he appeared atop the wall, all tattered ears and bent tail. "Ay-up. Your mutt got some more bacon for me?"

"Are you leading him astray?" Adams demanded. "He can't just steal food right in front of my parents."

"I was hungry, and he owes me." Thompson stretched luxuriously. "How's the holiday?"

"It's not a sodding holiday. Is my house safe yet?"

"No."

"Have you figured out what's behind the hexes?"

"A Gentry."

"Genius. I mean how they found me, and what they're up to." She hadn't told him about the demand in the vanishing note. The cat would only say she couldn't give the book to the Gentry, which she already knew, and she didn't want him getting distracted by details. Besides, if it was the only way to protect her parents ... Well, she still wasn't going to do it, but the cat didn't need to know she might use the *promise* of doing it. Things like this were never about what someone wanted anyway. It was always about *why*.

"Also no."

Adams took a sip of coffee. "Not much good, are you?"

Thompson narrowed his eyes at her. "Skipton's not my patch, you know."

"Oh, I do know. You mention it constantly."

"Nettie?" her dad called, and Adams winced, turning to look up the garden.

"Yes?"

"Your eggs are ready."

"Be right there." She pointed at her phone. "Just on a call."

"Don't be long. Your toast's getting cold."

She nodded, and watched him walk back inside before she looked at the cat again.

"*Nettie?*" Thompson said, whiskers twitching.

"I'll call you Mittens if you use that name."

The cat snorted. "Whatever. Names are just a way to

avoid saying *oi you* to everyone. Call yourself what you want."

"I do." She took a sip of her coffee. "I really need to know if my parents are targets. I can't do anything when they're around without letting on something's up. Can you try to find out if they're in any sort of danger? Because if not, I can pack them off back to London, or even leave them here to go and look at trains or whatever, then we can get this sorted."

Thompson looked past her at the house, his pupils narrowed filament-thin in the sunlight. "You don't think they know anything?"

"About Folk and hexes? Absolutely not. My dad's a maths teacher with a fixation on ancient *human* history and dead languages."

"You realise that's all tangled up in ancient Folk history?"

"Makes sense. But still no."

"What about your mum?"

Adams hesitated, thinking of the little bundles of herbs Gloria made, tied with twine and tucked behind clocks and into car doors, laid on windowsills and bedside tables and dressers, binding her loved ones to safety with thyme and rowan. Or the rhymes she repeated quietly over her cakes, to ensure a good rise, or had whispered over her kids' beds, chasing the bogeyman away. That was nothing but superstition and tradition, though. It didn't *mean* anything.

"No," she said aloud. "And they can't know anything. It's not safe." Knowing things was a slippery slope. One moment the world was unpredictable but logical to a certain extent, full of the vagaries of human nature and all its accompanying risks. The next moment it was goblins and weres and things with extraneous limbs, as well as dimensions. And once one was seeing *it*, seeing the hidden cities that existed under the ones everyone knew of, seeing the tails and horns and wings and teeth, it started seeing one back.

There was no returning from that, and she'd done the best she could to keep anyone who didn't need to know in a state of blissful ignorance. She still felt terrible that she'd pulled Collins in with her before realising just how dodgy it could be. And her parents … her parents would be going back to London. London with its rivers and bridges and *snap-snap-snap*. She shivered, violently enough to slop coffee over her fingers.

"Interesting," Thompson said, turning his flat green gaze on her. She found herself wanting to shift under it, as if the damn creature was *judging* her.

"What is?"

He looked as if he were considering how to answer, but her mum shouted from the little outside table, "Jeanette! Your dad's made you eggs, so come and eat them before they get cold!"

"Best get yourself to breakfast, Nettie." Thompson stood up, stretching and ignoring her scowl. "Nothing from the little witch or Posh Spice?"

"They're looking into it, kitty-cat."

He snorted. "Keep your head down, then. And get some kippers in for tomorrow, can't you?"

He was gone before Adams could respond, stepping off the fence and snapping out of being, leaving only the faintest whisper of air rushing in to fill the space where he'd been, barely heard under the birdsong. Dandy whined, and she let her fingers brush his head, her stomach tight with apprehension.

"*Jeanette!*"

"Coming," Adams said, trying not to let her scratchiness show in her voice. She didn't want to be here. More to the point, she didn't want her *parents* to be here. She wanted them to be somewhere safe, so she could be off figuring out what was going on, not sitting here kicking her heels and jumping at every butterfly that flickered past the windows.

But there was no telling what was safe anymore, so all she could do was listen to the cat.

It was not an improvement in circumstances.

7

A STRONG LINE IN TUTTING

HER EGGS WERE COLD AND HER TOAST, ONCE HER DAD HAD insisted on putting it back in again to warm it up, was distinctly on the crispy side, but she surprised herself by being hungry enough to eat it anyway, despite the unsettling start to the day. Plus anything tasted fine with enough hot sauce on, washed down with another mug of coffee.

"You're not eating right, are you?" Gloria asked

"I'm eating fine."

"*Fine.* I bet it's all noodles and takeaways."

"Not *all*," she protested, adding more butter to her toast.

"You're skinny."

"It's the running. It's different up here. Trails and that."

"I'd like to do some of those," her dad said. "Walking, mind. Would've been fun to see the ones around your place, really."

"Yeah, sorry about that."

"I've never heard of a fumigation taking a week," Gloria said.

"Like Maud said, it's all over town," Adams said. "Hard to get someone out to tackle it."

"Beer," her dad said around a mouthful of toast.

"What?"

"That's for slugs," Gloria said.

"Sorry?" Adams was starting to feel as if she were talking to the cat again. Or the Toot Hansell W.I., who were at least as bad.

"You give them saucers of beer and they drink themselves to death," Hugh said.

"Bedbugs?"

"*Slugs*," her mum said again.

"Oh. Well, these were bedbugs."

"You could take it internally. You'd be less likely to notice the bites then," Hugh said, grinning, and Gloria swatted his arm. "*Ow!* Assault! Arrest your mother, Nettie."

Gloria sniffed. "She should be arresting you for wearing that T-shirt. Who gave you that?"

Hugh examined his T-shirt, which read *Caseum Diem**, then, in smaller print, **cheese the day*. "I bought it. It's fun."

"It's not *fun*. It's not even funny. I know you're a maths teacher, but still."

"*Ouch*. Also, it's not maths related. It's Latin related. And cheesy." He grinned even more widely, and Gloria flicked a toast crumb at him. "Hey!"

Adams sighed deeply and had another bite of toast.

"Here, try this," Hugh said, forgetting about his wounded fashion sense and pushing a jar of marmalade toward her. "I got it yesterday. Made locally. Look at the colour!"

Adams and Gloria both looked at the marmalade dubiously, and Gloria picked up the jar, examining it. "It says 'Made in Spain.'"

Hugh frowned. "I'm sure they told me it was local," he muttered, looking around for his glasses.

"On your head, dear," Gloria said, getting up. "No wonder

you bought that shirt. Buy anything, you will. More toast all round?"

"No thanks," Adams said, as her phone dinged.

"All round," Gloria repeated firmly, collecting the plates and heading for the kitchen, humming softly to herself as she went, an unfamiliar little tune.

Adams sighed again and picked up her phone.

"No phones at the table!" Gloria shouted from the kitchen.

Adams looked at her dad. "How does she know?"

"Witchcraft," he said, not looking up from his examination of the marmalade label. "Ah, here we go. Made from Spanish oranges. Well, that's fair enough. Can't exactly get Yorkshire ones. Made … oh. *Packaged* in Hawes. Cheeky sods, they've just put their own label on it."

"*What?*" Adams' tone was sharper than she intended.

Hugh looked up, peering at her over his glasses. "I don't think you can arrest them for mildly misleading labelling, love."

"Not that. Witchcraft?"

"Oh, I didn't mean that. I'm not actually calling your mum a witch. Can you imagine? She'd tell her sisters and I'd end up skinned alive. Plus I wouldn't mean it, obviously."

"Right. Of course." She looked sideways at her phone but didn't touch it.

"Are you alright, Nettie? You're very jumpy."

"I'm not."

He just looked at her, and she sighed.

"Sorry. Work's been intense, then the whole bedbug thing …"

He put the jar down, watching her thoughtfully. "You do seem to be very busy, and across half the county, too."

"I know. I keep getting pulled into … stuff."

They listened to the birdsong for a while before he said, "I thought things were meant to be a little quieter up here. Wasn't that the whole point?"

"It hasn't quite worked out that way." *Hasn't quite* was the understatement of the century. Adams hadn't left London because of the kids that had been stolen. That had been terrible, and vicious, and ugly, but it *happened*. Bad things happened all the time, and that was why she did what she did, to try and push back a little against the ugliness of the world. If she hadn't been able to handle that, she wouldn't have become a police officer at all.

No, what had sent her fleeing London wasn't the kids, but what had taken them. Monsters stalking the Thames, ancient and metallic and multi-jointed, and savagely ravenous. Monsters her London DCI had neither confirmed nor denied, but only offered Adams the chance to keep fighting them. And she'd refused. She'd fled north, not wanting to deal with myths and legends sharing her streets, upending realities and beliefs. With *magic. Ugh.* She had more than enough work dealing with human monsters. She didn't need *magic.*

Only the north had brought dragons, and invisible dogs, and toothy goblins and moody sprites and talking bloody cats. And she hadn't even had the option to ignore them, since they kept turning up on her patch and expecting her to sort things out, even though she wasn't the law for Folk. That was the Watch, the exact details of which she was still somewhat unclear about. According to Thompson, it consisted only of cats and was older than most human history, established when Folk and humans had first divided, the Folk driven into hiding by the unrelenting expansion of humans and their hunger and panicked distrust of anything *other*. The Watch was apparently distinctly hostile to humans poking in its business, yet somehow she found herself doing just that, repeatedly, often to prevent ladies of a certain age from blowing the centuries-old cover of a bunch of tea-drinking dragons.

So … no. The north had not been quieter. The north had her questioning her very understanding of the world, and was also proving that Folk were every bit as annoying as humans, and required just as much people-skilling, which seemed unfair. Also she was developing something close to a phobia of women of a certain age, particularly if they came bearing baked goods.

"Nettie?"

She blinked at her dad. "Sorry. Distracted."

He nodded, his face serious, and she thought his hair had more white than the last time she'd seen him, the soft scuff of his stubble forming a ghost on his skin rather than a shadow. Her heart squeezed in her chest, and she thought suddenly of the milky coffee. But he'd probably just got muddled while making a tea at the same time. Had to have.

He played with the handle of his mug, but kept his gaze on her as he said, "Is London still bothering you? Are you sleeping?"

She smiled, trying to put all the reassurance she could into it. "No, it's not London. It's bedbugs. And also, I really don't want any more toast."

He pushed the jar of marmalade toward her. "Try some. It's nice, even if it is poorly labelled."

She made a face. "Pass."

"Here." Gloria reappeared, setting a plate laden with fresh toast in the middle of the table, and placed a jar of honey next to it. "That's *actually* local. There's an honesty box down the road. Someone has their own bees!"

"Probably just did a better job changing the label," Hugh muttered, and reclaimed his marmalade. "Well, we're supporting the local economy anyway, aren't we?"

Adams' phone dinged again, and her hand twitched

toward it. Gloria made a disapproving noise, so Adams stopped and stared at her toast instead, trying to ignore Dandy nudging her leg. She wasn't used to having people around all the time, and the last holiday she'd had with her parents had been when she was still in school. Back then it had been both her brothers, her, and their parents in a very dodgy caravan in Norfolk. At least she had her own bedroom here. Things could be worse.

"What d'you want to do today?" she asked, wondering if she could drop the toast to Dandy. Probably not. It'd be very obvious when it didn't hit the floor.

"Well, you're the tour guide," Hugh said.

She wrinkled her nose. "I'm hardly a local expert. You've probably looked into it more than me."

"Ribblehead Viaduct, then," he said. "We might be able to see a steam train!"

Adams braced herself against a shudder. Her last train encounter had involved weird underground beasts with far too many teeth. A completely disproportionate amount of Folk seemed to go in for excessive teeth, in her mind.

"I'd rather do something more interesting," Gloria said. "A nice walk and a picnic, perhaps."

"How is *that* more interesting than a steam train? Besides, we could combine it."

"What about a museum?"

"It's too nice a day to be inside."

Gloria frowned. "How do you even know your steam train will be running? We could sit there all day and see nothing but commuters."

"That's a good point." Hugh chewed on his toast for moment, then said, "The young lady who sold me the marmalade said there's a good sheepdog demo on tomorrow evening. Very impressive, apparently."

Gloria made an agreeable sound. "Spanish sheepdogs, are they?"

"Oh, ha."

"Well, we can have a look at that tomorrow. There must be a lot of other things to do around here today, though."

They both looked expectantly at Adams, and she tapped her phone. "Let me call Collins."

"Your partner?" Gloria asked.

"He's local. And he's into trains."

"Oh, ask him about the cheese factory too," Hugh said. "They've got a tour."

"A cheese factory tour? It'll just be a bunch of vats," Gloria said. "Like that brewery tour you made me go on. I don't really fancy that."

Adams agreed strongly on that. She also had no desire to go on anything remotely resembling a brewery tour. The last one she'd been on had got her almost eaten by weres.

"Well, what would *you* like to do, love?" Hugh asked Gloria.

"I'd like to go to Harrogate. Maybe do the baths."

"That's a long way," Hugh said.

"We just drove from London. It's not *that* far."

"Well, then we should go to York for the Viking Museum, too."

"I'm calling Collins," Adams said, getting up and taking her toast with her. She wasn't letting her parents go to Harrogate *or* York, or anywhere else she could be recognised. She'd have been reluctant to anyway, but given the hexes, she needed to ensure her parents kept a low profile until she was certain it was safe to pack them off back to London. It might have treacherous bridges and questionable toasties, but at least no one there knew they were her parents.

SHE RETREATED BACK DOWN to the bottom of the garden, in the hopes her parents wouldn't overhear. They were still discussing the relevant merits of York versus Harrogate, so the odds were they weren't paying attention anyway. She passed Dandy her toast and hit dial on Collins' number.

It rang, rang some more, and she was about to give up when the connection clicked.

"Ay-up, Adams."

"Alright?"

"Un-hexed, which seems like a good start. How's laying low?" His tone was light, but there was an edge of concern under it.

"I'm not sure I'm going to survive a week," Adams said. "There's no proper coffeeshop."

"And homemade isn't doing it for you?"

"I mean, it's *fine,* but it's not the same. And there's all the fussing. It took us half an hour to get out the door yesterday, and we were only walking into the village for a look at the shops."

"I can see where your tolerance for fuss might be low."

"And somehow I'm meant to eat a daily cooked breakfast, lunch, *and* dinner. Plus morning tea and afternoon tea, and Mum *tutted* when I turned down a biscuit last night."

"The horror."

"You evidently haven't been tutted at properly. Your mum doesn't strike me as a tutter." Collins' mum was more inclined to civil unrest, in the form of non-violent protests. Or mostly non-violent. Adams had lost a decent pair of trousers to cranberry sauce-filled water balloons in her first encounter with Rainbow.

"No, not really her thing," Collins agreed. "Are you calling to file a complaint about the tutting?"

"I should. But no. I need some local outing ideas. They're

threatening day trips to York and Harrogate, and that seems risky."

"*Hmm.* Yes, good call. Cheese factory?"

"Mum seems unconvinced."

"*What?*" Collins sounded as if he might be clutching his pearls, if he had them. "It's an institution! And they have a whole cheese-tasting room. You need to go."

"I'll pass that on."

"Then there's the Dales Countryside Museum, the Hawes Ropemakers—"

"The *what?*"

"It's fun."

"I think your idea of fun and mine are not the same."

"Fine. Do some walks. See some waterfalls. Ingleton has some good cave tours, if you don't mind going underground."

"Rather not." The unpleasant train encounter had also been an underground encounter, and Adams was starting to wonder if there was *anything* she could do that wasn't going to poke some nasty memories. "The waterfalls sound good, though." As long as there were no sprites. She couldn't be doing with sprites in her current mood.

"Great walking around there. And it's a good way to keep out of everyone's way."

"Perfect. Thanks, Collins."

"Sure. Have you heard anything from anyone yet?"

Adams sighed. "Only Thompson, and he's got nothing."

"Worth reaching out to anyone else?"

Adams made a doubtful noise. She knew Collins wasn't talking about police contacts. He meant her specific Folk contacts, dragons in the Dales and bartenders in York. "I imagine if anyone can find anything, it'll be Thompson. Besides, the more people who know about my parents being here, the more chances of a leak."

"Fair point. Do you need someone else up there, do you think? More eyes on the street?"

"No. I'll be fine." The last thing she needed was more people to worry about. She had Dandy, and that was plenty.

"Alright. Keep me updated. And don't go off running stuff down on your own, even if the cat comes back with something. He's not actual backup, you know."

"He'd probably argue that."

"He'd argue anything. And I'm sure he vomits a mean hairball, but you might need more than that. And more than invisible dogs, handy as they are."

"Sure. Thanks, Collins." She hesitated, then added, "Has Maud said anything?"

"About?" Collins asked, a little too innocently.

"The note being blank. I know you saw it too."

"Well, yes," he admitted. "But clearly there *was* something, else you wouldn't have been worried."

"So? Has she said anything?"

He was quiet for a moment, then said, "She asked me a few questions about how you've been coping with regular cases, if stuff's been compromised at all. If your behaviour seemed erratic. I said no, of course not, you're fine."

"Thanks," Adams said, her voice sounding reedy to her own ears. "She still seem suspicious?"

Another long pause, then Collins said, "She knows Toot Hansell stuff actually exists. I'm sure she doesn't think you … doesn't think anything's wrong."

Adams nodded, even though he couldn't see it. "What do you think?"

"That you're the least unbalanced person I've met. If you say there were runes and a note, there were. It'll be fine, Adams. Chin up."

He hung up, sparing her the need to thank him again, and she stood there looking at the jumbled flowerbeds, tapping her phone restlessly against her leg, her free hand finding her car keys in her pocket. Or not the keys so much as the duck, its metal wings smooth under her fingertips. She had the sudden urge to go to her jacket where it hung by the door and get her baton, just to have it handy. And Yorkies. She needed to buy some Yorkies, although she knew she still had at least half a dozen in her kit bag in the car.

Not that she was planning to go chasing down leads, not with her parents here. She hadn't lied to Collins about that. It would be spectacularly bad judgement. Although what if she couldn't find anything out before they were meant to go home? What then? She couldn't send them off when she didn't know if they'd definitely been targeted along with her, if the note's mention of *those thou lovest* had been mere hyperbole or concrete threat. The timing *could* be a fluke, but it might not, either. She groaned, rubbing the tight lines of stress on the back of her neck. She needed answers, and instead she was hanging around planning *day trips*, waiting on other people to get back to her, and she *hated* it. All of it.

Dandy gave a sudden, low growl, and she looked at him. His gaze was fixed on the wall, and she examined it, frowning. She couldn't see anything.

"What?" she asked, her voice low, but he ignored her, gathering himself for a leap. "Dandy?"

He launched himself at the wall. There was no way he should have been able to reach the top, given the size of him, but he hurdled it effortlessly, dreadlocks flying, and vanished over the other side.

"*Dandy!*" Adams hissed, and ran for the gate.

She had it open, already heading through, when her mum called, "Jeanette? Where are you going?"

Adams stumbled to a stop. She couldn't go. She couldn't leave them. What if this was all a ploy to call her away, to leave her parents unprotected? She retreated into the garden so quickly she almost tripped, spinning to scan the walls. Nothing. Some birds at the feeder, where her dad had put the bacon rinds, but nothing else, just her mum standing at the door.

"Jeanette?"

She checked the path beyond the gate again, then pulled it closed, thinking she might have to invest in that hasp anyway. For all the good it might do, when the hexes could drop the cottage out of this reality, if Thompson was right. She checked her own countercharms on the wall, frowning, but they looked fine. Well, they looked the same as they had, anyway. She had no way of knowing if they were actually doing anything.

"Jeanette!"

"Coming," she called, and walked slowly up the garden, her gaze still on the walls and that persistent knot in her stomach tightening to something that rendered her breathless.

What had it been? What kept calling Dandy away?

She couldn't even take five minutes out of bloody breakfast to search for the answers. This situation was getting untenable, but she couldn't see what else to do, except wait.

And go to bloody sheepdog demos and *ropemakers*.

THE DAY WAS LONG, and baked with unfamiliar Yorkshire sunshine, and fuelled by far too much food. Adams couldn't even sneak any to Dandy, not the cheese and chutney sandwiches her mum made for their walk to the waterfalls, or the flapjacks to fuel the walk back, or the nuts and crisps before dinner, or the generous servings of rice and beans, spiced and tasty and way too filling. At least thinking about her over-stretched stomach distracted her from scowling at rocks that might hold runes, and searching for suspicious mushrooms that could be faery circles, or thinking about what might have happened to Dandy. Because he didn't come back, not on the walk or after it, when they stopped at a pub for a drink, nor when they sat playing cards in the garden after dinner. He didn't even reappear when Adams made her post-dinner coffee, and that seemed like the worst sign of all.

If caffeine wasn't going to bring him back, what would?

She didn't think she'd sleep, between worrying about Dandy and being painfully aware that, without him, she had no one to warn her if any fae came sneaking around in the night – or anyone else for that matter. She checked the countercharms again once her parents were asleep, and sent a photo of them to Chloe, who sent it back with arrows and notes, like a teacher marking homework. Adams made the corrections, considered sending the photo back again, then decided they'd have to do. She didn't need Chloe rushing out here to fix them.

She lay awake for a long time, alternately staring at the ceiling and peering out of the window at the street below, but eventually, at some point, she fell into restless sleep.

It didn't feel like it was long before she woke again, although she'd slept deeply enough to be momentarily disorientated by the unfamiliar single bed and the placement of the window. She frowned at it until the lines and angles of the cottage's little second bedroom coalesced around her, and she sat up.

Still no Dandy, not crowding her out of her bed or sprawled on the room's second one, close enough to reach out and smooth the cover. There was no sound in the house, no doors or floorboards creaking, and no whisper of traffic from the road outside. She wasn't sure what had woken her, but she was fully awake, every dim shadow drawn hard on the world.

She got up, her stomach tight and uneasy, déjà vu crawling about her shoulders and worming into her breath, making her stop for a second, breathing in deeply. She steadied herself, then took her baton and duck from the bedside table and crept to the door.

The landing was empty, the cottage entirely silent. She eased the door of the main bedroom open, revealing the twin mounds of her parents under the covers. She didn't go in, but from here she could hear them breathing. Nothing seemed amiss.

She headed downstairs, the stairs creaking in unfamiliar spots before delivering her into the little hall. She peered into the living room, lit by a soft mix of streetlight and moonlight coming in through the open curtains of the windows. The sofa and armchairs were empty, the remotes neatly arranged on the coffee table. She withdrew and checked the front door. Locked. Under-stairs cupboard, empty. That just left the kitchen, which was as unremarkable as everywhere else. She stopped on its threshold even so, feeling the same sense of dislocation as the night the hexes had appeared, as if she'd stepped out of time and space, lost her grip on the world for a moment. She tightened her hand on the duck, rolled her shoulders, and crossed the room to the garden door.

She opened it slowly onto an empty patio, the trees and flowerbeds beyond edged with silver by the moon, the walls stern and silent, rendered larger and oddly mystical in the night, as if it had become a storybook garden. Or a faery tale one. She pulled on her trainers and stepped out, checking the charms almost reflexively. They were undisturbed, as far as she could tell, and she walked silently into the garden, snapping her baton out as she went, the sound making her wince.

Nothing reacted, though. The garden was as still as the house, no rustling in the bushes from foraging hedgehogs, no lurking cats, no one sitting in the flood of moonlight that spotlighted the garden bench. Not even a breeze disturbed the trees, and a rich green scent rose from the grass and the cluttered flowerbeds, something earthy and vital. Adams almost imagined she could hear the shoots growing. It was *too much*, in some way, the heady scents and the languid light and the implacable stillness, and it made the skin on the back of her neck tighten. She found herself wishing for someone to shout outside, or a car to rev, anything to prove the world was real.

But there was nothing, and she walked to the gate, which she'd bound with some twine she'd found in a drawer in the kitchen. It wasn't much, but at least it told her if anyone had broken it to come in.

They hadn't, so she broke it herself and unlatched the gate, pulling it open onto the narrow path between the wall and the stream. The water glittered softly as it ran through mossy banks, and Adams looked for a sprite automatically. It was the sort of scene that called for a sprite.

But there was no sprite. There was just Dandy, standing on the same side of the stream as the house, expanded up to the size of a Saint Bernard, his head hanging low as he stared fixedly across the water.

And on the other side, staring back, was the tall, lean form of what could only be the Gentry, the moonlight silver in their hair.

8

ALWAYS KNOW THE SAFE WORD

Adams froze, one hand tightening on the baton, the other finding the duck again, the metal of its wings hard and reassuring. Part of her wanted to dive back into the garden, to run to the house and lock the doors, to stand in her parents' doorway and guard it against all comers. But the answers were out here, not in there, so she stepped forward, straightening her back as she went, and said, "What do you want?"

The Gentry looked around at her slowly, without any flicker of surprise. "My lady," they said, the word barely a whisper, but it carried easily in the still night, curling around her neck and slipping into her ears almost lovingly.

She frowned. "Detective Inspector Adams, or any combination thereof," she said, her voice flat and clipped. "And you are?"

The Gentry shifted, the light doing excessively magical things to them. Their hair was long and sleek, spilling gently over their shoulders, and seemed to be spun of moonlight, while their face was fine-featured and almost as colourless as their hair, only their lips pinched pink and full. They regarded her with pale, limpid eyes and breathed, "I am fae."

"Well, I didn't think you were from bloody Asda," she said, and a flicker of expression crossed their flawless features. Startled? Annoyed? Hard to say, but it was something unguarded, and it made her feel at least a little better. "Name?"

"I am Velmyr Duskthorn, Lord of the Fae," they said, flicking their hair over one shoulder and regarding her in a manner which indicated fairly clearly she should be impressed.

The author of the note. Not surprising. She wondered if *lord* was genderless for fae, as it was for dragons. "Preferred pronouns?" she asked, just to be sure.

"*He,*" Velmyr snapped. "*Clearly.*"

"Sorry. I'm sure it's clear to fae, but not to me." She folded her arms over her chest, feet planted wide, feeling solid and earthbound compared to the ethereal creature in front of her. "Why are you here?"

"I seek you," Velmyr said, and indicated Dandy with a disdainful little flourish. "But this traitorous mutt won't let me cross the water."

Adams looked at Dandy, and realised he was standing at one side of a plank of wood that had been laid across the stream. "I'm sure he has his reasons," she said. "Why're you looking for me? Want to leave me another note, do you?"

"I wanted to talk to you, as I did the other night, but the creature is problematic."

Dandy huffed.

"The *note* was problematic. You're threatening a police officer."

"The police have no hold over the fae."

Adams resisted the urge to say *watch me,* and instead said,

"I assume I have you to thank for booby-trapping my house as well?"

Velmyr's perfect brow creased. "There were no birds involved."

"Birds?"

"Boobies." They frowned at each other, then his eyes widened. "Wait, *boobies?* Are you a *child?* Do you mean breasts? The beautiful—" He cupped his hands in front of his own chest, raising pale eyebrows.

"*No.* Did you set booby-traps for me?"

"I'm not interested in your breasts."

Adams took a deep breath, wishing she didn't have both hands occupied. She could feel a twitch threatening to start over one eye. "Good to know. Did you or did you not put hexes on my doorsteps?"

"Oh. Yes."

"Why?"

"I wished to talk to you." His tone said *obviously.*

"Why didn't you just knock on the bloody door, then?"

"Far too many cats," he said. "Nosey creatures." He glanced around, scowling, and Adams did too. In this, at least, she shared his opinion.

"I was told the hexes could pull my whole house out of time."

"It's the most secure way to talk," Velmyr said.

"Right. And the note? Hardly secure, that."

"The mutt complicated things." He drew himself up abruptly, the light seeming to tighten around him like an actor on a stage, and he tilted his head imperiously. "Where is the book?"

"What book?"

He scowled. "*The* book."

"The Encyclopaedia Britannica?"

He hissed, revealing alarmingly sharp teeth – Folk and

their damn teeth again – then clicked his fingers at her imperiously. "The sorcerer's book. Give it to me, woman."

She matched his scowl with her own. "*Detective Inspector.* And I don't have it."

The night seemed to be getting darker, as if he was drawing all the light out of it in his fury. "Then you will find it."

"I'm not giving you the book."

He laughed at that, the sound incongruously high and tinkling. "You will, or your parents will pay."

She shifted her grip on the baton, half raising it, the movement automatic. "You don't *touch* them."

"My safe word is mint sauce," Velmyr said, eyeing the baton.

Adams started forward, not even sure what she was going to do, just that she had to do *something,* she had to get answers out of this smug bloody fae, and then Dandy was in front of her, leaning against her legs, blocking her way. She stopped short, swallowing hard, and glared at the Gentry.

"The mutt likes you," Velmyr said, the words a sneer.

"If you so much as *think* about my parents, I'll destroy you."

A small smile curled around his lips. "It's too late for that, Detective Inspector."

"*What?*" She glanced back at the house, unable to help herself.

"Oh they're still there. For now." He crouched, making her step back quickly and Dandy growl. The Gentry looked up at her, his face all flat planes and hard beauty, and gave her that sharp-toothed smile again. "Look." He touched the stream and the water stilled instantly. And it wasn't just the surface that smoothed. The entire waterway stopped flowing, and light bloomed in its depths.

Adams stared at it, then tipped her head to one side,

trying to make sense of what she was seeing. The light was beautiful, all purples and blues, but it had no shape. It rather reminded her of underwater photos of deep-sea jellyfish.

"Witness," Velmyr said, standing up again and doing one of his flourishes at the water.

She tried tipping her head to the other side, then shrugged. "I can't see anything."

"You—" He stopped, sighed, and said, "You're looking at it from the wrong angle. Come over here."

"Not bloody likely."

He put his hands on his hips. "Well, I can't show you from there."

"Use your words, then. I didn't come here for show and tell. *What have you done to my parents?*"

He waved impatiently. "It's so much less fun this way, but fine. I may have given them a teeny bit of cake."

"You *what?*" She stared at him. "But that's ... isn't that how you trap people in Faery forever? Eat or drink anything, and you can never leave?" She suddenly wondered if she should've given him her name. Too late to take it back now, though. And the cat had said names weren't important, although who knew if that meant to cats, fae, or the world in general.

"Don't be so *dramatic*," Velmyr said, which she thought was a bit rich coming from someone calling himself Lord Duskthorn and waving his robes about the place. "If they were *in* Faery, yes. On this side, though, it merely binds them to me. So I could do this"—he clicked his fingers, setting up a ringing on the edge of Adams' hearing—"and they will wake and join me, to dance forever in the faery realms."

Adams pointed the baton at him. "Un-do that, then."

"Won't," he said smugly.

"Oh, you've got a door to Faery open right here, then?

What're you going to do, piggyback them away while I show you what a baton's for?"

His smug look vanished. "Oh, horseshoes." He hurriedly clicked his fingers again, setting up a deeper tone that echoed in the trees. "There. They sleep again."

Adams looked around at the gate. She couldn't see anyone in the garden, so she turned back to the Gentry, clenching her hands even tighter on the baton and the duck to hide the shaking that had started somewhere in her belly. "If you even *try* to touch them—"

"Bring me the book. Once I have that, I shall release them unharmed. It's very simple."

They stared at each other across the water, so close they could have reached out and touched hands, and Dandy growled warningly. Neither of them looked at him.

She couldn't give him the book, even if she had it. The book was dangerous in ways she didn't fully understand, but more than that, this overgrown bloody faery was putting her parents at risk, using them like playthings. She wasn't going to let *anyone* get away with that. But aloud all she said was, "Alright."

He raised his eyebrows. "Just like that?"

"It's my parents."

"*Huh*. Humans really are very soft." He examined her, and for one moment she let the fright of it bubble up, the terror of losing them, feeling it surface on her skin. Velmyr nodded, apparently satisfied. "You have until the solstice."

Adams couldn't answer straight away, shoving the emotions back down, abruptly scared that now her grip on them had slipped she wouldn't be able to catch hold again. But she squeezed the duck as tightly as she could, the wings gouging her palm, and finally said, "When's that?"

Velmyr blinked at her. "You don't know when the solstice is?"

"I'm not a sodding astronomer."

He gave a long-suffering sigh. "Three nights hence. You must bring the book to the Huntress in the woods in Skipton, and I will release your parents. If you do not do it, or if you try to evade me, I will claim them. Choose your actions carefully." He turned, swirling his cloak in a manner that would've been a lot more elegant if it hadn't caught on a patch of thistles. He tugged it free irritably, then looked over his shoulder at Adams, raised one hand, and clicked his fingers once more.

Adams expected him to vanish, but he just stood there, smiling slyly, while the echo of the click drifted away. "What've you done now?"

"You may return. The house is released."

"Released?"

"From its stasis." When she still looked at him blankly he sighed and turned back to her. "Do you think it's *chance* you're the only one awake? That the streets are empty and the world silent?"

"Did you just pull my boss's house out of space and time?"

"*No.* I put it in *stasis.* Honestly, *humans.*" He spun away and stomped off into the woods, rather less dramatically than might've been expected. "Three nights!"

Adams watched him go, then looked at Dandy, who whined. "Yeah," she said. "Maud's never lending us her house again."

Then she turned and led the way back into the garden, still feeling sick and weak and a little shaky. Her *parents.*

SHE DIDN'T SLEEP any more that night. Her parents were still asleep – or asleep again – when she got inside, although her dad was sprawled on the floor in the hall and her mum was curled up in the bedroom doorway, so evidently Velmyr hadn't been lying about the cake. Adams got them back into bed, both moving with the slow deliberation of sleepwalkers, as if still half under the Gentry's spell. She pulled the covers over them, tucking them in securely before she headed downstairs to make some coffee and wait out the night. She wasn't leaving them unattended again. She couldn't risk it.

She and Dandy saw out the rest of the night with generous servings of caffeine, and, in Adams' case, a lot of reading about faeries online without finding anything useful. Dawn came in rich and heavy, and she went upstairs to shower, leaving Dandy guarding her parents' room. At least things seemed somewhat more manageable in the light, even if she was too tired to appreciate what was looking like another strangely beautiful day. She managed to be cheerful when her parents woke up, neither of them with any memory of their little bout of enchantment, and she leaned on the table as she watched her dad breaking eggs into a bowl to scramble.

"Your trip up okay, was it?" she asked him.

"Not bad," Hugh said. "We ran into traffic around Birmingham, and there were awful roadworks on the—"

"Nothing unusual happened?"

He frowned at her over his glasses. "Such as?"

"No one gave you any free samples of cake or anything?"

"Oh! Funny you should ask. Yes, they did. That was up here, though, after we left yours. We stopped for a cuppa at this nice farm shop place – bit fancy, but nice scones – and someone was giving out samples of fairy cake." He made a face. "Quite rubbery, though. Don't think it'll be a winner for them, although their representative or whoever looked the part. Very pretty sort."

"Faery cake?" Adams asked, clutching her mug more

tightly. She'd already known, but … he'd openly called it *faery cake?*

"Yes, you know. Little pale cupcake thingies. Your mum and Caleb used to make them, but theirs were much better." He peered at the eggs. "Is this enough, do you think?"

"Plenty," Adams said. "I'm not hungry." She turned and went out into the garden, her head pounding with caffeine and sleeplessness and stress. He'd been in Skipton, trapping her parents while she'd been poking runes and going bloody *shopping.* But it also meant he hadn't had his claws in them when he'd written the note, and she tried to figure out if that was good or not. She thought it might be. It meant he hadn't tracked them to London, and that likely meant her brothers were safe. For now, at least. She squeezed her forehead, trying to push the headache back down. *For now.* She grabbed her phone from her pocket.

Breakfast was calm enough, despite her mum holding her phone up and saying, "Jeanette, have you been telling your brothers not to accept free cakes from anyone because there's a scam going on?" which necessitated her coming up with a very convoluted story involving contacts at her old station and cake as a street name for an entirely new class of drug. At least they'd listened, she supposed.

After that, the morning ticked quietly away. They went to the shop for more food (Adams had no idea why, as there was more jammed into the cottage's little fridge than her own saw in about a month), went home again, had morning tea, went out for a small walk so her dad could break in his new hiking shoes, went home for lunch, and finally set off for the cheese factory in the heat of the afternoon, walking along the main street and past drinkers already gathered at the picnic tables outside the pubs, soaking in the sun. A table of three large men of around her own age or a bit younger, all in wellies and stained jeans, waved at them cheerily, and the biggest shouted, "Nice day for it!"

"Lovely," Hugh agreed, and Gloria waved back.

Adams ignored them. She'd spent the whole day on edge, every nerve snapping. Waiting for the Gentry to reappear, or Thompson, or for *something* to happen. Another hex, a fae attack in some corner of the endlessly picturesque streets. She searched for a sprite in the stream, but didn't see one, looked for gargoyles on the roofs or faeries lurking in the tearooms, but didn't spot any of those, either. Maybe the endless rush of tourists had forced them out, although there was a faun in the fancy florist and a dryad in the second-hand shop, as well as what looked suspiciously like a troll moving furniture out the back, so Folk were evidently around, as they were everywhere. Not that anyone noticed they were anything other than human, of course. Folk's greatest protection was how unobservant humans were, and how neatly they dismissed what was right in front of them if they did see it. She eyed her parents carefully each time she spotted Folk, just in case Thompson was right, but the only thing that happened was Hugh saying brightly, "Cor, he's a big lad, isn't he?" when he noticed the troll. So she could tick that off her list.

The cheese factory was ... cheesy. And somewhat difficult to navigate while trying to stop Dandy taking bites out of everything. But Adams had to admit the tasting room was worth the entry fee – when they finally made it there – even if Hugh had resurrected his *Caseum Diem* T-shirt, which proved popular enough with the staff to make him unbearably smug. Afterward they were ushered into the gift shop, where Hugh selected three varieties of fruitcake, six cheeses, and two jars of chutney, and Gloria had to almost physically restrain him from picking up a cheese board and knife set.

"We already have two," she told him.

"But this is a Yorkshire one," he pointed out. "We don't have a Yorkshire cheeseboard."

"I fail to see the difference between it and a London cheeseboard."

"You see? You don't even remember. Neither of them are London. The old cheeseboard we bought on our honeymoon in Cornwall, and the new one's from that trip up to Scotland we took when we finally got rid of all the kids."

"Hi," Adams said. "Still here."

"Yes, but not at home. Trust me, we did some celebrating when that finally happened. In every room—"

"*No*," she said, and went to buy a travel mug with the cheesemaker's logo on the side. She didn't really need one, but she wasn't listening to her parents reminisce about kid-free shenanigans. She'd take the monsters under York over that.

"Holiday, is it?" the young woman behind the counter asked as she scanned the label on the mug. She was pink-cheeked and rounded, and smiling so brightly it made Adams' cheeks ache in sympathy.

She wondered if that was the woman's normal disposition, or if she had a little chemical help in the large water bottle sitting next to her. No one could be *that* happy about cheese. Aloud, Adams said, "Yes, just visiting."

"*Ooh*, where from? Down south, is it?"

"Yes."

"Do you like it? Where are you staying? How long are you here for? Have you gone to the waterfalls yet?"

Adams frowned at her, but Hugh set his armload of purchases on the counter and said, "I'll get the mug. And don't mind my grumpy daughter. She's a copper, and she hasn't been able to arrest anyone for *days*. Puts her in a terrible mood." He winked, and the young woman giggled.

"Oh, I don't mind. I can talk enough for all of us! My dad

said, Shell, you need to get yourself a job at the cheese shop so you can talk to all the tourists. You'll be right good at that! And I didn't think I'd get it, on account of me not being good with numbers and all, but Mary – Mary's the manager—"

Adams stepped back from the counter, leaving her dad nodding agreeably to Shell's story, and looked at Gloria. She held up an apron with *Big Cheese* printed on it. "For your brother?"

"He'll hate it. It's not Gucci."

"You're right," Gloria said, putting it back. "I need to find something tackier, so I can guilt him into wearing it every time I go around to his."

Adams snorted laughter, and looked at her dad, still listening to Shell. "He never gets any better, does he?"

"One could argue he's better than either of us at this sort of thing," Gloria said, which Adams thought was a fairly tactful way of saying she hadn't inherited either of her parents' abilities with people.

Gloria put a couple of fridge magnets next to Hugh's haul, then hooked her arm through her daughter's. "Come on. Let's get a cuppa while he's talking."

"My mug—"

"Your father can buy you a mug." Gloria all but dragged her into the cafe attached to the cheese shop, past a large blackboard advertising cheese scones, cheese plates, and cheese sandwiches.

"No wonder Collins loves this place," Adams muttered as they sat down at a table by one of the big windows, the hills rolling in variegated greens away from town, smudged with sheep and trees and drystone walls, and likely hiding all sorts of fae up to nefarious doings. She touched the baton in her coat pocket. It was too warm to be wearing a coat, but she could hardly shove the baton into the pocket of her jeans.

And she certainly wasn't going to be without it. Or the duck, which was in her other pocket.

"Now, what's really going on?" Gloria asked, once they'd ordered a pot of tea with two cups, as well as a coffee for Adams (thankfully not cheese themed. She'd half expected them to offer her a dusting of parmesan on top).

"What?" she said, as innocently as she could.

"Bedbugs? Really?"

"Well—"

"*Jeanette.*"

Adams grimaced, looking at the table. It was proper wood, not laminate, the top softly scratched and ringed with old cup marks. "It just seemed better for you not to stay in Skipton."

"Why? Is it one of your cases?"

"So to speak."

Gloria sighed, shaking her head. "We thought, well, give you a day and you'll be sure to tell us what's actually going on, but no. *So to speak?* Who do you think you're talking to?"

"I just can't tell you much." Movement outside caught her eye, something at the far side of the field that bordered the cheese factory, near a stand of trees, and she narrowed her eyes, trying to spot it again.

"I'm sure you can tell us more than *bedbugs.*"

No sheep in the fields, and it had been too big for a bird. She leaned toward the window, her chest tight, and Dandy put his paws up on the sill to peer out.

"Jeanette? Are you listening?"

"Ah—" The trees weren't thick. Had it been walkers?

"What're you looking at?" Gloria touched her arm. "Are you alright?"

Adams looked away from the window reluctantly, but was saved from answering by the drinks arriving, followed by Hugh, clutching his shopping. He set the bag on the floor next to his chair and rubbed his hands together, smiling at the young man offloading the tray of tea things.

"Could I have one of those millionaire shortbreads? They look amazing!"

The young man nodded and wandered off, swinging his tray. Hugh looked from Adams to Gloria. "Has she come clean yet?"

"No."

"*Nettie*."

Adams spread her hands on the table. "You just have to trust me. We couldn't stay in Skipton, alright? But it's all in hand. You don't have to worry."

Gloria raised her eyebrows. "So I shouldn't be wondering what my daughter was doing drawing under the doormat at three a.m. the first morning, and creeping about the kitchen the same time last night?"

Adams scowled. "You should've been asleep."

"So should you."

They stared at each other. The young man brought the millionaire's shortbread over, started to say something, then looked from Adams to Gloria and fled.

"Now you're scaring the locals," Hugh said, cutting the shortbread into uneven thirds and setting it in the middle of the table.

"I'm *worried*," Gloria said.

"You don't need to be," Adams replied. "Really. I've got this." Or she would have. Somehow.

"I'm not worried about *us*. I'm worried about *you*."

"I can look after myself."

"That's not what I mean."

The table fell silent, and Adams picked up her coffee, sipping it carefully. It was okay. Not instant, at least, although it tasted a bit scorched.

"Nettie," her dad started, and she shook her head.

"No. This is not like London, and don't go looking at me like I'm *delicate* or something. You just need to believe me when I say we couldn't stay in Skipton, but there's no risk here. I'll make sure of it."

"We're allowed to worry. We're your parents," Gloria said, but without the force she'd had a moment earlier.

"Sure," Adams said, getting up. "I need to make a phone call." She took the coffee with her, walking through the back doors of the cafe into an outdoor seating area, Dandy trotting after her. Two older women with matching black labradors were sitting at one of the wooden picnic tables drinking wine and sharing a cheeseboard. The two dogs watched Dandy pass with wide eyes, but the women ignored them, and Adams walked to the wooden fence that held back the field, shading her eyes with one hand as she examined the clump of trees beyond. Nothing, or she didn't think so. She could go and have a look, of course, but that would mean leaving her parents here, and what did she tell them then? Was that even *safe?*

She pressed her hand to her forehead, taking a deep breath. She needed sleep, and she needed to talk to Thompson, or someone who knew how to undo the faery cake, but in the meantime she just had to hold it together. She stepped back from the fence and leaned against the nearest picnic table, taking a moment to gather herself, to let the copper-salt taste of the Thames die out of the back of her throat, the memory of the *snap-snap-snap* fade to an echo. She wasn't angry at her parents for bringing it up, not really. She was angry she'd made them feel they needed to.

She was just taking a sip from the chunky cafe mug when her phone rang, startling her enough that she spilled coffee on her T-shirt. She scrabbled the phone out and hit answer without checking the display. "*What?*"

"Lovely to hear you, too," Rory said, sounding amused.

"Sorry."

"Everything alright?"

"No," she said, and was startled by both her answer and the catch in her voice.

"That seems like a reasonable response," he said, his voice quiet. "Want to look at some boring books?"

"I can't come over."

"I know. What's the address for the cottage?"

"You don't want to drive all this way."

"Well, I'm already here, so …"

Adams looked around as if he might be standing in the cafe waving at her. "Where's here?"

"Middle of Hawes. You?"

"Cheese factory, but I've got my parents with me."

"Oh, send them to the Ropemakers. It's fascinating."

Adams shook her head. "You and Collins are destined to be besties, you know. And I'm not sure it's safe to send them off anywhere."

"Why? What's happened?"

She glanced at the women at the table, but they still weren't paying any attention to her. She dropped her voice anyway. "The Gentry's been in touch."

"Ah. Are they in danger right now?"

She tapped her fingers on her legs. Velmyr *had* given her three days, and she wasn't going to be able to look at Rory's weird old books with her parents around. She looked at Dandy. "No. Probably not. Alright, I'll send them to the Ropemakers."

"Meet me in the pub, then. Want me to order you a coffee? Or something stronger?"

"Yes," she said, and hit disconnect, trying to ignore the sudden easing of tension in her shoulders. Rory was as much a liability as anyone else.

On the other hand, at least he knew why she was drawing under doormats at three a.m. That counted for something.

9

TICK-TOCK

Packing her parents off didn't exactly go smoothly. For a start, her dad had collared the lad who'd been serving them, and was endeavouring to find out where the millionaire's shortbread was made, as he swore it was the best he'd ever tasted. Adams was fairly sure he was just trying to make up for the young man stumbling into the middle of a family dispute, and it didn't look like it was working as she arrived back at the table.

Gloria slid the plate holding the last third of the slice toward her. "That's yours, love."

"No thanks. I—"

"You need to eat."

"I'm already eating twice as much as usual."

"My point exactly. Eat it!"

"I need to go," the young man said, backing away, and Hugh gave the two women an admonishing look.

"See, you've scared him again."

"Uh, no, I just …" He gave up on excuses and fled to another table.

"I need to go and do a couple of things," Adams said,

sitting down and clicking her fingers quietly under the table at Dandy, pointing to the floor. "Apparently the Ropemakers comes highly recommended."

"Oh, that does sound interesting," Hugh said, and pointed at the shortbread. "Are you going to eat that?"

Adams pushed it toward him while her mum tutted, then said, "Ropemakers? Are you sure there isn't a Paint Dryer's we could look at instead?"

Adams snorted. "There's a Countryside Museum? Sorry, I just really need to do this. We'll do something more fun tomorrow."

"Of course, love," Hugh said, somewhat indistinctly around the shortbread. "Anyway, there's that sheepdog demonstration this evening. Shell said it's really good. And Paul said we should definitely go to the viaduct for the trains, so there's tomorrow's plan."

"Who's Paul? That lad?"

"No, Paul from the cheese-tasting room. He grew up here. Spent his whole life in this valley. Or dale? I suppose you call it a dale."

Adams thought briefly that if her dad did get kidnapped by anyone, he'd at least get their full life story, date of birth, and favourite hobbies, which would make catching them later much easier. She winced. No one was getting kidnapped, and even if they did, she'd know who was behind it. She looked at Dandy, and, with her hand still under the table, subtly pointed at each of her parents, hoping he got the hint. She didn't think they could get in much trouble at the Ropemakers, but Dandy seemed fairly hostile to fae stuff, so it could only help. Aloud she said, "Right, well, let me know how you get on, alright? Message me."

Hugh put an arm around her shoulders and gave her a quick squeeze. "We'll be just fine, Nettie. Off you go and do your stuff."

Her mum nodded, shooing her away. "I still wish it was a secret date."

"Definitely not." Adams pressed her fingers lightly onto Dandy's head before she got up, and he whined but stayed put as she headed for the door, nodding at Shell as she passed through the gift shop but not lingering enough to be caught in a conversation.

It was a quick walk down to the main street, and along to the crowded picnic benches in front of the pub, which were even busier than they'd been earlier. There was no sign of Rory, but she supposed, given the weather, they'd have more chance of privacy inside. She headed into the shadowed interior, scented with old beer and warm wood, blinking around as her eyes adjusted. She'd barely oriented herself when a cold nose shoved itself into her hand, and she looked down. Midge peered past her, disappointment evident.

"Sorry," she said, scuffing the border collie's ears. "He's busy."

Pinto had stayed with Rory, tucked into a booth in the corner, well away from the scattering of afternoon drinkers who remained inside. Most people were making the most of the unfamiliar heat, working on sunburns and dehydration at the tables outside, and in here there was only an elderly man perched on a barstool, four teenagers who looked like they'd probably only turned legal drinking age last week (if they had), and two large men arguing loudly over the tile design for a new bathroom.

Adams headed over to join Rory, Midge trailing her.

"Alright?" she asked, sitting down opposite him. A large supermarket bag sat on the wooden seat between them, and she eyed it mistrustfully. He'd brought a *lot* of books, by the look of things.

"Not bad. Surviving?"

"Sort of." She nodded at the bag. "Brought the whole library?"

He seesawed his hand. "I found a bunch of things in different books. Nothing's *quite* right, so we might need to do some piecing together."

"Great." She paused as the bartender set a cup of coffee in front of her. "Thanks." She waited until the woman was gone again, then looked at Rory. "Give me the condensed version of what you think you've got so far."

He hesitated, then said, "I don't want to make wild guesses. I ran it past Chloe and she's not sure either. Says she needs to look into it more."

"But?"

"But." He tapped his fingers lightly on the table, looking at his bottle of dandelion and burdock. "Casting hexes like the ones in your photos takes a lot of power, and vanishing ones aren't even mentioned. Whoever this Gentry is, they're powerful. Plus they could well have others working with them."

Adams sipped her coffee, thinking about Velmyr and his clicking fingers, then said, "So a super-powered fae gang, basically."

"Basically."

"Sodding *hell*. As if average faeries aren't bad enough."

Rory scratched the back of his neck. "Met faeries, have you?"

"Met them. Fought them with Christmas puddings. Had to put Santa in a sack."

He made a thoughtful noise. "Not exactly the response I was expecting. But you see what we're getting into, then."

"Me. What *I'm* getting into."

"Keep telling yourself that."

She narrowed her eyes at him, and he grinned. She sighed, and said, "Any idea how we counter the hexes?"

"Working on it. So what happened here? You're looking a bit weary on it."

Adams watched the kids at the table. One of them was attempting a Guinness and already looked a bit queasy. "Do you believe there's actually a faery land people can be stolen away to, like in the stories?"

He made a thoughtful noise. "There's some debate. It might be that there's not an actual other world, just pockets of time that are frozen, and the rest of the world washes past it. Either way, the fae have a place out of this reality." He tapped the table lightly, knocking on wood or demonstrating its solidity, she wasn't sure.

"So you do think there's *something*."

"Yes." He said it simply, and she waited, letting silence fill the space between them. Finally he said, "You know my mum had problems."

"You said she could see the Folk world, but couldn't reconcile it with the human one. That seeing both when everyone was telling her one couldn't exist was too much to cope with."

"Pretty much." He fell silent again, and she wondered if it was too painful for him to recall, or if he was choosing how to tell her – or how much to. One of the big men who'd shouted out to them earlier came in, stripped down to a white singlet, and leaned over the bar, his shoulders violently red.

"I went looking for her in York," Rory said, his voice quiet. "I told you that, right?"

"You did," Adams said.

"She spent a lot of time there before she vanished, and I spent a lot of time there after, trying to figure things out. But it's not where she disappeared."

Adams blinked. "She disappeared? I thought ..." She

wasn't sure how to continue. There was probably a polite way to finish the thought, but she couldn't think how.

Rory gave her a half smile. "I never said she'd died."

Hadn't he? She supposed he hadn't. "Oh. I mean … that's good?"

"Other than the fact she vanished."

"Well, yes." She waited, watching the big man collect three pints and amble out again. When Rory didn't continue, she said, "You think faeries took her?" It should've sounded more ridiculous to say than it did.

He ran a hand back through his hair, setting it in dishevelled angles. "I don't know what I think. She wasn't right for a long time, and maybe she just fell through the cracks somewhere, you know? People do, all the time. But she had a thing about faeries. As in she was scared of them, always looking for faery rings and warning me not to use their names. She had iron horseshoes on my bedroom door, and salt on all the windowsills, and there's this." He reached into his shirt and produced a necklace, a chunk of burnt, striated gold stone set into a frame of tarnished metal, and hung from a chain.

Adams frowned at it. "Amber?"

"Yes. It's meant to protect you against abduction. She used to wear it, but she gave it to me the night she vanished."

Adams didn't know how to respond to that, so after a moment she said, "Is there anything else that protects against abduction?"

"Sure. Certain bones, stones with holes in them, some plants."

She nodded. "We should get some. Chloe might have them at the shop."

"Probably." He took a sip of his drink, the ice clinking in the glass. "Are you going to tell me what's happened?"

She looked at her mug. "I'm sorry about your mum."

"Thanks."

They were both quiet for a bit, then Adams said, "I spoke to the Gentry. He turned up at the house last night. He found my parents in Skipton and gave them faery cakes, and now he wants me to get something for him or else he'll click his fingers and steal them away." There was a strain in her voice she didn't like, something stretched taut and fragile, and she hoped he couldn't hear it.

"He came to the cottage?"

"Yes."

Rory swore, then was quiet again before he said, "This thing he wants, is it something you can get easily?"

"I'm not sure it's something I can get at all, and even if I did, I think giving it to the Gentry is a truly terrible idea. World-ending level terrible."

He tapped on the table again without speaking, then got up. "Want that something stronger I mentioned earlier?"

"Make it a double."

"Done. And you can tell me all about Christmas puddings as a deadly weapon before we get into this."

He headed for the bar, and Adams watched him go, fingers pressed into her mug hard enough to hurt. His mum had never come back. She couldn't let that happen to hers. She *couldn't*.

AN HOUR later they were still huddled in the corner booth with the dogs at their feet, half a dozen old, leather-bound books in varying degrees of slow decay cluttering up the table in front of them. Every now and then Rory would push one toward Adams, tapping a picture or a passage, and she'd switch her attention to it dutifully, but she was starting to feel like she'd read the same thing half a dozen times over, mostly old posh men getting hot under the collar – and elsewhere – as they described the Gentry. Not that their descriptions were particularly helpful, either. They didn't sound anything like Velmyr. It was all *glowing, luminous skin* and *lips honeyed with dew* and *eyes like dawn mist,* which was giving Adams uneasy images of creatures with glow-in-the-dark faces and murky orange eyeballs. She was trying not to picture the lips, as they just sounded sticky and a bit messy. The old toffs were evidently the original rabid fanboys.

And none of it was helping them. Nothing told them how to counter the effects of eating faery cake, or even suggested the possibility of it being used on this side of Faery. The only mention of it was as some sort of common lore, that once one ate or drank anything in Faery, there would be no returning. The hexes were just as elusive, the runes in the books all looking *almost* but not quite like the ones in Adams' photos, off by a cross-hatching or the thickness of a line, so subtle she kept being sure she'd found them, then Rory would point out the difference. She had no idea how he could even tell.

The one thing they did discover was that Chloe was right about the Gentry being banished to Faery. The average fae could move as freely as Folk, but it seemed sorcerers had taken serious exception to their fae counterparts, and Velmyr was breaking half a dozen treaties even by being here, which probably explained why Thompson was so antsy about the Watch. The sorcerers sounded like they'd taken rather a scorched earth approach to getting rid of the Gentry, which wasn't something that'd be easy to hide, should things kick off again. According to the books, towns and villages had been flattened, half the country's sorcerers had been killed, and the humans were so traumatised it had set the entire anti-Folk movement going. All of which made it seem even more imperative that she didn't give Velmyr the book, as he couldn't be up to anything good with it after all that.

The books didn't mention the Watch, or the cats, and Adams found herself unsurprised. She doubted old rich men gave much credence to the idea the world was run by cats, or anyone else small and un-endowed with double-barrelled surnames and titles.

She finished her whisky and leaned back in her seat, pinching the bridge of her nose.

"Okay?" Rory asked.

"No."

"No," he agreed, and checked his phone. "Still nothing from Chloe. You?"

Adams shook her head, and checked her own phone. Her dad had sent a photo of some rope, which at least proved she wouldn't have been having any better a time with them. That was over half an hour ago, though. She hit dial, waiting while it rang.

It clicked onto voicemail, and she hung up without leaving a message. He never heard it ring, even when he had it on him.

She knew that. She knew that, and yet … She pulled up her mum's phone number and tried that instead, her stomach tightening even past what seemed to have become her normal, unpleasant level of tension. The whisky and extra coffee weren't helping, admittedly.

It rang once. Twice.

"Adams?" Rory said.

Three times. Four.

"What's happening?"

She got up on the fifth ring, already heading for the door as the phone cut to messages. It didn't necessarily mean anything, maybe the Ropemakers didn't allow phones in case they upset the ropes, or her mum was on the phone to one of her brothers, or an aunt, or anyone. It could mean *nothing*.

Or it could mean everything.

"Adams." Rory grabbed her arm and she jerked away from him.

"They're not answering."

"Okay. What's your plan?" He didn't move to touch her again, just stood there watching her, dust on his fingers from the books, which they'd abandoned on the table. Midge and Pinto had followed them, staring up at Adams earnestly.

"I need to find them," she said. "Dandy was with them, but …" But he kept vanishing at inopportune moments, and she didn't know why, and what if this had been one of those moments?

"Yes. How do you want to start?"

"They were going to the Ropemakers. I'll try there, then the cottage, then I'm calling in a trace on their phones."

"Right. I don't know where the cottage is, so why don't I take the Ropemakers? I just need to grab our stuff." He gestured back at the cluttered table.

"You don't—" she started, then cut herself off. This was her *parents,* lost in some Dales village with sneaky bloody fae lurking about the place. She couldn't afford to waste time. "Thanks," she said instead, but he was already on the way back to the table, not waiting for her answer. Midge whined at her instead. "I know," she said. "Useless bloody invisible dogs."

Rory didn't waste time, just swept the books unceremoniously into the bag and hurried back to join her while she tried both phone numbers again.

"Still nothing?" he asked.

"Nothing." She headed for the door, stepping back quickly as a large, sweaty man with a luminously pink face and sunburnt shoulders under his white singlet trundled in, either the same man from earlier or one who looked astonishingly similar. He almost tripped over Pinto, made a smooching noise at Midge, and grinned at Adams and Rory.

"Chuffing great, innit?" he said. "Can't beat summer in the Dales!"

"It's a blinder," Rory said agreeably, and Adams gave the man a quick nod, hurrying through the door as soon as it was clear.

Outside, the sun made her squint painfully after the dim interior, and there was such a clamour going up from the tables she almost flinched. There were even more people out here now, standing on the pavement and wedged onto every scrap of the benches, leaning against the walls with pints and Pimm's and clinking glasses of gin and tonic. She scanned the crowd automatically, the same way she did any group, particularly at pubs, and particularly when the weather was hot. It was a reflex, listening for the edge in a voice that tipped it from jovial to jagged, the slam of a glass that slipped out of amused and into aggression. Rory was already walking past her, wending his way through the drinkers, and she caught the bag of books, pulling him to a halt.

"What?" There was an anxious edge to his voice.

She nodded through the crowd, to the furthest table, which was crowded with empty glasses and mostly taken up by the same trio of large men as had called out to them earlier, minus the one who'd just gone inside. The remaining two were as alarmingly red-faced as he'd been, and one had his shirt off, revealing an untoned but solid torso that spoke of physical work rather than gym time. The other had managed to keep his T-shirt on but was slamming his fist into the table, walking that very fine line Adams had just been looking for.

And next to them were her parents, Gloria swatting the arm of the truly enormous fist-slammer and clearly trying not to laugh at whatever he was roaring about. Hugh was gesticulating wildly with a half-full pint, and the shirtless man kept trying to fist bump him, but Adams had never seen her dad fist bump anyone in his life. Instead he kept offering either a flat hand or two fingers in the time-honoured paper and scissors gestures, looking faintly puzzled but cheerful.

"Oh," Rory said, and the relief in his voice was so clear she looked at him, startled. "I guess we don't need to rush to the rescue, then."

"You didn't in the first place."

"*Adams*. I'll call you Jeanette if you keep that up."

"I will definitely arrest you for that."

"You keep promising," he said, grinning at her, and she looked away before she could grin back. He got more annoying all the time.

She led the way through the tangle of drinkers to the end of the table, looking for Dandy as she went. There was no sign of him, and as they got closer the shirtless man was the first to notice her. "*Oi oi*," he said, raising his glass. "Is this the daughter?"

"*Ooh*, best behaviour, Stu," the other man said, grinning. "She's dying to arrest someone!"

"Honestly, it's not that easy," Rory said. "I keep trying."

"Nettie!" Hugh exclaimed, and looked at the glass-cluttered table. "These aren't all mine."

"What happened to the Ropemakers?" she asked.

"Far too nice a day to spend it all in there," Gloria said, and waved at Rory before looking back at Adams. "And what about you? Is this the thing you were sneaking away to do?"

Fist-slammer choked on his pint, and Gloria gave him a disapproving look. "*Eric.*"

"Sorry," he said, wiping his mouth.

"Disgraceful," she said, but the corners of her mouth were twitching, and Hugh shook his head.

"*Gloria.* One G&T and all decorum's gone."

Adams pinched the bridge of her nose. "Why weren't you

answering your phones?" She frowned. "And since when do you drink gin?"

"I'm allowed to drink whatever I want," Gloria said. "It's refreshing in this heat."

Adams started to answer, and Rory grabbed her arm. His grip was tight, and she looked around at him, meaning to ask what he was playing at, then she felt it. A shudder passed over her, and she felt it reflected in him, full-bodied and visceral, starting somewhere deeper than thought, the same cold, otherworldly sensation as she'd had the night before. The whole street darkened, as if a cloud had passed over the sun, and the conversation paused, a collective catch of the breath, then resumed again as the feeling faded.

"There," Rory said, his voice low, and she followed his gaze. Someone stood watching them from across the street, their back perfectly straight, the sun gleaming on their pale hair, and there was no doubting who it was. Velmyr was edged with brilliance, not simply in the sunlight shining on his glossy hair, but in the way Folk were always more clear-cut, more in the world than humans. Only with him it seemed amplified, as if reality itself dimpled around him. And as if he needed to make any more of an impact, he was clad in a full-length, swirling cloak in some darkly hued fabric that was shot through with silver, his collar high and a waistcoat hugging his chest beneath it. He also seemed to be wearing an actual crown of some sort, which seemed like an overkill. He didn't need it to set himself apart from everyone else here.

"Stay with Mum and Dad," Adams said to Rory, her voice low. She didn't take her eyes off Velmyr, as if he'd vanish the moment she looked away. For all she knew, he might. She headed for him, moving fast through the crowd, not bothering with *excuse me*'s or *coming throughs*, just making her own path, quick and efficient. Velmyr watched her come, a smile tipping up the corners of his lips, and as she reached the street he raised one hand, tapping his wrist softly, perfect eyebrows raised.

It couldn't have been clearer. *Tick-tock.*

Adams clutched her baton in her pocket as she crossed the road, scowling as Velmyr turned, strolling away with his hair rippling softly over his shoulders. No one paid him any attention, as if cloaks and crowns were perfectly normal hiking attire, and Adams called, "*Hey!* I want a word."

The Gentry looked back at her, still smiling, and raised one hand, fingertips touching softly.

"*Don't—*"

He clicked them, and the world shivered, Adams' ears crackling with a shift in pressure. A dog started barking behind her, regular, sharp yaps of alarm. She spun around, her chest tight with fright, searching for her parents. They were still there, but Midge hadn't stopped barking. Pinto joined in, Rory trying to quiet them both, and Adams hesitated, looking back at Velmyr.

"Hurry up, Detective," he said, the words sounding as if he was breathing them into her ears. "My patience isn't infinite."

"It's not even been a day—"

"I think you need a little nudge."

"I *don't.*"

"See you soon." He kept walking, and Adams started after him.

Then Rory shouted, "*Don't touch it!*"

She swung back in time to see the crowd erupt into motion, everyone pushing and shoving, and somewhere at the back of her mind she heard the Gentry's high, dangerous laughter.

She gave up on Velmyr and sprinted toward her parents. It wasn't like she had a choice.

10

A COMPLETE SHEEP SHOW

THE CROWD WAS IN UPHEAVAL, MIDGE AND PINTO STILL barking, and Adams' sprint turned into a wade through the drinkers, all but manhandling them out of her path as she fought her way to the table.

"Leave it!" Rory shouted, and she wasn't sure if he was talking to the dogs or the humans, his voice sharp with alarm. She detoured around a scrum of grey-haired men and women in bright walking shirts, all scrabbling after something on the ground and trying to elbow each other out of the way, and got a clear view of the table in time to see Hugh pointing at something.

"It's bothering them," he shouted over the dogs' barking. "It's just a coin. Whose is it?"

"Don't touch it," Rory said again, trying to silence the dogs.

"There's another one," Gloria said, indicating the ground by her feet, and bent to reach for it.

Eric – the fist-slammer – caught her shoulder, not roughly, but firmly enough to make Adams push a young man to the side rather more harshly than she might normally have.

"It's mine," Eric said.

"I don't *think* so," Gloria replied, trying to shake him off.

And Adams was too far away to see the things clearly, and wasn't even sure she'd have known what they were if she could, but she could *feel* them, feel the ugly intent bleeding through the crowd, even as Singlet, who'd returned with more drinks, peered at the one on the table and said, "It's right nice, that. Here, let me get it."

"No, I saw it first," Shirtless Stu said, pulling Singlet back.

"I've got it," Hugh insisted, and Rory caught his arm to stop him touching it, but *someone* was going to grab the bloody things, because whatever she and Rory and the dogs were feeling, it wasn't what the others were. There was a nasty, hungry look on everyone's faces, even her mum's, and Adams shouted, "Leave them! Don't touch them!"

No one was listening, though, and more people were turning toward the coins, ducks fighting for food at a pond. It wasn't just the two at her parents' table, but others as well, as if someone had tossed a handful casually into the crowd, turning the happy hour into a feeding frenzy. The scrum she'd just worked her way past was blooming, and others were forming and building violently.

"*Stop!*" she bellowed, but no one was listening, and the only reason no one had grabbed one of the coins yet was because *everyone* was trying to be the first to reach them, pulling each other back, scrabbling and struggling, and it was going to get ugly any moment. She could feel it, the heat setting light to a barely subdued fury.

"Adams, I don't want to touch it," Rory said as she finally reached the table. He was still trying to keep her dad away from the coin.

"Excuse *me*," Hugh said, trying to push Rory off. "That is *my* coin."

"I've got it," Adams said, finally breaking through the crowd and reaching the table. She had no gloves, nothing she could use to pick the coin up, so she grabbed a book from the bag Rory had abandoned and simply slammed it down on top of the glittering token.

"Hey," Hugh started, then blinked. He looked puzzled for a moment, then said, "What book's that, love?"

Adams slipped her foot in front of Gloria and put it on top of the second coin, wishing she had boots on instead of trainers, and preferably ones with steel plates or something in the bottoms of them. She felt like the thing might be leeching poison into her sole. All around them drinkers were still straining to reach the other coins, and she didn't know how she was going to manage to get to them all, or what to do with them once she had, but at least her parents couldn't reach these ones.

"This looks really interesting," Hugh said, picking up the book and exposing the coin again.

"*No,*" Rory yelped, trying to snatch the book back, and Gloria and Eric both lunged for the uncovered coin. Adams grabbed them, a shoulder each, and Eric flung her off easily, bumping Gloria out of the way the same time.

"How *dare* you?" Gloria demanded, but rather than taking him to task she lunged for the coin again.

"Mum, *stop!*" Adams shouted, and jammed her shoulder between the two of them, using her baton to flick the coin into the air.

"*Hey!*" Eric yelped, and he and his two mates lunged for the token together. Adams tried to heft herself over the top of them, to catch it before it landed, because she didn't *want* to touch it, but she certainly wasn't letting anyone else do so. She wasn't going to make it though, the men's reach longer than hers, and just as Eric was about to snatch the coin out of the air, the clutter of empty and half-empty glasses on the table exploded into motion. They surged down the slatted wooden top, tumbling into laps and to the ground, spilling dregs of beer and smashing apart as they hit the concrete below. Dandy rode the wave of crashing glassware with his teeth bared and his dreadlocks flowing, and slammed into the men, sending them backward with startled cries.

Gloria gave a shout of triumph as she reached for the falling coin, and Adams smacked it with the baton, a glancing blow that sent it off course, missing her mum's fingertips by a breath. Dandy bounded after it, leaving devastation in his wake, and Adams was almost sure she heard the coin clatter off his teeth as he seized it. He landed lightly on the glass-strewn ground, spun back, pounced on the coin she'd had covered with her foot, then plunged into the crowd, Midge and Pinto scampering after him.

Adams turned to watch him darting through the knots of struggling drinkers, her heart going so fast she could barely catch breath. So close. It had been *so close*. And everyone here had been put at risk. Dandy didn't come back, snaking through the crowd, and in his wake the skirmishes eased, people straightening up and looking around as if startled to find themselves out of their seats. Adams wondered if she needed to make an announcement of some sort, call it a gas leak or bad beer (not that the pub would appreciate that), but it was almost immediately clear she wouldn't have to. Everyone simply turned back to their drinks and conversations as if nothing untoward had happened, glancing at their torn sleeves and grazed knees with a complete lack of curiosity.

All except one woman, anyway. She emerged from the crowd with her hair rumpled and her T-shirt torn at the neck and walked slowly off down the road, her hands clutching something to her chest. Dandy stepped onto the tarmac then stood silently watching her go, his ears back. Adams hurried toward the street, but when she reached it Dandy stepped in front of her, just as he had at the house.

"What?" she murmured, her voice low.

He leaned against her legs, pushing her back, and when she looked up again the woman was vanishing. Not around a corner, or into a shop. Just … fading out, as if she'd never been. Adams blinked, and looked around at Rory, who was staring after the vanished woman just as blankly as she was.

She looked at Dandy. "What the hell was that?" she asked him. "Was it like the hexes? Faery traps or something?"

He tipped his head.

"Helpful," she muttered, and turned back to the table, her chest tight and her stomach sick. There had been coins in the crowd, sure. But there had been *two* at her parents' table.

That wasn't a *nudge*. It was a test.

*

"Come on. We're going," Adams said when she made it back to the table.

"Oh … but Mike's just getting another round in," Hugh said, waving vaguely toward the pub door. He still had Rory's book in front of him, and had opened the front cover, but was wearing his sunglasses instead of his reading glasses, so hadn't got any further than peering hopefully at the page.

"Someone can tell him to leave yours off," Adams said, looking pointedly at the shirtless man. He blinked a couple of times, and Eric clapped him on the shoulder.

"Off you go, Stu."

"Right." Stu got up and trailed inside, pulling a T-shirt on as he went, and Eric looked at Adams.

"Sure you don't want to join us?"

"We need to get back," she said, picking up her dad's bag of cheese shop goodies.

"Spoilsport," Eric said and grinned, showing off a couple of impressively chipped teeth.

"I'm not done with my G&T, Jeanette," Gloria said, raising her glass, which had somehow escaped the Dandy-based carnage. "There's no rush. Have a little drink while I finish this."

Adams took a deep breath, holding back the desire to make it *very clear* that the entire bloody table had just about got stolen off to Faery, so no, she did not want to have a *little drink* with anyone.

"You off to the sheepdog demo, then?" Eric asked before Adams could find any civilised words, looking at Gloria. "Should be starting in ten minutes or so, and it's right good."

"It depends what our daughter's got planned for us."

Eric looked at Adams, and she scowled at him. "Why? You from the Hawes tourist board or something?"

"It's local colour, like," he said. "And it's just up the road. You'll be there in five minutes."

Adams thought she'd had enough local colour, as she watched Stu amble back to the table, his shirt already off again.

"We heard about the demo," Hugh said, looking up from the book. "Anyone you lads know?"

"'Cause all us farmers look the same?" Eric asked, grinning, and Gloria swatted his arm again.

"I wouldn't think it was hard to know everyone here," she said.

"You should go," Stu said, scratching his chest. His sunburn looked painful, and he had a muppet tattooed on his chest. It was spectacularly bad, and Adams wasn't even sure which one it was meant to be. "Your dogs might learn something. Stop them barking so much."

"They're not usually so bad," Rory said, looking at Midge and Pinto. They were fawning over Dandy in such a way that Adams couldn't imagine how anyone could miss the fact there was an invisible dog sitting right by the table.

"Not the dogs' faults," Eric said. "That's training, that is." He gave a short nod of satisfaction and drained his glass.

Rory nodded back amiably. "Probably." He had his hands in the pockets of his jeans, his arms bare below his T-shirt sleeves, and despite the warmth of the late afternoon sun Adams could see goosebumps on his skin. He was as unsettled as she was.

"Let's go, then," she said, taking the book from her dad and handing it to Rory.

"I was reading that," Hugh protested.

"Not without your glasses, you weren't. Come on. You wanted to experience Yorkshire? Watching some sheep get chased around a field seems pretty on-brand." She wasn't actually sure it was *Yorkshire*, exactly, more *country*, but it certainly wasn't London, and if it got her parents out of the crowd, away from the press of people, that was the most important bit. It felt too easy for another coin to appear, or the Gentry to come back, or … something. She didn't know what else could happen, but there would be something, and she wanted to be able to see it coming.

Hugh shrugged. "Fair enough. Come on, Gloria. You can't nurse that all night."

"I was enjoying it," she said, but put the glass down. Eric got up hurriedly, and she let him take her hand and help her to her feet. "Thank you, love."

"A pleasure," he said, looking as if he didn't really want to let go. But he did, and held his hand out for Hugh to shake. "Enjoy the sheepdogs. It's a right good show."

"Thanks," Hugh said, shaking hands with both men. "Say goodbye to Mike for us. It was a pleasure to meet you all."

"Great," Adams said. "Shall we go?"

"You should really let her arrest you, mate," Eric said to Rory. "She needs to do something with all that aggression."

"It's not healthy, holding onto it," Stu said. "I usually take it out wrestling sheep, myself."

"Wrestling what, sorry?" Hugh said. "I've heard of pigs, but—"

"No, to get them dipped and shorn. It's not *weird*."

Rory looked at Adams, and she held a hand up. "Don't suggest wrestling."

"Really? So tempting," he said, grinning.

Gloria linked her arm through Rory's. "She's very prickly, my daughter. But only on the outside."

"Are you sure? It seems quite heartfelt."

Adams shook her head, and led the way onto the road. "Which way?"

"Right," Rory said.

Adams turned that way, her chest tight with unease. The Gentry had gone this way, and the vanishing woman. The town looked just as it had before, the shops lining the street, display windows full of souvenirs and the names still painted above the doors in old-fashioned font, the cars jammed into the parking spaces and the meandering tourists. But nothing *felt* the same. The world had too many layers, and it seemed she saw them more and more all the time, until she feared she was never going to be able to *not* see them, passing some point of no return where the world could no longer be as she'd known it ever again.

"Are you alright, love?" Hugh asked, catching up with her and taking the bag of books off her. "We didn't mean to intrude. It was just such a nice day, and those lads said we could share their table, so … it felt like a holiday thing to do."

"I'm fine," she said. "Really."

"You need to learn how to lie better," he said, and put an

arm around her shoulders as they walked. And for a moment she really *was* fine, under the familiar weight of his hand, as if he could make everything better, the way he had when she'd been a kid and had fought with her brothers, or fallen in the playground, or her mum had yelled because she'd come home with her clothes torn and her lip bloodied.

Only he couldn't fix this. He couldn't even understand it. But she let his arm stay where it was. It was nice, plus it made her feel a little less like he could be snatched off to Faery any moment.

THEY WALKED to the edge of town, where a small crowd had already gathered at the gate to a field, leaning on the drystone wall and peering expectantly at a couple of dozen sheep inside it. They were grazing, unbothered by the spectators, and nothing seemed to be happening in a hurry. Adams shepherded everyone away from the other tourists, giving them enough space that no fae in disguise could sneak up on them without being seen. Or not if they were walking like normal people, anyway, and she had no way of preparing for anything else, other than relying on Dandy. He was nosing around a group of kids who were eating ice creams and asking if they could try herding the sheep too, and Adams whistled to him, hoping he wasn't going to start thieving off small children. The general thieving was bad enough.

Midge and Pinto looked at her curiously, and her dad said, "Are you getting in on the sheepdog thing too?"

"Oh. No." She couldn't think of anything else to add, so checked her phone instead, while Rory fielded questions about his own dog training techniques. As far as Adams could tell, they involved a lot of dog biscuits and YouTube videos, and the fact that Midge and Pinto really liked learning things. She had no such luck with Dandy, even with the use of coffee as a bribe.

He did come loping back to her eventually, licking his chops, while behind him a small boy wailed he'd dropped his ice cream and it had vanished. His parents were telling him not to lie, and she gave Dandy as much of a scowl as she dared, hoping he hadn't helped with the dropping part as well as the vanishing bit.

An old green Land Rover, almost as decrepit as Rory's, ambled up the road, and an elderly man clambered out with a woolly hat pulled down to his impressive eyebrows. He looked skinny enough that a decent breeze could whisk him away, if it wasn't for his large and battered wellies anchoring him to the land.

"Evening," he called, as two equally ancient dogs stumbled out of the back. He turned and lifted out a third, who had milky cataracts in her eyes. One of the slightly less elderly dogs leaned against her, and they walked together to the gate, which she went up and over with surprising grace. "I'm Jacob. The dogs here are Patch, Dipper, and Millie. Who's here to see some *magic?*"

Adams twitched at the word, even as the kids cheered.

"The bond between man and dog is unlike any other," the old boy intoned, strolling to the gate. "We think as one, move as one, *are* as one on the field, and this is how we bend the sheep to our will."

"Worth it for the monologue," Hugh said, and Gloria poked him.

"Behave. And get some money out."

"Why am I paying?"

"Because you're a gentleman."

"I am as well," he said with a sigh. "It's such a trap."

Adams took a step away from the wall, checking the road. No cars rushing down it, no charging fae army, just a trickle of people ambling up from town to check out the sheepdogs, mostly families with kids. In the other direction the road was empty, curling away into the Dales, where the hills were still bright with the afternoon light, sunset a long way off yet. And it normally never unnerved her, these ancient slabs of dale and fell, carved by humans into fields and farms and counties, but never quite tamed. They'd been unfamiliar when she arrived, but never unsettling. There was something almost reassuring about their wildness, in fact, something that spoke to her the same way the old waters of the Thames did, the bones of the land on display here just as surely as its veins were in London's endlessly persistent waterways.

But today she wasn't so sure. Today something was *off*, and they were out here unprotected, just waiting for the Gentry to return and pluck them out of the world. She caught Rory's arm, pulling him a little away from her parents.

"Where's your Land Rover?"

"Car park just out of town."

"Can you get it?"

"Sure." He looked around. "You alright here?"

She started to say *of course*, and stopped herself. It wasn't going to help her parents, pretending things were fine. "I don't know. I can't quite figure out what's going on – the Gentry said I needed a *nudge*, to hurry things along, but that was more than a nudge. That woman vanished."

He puffed air over his lips. "You think he knows you can't give him what he wants?"

She rubbed the back of her neck. "Maybe. Either way, I need to be ready to move my parents fast." She took a deep breath, making herself say it. "I need *you* to move my parents, if it comes to it. Keep them safe."

"Sure," he said simply. "Won't be long." He turned and

jogged off, a tall, lean man with a long gait, the dogs loping next to him.

"Nice," Gloria said, and Adams looked at her. She was watching Rory go, and flashed Adams a grin. "I see why you keep him around."

"*Mum.*"

"I can look!"

"Where's he off to?" Hugh asked. "I thought he wanted to get some tips."

"They're starting," Adams said, stepping closer to the wall. The sheep were watching the farmer and his dogs with very little alarm. The near-blind collie, ears pricked and grey muzzle twitching, lay in the grass next to her owner while the other two ranged down the field, moving a little stiffly but still with a certain assured grace. The farmer whistled, and the two dogs dropped to the grass, eyes fixed on the sheep, who clustered together a little more tightly.

A pen built of moveable metal gates stood in the middle of the field, barely big enough to hold the small flock, and as the farmer gave a series of short whistles the dogs started to work, slipping across the field in sharp little bursts of move-ment, dropping to their bellies whenever they stopped, here prowling forward step by step, here darting to cut off an escape, eyes never leaving the sheep. The sheep, for their part, gave a few disgruntled bleats, and made a couple of half-hearted breaks for freedom, but mostly seemed some-what resigned to the process as the dogs moved them around the field, not heading for the pen just yet. Adams was fairly sure they were almost as well-trained in this as the dogs themselves, and once the farmer had them gathered in a corner of the field he turned to the little crowd.

"As you can see," he said solemnly, "them dogs has a psychological hold on the sheep. They stare right into their souls and cast an enchantment on them, so the sheep will do whatever they wants. They'd trot right on into the river if the dogs told them to!"

"What if they drown?" the little boy who'd lost his ice cream asked, eyes wide.

"All that wool's a flotation device," the farmer said cheerfully, which seemed to calm the small critic.

Dandy growled, the sound pitched low, and Adams looked at him. He had his paws up on the wall, gaze – as much as she could see, given his hair – fixed on the sheep. Adams nudged his back paw with her foot, since she couldn't grab him, hoping he wasn't planning on charging in there and messing up the display. He quieted, not moving, and she looked back at the field, where the blind collie had climbed to her feet. The other two were still belly-down to the grass, staring at the sheep, their muscles coiled and tight.

"Now who wants to see the sheep do a figure eight around the field, then straight into the pen?" the farmer asked.

"Yeah!" the little boy shouted, accompanied by some slightly less enthusiastic but still positive responses from the older viewers.

"It really is impressive," Hugh said. "The control— *Oh!*"

The *oh* was because the blind collie broke into a sprint, startlingly smooth and swift, her unseeing gaze fixed on the sheep. Dandy shot up and over the wall, knocking a stone loose in his wake, which made her mum say, "Careful, Jeanette!"

"It wasn't me," she said, more on reflex than for any other reason.

The farmer whistled sharply, waving to the other dogs, and they burst into motion, rushing to intercept the blind dog – until they saw Dandy, at which point they stopped so hard that one smacked his muzzle into the ground, almost somersaulting, and the other barely managed to avoid falling over his partner. "*Oi!* Useless bloody mutts!" the farmer roared, as the sheep broke for the field's gate. He waved wildly. "Get out of it, Millie! Get out, you daft old bitch!"

"Mum, he *swore!*" the little boy shouted gleefully.

"Um, not really," his mum said, but Adams wasn't paying a lot of attention to the explanation of dog genders. Rory's old Land Rover was wheezing up the road, and she grabbed her parents' arms.

"*Move.* Now."

"What? But I want to see how he gets them back under control. This must be part of the demonstration," Hugh protested.

Adams glanced back at the field, propelling her unwilling parents toward the 4x4. Dandy had intercepted Millie, blocking her gently, but the sheep were still bearing down on the gate as the farmer whistled frantically, starting to back up. "*Bollocks,*" she hissed, and shoved her parents toward Rory as he brought the Land Rover to a sharp halt in front of them. "Get them out of here," she said to him, already running for the gate.

"Nettie?" her dad called, but she didn't stop.

The farmer had reached the gate, swinging himself up and over the top, out of the field, and she grabbed him as he landed, spinning him into the shelter of the wall as she yelled, "*Everyone out of the way!*"

They stared at her.

"*Now!*" she bellowed, and she'd like to have thought they listened, but it was more likely the gate crashing open under the charge of the sheep that got them moving. The latch burst out of the old wood of the fencepost and the flock poured through in a sea of woolly backs, while the farmer pushed her off and whistled frantically, waving his arms at the dogs still in the field.

"*Get in back!*" he roared. "*Get in, get* **in,** you useless creatures!"

The dogs were trying, shooting through the gate after the sheep and trying to get ahead of them, but the flock thundered down the road in furious pursuit of the rapidly reversing Land Rover. Rory spun the wheel across, backing into a gate on the opposite side of the lane, then jolted forward again, turning and roaring toward town in a belch of heavy black smoke. The sheep kept up their pursuit, and the two elderly dogs ran after them, trailed by the still yelling farmer.

Adams stayed where she was, both hands on her head, and one of the tourists started clapping uncertainly, then trailed off. After, there was only silence.

11

STAIRWAY TO SOMETHING

Adams turned to the field, looking for Dandy, who was doing almost as poor a job at protecting her parents as she was. He was busy pushing Millie toward the gate while the old dog snarled enthusiastically, her hackles up and her blind eyes rolling, trying to get past him and back to attack something in the field. There was nothing that Adams could see, nothing that should be setting the dog into such a fury, and she touched the duck in her pocket lightly, checking the other pocket at the same time. Baton. Dog biscuits. She still needed to get the Yorkies.

She stepped through the broken gate into the field, ignoring the little crowd.

"Unexpected," a man said in a strong American accent. "I liked the twist."

"Are you sure it was a twist?" his companion asked. "Seemed more like it went wrong."

"No, that bit with the old guy coming over the gate? Genius!" They both looked at Adams expectantly, as if waiting for her to continue the show, but she ignored them, her fingers tightening on the baton as she ventured across the field, smelling damp wool and trampled grass. Millie's head snapped toward her, nose twitching, and Adams took two dog biscuits from her pocket.

"There you go," she said, holding one out in each hand, and keeping her back to the gate so no one would see one vanish. "Quiet, now."

Millie snarled, and Dandy bumped her again.

"Behave," she said to him, and added, "Good girl," to Millie. Millie showed well-worn, yellowed teeth, but her snarling quieted, and Adams kept talking, her voice low and soothing, until Dandy stepped back and she felt safe enough to set the biscuit within sniffing distance of the collie. Millie took it hesitantly, crunching it slowly as her tail gave a couple of uneasy wags. "Well done," Adams said, and flicked the other biscuit to Dandy, then found a third and gave it to Millie, who took it from her happily enough. She looked at Dandy. "What was it?"

He looked across the field, then trotted to a spot of grass that was hidden from the spectators by the pen. She followed, stopping when he looked up at her and gave a small growl.

Not that she needed the growl.

Mushrooms scattered the grass, fat pale heads poking out of the green, some broken by the sheep's hooves, unevenly spaced and looking a little rotten even where they weren't trampled. There were still enough in place to tell it had been a ring, though.

"Bloody *hell*," she muttered. Couldn't go anywhere in this damn village without tripping over fae traps, apparently. Dandy whined, moving to intercept Millie, who stopped short as Adams turned to look, seemingly staring directly at her. "What did you see?" she asked, but the collie didn't answer.

The ones she wanted to talk never did.

"Do we follow the old guy?" the American man asked as Adams headed back through the gate, leaving it open behind her. She'd hurriedly snapped a few photos of the mushrooms, for all the good it'd do. Whatever Millie had seen, it was apparently gone now, and the old dog was trotting stiffly at her side, Dandy acting as a guide when she veered off course.

"Is the show down the road now?" the man persisted.

The rest of the little crowd looked at her expectantly. The sheep had left a trail of droppings leading toward town, but there was no sign of anyone returning. A few people had wandered off, but most were still waiting for Act Two.

"Ah … don't know. Sorry." She turned down the road, giving Millie a worried look as the dog stayed on her heel. "Sit," she tried, but Millie just looked at her blankly. "Stay?" Millie gave the impression she'd decided to be deaf as well, and Adams sighed. Great. Not that she expected she was going to be able to catch up to Rory and her parents on foot, blind dog for company or not, but now she was going to have to find the bloody farmer, too. Unless she put the dog in the old boy's Land Rover. She looked at it speculatively, but the back was open. If the collie tried to jump out and follow she'd only hurt herself.

"Aren't you part of the show?" the woman with the small boy asked Adams.

"No." She kept walking.

"But we haven't even paid," the American woman said. "We can't just *leave.*"

"There's a QR code," a skinny kid in baggy shorts said, pointing at the homemade sign on the gate that read *Sheep Dog Demo Here!!! Come and See the Magic!!!* It was decorated with a photo of the three dogs sitting on a quad bike, peering over the shoulders of the farmer at the viewer.

Adams left them milling about, alternately trying to get the QR code to work and discussing the possibility that this was just part of the show and they should stay put. She wasn't worried about them right now. Whatever had set the sheep off had never been intended for the tourist crowd, she was sure of it. It was another *nudge*, a show of strength from the Gentry. A reminder that she needed to get the book, one way or another. She shot Millie a look.

"Stay?" she tried again, but Millie kept trotting along, skinny haunches hitching a little, her path wobbly but mostly keeping on in a straight line. "Great," she muttered, pulling her mobile out. "I'm a dog thief now."

Rory didn't answer the phone. Neither did her mum or her dad, and by the time she reached town the only reason she wasn't running was the fact that Millie was already struggling to keep up. She kept following the path of sheep droppings, assuming the flock had kept up their frenzied pursuit of the Land Rover, and it led her straight down the main street, where the tables outside the pub were in an uproar. Half a dozen sheep had broken ranks and were stealing crisps, head-butting drinkers, and knocking over glasses, and one man in cycling shorts was standing on top of a table, hands clutched to his chest, shrieking, *"I have ovinophobia!"*

The table of big lads were wrestling a couple of sheep back onto the road, and as Adams drew level with the pub the door flew open and a skinny young woman ejected another sheep straight onto the pavement before roaring, "Whose idea of a joke is this?" She pointed down the street, where a man not much older than her was standing outside the next pub along, arms crossed over his chest and a wide grin on his face. *"Dan!* You *divot!"*

"Not me!" he shouted back.

"Just like the ducks weren't you?"

"Bloody ducks," Adams muttered, and shouted at Eric, "Hey! Have you seen my parents go past? In a Land Rover?"

He straightened up, face red and his knees still pressed into the back of a recalcitrant sheep that was trying to reach the flower planters on the windowsills. "This you, is it? Thought you were all law and order."

"I'm on holiday."

"Evidently," he said, and nodded at Millie. "Nicking dogs, too?"

"No. Have you seen them?"

He frowned, and tipped his head down the road. "Saw a Land Rover tearing off that way. What's happened?"

"Nothing." She pushed Millie toward him. "Look after her until the farmer comes back for his sheep?"

"Hang about, is your mum okay? Do you need some help?"

"What's this?" Stu asked. "Is Gloria alright?"

"She's lost her," Eric said.

"*What?*"

"No," Adams said. "They're with Rory."

"That posh bloke?" Mike asked. "What's he going to do, send the servants after them?"

"Who's them?" Adams asked sharply.

"Ah … dunno. Whoever's after your parents."

"The *sheep* are after them, Mike," Eric said. "Don't be a pillock." He abandoned the sheep and came to grab Millie's worn collar, patting her side with a heavy hand. "Come on, then, lass. Want some pork crackling?"

Millie whined, looking at Dandy, but Adams just said, "Thanks."

"Sure. Come back for a pint once you're sorted."

She nodded at him and headed down the street again, breaking into a jog now they weren't worried about geriatric sheepdogs keeping up. Dandy bounded ahead, and they followed the sheep's trail of devastation down the narrowing road, to where it split into two one-way lanes, divided by old stone buildings. Toppled planters and postcard stands pocked the street leading out, and one sheep was involved in an enthusiastic tug of war with an elderly woman over a wicker basket. But the trail still led on, and she ran past the downhill shops and over the hump of the one-lane stone bridge, water plunging through the buildings that formed its banks on her right, and kept going. The lane toward the holiday cottage yawned on her left, and she hesitated, but further along the main route through town she spotted a woman clutching a basket half-full of vegetables to her chest, leaning against a low garden wall. Adams jogged up to her.

"Was it sheep?" she asked.

"*Yes,*" the woman said, looking up at her with eyes that refracted the light, as if they had prisms rather than a smooth surface. Adams realised, with something bordering dismay, that she hadn't even noticed the woman's sharper edges. "Was that you?"

"No. I'm trying to track them down, though. Did a Land Rover go through?"

She nodded, looking Adams up and down with her eyes narrowed slightly, then her gaze slid to Dandy, and her arms tightened around the basket, as if worried she might lose her remaining few carrots. "Interesting dog."

"Yeah. Thanks." She headed off again before the woman could say anything else, swearing to herself softly. So much for keeping a low profile, for either her *or* Dandy. Not that the woman necessarily recognised them, or was fae herself, but she was definitely Folk, and if anyone was asking questions about unusual dogs, they had a nice clear lead now. Although she was less worried about the Watch than the Gentry, if she were being honest about it.

Another couple of uneven blocks and she was at the other

edge of town, discovering a pocket of allotments pressed up to the road, surrounded by the ubiquitous drystone walls and maintained in an impressive range of fastidiousness. One looked as though the owner was engaged in small-scale commercial growing, all climbing frames and plastic-covered beds, not a weed in sight; another had been given over entirely to rampaging courgettes; a third walked an enchanting line between order and chaos, giving the impression that anything and everything could grow there, as long as they behaved themselves; and yet another was home to nothing but a crumbling wooden shed and an explosion of wildflowers.

What they all had in common, though, were the sheep lawnmower-ing their way across the patches with utter disregard for any human order. Jacob the farmer stood in the gateway, whistling furiously, and his two dogs were visible here and there as an ear or a tail, but mostly only by the sheep's movement as they reluctantly edged back toward the gate.

"Hi," she called, and the farmer looked around at her.

"*What?*" he demanded. "Come to sabotage me again?"

She frowned. "I didn't do anything."

"Fair tackled me off the gate, you did!"

"You mean when you were about to be run down by your own sheep?"

He narrowed his eyes at her. "Still your fault. I know trouble when I see it."

Adams wondered if he meant trouble came in non-white skin in his world, or if he could pick up on the Dandy-ness around her, and decided she didn't want to know the answer. She didn't have time to deal with it, either way. "How did you get the sheep in here?"

"What d'you think my dogs are for?"

"So the sheep stopped chasing the Land Rover?"

"Chasing it? They're *sheep*. They don't chase cars."

"Fine. They stopped doing their little stampede or what-ever on their own? Or you made them stop?"

"They stopped," he said. "Not made for all that sprinting."

"Great." She stepped back from the gate. "Millie's at the pub."

"*What?* You stealing my dogs now?"

"Yes, by leaving your old blind dog with someone who'll keep her safe, rather than abandoning her by the road in an open field," she snapped, and walked away, taking her phone out again as she went.

"That's right, sod off," he shouted after her. "We don't want your sort around here, bringing trouble!"

Adams ignored him. She'd had worse things shouted at her. She thought she might check on what sort of business licence Jacob had for those demos, though.

After she found her bloody parents.

No ANSWER on any of the phones still, and Adams and Dandy followed the road past the allotment and into the edge of the fields. The sheep had evidently abandoned the pursuit once they'd run the Land Rover out of town, but where was it now? The vagaries of the landscape, all clefts and folds, with high, grey-sided fells streaked with heather lifting themselves over rivers that chattered and danced along the bottoms of valleys, plus hills and villages and farms and fields curling and snaking out of sight around every curve, meant that mobile reception was never guaranteed. She didn't even have full signal here, barely out of town.

She tapped her phone against her leg, then turned for the cottage, not jogging, but her pace quick, Dandy loping effort-lessly next to her. He burped every now and then, and she glanced at him. "Is that the faery coins?" she asked, and he burped again by way of answer. "Better out than in," she said. "Just don't choke on Tinkerbell."

Dandy tipped his head at her a little curiously, and she sighed. The enforced holiday wasn't suiting her. And neither was the enforced silence. She tried Rory's number again as she rounded the lane toward the holiday cottage, then her parents', but there was still nothing. Just straight to messages, which indicated they really were out of range, but *where?* Had Rory hidden them away somewhere, or were they upside down in a ditch? Or whisked away to Faery, the sheep driven them into some sort of portal, maybe like the faery ring in the field?

She took her keys out, bouncing them in her hand as she checked the street. Her car was still parked outside, along with her parents', but there was no sign of the Land Rover. Did she go out and try driving around, see if she could track them down?

Even as she considered it, she drew level with the cottage and noticed the doormat on the front step.

It was askew.

She stopped on the pavement, scanning the road again. It was quiet, a little back lane of holiday cottages and residential ones, a few cars in evidence but no one out and about. Not even a cat in sight, although she was sure they were lurking somewhere.

"Dandy?" she said, nodding at the step, and he prowled forward then stopped, whining. Adams licked her lips, stepping up next to him, and they both stared at the mat. It was plain hessian, and had a white rose printed in the middle, a little faded by feet and mud and time. She'd placed Chloe's runes under it, but she was the first to admit she was no expert. Had someone come along and wiped them off?

Replaced them with their own, rather more treacherous ones?

Standing here wasn't getting them any answers.

"Ready?" she said, and Dandy whined again. He was still keeping to his Labrador proportions, but his ears drooped unhappily.

"Great." She took her baton out, snapping it to full length, and edged forward until she could use it to gingerly prod the mat. It didn't vanish into a black hole, and nothing tried to jump out and grab her, so she crept a little closer, sliding the mat out of place. Her runes stared back at her, the pebbles knocked out of alignment by the movement, but everything else looking much as it had before. She frowned at them. *Almost* as it had before. Something felt … not uneasy, nothing like the ugly chill rising off the hexes at her house, but something was different. The runes hadn't felt like that before.

She reached cautiously over the mat and tested the door. The handle turned easily, and she paused. It had definitely been locked when they went out, the key left in the lockbox that was tucked mostly out of sight in the shelter of the window frame. She hesitated, but of course she was going in. What else could she do? She had Dandy, she had her duck, and she had her baton. There wasn't anything else that could help her.

She pushed the door open, baton held to her side, ready to jump back if anyone rushed her. The little hall was empty, the sunlight spilling across the wooden flooring and reflecting on the framed photos of the Dales on the walls. She stepped over the mat and into the faintly lemon-scented hush of the cottage, Dandy slipping in behind her with his ears firmly back. Still no movement, no sound, no indication that anyone was about. Maybe they'd been and gone, but what traps had they left? Or already sprung? Was that where her parents were? And Rory? Was he *part* of the trap, and he'd actually spirited them off himself?

She clamped down on the questions. There was no time for conjecture. Treat it like any other scene.

Moving quickly, but trying to keep her footsteps light, she checked the front room. Empty. Into the kitchen, which was bland and silent, upstairs to check the two bedrooms and the little bathroom. Nothing, and nothing, and nothing again. She was starting to wonder if they really had left the door open in their jumbled departure earlier.

She didn't linger once she was sure no one was upstairs, just headed back down again, and she was mid-step when she heard a *scuffle*. She stopped, frowning, and looked around. The scuffle came again, a scraping, scrabbling sound, as if a rat – a very large one – was trying to drag its way through the walls. It was coming from beneath her, from the cupboard under the stairs.

She shifted her grip on the baton, and descended the rest of the steps slowly, trying not to let them creak. The door to the cupboard was closed, and there were no more sounds until she was standing outside it, which was when another little scrabble went up. It did *sound* like a rat, if a very big one. Somehow she thought her luck might not run to rats, though. Unless it was some super-powered, pixie-altered one, probably with a stinger on its tail.

"What do you think?" she asked Dandy, who whined, and she stared at him. At some point since the scratching had started, he'd become terrier sized. "Great," she muttered, and wondered if she was better arming herself with the duck or the baton. The duck had its own curious properties, but the baton felt rather more reassuring, so she took a steady stance, held it at the ready, and put one hand on the door.

One deep breath, and she threw it open, not bothering to announce herself, ready to wallop any rats, pixies, or faeries that might be lurking inside. But nothing jumped out at her. Instead, she found herself lurching *in,* caught in an inexplicable gravitational pull, the interior of the cupboard partially taken up by a sinkhole that spread across half the floor and up one of the walls. It opened not onto dirt or stone but onto the distant view of a rumpled land under strange, alien skies, lit by constellations that she recognised in some primal part of her, even if the actual shape of them made no sense, as if they were the stars her ancestors had stared at, their familiarity sunk into her very DNA. With the door open, a high, sweet sound drifted from the … well, *portal,* she supposed. It wasn't tempting or enticing, though. It was the sort of sweetness that spoke of rot and decay.

"What the *hell,*" she breathed, catching the doorframe in one hand before she could stumble any closer, Dandy giving a yap of alarm behind her.

"*Mmmip,*" came a very indistinct and slightly plaintive answer, and she spotted two sets of metallic claws sunk deep into the floor of the cupboard.

She knew that sound, and those claws. "*Fergus?*"

"*Mmmip!*"

Adams started to step forward, but the suck of the portal made her stagger, and she grabbed the doorframe again even as Dandy barked another warning, scuttling forward to join her.

"Get back," she snapped at him. She didn't need him vanishing in there too. She dropped to her knees, giving herself a more stable base, and shuffled forward, careful not to get too close to the edge of the gap. She could still feel the pull of it though, so she stretched out on her side, hooking her legs around the doorframe. That seemed secure enough, and she could just reach Fergus, abandoning her baton to use both hands, finding the gear shafts that formed his forelegs. "Come on, then," she said, and tried to heave him up.

"*Mmmip!*" He was inordinately heavy, and with her twisted angle all she got was a twinge in her back for her trouble.

"Bloody hell. You weren't this heavy before. What've you been eating?"

"*Brrrip!*" He sounded offended.

"Hang on." She unhooked her legs from the doorframe and rolled onto her stomach, working forward until she could peer over the edge and see if he was caught on anything. The metal cat was spaniel-sized, staring back at her with round black eyes, his concertinaed wings flaring and making her wonder why he didn't just fly out. She'd have put it down to the pull of the portal being too strong, except then she looked past him. The edge of the gap was sheer but also *thin*, as if it was a hole punched into a glass dome above the distant landscape. But that wasn't the issue. The issue was Collins, swinging gently in midair below Fergus and clinging to his back paws with both hands. And below Collins, her arms wrapped around his waist, was Chloe.

"What the actual hell?" Adams said, hearing the bewilderment in her own voice.

"Adams!" Collins bellowed, the sound inexplicably distant. "Adams, I can't hold on much longer!"

"Coming!" she yelled back, and scrambled backward out of the cupboard. Questions could wait. Some things were the same no matter what dimensions were involved, and one of those was the need for rope. She ran for the car.

ROGUE SHEEP & FAERY CIRCLES

IT WASN'T AS DIFFICULT TO GET COLLINS AND CHLOE OUT AS Adams had feared. She dropped one end of the rope to them, then backed up until she could sit outside the door with her feet braced against the frame and loop the line around herself for added purchase. She barely needed it, though – Chloe was stronger than her meagre frame suggested, and scrambled out over Collins with Adams doing very little other than keeping the rope taut. Adams reached into the cupboard and grabbed the back of the young woman's singlet as she emerged over the edge of the hole, or door, or portal, or whatever the hell it was, and helped her into the hall.

"Alright?" she asked, as Chloe rolled herself to sitting and untied the rope from around her waist.

"I mean, it's always an experience with you," Chloe said, and wedged herself into the doorway with Adams, both of them peering back at the portal. "*Next!*" Chloe yelled, and Adams winced.

She fed the rope back past Fergus, scooting forward on her belly until she could peer down at Collins. "Can you get it?" she called.

"Sure." His face was red with effort, and Adams could see the muscles of his forearms in hard relief against the skin. Clinging to the metal cat's skinny legs couldn't be easy, and he'd been holding both himself and Chloe up. Even so, he braced himself, let go with one hand, and snatched at the rope. His grip on Fergus slipped almost immediately and he abandoned the line, clutching the metal cat's legs with both hands again and swearing enthusiastically. The rope bumped against his arm in a friendly manner, but there was no way he was going to be able to tie it around himself.

"Hang on," Adams said, pulling it back up rapidly. She tied a bowline in the end, creating a loop, then lowered it again, stopping when it was roughly at the level of Collins' feet. "Step in."

He didn't argue, just waved around with one foot until he could get it in the loop. Adams shuffled back to the doorway to take up her position again, and said to Chloe, "Tell me what's happening there. I can't see anything from here."

"On it," Chloe said, and they scuffled around each other to reposition, Adams settling herself outside the door so she could brace a foot to either side of the frame again, and Chloe flopping belly-down on the cupboard floor, staring straight into their brand-new void.

"Is he ready?" Adams asked Chloe.

"He's saying hurry up, only slightly less politely."

Adams couldn't hear any of it from outside the door, which took some of the fun out of things, in her opinion. She adjusted her legs, tightened her grip on the rope, and nodded. "Tell him to start climbing."

"Start climbing!" Chloe shouted into the hole, and weight came onto the rope instantly.

Adams leaned back against it, and felt the shift as Collins began to pull himself over Fergus. She took up the slack, keeping the rope taut, and heard Fergus give a *"Brrrip!"* of protest, presumably as Collins stood on something delicate, whatever that might be for a metal cat.

Collins' hands appeared first, Chloe grabbing his wrists and trying to wriggle backward, but there wasn't room in the tight confines of the cupboard, and she just bumped into the wall. She pulled her knees under her instead, and Adams called, "Careful!"

"I'm okay," Chloe said, keeping her grip on Collins' hands, although Adams doubted she'd be able to do much if he slipped, other than go in after him. The thought was there, though.

A moment later Collins' short-cropped hair emerged out of the gap, and he clawed his way onto the floor. As the weight came off the rope entirely Adams abandoned it, keeping one hand on the doorframe in case the pull of the portal suddenly increased as she waved Chloe into the hall. Collins followed, wriggling to the doorway on his belly, where she caught the back of his shirt to help him along. He collapsed on the hall floor as soon as he was over the threshold, puffing dramatically, and Adams crawled back into the cupboard, peering into the hole. Fergus looked up at her, eyes gleaming.

"*Mmmip?*"

"You need help?"

"*Mmmip.*"

Adams reached into the gap, feeling an intense, sticky heat on her arms, as if she'd leaned into the humid confines of a terrarium. Below them, mist swirled over greenery and glittering lights, warm dots that might be lanterns, or village lights, or bonfires seen from afar. It was impossible to be sure of distance, everything smudgy as a watercolour through the murky air, and it made her think of the disjointed incoherence of dreams, urgent and insubstantial all at once. She edged a little further forward, a nervous snorkeler dipping their head below the surface before leaving the shore, trying to make out more detail. The trees were vast, or so similar as to be impossible to tell apart, and something glittered – a lake? – amid the lights. She could make out some shapes that looked too regular to be natural, too, and she strained forward, trying to see more. Just a little closer …

"Brrrrrippp!"

She shot backward so suddenly she yelped, her T-shirt riding up and her belly scraping on the floor, and just had the presence of mind to grab Fergus's forelegs as she was hauled out of the cupboard. Her rapid exit stalled for a second as they both struggled to get his claws out of the floor, then they were moving again, and a moment later she was sprawled in the hall, still clutching Fergus and with her heart beating far too fast, as if she'd just jumped clear of an oncoming train.

Dandy was barking furiously, and she released Fergus to roll over. Collins rocked back onto his heels from his spot at her feet, red-faced and wide-eyed.

"Bloody hell, Adams. Thought you were a goner."

"I was getting Fergus."

"You just about went in head-first," Chloe said. "Looked like you were planning to skydive into Faery."

Adams petted Dandy, quieting him until his barks gave way to a steady growling directed at Fergus, who just blinked lazily, his eyes whorling down to a pinpoint like an old-fashioned camera shutter. "Right," she said, thinking of those drifting, inviting lights, and shivered. "Thanks."

She got up, and they gathered around the door – careful not to stand close enough to feel that hungry pull – and stared at the hole in the floor. Adams waited for it to snap closed, or fade gently away, but it just sat there, shimmering with threat, and she wondered how she was going to explain to Maud there was a portal in her broom cupboard.

"*Mmmip.*"

Fergus looked up at Adams, and she petted his head awkwardly. She was never sure if he could feel it or not, but he gave a ratcheting purr.

"Adams?" Collins said, looking from the cat to her. He had one hand on the wall to brace himself against an accidental slip into the void.

"Yes?"

"Did you really go back in there to lift the *flying* metal cat out?"

"I— Oh." She looked at Fergus, and he twitched his ears at her, then flopped onto his back, offering her his stomach to pet. "He gets more cat all the time."

"He's useful, though," Chloe said, standing on her tiptoes as she peered around the frame. "We would've been whisked away to Faery if he hadn't caught us."

"Or sucked into nothingness," Collins said. "I thought being whisked away to Faery would be all dances and cupcakes. That was more like one of those whirlpools on old maps. The ones with the sea monsters in the bottom."

"I'm sure the whisking would've kicked in at some point," Chloe said. "Not much point in it if everyone arrives squished."

Adams scuffed Dandy's ears. He was leaning on her legs, keeping his gaze on Fergus, and had stuck to his terrier size, which made him around the same proportions as the metal cat. "How the hell did you end up in the cupboard, anyway?"

"Can we shut the door before we talk about it?" Collins asked. "I feel like it's listening to us."

They all looked at the portal, and Adams said to Chloe, "Is it?"

She shrugged. "I don't know. I've never seen one before."

"Do you think it'll stay in there?" Collins asked.

"I hope so," Adams said. "We can't have it eating the whole bloody house."

Chloe rubbed the back of her neck lightly. The small head of a snake poked out of her hair, which was bundled into a bun that was likely messier than it had started out that morning. "I can put some charms on the door," she said, sounding dubious. "No idea if they'll work on portals, though."

"Give it a go anyway," Adams said. She closed the cupboard, taking a last wary look at the portal before she did so. It didn't appear to have grown, but she had an idea it had eaten the vacuum cleaner. That would be coming out of her wages.

Chloe had somehow held onto her satchel, and she produced some chalk from it, which she used to sketch runes all around the cupboard doorframe, muttering to herself as she did so. Collins watched for a bit, then vanished into the kitchen, trailed silently by both Fergus and Dandy. Adams heard the kettle go on, and a moment later a yelp as he ran into one or both of them.

"Adams!" he shouted. "Keep your menagerie under control, can't you?"

"Nothing to do with me," she called back, watching Chloe put a final flourish of chalk on the wall then step back, frowning.

"That's the best I can do," she said, dropping the chalk back into her bag. "I'd keep the door shut, though."

"I fully intend to," Adams said, checking her phone. Still nothing from Rory or her parents. "Is this like a faery ring? You know, mushrooms?"

"I can honestly say I was not checking for mushrooms when it sucked us in," Chloe said. "But I kind of doubt it's an entirely unrelated portal."

"Fair. What were you doing in the cupboard?"

"Looking for you," Collins said, leaning out of the kitchen. "Chloe, you want tea?"

"Unless there's anything stronger in the offing."

"Mum's got some wine in the fridge, I think," Adams said, following Collins into the kitchen. He'd set up the cafetière on the worktop next to some mugs, and Dandy, having grown enough to put both paws up next to it, was just finishing licking the coffee grounds out. "*Dandy!*"

He dropped back to the ground and glared at Fergus, who gave a questioning "*Mmmip?*"

Adams picked up the cafetière and went to wash it in the sink. "Why would I have been in the cupboard?"

"Well, not you specifically," Collins said, as the kettle clicked off. He topped up one of the mugs, then looked at Chloe questioningly. She nodded, and he poured water into a second mug as well, then waited as Adams scooped more coffee. "The front door was open when we got here," he said. "We searched the place, then heard something in the cupboard. We were looking at the ... whatever the hell that hole was, when someone shoved us in and slammed the door."

"*Shoved you?*" Adams asked, frowning. "Did you see anything?"

"Nothing," Collins said. "I was too busy trying not to inadvertently take up base-jumping."

Chloe nodded. "It all happened too quickly to know if it was even a person. It didn't *feel* like hands, to be honest. It hit me, and I fell into Colin, then we both went into the hole. Maybe it was part of the trap, an automated thing we tripped by opening the door."

"Just bloody lucky Fergus was there," Collins said. "I got hold of the edge, but I couldn't get any purchase. He dived right off and got his claws stuck in the floor just before my grip slipped, then I managed to grab him."

"And I was just hanging onto anything I could," Chloe said cheerfully.

"More damn faery traps," Adams muttered, making a face, and found the Tupperware full of her mum's ginger biscuits, setting them on the table. "What was even the point of coming all this bloody way? We've not avoided *anything*."

"It's hardly Outer Siberia, Adams," Collins pointed out, helping himself to a biscuit. "It's Hawes. Plus it seemed like a good option at the time."

"There's a sodding *wormhole* in the broom cupboard. Not helping my parents, is it?"

"Where are your parents?" Collins asked.

"I don't know." She rubbed her face with both hands, her stomach sick with the build-up of tension. She probably needed to lay off the coffee, but she poured herself a mug anyway. "They got chased out of town by a pack of rogue sheep, who I think were set off by a faery circle."

There was silence for a moment, then Collins said, "I had actually thought nothing could surprise me anymore, but it turns out it can. Rogue sheep?"

"The faery circle's more interesting," Chloe said. "Was that why you were asking about mushrooms?"

Adams found the photos on her phone and slid it across to Chloe. "I found what looked like the remains of one at a sheepdog demo, before the silly creatures stampeded. We'd just had a run-in with the Gentry, too."

"*The* Gentry?" Chloe asked. "The one from the hexes?"

"Pretty sure."

"Rogue sheep and faery circles," Collins said, taking a bite of biscuit. "Naturally."

"Naturally," Adams agreed. "Anyhow, Rory got my parents out, but now none of them are answering their phones." There was a creeping, niggling concern worming through her. What if the sheep had been infected, somehow, the way the coins had infected the crowd? And what if it had got to Rory, whatever *it* was? What if he really had driven the Land Rover off the road, not by accident but by *design*, because the mushrooms were telling him to? She took a gulp of too-hot coffee, trying to push the thought down.

Chloe handed the phone back. "Call them again," she said.

Adams nodded, tapping her mum's number. "Was it a faery circle?"

"It was mushrooms. Hard to say much else from a photo."

"*Mmmip?*" Fergus tried to put his paws on Adams' leg, and she pushed him away. His claws were basically scalpels, and she didn't fancy a trip to A&E for stitches as an added adventure.

"When did you pick him up?" she asked, and Collins and Chloe looked at each other.

"I thought you must've got him from Kaz," Collins said.

"Yeah, he was here when we arrived," Chloe agreed, and they all looked at Fergus. He still had his gaze fixed on Adams, and he blinked, eyes pinwheeling down to dots then swirling open again.

"*Mmmip.*"

"He's very cool," Chloe declared, and Dandy whined again. He was sitting in the sink, looking mournfully at the coffee canister.

"No answer." Adams disconnected and tried her dad, without much hope.

"The signal can be right dodgy out here," Collins offered.

"Sure." She tried Rory next, but with the same result. "I'm going to have to go after them."

"You know where they've gone?" Chloe asked.

"No, but I know what direction they headed out of town. I'll just go the same way."

Collins and Chloe looked at each other.

"What?"

"There's loads of little lanes out here," Chloe said, almost apologetically. "It's not going to be that easy."

"Of course it isn't." Adams took another swig of coffee, wondering if she should be breaking into her mum's wine after all.

"*Mmmip*," Fergus said, pawing her jeans lightly.

"Don't tell me you drink coffee too."

"*Mmmip. Brrrip. Mmm-mmmip*," he insisted, and clattered his wings pointedly.

She stared at him. "You can find them?"

"*Mmmip*," he said, in a tone that very clearly meant *obviously*.

The flying metal cat was probably going to be a bit of a giveaway that things weren't quite situation normal in Hawes, but Adams didn't really care at this point. If anyone spotted him she had a handy reporter who could spread a story about it being a drone. Or he would if he ever wanted a sniff at any of her cases, ever again.

"Let's go," she said, setting her mug in front of Dandy. He shoved his snout into it, lapping frantically, and she headed for the door, Fergus trotting next to her. Collins and Chloe scrambled to catch up, and a moment later they were out on the pavement, the sun still rich and warm, and the scent of cut grass drifting from somewhere.

"You want me to see if we can get a ping on their phones?" Collins asked her as she beeped her car open.

Adams hesitated, thinking of Maud and her *don't use station resources*, then said, "Let's see what Fergus can come up with first." She frowned at Chloe as the young woman reached for the front passenger door. "What're you doing?"

"Coming with you."

"You almost got eaten by a cupboard. I think you should leave this one to me."

"Absolutely not," Collins said, opening the back door.

"Well, you, maybe, but—"

"Either of you know how to defuse a fae trap?" Chloe demanded, and when Adams and Collins looked at each other she said, "That's what I thought. Let's go."

They piled in, Dandy panting eagerly over Chloe's shoulder and making her flinch, and as Adams tried to close her door Fergus scrambled in too.

"Hey! You need to follow the Land Rover."

"*Mmmip,*" he said, trying to sit down.

"No—"

Dandy barked imperiously, glaring at Fergus, who hissed like a pressure cooker about to explode, and Chloe ducked. "Is he hissing at me?"

"No, Dandy's barking— *Dandy!* Shut up!"

Dandy kept barking, and Fergus showed off needle teeth, and in that moment a flash of tabby fur appeared on Chloe's lap. She shrieked, more in surprise than fright, and pushed Thompson into the footwell.

"Hey! That's no way— *What in the name of the Old Ones is that?*"

Fergus swung toward Thompson, ears swivelling stiffly, and Dandy tried to lunge into the front; whether to get between them or to grab one of them was impossible to say. Thompson hissed, his pupils huge, and belted Fergus's snout, but his claws slid straight off the smooth metal and dug into Chloe instead.

"*Ow!*"

Dandy redoubled his barking, and Adams threw her door open. "Everyone *out,*" she shouted, and grabbed Fergus around the middle, hauling him out with her. Dandy followed, still barking furiously, and Thompson bounded out in pursuit, his crooked tail puffed and his eyes wild. Fergus hung stiff-legged in Adams' hands, needle teeth bared and segmented tail twitching, but didn't try to escape.

"Why the *hell* do you have a guardian?" Thompson snarled. "That thing— Is that meant to be a *cat?* It's an *abomination.*"

"*Brrrip!*"

"He's not an abomination," Adams said.

"It is!"

"Adams," Collins said.

"Sodding devil dandy dogs, now robot-cats—"

"*Brrrip!*"

"Adams!"

"*Brrrip* to you too, you clockwork cabbage!"

"Shut *up*," Adams hissed at Thompson.

"Oh, *now* you want me to shut up. It's all happy days having a talking cat when you want something, and then when you think you can replace them with a bloody computer—*Mmph!*"

The *mmph* was because Collins had scooped him up and placed one hefty hand over the cat's face, clamping his mouth closed just as Rory's battered green Land Rover came to a halt in front of them. Adams tried to arrange her face into something like a welcoming smile, hoping Fergus took the hint to be quiet, then her expression froze.

Rory climbed out and stood there looking at Adams, his hands loose and empty at his sides.

"I don't know what happened," he said, his voice quiet. "I tried … I just don't know."

Adams stared at the empty 4x4, as if expecting her parents to pop into sight from below the windows, like a couple of kids messing about.

They didn't.

13

GETTING PUNCHY WITH IT

"Where," she started, but the word was a wheeze. She couldn't seem to get enough air into her lungs. Fergus tipped his head to look up at her, and then Chloe was there, putting a hand on Adams' back, up between her shoulder blades as if she was about to whack her a few times to stop her choking on the reality of the situation. Or the *unreality*.

Rory stepped forward, reaching out as if to take her hands, then stopped. Midge and Pinto hadn't climbed out of the Land Rover, but just watched silently, not moving, seemingly aware that something had gone terribly, *horribly* wrong. "I'm sorry," Rory whispered again.

"Let's get inside," Collins said, and Thompson growled. Collins released his grip on the cat's jaw.

Thompson shook himself off, huffed a few times, then said, "If you do that again I'll take your tonsils out with my teeth." His tone was quiet, though.

Collins headed for the cottage door, and Adams turned automatically under the pressure of Chloe's hand. She was still clutching Fergus, but Dandy bumped her free hand gently, and she barely glanced at him. *Gone? They were *gone?* She lost them because of some bloody *sheep?*

There was no way, in any world, she could have messed up more spectacularly than this.

She wasn't quite sure how she ended up sitting at the garden table in the late afternoon sunlight, staring at a mug of murky herbal tea, but suddenly she was, without any real memory of getting into the house or out of it again. Fergus leaned against her chest, and Dandy had his head in her lap, and she petted him mechanically. She wasn't crying, and her breathing was slow and even. She had just … stopped, watching herself with a curious detachment, waiting to see what would happen once she kicked into gear again. The world was distant, and the sounds of the garden had faded away, but she could hear the others talking.

"Is she in shock?" Chloe asked. "I mean, I'd do the whole checking her pulse and hands thing, but I don't fancy getting arrested over it."

"I don't think she is," Collins said, and Adams heard the click of the cover coming off the biscuits. "Just give her a minute."

Adams watched the mug for a little longer, while the others joined her at the table. No one spoke, and she couldn't decide if it was claustrophobic having all these animals and people crowded around her, or if there was comfort to be had in it. It could go either way.

Finally Chloe nudged the mug closer to her. "Drink it."

Adams licked her lips, rousing herself. The birdsong washed back from wherever it had been hiding, absurdly loud, and she winced. "Right. Thanks."

"Sure." Chloe wrapped her hands around her own mug as Collins offered the biscuits to the others, and then there was silence again for a little.

Adams fiddled with the handle of the mug, and Dandy

whined. She looked at him, and he licked his chops. "It's not coffee, sorry."

He huffed, pressing his jaw more firmly into her leg, and stared up at her with his eyes wide and red. She rubbed his ears, not sure who was comforting whom, and noticed her jeans.

"You're slobbering."

"Dog," Thompson said. "It's all they do." Midge whined, and Thompson looked at her. "You're no better. Can't even keep hold of a couple of humans. Useless canines."

"Not their fault," Rory said. "It's mine." He didn't apologise again, just said it matter-of-factly, and sipped his tea before continuing. "I headed straight into the middle of the village, because I figured it was safer to be around people. Thought that if the sheep chased us out of town and there were just fields, it might be easier for the fae to trap us somehow. But the village isn't that big, and I ended up out the other side, and there were even more sheep on the damn road. I had to stop, and that was it."

"That was it how?" Adams asked.

He scuffled Pinto's ears. "I'm not quite sure. We didn't hit anything. Nothing hit us. These two started going bonkers, then the next thing I woke up in a lay-by, and your parents were gone."

"The Gentry?" Adams didn't see who else it could be, but she had to ask.

"Got to be," Thompson said. "Used the sheep to stop the car long enough to zap everyone with a stun spell or something, dragged the olds off, and left the rest somewhere out of the way."

"A *stun spell?*" Chloe said. "Really? I've never heard of that."

"Well, whatever they did. This is Gentry we're talking about. Who knows what the hell they can do? It's been so long since they've been around they could've learned all sorts of new tricks."

"Yes, but a *stun* spell?"

"Well, what else is it going to be? Carbon monoxide poisoning?"

Collins made a thoughtful noise, and Rory gave him a reproachful look. "My car isn't that bad!"

"I'm finding it easier to deal with than the idea of a stun spell."

"It can't be a stun spell," Chloe said. "That's just silly. Next you'll be saying they whipped past on their broomstick with a magic wand."

"That's you," the cat said. "The broomstick bit, anyway."

"See? You don't even know what a witch really is, and we're meant to listen to you on the Gentry?"

"I know fae," Thompson protested. "And I just generally know *a lot* more than you, witch."

"Listen, *cat—*"

"It's irrelevant if it was a stun spell or some other charm," Adams said. "The important part is they jumped you somehow."

"Yes," Rory said simply. "And I didn't see who, or how."

"There was a faery circle at the sheep demo," Adams said. "It must've been a distraction, because with both of us and Dandy, the fae couldn't get hold of them at the pub. I thought … he said it was a *nudge*, but even then I wondered …" She pushed the palms of her hands into her forehead and swore. "*Dandy*. Why did I keep him with me? He should've gone with Mum and Dad. We both should've. How did I not see this?"

Dandy whined, putting his paws on her legs to try and lick her face, his tail down, his fear of Fergus apparently forgotten, and Chloe rubbed Adams' shoulder. "You couldn't foresee any of this. It's a *Gentry*. That's, like … the boss faery.

The big magic cheese. The dream queen. Whatever you want to call it, they're *powerful*. How were you meant to know what they were going to do?"

"Because he told me," she said gloomily.

"*What?*" Everyone except Rory spoke at the same moment, and Thompson said, "Tell me you've not been chatting with a bloody *Gentry* and not telling me about it."

"I'm sorry, I didn't realise I reported to you." Her heart wasn't in it, though. He was right. She should've told him. She wrapped her hands around her mug.

"I outrank every bloody one of you when it comes to dealing with this stuff," the cat said.

"Go easy," Rory put in. "This is my fault."

"Yeah, well, I didn't miss the fact *you* weren't surprised by this revelation, Posh Spice. Keep your nose out. You don't know enough to be poking around in this."

Chloe snorted. "Posh Spice? Can I be Scary Spice, then?"

"You're about as scary as my morning hairball, witch."

"Gross, cat."

Adams pinched her forehead. "The note I got, the one that vanished. He said if I didn't give him the book, he'd hex me and everyone I love."

"What book?" Collins asked.

"I can only think of one," Adams said, looking at Thompson. He hadn't been around when she'd captured the sorcerer's book, but she had an idea he'd know about it anyway.

"*Huh.* Well, that stinks like week-old sardines."

"Seemed dodgy to me, too. He rocked up outside the gate last night and told me I had three nights, but then all this stuff started happening today. Said I needed a *nudge*, but I guess he decided a nudge wasn't enough."

"It's the solstice in three nights," Chloe said. "Was that it?"

"Yes. Is that important?"

"Well—"

"No," the cat said, ignoring Chloe's offended huff. "Not to the fae. It's mostly symbolic. It matters to little witches and human magic-workers, but barely ever to fae, and not at all to Gentry."

"So why mention it?"

"I'm more interested in why he wants a sorcerer's book," Thompson said. "Fae magic and sorcerer magic work on two entirely different systems. It's like one's a fish and one's a bird. They both work perfectly well, but there's no crossover."

"Penguins," Chloe said. "Shags, too. And—"

"Old Ones take me, can you actually *do* magic or do you just annoy people to death?"

"More like operating systems, perhaps," Collins said. "Mac and Windows."

"They work together, though," Rory pointed out. "Things might be a bit glitchy here and there, but they're not incompatible."

"*Hmm.* Power, maybe? Like 110 and 240 volts?"

"You can get adapter thingies for those."

"Technical term, is that?"

Adams looked at Thompson, whose ears were so far back they looked in danger of cramping. "I think we get the point," she said. "But if the magic systems aren't compatible, why would the Gentry want the book?"

"Glad one of you isn't completely useless. Exactly my question. He can't use it."

Adams tapped her fingers on the mug. "Would it be so dangerous for him to have it, then?"

"Out of the question."

"For those of us a little slow on the uptake, what book?" Collins asked. "I take it we're not talking about the Dales guide?"

Adams sighed. "When I first ran into Folk stuff properly

in Leeds, I recovered a book and a necklace belonging to a dead sorcerer—"

"Eh," Thompson said. "Not sure sorcerers can really die."

"Well, as far as I know she's dead. She's *gone* anyway, and her companion inherited her house and all her stuff, which included the book and necklace. The Gentry wants the book."

"You've got a *sorcerer's book?*" Chloe breathed. "Why didn't you say?"

"I don't have it anymore."

"What happened?"

"I gave it to someone for safekeeping," Adams said.

"And that's where it has to stay," Thompson said. "You can't give it to the Gentry."

"But you said he can't use it."

"Even more reason for them not to have it. It makes no sense, and I don't like it."

It was a fair point. Adams hesitated, and Collins said, "The important bit here is Gloria and Hugh." He held his phone up. "I've called Lucas and asked him to see if he can get a ping on them."

"Good. Thanks," Adams said.

"Ninety-nine per cent sure mobile network doesn't work in Faery," Thompson said.

"Do you have a better suggestion?" Collins asked him.

"Just saying. You lot have your tails in a right knot, don't you?"

"Adams' parents are *missing,*" Rory said sharply. "Kind of worth being in a knot over."

"Well, that's on you, Posh Spice."

"It's not," Adams said. "It's on me." Why had she let them go on without her, and without Dandy? She should have been there, not messing around chasing sheep and taking photos of bloody mushrooms. She took a breath, stopping herself. That was going to get her nowhere but into a lovely little guilt spiral, and she could do that on her own time, once her parents were back safely. "We need a plan, whether we get a location on them or not."

"I just wish I'd *seen* something," Rory said, pressing the fingers of both hands to his forehead, as if he could force a memory out of it. "But there's nothing. They were there and then gone, and all I knew about it was the dogs going absolutely bonkers."

Adams saw the shadow of grief on his face, and wondered if he was thinking of his own mum. He kind of had to be. "It's not your fault," she said. "Bloody fae. Nightmares, all of them. And I don't even have any Christmas puddings."

Rory gave a reluctant snort, and Collins said, "*Ohhh*. Oh, no. I don't want to do that again."

"What, you've only just realised faeries are fae?" Thompson asked. "I thought you were a detective."

"Don't listen to him," Adams said. "They're not the same as faeries. Less teeth."

"Well, that's something."

"Can someone explain the Christmas puddings to me?" Chloe asked.

"Later," Adams said, and finally picked her mug up, sniffing it. An earthy, mulchy scent rose from it, like water that had been festering in a bucket all winter. "What is this?"

"Drink it," Chloe said. "It's very soothing."

"A coffee would soothe me much more."

"You're not having any more coffee," Chloe said firmly. "It's this or whisky, but Colin thinks that might make you a bit punchy."

"Only if the Gentry turns up."

"I'd pay good money to see that," Thompson said.

Adams swirled her mug, watching the murky liquid sloshing inside. She'd pay good money for it too, especially if it meant she could face the damn creature alone. But there was no chance of that, and even if there had been, she didn't think she *could* do this alone. She didn't know enough about any of it, and this was her parents. She'd do anything to get them back. Anything at all, which meant the book was still in play, as far as she was concerned. But she wasn't going to share that. She looked around the table. "Any of you want to step back?" she asked. "Because it's completely fine if you do. They're not your parents, and this could get nasty. But I'm going after them no matter what."

"Well, that was never in question," Collins said, taking a sip of his tea.

"I'm in, obviously," Rory said. "Can I have a go at punching them, though? After you, of course."

"That's technically assault," Collins pointed out.

"Even if it's a fae?"

"No real grey area with assault."

"Self-defence?"

"I'll vouch for you," Chloe said. "I will swear up and down they hit you first. I mean, they did knock you out or steal your memory or whatever, so it's not really a lie."

Thompson huffed. "Well, I'm in too. I'm not missing this."

Adams pinched the bridge of her nose. "Look, they've already taken my parents. They could take any one of you next. You get that, right? This isn't a game."

"She's not kidding," the cat said. "You know the whole dancing for a thousand years thing? That's not an exaggeration. Well, not a big one, anyway. Sometimes it's a hundred years, sometimes it's ten years, sometimes there's no way of knowing. Not everyone comes back, or it's so late when they do no one realises it's them. The ones that do come back are never the same. And none of them look like they've been having a good time if they do make it home."

No one spoke for a long moment, staring at him, then Chloe flicked his ears.

"*Ow!* Hands to yourself, witch."

"Stop calling me that."

"Is it not correct?"

"It's your tone," Chloe replied. "And you're being unhelpful."

"Truthful."

Chloe looked at Adams. "We're going to get your parents back."

Adams took a sip of her tea and made a face. "This is *awful.*"

"Only because it's not coffee."

"*Do* we have any whisky?"

"This is your holiday cottage," Collins pointed out.

"Eh."

Chloe dug in her satchel and passed Adams a small silver flask. "Here."

Adams took it and unscrewed the top to sniff the contents. It actually smelled decent, and she put a dollop in her tea, hoping it made it drinkable. "You came prepared."

"Always. You never know when you might need it."

Adams passed the flask on to Rory, and then there was silence, full of unsaid things and anxious energy. She tried the tea and winced. It was still awful.

Finally Chloe looked at Rory and said, "What I find weird is that you didn't go anywhere."

"Chloe," Collins said.

"I'm not saying Rory did anything, or didn't, or whatever, but why not take him too?"

"Well, we're guessing Adams' parents were the targets," Collins pointed out. "There was no point in taking Rory too."

"But why not, since he was there? Then there'd be no one

to come back and tell us it was definitely a fae thing, or where it had happened, or anything. We'd've spent ages searching for all three of you before even realising they'd been snatched."

There was a moment of silence while Adams wondered why the only person who seemed to be thinking straight here was both the youngest of them all and the one currently wearing a snake in her hair.

Rory reached inside his shirt, pulling out the amber pendant. "Would it be this?" he asked.

"*Absolutely,*" Chloe said, leaning closer. "Where did you get that?"

"My mum," he said, and didn't expand any further, his gaze drifting to Adams. She picked the flask up from the middle of the table and offered it to him again, and he took it, giving her a slight smile. "Thanks."

"Sure." She looked at Chloe. "We tried texting you, actually. We wanted to see if you had some in the shop."

Chloe grimaced. "I have some protective amulets, but *this* ..." She trailed off, still peering at the necklace, then straightened up. "That's hefty. I don't have anything that good."

"If we could get some, would it protect us if we went after them?"

"Hold your whiskers," Thompson said, before Chloe could answer. "Clarify *go after?*"

"The longer we wait around, the more likely my parents are going to get stuck, right? Eat the food or drink the wine or whatever else you're not meant to do."

"I mean, if they don't know not to eat the food in Faery, then honestly—"

Chloe flicked his ear again.

"*Would you stop that?*"

"Would you think before you speak?"

He hissed at her, and the snake swung out of her hair to hiss back. "Oh, sod off, Medusa."

"Ooh, I like that," Chloe said.

"It wasn't meant as a compliment."

"Taking it as one anyway."

"Are you thinking …?" Collins asked, tipping his head toward the house, and the gap in reality lurking in the broom cupboard.

"He's not going to expect it."

"Excuse me, are you talking about a faery circle?" Thompson asked. "Tell me you don't think you're off after the mushrooms."

"More a portal under the stairs," Adams said. "It just popped up and tried to eat Collins and Chloe."

"*Mmmip.*"

"And Fergus."

Thompson hissed. "*Absolutely not.*"

"Is that in the Airbnb listing?" Rory asked. "Because I'm not sure it's really a selling point."

"It's got to be there for a reason," Chloe said.

"Yes, because the bloody fae have been chucking charms at the house, and you lot"—Thompson glared from Chloe to Adams—"have been throwing countercharms about the place with *no* sense of what you're actually warding against, and now it's gone and created a rift. *That's* the reason. I knew I could smell some sort of mess."

"Well, we can still use it, can't we?" Adams asked.

"*No.* You have no idea where the bloody thing goes."

"But it's got to be a fae portal, right?" Chloe said. "If it's a reaction of some sort between our charms and the Gentry's? He's been trying to hex the cottage into Faery, and this is a bit that's slipped past the countercharms. It's not going to be a wormhole to the stars, is it?"

"No, but we don't know where it goes. It could be

unstable and you'll come out the other end with your head where your hands should be, or your intestines on the outside. Or it's not a rift at all, but a trap that'll chuck you into an oubliette. Or it's always been there and is just a rubbish chute into a different dimension. We can't know, and you don't just go jumping into unknown portals. That should be Folk 101." Thompson's tail was lashing furiously, his ears back.

Adams sipped her nasty tea. "It still seems like a possibility to me. No one's put me on a course for this, you know."

"*Read the books*," the cat all but yowled at her.

"You know so much, just tell us."

"I am *not* your personal reference library. Posh Spice there's got all the books. Just go and bloody read them."

"To be fair, the books are pretty dire," Rory said. "It's hard to work out what's true and what's down to the various substances they used to enjoy back then."

"I think quite a bit of it's the substances," Adams said. "Especially when it comes to the fae. They get very funny about the fae."

Thompson gave the impression that if he had hands to throw up, he would. "*Fine*. Then listen to me. If you go jumping into that portal, anything could happen. You could end up anywhere. And then what's going to happen to your parents?"

Adams didn't answer straight away, trying not to flinch from the sting of the words, and no one else spoke, until Rory said, "I feel like amulets would be handy anyway."

"If it gives us half a chance of not being whisked away to Faery, it seems worth it," Collins said, and looked at Chloe. "You sure you don't have any in stock?"

"Yes," Chloe said. "But I know where we can get some."

"No," Thompson said.

"Just for protection," Rory said. "You know, in case the fae try to catch us."

"*No.*"

"Can we get them now?" Collins asked.

"*No!*"

"Sure," Chloe said, getting up. "We need to go to York."

"Are *any* of you listening to me?" Thompson demanded.

"Ash & Yew?" Adams asked.

"Of course," Chloe said. "Heather'll have them in stock."

"Oh, stuff your ears with parsnips, then," Thompson said. "You can't say I didn't warn you."

"And you can't say the amulets are a bad idea, can you?" Adams pointed out.

"It's what you're going to do once you have them that worries me."

14

GOING ON A DRAGON HUNT

"I'll go now," Collins said, getting up. "I can be up in York in an hour and a half or so. Can you call ahead, have them waiting for me?"

Adams nodded, fishing her phone from her pocket. "Hang about. Let me make sure she's got them." She scrolled through her contacts and found Heather's number, which had somehow grown curling vines over the name, and she was quite sure that was a feature her phone didn't have. She hit dial and put it on speaker, waiting. It rang three times before a warm voice, a little throaty around the edges, answered. The garden seemed to lean toward it, the trees shivering and the scraggly flowerbeds standing to attention, as Heather said, "Detective Inspector Adams. To what do I owe the pleasure?"

"I'm hoping you can help me," Adams said.

"Oh, well, this is a turnaround." There was a smile in Heather's voice. "Last time I saw you, you wanted to arrest me."

"Not the *last* time. I think the last time was when I

stopped you tearing York apart, got your charm back, and put down the bloke who was after the guardians."

"With our help."

"True. But I still think it could be said that you owe me a favour."

Heather chuckled, and blossoms burst into life on one of the wizened fruit trees, making Chloe give a little *oooh* of delight. "I've seen cities fall and rise and fall again, Detective Inspector. I'm sure I'll see many more. The end of York would not have been the end of our story."

"Yes, but it would have been a hassle," Adams pointed out.

Heather laughed properly at that, and this time the garden ignored her, as if she'd stepped down to something closer to human. "There is that. Plus I'd hate to miss whatever you're going to do next. What do you need?"

"I don't actually know what they're called," Adams said, looking at Rory, who shrugged. "Bits of amber on a chain. For warding off the fae."

"Amulets," Chloe suggested, leaning closer to the phone. "But strong ones. Not just the average hags' stones and stuff."

"Strong ones? Are you having issues with the fae, DI Adams?" Heather asked. "That's dangerous territory."

"That's what I keep telling them," Thompson growled.

"And *cats?* This gets better by the moment."

"It does," Adams said, her voice clipped. "So can you help me or not?"

"Oh, yes, I always have amulets in stock. The threat of being stolen away by the Fair Folk is ever-present, as much as the Watch tries to keep it under control. Have you missed a live faery circle again, kitty? You're getting careless."

"*Thompson.* And no. This lot are determined to jump in a portal."

"Portals, now? Well, yes, I would hate to have missed this.

You can have as many as you want as long as you tell me what happens, Detective."

"How much? We'll need five."

"No charge. The entertainment alone will be worth it." The smile in Heather's voice deepened. "Plus, we were talking about favours, weren't we? Call this an investment in future assistance."

Adams didn't much like the sound of that. Favours were a slippery slope already, and the idea of an *investment* made her skin crawl. But she wasn't about to argue it now. There wasn't time. "Alright. My colleague's going to come up and collect them. Any chance you can tell us how they work, or what else we can do to protect ourselves? You must've had run-ins with the Gentry before."

"The Gentry." Heather's voice faded for a moment, and they heard her call, "Charles! Charles, the detective's meddling with the Gentry now." Faintly, someone gave an exclamation of astonishment, then she was back. "Are you really talking about actual Gentry? Not your man with the dogs?"

"I knew that would come up," Rory muttered, and leaned toward the phone. "I'm not landed gentry. I'm just a penniless landowner."

"That accent, though," Chloe said, giving him a dubious look.

"A Gentry took my parents," Adams said, ignoring them.

"And you think you're going to jump in a portal and drag them back?"

"I don't see any other option."

"Well, I'm sure you know best. I'll be waiting," Heather said.

"Wait—" But she was gone, and Adams scowled at the mobile. "Did that sound like she was *hoping* it all goes pear-shaped?"

"It sounded like she was off to make popcorn," Chloe said.

Adams looked at Collins, and he nodded. "I'll talk to her when I get there, see if she can tell us anything else."

"Thanks. I don't think my people skills are up to much today." No one said anything, and she scowled at them. "I usually have *some*."

Collins turned for the house. "I'll be back as soon as I can. Don't go walking widdershins around anything without me."

"I'm coming too," Chloe said, jumping up. "You're not going to even know what questions to ask her."

Collins raised his eyebrows, pointing at himself. "Police."

"Witch," she responded, pointing at her own chest. "So I think I outrank you in this area."

"Fair point." He looked at Adams. "You alright here?"

"Sure. Let me know when you're on the way back."

He gave her a thumbs up and led the way to the house, Chloe trotting after him, and they were just going in the door when Adams looked at Fergus, still leaning against her. "Wait," she called, and they looked back. She set Fergus on the ground, and he gave a puzzled "*Mmmip?*"

"Take him with you," she said.

Fergus looked at her, his tail drooping.

"Please," she said to him. "You did such a good job of looking after them before."

The metal cat watched her for a moment longer, whiskers twitching, and she had the idea he was having reservations about the fact he'd already dived into a rift in reality for the pair once that afternoon, but then he turned and padded toward Collins and Chloe.

"Cheers," Collins said, either to her or Fergus, or both, and then they were gone.

"Good riddance," Thompson said, then for a moment the garden was quiet, just the birds filling the silence. They listened to a car start up on the street outside, and Rory dug in his pockets, producing some dog biscuits. He gave one each to Midge and Pinto, then held a third out vaguely.

"Dandy?"

Dandy lifted his head off Adams' knee and took the biscuit delicately.

"Favouritism," Thompson said.

"Go and check the wards or countercharms or whatever, and I'll get you some mackerel," Adams said.

He narrowed his eyes at her. "You have some?"

"Mum loves it."

"A woman of good taste." He jumped to the ground. "Don't go diving in any portals while I'm gone."

He trotted off, tail high, and Adams leaned back in her chair, rubbing her face. Rory slumped forward with his forearms resting on the table, staring at his empty mug, and Adams hesitated, then reached over, putting her hand on one of his arms lightly. He looked at it, then up at her.

For a moment she didn't think she knew what to say, or even what she wanted to. This was the sort of thing she needed more time to prepare for, with notes and reference material, and probably advice from Collins. So finally she just said, "Sodding fae."

He gave a half-hearted snort of laughter. "Yeah. I kind of wish they'd taken me as well. Maybe I'd have been able to do something."

"Get kidnapped too, you mean?"

"Thanks for the vote of confidence." But he gave her a half smile.

"You couldn't have done anything even if you'd been conscious."

He fiddled with the amulet, frowning. "I suppose."

She pointed at the necklace. "Did you ever try to find a portal and go after your mum?"

He nodded, a very small, sharp nod.

"What happened?"

"It's not that easy." He watched Thompson prowl past, drifting from one side of the garden to the other like a tabby ghost.

"To find one?"

"That too." He looked at her finally. "It took me a long time. A couple of years, really. And in the end I ... I couldn't go through with it. I wasn't sure I'd ever get back. The faery that opened it took pity on me, I think. Told me it'd be too late anyway, that she'd have drunk the wine for too long and probably wouldn't even remember me."

She still had her hand on his arm, and she tightened her grip, not sure how to answer. Anything she said would be pointless, a platitude.

They were quiet for a moment, then Adams got up.

"What're you doing?" he asked her.

"I have to find them before they drink anything. Or eat anything, whatever."

"There's time."

"You don't know my dad. He'll want to try the local delicacies. He'll be all, *Well, it'd be rude not to.*"

Rory laughed, then immediately looked horrified. "Sorry."

"No, it's fine. But I need to get moving."

He got up. "We do."

"There's no we."

"Give it up, Adams," he said, his tone weary. "I've already lost my mum. I'm not losing your parents too."

They stared at each other, then she nodded, a small movement. "Come on, then."

"We need to get you an amulet before we go jumping in portals, though."

"We're not doing that. We're going to see some dragons about a book." Adams led the way into the kitchen, Rory following her.

"Dragons," he said. "Like, actual ones?"

"You can't be that surprised," she replied, collecting the last of her mum's biscuits, a large bag of sweet chilli crisps, and a couple of apples.

"Well, there's many things I wouldn't be surprised by," Rory said, rinsing their mugs in the sink. "I've never come across dragons before, though. I thought they were mythical, even given all the other Folk."

"I have an idea that's what you're supposed to think."

"Right. And are they going to try to eat us?"

Adams grinned slightly as she set the supplies on the table then, after a moment's thought, added one of her dad's fruit-cakes to the pile. "Most of them won't. One might. Depends how polite you are."

"I can be exceptionally polite. Particularly when it comes to avoiding being eaten."

"Who's being eaten?" Thompson asked, appearing on the windowsill, and Adams jumped.

"No one, preferably," she said, wishing she could suggest he wear a bell. That was unlikely to go down well, though.

"I can get behind that. I've checked the charms, and honestly I'm surprised the whole house hasn't fallen into a pocket dimension. It all seems to be holding for now, though."

"For now?"

"Sure. Long enough for a mackerel break, anyway."

"And here I thought dogs were food-motivated," Rory said, sneaking another biscuit out of the tub.

Adams found a tin of fish in the pantry and tipped some into a bowl. Thompson barely waited for her to get it onto the floor before he pounced, gobbling it down hungrily.

"You'll get indigestion," she told him, but he ignored her, and she looked at Rory. "Let's go."

"*Mmph?*" Thompson said, looking up with a mouthful of scales.

"Not you. You keep an eye on Collins and Chloe. We're just going to pick a few things up so we're ready to go when they get back."

"*Mmph,*" Thompson said, his eyes narrowing, but as she and Rory collected the supplies from the table and headed out of the kitchen he stayed where he was.

Adams beeped her car open and shoved the food in her backpack in the boot, then looked around as Midge and Pinto piled into the back seat. She frowned. "Where's Dandy?"

"Can't help you much on that," Rory said, checking the street anyway.

"Oh, bloody *hell.*" Adams looked back at the cottage, considering. Dandy could catch up, of course, but she didn't like not having him around. She also didn't like how he was making a habit of vanishing ever since the fae had turned up, but she could hardly interrogate him about it. And now he'd either follow or he wouldn't, and she wanted to go before the cat finished his fish and started asking questions. "Fine. Let's go."

THE ROAD through the village felt painfully slow, cluttered with walkers striding back from the fells, flocks of cyclists coming in to rest, and wandering tourists still gawking in the shop windows. It seemed to take forever to get through it, and as soon as they hit the road beyond the last of the houses Adams accelerated, overtaking dawdling camper vans and sweeping past slow-moving cars, not taking her eyes from the road. Midge and Pinto panted out of the same window, jammed together like one bulky beast.

She had an idea this was going to be a wasted trip, but she had to try. She had to do *something*. It was better than the alternative.

Thinking about how to find the dragons was a distraction, too. She wasn't sure how they were going to find the mount. It was hidden by deep, old charms, things that not only meant the gaze slipped away from it, but the feet did, too, bouncing the walker off the dragons' borders the way one magnet repels another. No one was going to stumble on the mount by accident, and anyone looking for it was only going to find themselves hopelessly turned around in the woods that surrounded it. Adams could've asked Thompson to lead them there, of course, but it was clear he was firmly against the idea of the book going anywhere near the fae, so he'd be zero help.

There was also the option of going into Toot Hansell and asking the members of the Women's Institute if the dragons were around, but that would be even worse than the cat. Not that the W.I. wouldn't help. They problem was they *would*, with great enthusiasm, then next thing she'd have a bunch of ladies of a certain age poking not just into her case but into the world of fae, and that really was the last thing she needed. Everything they touched turned to chaos. Chaos with homemade jam and doilies, admittedly, but it was still chaos, and she couldn't afford that.

So her plan as it stood was to head for the woods and stumble around a bit, in the hope the dragons came to see what was going on. It was thin, but she had no choice. She *needed* the book. It was the only way she was sure to get her parents back, and if the fae couldn't even use it, it was hardly an issue to give it to them, was it?

Her mind slid away from that. It wasn't true, and she knew it. If Velmyr wanted the book, he had a reason, and that reason wasn't going to be a good one. But she had no intention of *actually* letting him have it. It would give her a bargaining chip, was all. She'd be able to keep hold of it. She was sure of that. Mostly, anyway.

The roads unrolled ahead of her, tarmac patchy with frosts and wear, the fields to either side green and rich and speckled with sheep or cattle, the weather still behaving in a very un-Yorkshire-like manner, and she was just wondering if walkie-talkies would be a desperately bad thing to introduce to dragons when Midge and Pinto gave matching howls of horror, and tried to pile into the front seat.

"What the *hell?*" Adams demanded, trying to fend Midge off with one arm at the same time as not drive into the drystone wall that bordered the road.

"*Sit,*" Rory said, trying to force the dogs back, and Pinto gave a piteous wail of fright, both of them still scrabbling frantically to get out of the back. "What? What is it?"

Adams jammed the brakes on as Midge landed on the gearstick and tumbled into Rory's lap with a yelp, and behind her a wordless feline snarl went up.

"Bollocks," Adams said with a sigh.

"What in the Old Ones' names are you doing?" Thompson demanded. "You know how hard shifting into a moving car is. I just about ended up in the engine!"

"What are *you* doing?" Adams asked, peering past Pinto into the back. "I told you to keep an eye on Collins and Chloe."

Thompson's tail was lashing violently. "I *was* keeping an eye on them. But then I started to wonder what sort of *things* you thought you were going to need, and decided I better check."

"You just *left* them?"

"I'm not worried about what they'll do. Collins is pretty predictable. You, on the other hand ..." He narrowed his eyes at Adams.

"I'm perfectly reliable."

"I didn't say anything about reliable. Unpredictable is another question. What the hell are you doing out here?"

Adams looked back at the road, checking her mirrors to make sure no one was racing up behind them. "I need to talk to Beaufort."

"They're not getting involved in any of your little fae dealings," the cat said. "Dragons are neutral. They don't tangle with anything outside dragon business." He hesitated, apparently rethinking. "Well, these ones do, but only because of the bloody W.I."

"I know that," Adams said. "But they've got something I need."

Thompson was quiet for a moment, then growled. "The book. You gave them the book?"

"Yes."

"Good call, to be fair. Dragons are about the only kind that won't be tempted by it. Well, and cats, but even I wouldn't trust us not to forget it in the back of a pantry in some cat lady's house, which would be a doily-decorated disaster, probably involving cat costumes and fluffy thrones. So, nice spot for it. And it needs to stay there."

Adams pulled the car in as close to the wall as she could. The road was wide enough here for another vehicle to pass, and she cut the engine, wincing as Pinto pushed past her to join Midge, both of them trying to fit on Rory's lap without much luck.

She twisted in her seat to look at the cat. "I'm not going to let Velmyr have it. It's just for negotiating."

"Who?"

"Velmyr Duskthorn. That's what he called himself. Lord of the Fae."

"Pretentious rubbish. They all reckon they're lords and ladies of some sort, and it's just because humans called them

Gentry so as not to offend them." He huffed. "Anyway, look, I know you think the sorcerer's jewel was the dangerous bit—"

"It was."

"Not as much as the book. Sorcerers sink a portion – sometimes a large portion – of their power into their books, because they can't carry it all around and still pass as even remotely human. So those books are basically sentient, and they *want* to be used. They'll get up to all sorts of mischief, given half the chance. You can't let Vilma Dustyhorn have it. Did I not tell you about the Gentry and the sorcerers being at war forever?"

"Hang about," Rory said. "You said before the fae can't use it. So what's the risk, exactly?"

Thompson looked at him. "I'm not sure, which makes it worse. Maybe they've figured out a way to tap into the power, or are working with a human or a magician or *whatever*. Doesn't matter. They can't have it."

"But it's my *parents*," Adams said, and had to swallow against a little catch in the back of her throat.

No one spoke for a moment, then the cat said, "Sorry. Bigger things at stake. You need a better plan than *Give them what they want*, anyway. What happened to throwing Christmas puddings at faeries and shoving Santa in a sack? *That's* how you deal with fae of any kind. Play to your strengths, Detective Inspector. Plus it's hilarious to watch." He craned his neck to look at the dogs. "We should do this all the time. Much more comfortable back here without those two cluttering things up."

Adams sighed, and rubbed the back of her neck, hard enough to tug the hairs caught up in her bun. The cat was right, and that was the worst of it. She needed a proper plan.

15

FAIR GAME

Rory got out, dragged Midge and Pinto to the back door, and loaded them in again, which they acquiesced to only once Thompson had jumped through to the front. Dogs secure, Rory tried to get back in his own seat, and the cat hissed at him.

"No," Rory said, and pushed Thompson into the footwell.

"Excuse *me*. I was here first."

"You weren't, plus my legs are longer than yours," Rory pointed out, getting in.

"I was, if you consider the big picture. Plus your legs are excessive. No one needs legs that long."

Adams looked at Thompson. "Can you go and check on Collins and Chloe again? I can see Chloe joining Heather's bloody nature cult or whatever, and Collins being too responsible to leave her."

"Absolutely not. You'll be raiding the dragon's mount the second I'm gone."

"Obviously I'm not going to do that. How the hell would I raid a dragon's mount anyway?"

"I'm sure you'd come up with something," Thompson replied. "Between you and Metallicat and the damn dandy."

"Neither of them are here," Adams pointed out.

"There's us," Rory said, nodding at Midge and Pinto watching Thompson warily from between the seats.

"Of course," Thompson said. "You could lecture them on cutlery etiquette or something."

Adams snorted and tried to turn it into a cough.

Rory frowned at her. "Don't you start."

"We're going back to the house," Thompson said, jumping to Rory's lap. "Drive."

Adams started the car and pulled back onto the road.

"You're going the wrong way."

"I can't turn here, it's too narrow. And yes, I get it. This was a bad idea. But we have to do something. You say we can't go through the portal—"

Thompson huffed. "You *can,* you just don't know where you're going to come out. Or when. Or in how many pieces."

"And if we can't use the book to negotiate—"

"Well, if you had it you could, and if you wanted to start a war. Kick off the hostilities between the fae and the sorcerers again. Just about turned the world inside out last time, but sure."

"But there has to be *something.*" She pushed her hands against the wheel, her face hot and eyes suddenly stinging. "I have to get my parents back."

"We've established that," Thompson said, and his tone softened. "Look, I don't know why Velma Dusseldorf wants the book. It doesn't make any sense. But that makes it even more important you don't give it to him, because we have no idea what the hell he has planned. And I can't find out from the Watch, you understand that?"

"Why not?" Rory asked. "I thought you were some sort of Watch higher-up."

"Eh. We don't do hierarchy in the Watch. I mean, there's a leader, and the leader's got a lieutenant. But the rest of us are just Watch. Some of us are a bit older, seen a few things, had our tails bitten a bit more, but it's all about respect. I know kittens in their second lives who've done more than old toms in their seventh."

"Can't you talk to one of them, then? The kittens, I mean. Or the leader."

Thompson didn't reply straight away, shifting his position. "The Watch isn't entirely trustworthy at the moment."

"How so?" Adams asked.

"I wish I knew. Things are in flux, and I haven't figured out the details yet. I can't find the cats I'd normally rely on, and the others … well, I don't want the wrong cats getting a whiff of things. Plus I'm so bloody busy trying to stop ladies of a certain age running afoul of goblins, and dragons getting exposed by journalists, and you lot jumping into faery portals, that I don't have time to keep up with the current political climate. But what I do know is that right now there's no one I can ask for help, and it's more important than ever that we keep this quiet. Because either we're going to have the cats we can trust coming to help when they're needed elsewhere, or else we're going to have the cats we *can't* trust coming to take advantage of the situation. So do you understand how important it is to not set loose an uncontrolled book?"

Adams sighed. The intricacies of the Watch sounded almost as bad as the political machinations of the police. She spotted a gate and swung into the space in front of it, checking the road then pulling into a tight three-point turn that barely squeezed them around. "You can't trust the Watch, and I'm not sure I can trust the police. They had their hands on the book *and* the necklace, then there was the whole incident with the beer. Plus Jasper after the guardians in York, and I still don't think he was working alone." She hesitated, then took a deep breath. "And there suddenly seems to be a bunch of rumours about me possibly having a mental break. That's what they called it when I left London. It wasn't, though. It was the bridges."

"I know about the bridges," Thompson said, and she gave him a startled look. "Watch are everywhere."

"I don't know about the bridges," Rory said.

"I told you."

"You said there was an *incident*."

"There was." She left it at that, and after a moment he sighed.

"Thank you for the additional details. Most enlightening. You think this is all related, then? Tied up with the Watch? It doesn't really sound like cat territory."

"Everything's cat territory," Thompson said.

"Yes, alright," Rory said. "So, what … the fae are trying to get the book even though they can't use it, but they're going to give it to someone who can? Someone who can replace the sorcerer in Leeds, perhaps? Maybe someone who was trying to get the book before, but you stopped them?"

Both Adams and Thompson looked at him, and the cat gave a thoughtful purr. "There is at least one other sorcerer in the Leeds area already, but maybe. It's not a *there can be only one* type situation."

"It has to be part of a bigger picture," Adams said. "As far as I know, I'm the only one dealing with Folk cases, and suddenly I'm not just being targeted, but they're using things like vanishing hexes, which are making me look … well, they're feeding the mental break narrative. Maud even mentioned it. And questioned Collins, apparently."

"Curiouser and curiouser," the cat said.

Adams glanced at him. "I didn't think you were a reader."

"I'm not. But there was a cat in that one."

"Alright. Is there another way we can find the Gentry? How do they travel? Do they do your thing, the teleportation?"

"You're doing this deliberately now," Thompson said. "You know it's not teleportation."

"I do, but you get so annoyed. It's fun."

He bared his teeth at her, a little lazily. "They don't shift. They have to use a portal. A stone circle preferably, although a faery ring will do at a pinch. Not as stable, though, and tougher to get captives through."

"What about coins?" Adams asked, thinking of the vanishing woman at the pub.

"That'll do it, but you're not coming back once you touch fae gold. It gobbles you up, that stuff."

"Nice," Rory muttered, and Adams shivered.

"Can we find a circle or something, then?" she asked.

Thompson sighed. "You make my job very difficult, you know. You really want to walk into Faery?"

"He's not going to expect us to come straight at him." Something about Velmyr wouldn't stop niggling at her. The *Kind regards* on the note. The little flares and slips of irritation. He didn't act like he was some all-powerful being. He acted like someone who *wanted* to be one. And that was different enough that it might just give them a chance.

"I'm in," Rory said, and she glanced at him. He shrugged. "I'm hardly going to miss out on the chance to launch a sneak attack on Faery, am I?"

"There's something wrong with you both," Thompson said.

Rory nodded. "Well, we are talking to a cat."

The phone rang twice while she was driving, Maud's number flashing up on the screen. The first time the signal was too patchy to hear anything, but the second time it connected.

"Adams," Maud said. "How're you doing out there?" Her voice was oddly diffident.

"Yeah, good," Adams said, glancing at Rory with a frown. He was fiddling with his phone, but returned her frown with raised eyebrows.

"Parents okay?" Maud asked.

"Great. Loved the cheese factory, but Mum was less enthusiastic about the Ropemakers."

"Really? It's very interesting."

"I'm sure it is," Adams said. Why was everyone in this part of the world so fixated on weird museums? Was there really so little to do?

"Good, good." Maud still didn't sound like herself, and Adams wondered if there was someone there with her. "Cottage alright?"

"Great, thanks. Really comfy." Other than the rift in reality under the stairs, but hopefully they could clean that up.

"Excellent. Ah … have you seen Collins at all?"

Rory lowered his phone, and Adams frowned again as she answered. "He popped by this afternoon. Why?"

"Oh, just checking in. Are you … are you feeling alright, then?"

Adams realised her hands were aching, and forced herself to ease her grip on the steering wheel. "Yes, good. It's nice to get away for a bit."

"Right. And nothing odd's been happening?"

"Nothing at all. Nice place, Hawes." She wasn't even sure why she was lying, just that this was *off*, this wasn't Maud's usual manner. Something was going on.

"Okay. Well. Good to know. Keep in touch."

"Sure." Adams listened to the phone disconnect, then looked in the rear-view mirror at Thompson, who'd moved into the back seat and sent the dogs huddling together against one door. "Go and check on Collins."

"Look, you can't get rid of me that easy—"

"*Now*, Thompson. Something's up, and if you don't sodding well go and check on him, I'll take you to the vet and get you the snip."

He narrowed his eyes at her reflection. "You wouldn't."

"Try me."

"You'd have to catch me first," he pointed out, then was gone, flashing out of existence and making Midge give a startled bark.

Rory glanced at her, then held his phone up. "There's a stone circle on a fell top not far from here. Private land, no rights of way, but it's a known site of significance in occult fields, apparently."

"Find the nearest road up."

"On it."

She accelerated, trying Collins' number again, something panicked clawing at her chest. Collins and Chloe would be alright. They weren't targets. *Surely.*

There was no answer from either of their phones, though.

They wound their way through the maze of deep dales and fells, up B-roads and C-roads and others that didn't really justify the title of *road*, Rory guiding Adams with quick, concise directions. She recognised some of the landmarks and junctions, but she wasn't paying as much attention as she should've been. She tried calling Collins a couple more times, as well as Chloe, then gave up. She wasn't sure she wanted to be certain they weren't answering. The longer she could put it down to patchy signal, the better.

"Turn here," Rory said suddenly, and she jammed the

brakes on, hauling the wheel over. Midge and Pinto tumbled into the back of the front seats with little yaps of protest, and Rory grabbed the door handle. "Bloody *hell*, Adams."

"Well, give me more warning," she said, taking the track they'd just turned into rather more slowly. It was a single lane between weather-scarred stone walls, crumbling in places and patched with wire and wood fencing. Potholes yawned to either side of the track's central, weedy ridge, and she could hear the long grass brushing the underside of the car as they passed. She hoped the potholes didn't get any deeper, or she'd start bottoming out. "Are you sure about this?" she asked. "I don't fancy having to reverse back all the way."

"It's the closest drivable access," he said. "Far as I can tell, anyway."

"Alright." She glanced at him. "Any chance you've got a decoy book we can use?"

"Not on me. But we're not going in yet, right? We're just scouting? You don't have an amulet."

She didn't answer.

"Adams? We need an amulet, and we need a book. I've got one I think could work – it was my mum's, but someone else gave it to her. It's pretty old, and it *looks* like a spell book."

"Perfect."

"Right. So we need to go and get it from my place."

She sighed, not looking at him. "We don't have time."

"We need to make time. I know you want to get straight after your parents, but we need to be prepared. You don't even have Dandy." He hesitated, looking in the back of the car. "Do you?"

"No," she admitted. "But the longer we wait, the harder it's going to be to get my parents back. You know that."

They were silent then, bumping their way up the track, leaving the road further and further behind. The lane meandered and switchbacked, dipping into a gully to cross an almost dry ford before climbing up the hill on the other side. They didn't appear to be heading to a farmhouse. In fact, the only buildings they saw were broken down old stone shepherd's huts, abandoned in the wash of green and grey and crumbling slowly to nothing. The route seemed unused by vehicles or anyone else, not even any sheep in the fields, or the ubiquitous, weather-beaten wooden signs of footpath routes pointing off into the distance. It was an empty, silent space in the middle of prime rambling country, and Adams wondered if there were charms on it to turn people away, just like at the dragons' wood, ones she couldn't feel. It wouldn't be the first time she'd missed such things.

The track grew rougher and more broken, the potholes deepening to troughs as they climbed toward a long, rugged ridge that capped the fell. Finally it became impassable for the car, and Adams stopped amid a rubble of loose stones before it got to the point where she wasn't going to be able to go back again.

"We should've taken my Land Rover," Rory said, and she gave him a sideways look.

"Yours wouldn't have even made it up the hill."

"It would. Land Rovers can do anything."

"Sure, if they're actually maintained."

"Ouch."

They got out of the car, Midge and Pinto scrambling to join them, and stood looking up at the rugged flank of the fell rising grey and stony to the dimming sky. The low sun was still warm, but a stiff breeze curled around them, plucking plaintively at their clothes. The place felt empty, desolate, and Adams could almost imagine no one had been up here for years, shying from the hostile slopes, scared away by a threat they couldn't quite explain.

"Up there?" she said to Rory, nodding at the fell top.

"Apparently. Local witchy groups come out and stake out the stone circle at the solstice and stuff, it seems. The site I read said the farmer's pretty hostile, so it's best to avoid him."

"Well, we'll certainly try." Adams dug into the boot to find her workout jacket, pulling it on, then grabbed her backpack, added the coil of rope on top of the food supplies, and tucked her baton into the pocket on one side, her duck and keys on the other.

"I really need to get a big stick," Rory said.

Adams paused, then said, "Actually, I've got one. It's been living in the boot for ages." She dug in behind her kit bag and gym gear and lurking six-pack of water, finding the staff she'd taken from the sorcerer's house in Leeds. It wasn't ornate or fancy, but it had a nice weight to it as she pulled it out, and for a moment she considered keeping hold of it and giving her baton to Rory instead. But that was ridiculous. She handed the stick over, and he took it with both hands, bouncing it gently.

"Nice."

"Try not to cause any injuries I'm going to have to explain to Maud."

"I shall do my best."

They headed straight up the fell, not bothering to hunt for a path, the dogs bounding up easily but the humans having to scramble and use their hands to steady themselves, skirting patches of loose scree. Rocks slipped away under their shoes, bouncing down toward the car, but it was manageable, and they kept going steadily, the wind intensifying as they climbed.

They crested the top abruptly, a sharp edge opening to a flat summit, as if the peak had been sliced neatly away. Adams turned to check on the car, breathing hard, and looked out over a wild sweep of country, a patchwork of fields and trees and walls punctuated by shattered stone buildings. Dimly she could see the road they'd taken, and even the bright flash of a car, but it seemed distant and uninteresting, alien and pointless. She knew that all those carefully sectioned fields, the trees pushed into their corners, the wobbly yet defiant lines of the walls, all spoke of the human taming of the land. And yet at the same time, it seemed to exist only on the surface, like someone trying to trim the pelt of some vast beast, the skin of it untouched and powerful beneath. The wild presence of the land was still evident in the curve of the slopes, the coil of the rivers, and the muscular upheavals of the fells. It wasn't something that could be contained so easily.

Rory joined her, panting slightly, and when she turned away he said, "Hang about. I need a moment to appreciate the view. If I meet a fae now I'm not even going to be able to run from them. My legs are dead."

"Lightweight," Adams said.

"Yeah, well, not all of us are running daily half-marathons," he said, grinning at her.

Adams snorted, but didn't move to leave their vantage point. She just looked the other way, over the flat expanse of the summit, rocky and grey. Patches of heather scoured flat by the wind bloomed with tiny flowers, and everything else was pale stone and scrappy grass, short but persistent. Despite the greenery, compared to the lushness of the valley below, it was a moonscape. Adams frowned. She hadn't expected mushrooms, obviously, or a sign saying *Faery this way,* but there was *nothing.* It was just a fell, like any other.

"It's there," Rory said, following her gaze.

"Where?"

"Look." The top of the fell had a long, flattened spine, like the hull of a boat turned upside down, and it rose at one end. Rory led the way toward the highest point, Midge and Pinto drawing closer and closer to him, until they finally stopped, whining. Adams scratched their heads as she passed, and joined Rory when he paused not far beyond the dogs. "There," he said.

She scanned the ground, about to say she didn't see anything, then, like one of those 3D paintings that need to be looked at just so, it swam into view. Nearly indistinguishable from the rest of the rocks was a circle of stones. Adams couldn't have said *why* they stood out, but now she'd seen them they were unmistakable, regularly spaced across the top of the fell and forming a large ring. They were a little bit smoother than their neighbours perhaps, a slightly different colour or texture, *something*, but she couldn't quite articulate it. It was just *different*, the way Folk were, and those who saw Folk. The crispness of them was similar, yet Adams thought that, where Folk always gave her the sense they were more *in* the world than non-Folk, the rocks were perhaps *less* in the world. They weren't right, anyway, and she shivered slightly, grateful for the lack of footpath signs and walkers. She didn't know how easy it was to fall into a faery circle, but she was glad there weren't too many people around to find out.

She licked her lips and said, "What do we do? Walk around them widdershins three times, is that it?"

"I suppose so," Rory said. "That's what the stories say, anyway."

Adams nodded. "Alright."

"I really think we should wait for the amulets, at least. Or Dandy."

"You don't have to come."

"Well, I am," he said, and unlooped the necklace from around his neck, holding it out to her. "Here."

She looked at it, then at him. "No."

"Please."

"I have a duck," she said, holding it up.

"Explain how that helps."

"I have no idea, but I'm not taking your mother's necklace."

He held it out to her for a little longer, but when she didn't budge he sighed and put it back on, then held his hand out. "I'll wear it, but I'm going to hold onto you, alright?"

"You think *that*'ll help?"

"It can't hurt."

She grimaced, and took his hand. "Fine."

"*Finally*," he said. "It only took a couple of abductions and an ill-judged assault on Faery to get you to hold my hand."

"Well, it's no fun if it's not a challenge," she replied, and they started walking, the wind cold and wild and smelling of strange and unknown places.

Adams expected a frisson of magic to start up, something deep and harsh and dangerous, or perhaps some gravitational pull to begin building, like with the portal. But there was nothing except the endless, peevish wind, pinching her ears and reminding her that summer in the Dales was nothing more than a suggestion.

They circled the stones once, Rory's hand uncomfortably warm on hers, and making her feel like a child in a nursery rhyme. "Do we have to say anything?" she asked. "Should we be chanting something?"

"I don't think so," he said, not sounding particularly sure. "They want people to fall in, after all. I imagine the idea is that anyone silly enough to go widdershins three times around the spooky rocks is fair game."

They kept walking, and she said, "Can you feel anything different?"

"No."

"Was it like this when you tried before?"

"No," he said again. "I used – tried to use – an existing portal. A faery had already opened it."

"Right. Maybe we should've looked for one of those."

"Maybe."

There was a buzzing sound rising in her ears, rough and hungry, and she wanted to ask if he could hear it too, but surely he'd say something if he could? She shot him a sideways glance and he was frowning, looking as uncertain as she felt, but before she could speak Midge and Pinto started barking in even, sharp yaps, not panicked but full of warning.

They stopped walking, and waited to see what would come next.

16

NEW BAND NAME

THE NOISE WAS ODDLY FAMILIAR, AND DISTINCTLY UNMUSICAL, and Adams suddenly realised what it was.

Engines.

Unless the fae were patrolling the hilltop with motorbikes, they were about to be busted for trespassing. "What did the site say about the hostile farmer?" she asked Rory.

"Shotguns and dogs were mentioned," he said, looking along the hill.

Adams swore, pulling her hand out of his. They couldn't risk it, not least the possibility that if the circle *did* open, she'd end up dragging some gun-wielding bloody Yorkshireman into Faery with her. That'd start a whole other war to the one Thompson was worried about. "Let's go."

Rory didn't argue. They sprinted for the edge of the fell top, not bothering to get back to the point where they'd summited. The bikes sounded to be coming up from the other side, still out of sight, and a moment later Adams and Rory were scrambling and sliding down the rubbly, scree-filled slope, trying to keep their feet and riding miniature avalanches all the way down, the dogs bounding delightedly past them.

"*Oi!*" someone shouted from above, and they didn't slow. Adams didn't think they *could* slow, and all she could hope was that the bikes would have to go back the way they had come and circle the fell – and that no one was going to take a pot shot at them.

They made it to the bottom with no one flinging more than a couple of shouts after them, none of which Adams could make out over the clatter of stones. She paused when she reached flatter ground, looking up to see four indistinct heads peering down at them, like they'd grown out of the land. One shook a shotgun but didn't take aim, and she raised her hands in a gesture of defeat as Rory stumbled to the grass next to her, panting.

"Alright?" she asked.

"Not shot or grabbed by faeries, so it's a start."

She didn't bother answering, just broke into a run again, not quite trusting that situation to continue until they got out of here. Rory fell into step with her, the dogs bounding ahead joyously, and they bolted for the car.

They made it unscathed, although the heads had vanished from the fell by the time they reached it, and would presumably be back on their bikes to give chase. Adams got the Golf turned around without getting stuck on any of the larger bits of rubble, then headed back down the farm track, bouncing and clattering and apologising silently to her poor car. It wasn't made for this. She didn't pause until they were about to join the road, when she slammed the brakes on so hard Rory, Midge, and Pinto all yelped in unison.

"Do you have to keep doing that?" Rory complained.

She didn't answer, just pointed at the gate. It was lying open, which was why they'd barrelled past without noticing it when they first came off the road. There was a *Private Prop-*

erty sign on it, but there was another notice next to that, a simple laminated A4 poster.

A photo of a quad bike, a farmer, and three dogs.

Sheepdog Demos in Hawes!!! Come and See the Magic!!!

"Oh, sodding hell," Rory said. "The *sheep*."

Adams thumped the steering wheel with both hands, swearing with such enthusiasm Midge and Pinto put their heads between the seats to stare at her in astonishment.

"Better?" Rory asked.

"Yes. No. That bloody farmer! I should've arrested him on the spot."

"On what charge?"

"Reckless use of livestock." She checked the rear-view mirror, but there was still no pursuit in sight. "We need to get back in there. Where's his farm?"

He raised his phone. "Not enough signal yet. The whole place is a dead spot."

She growled. "Where's the damn cat when you need him?"

"Look, this is good," Rory said. "If we head back to Hawes and pick up Collins and Chloe, we can get some signal and find the farm, plus we'll have more bodies *and* the amulets. We can make a better plan."

She glanced at him. "*A* plan, you mean."

"I was trying to be polite. You know, in case you got twitchy with the baton."

She snorted, and got the car moving again. "Alright. It's good enough."

It wasn't like they had much choice even if it wasn't. The circle was evidently watched for the farmer or his mystery guards to have got there so quickly. She poked the car's display, checking her own mobile signal, but it was still too low to try Collins again. She wasn't sure if that was good thing or not.

The road was empty and smooth, evening gathering its skirts on the edges of the hills and the last of the sun turning the tops of the fells to brushed gold. The sky's blue deepened and mellowed, and the rich greens grew mysterious hues. It was utterly idyllic, and Adams wished her parents could see it. They should be looking out at this from a pub beer garden, listening to her dad ramble on about trains and cheese and sodding fruitcake. Instead the two of them were either being held in some farmer's pigsty, for reasons presumably fae-related, or they'd already been thrown into Faery, while she was out here running in circles trying to get any sort of a grip on the case, as if she'd never encountered so much as a missing sock in her life.

She sighed, pinching the bridge of her nose, and Rory started to say something that was sure to be well-meaning but unhelpful, but he was cut off by the dogs exploding into movement, both fighting to get out the window at once. Adams slammed the brakes on as Rory tried to dive into the back seat, grabbing for the dogs' collars. Midge was already out and leaping the wall, sprinting into the nearest field, and Rory barely managed to keep hold of Pinto as she wriggled and barked.

"Is it the cat again?" Adams demanded. She was stopped in the middle of the road, and given it was only wide enough for one car, she couldn't stay here. She needed to find a passing bay, at least.

"No, Midge is after something," Rory said, managing to get the back window up, then he struggled out of his seatbelt while still keeping Pinto trapped in the back. "Don't let her follow me."

"Wait—" Adams started, but he was already swinging out of the car, and she grabbed Pinto's collar to hold her in place. The collie whined plaintively as the door slammed again. "I know, girl. I know."

They waited, Adams expecting a tractor or another car to round the curve from behind or ahead and plough into them at any moment, but the world was still and silent and empty, and when her phone rang she jumped so badly she knocked her knee on the door, and Pinto gave a wobbly little howl. She punched answer on the handsfree, rubbing her knee urgently.

"Collins?"

"No," a male voice said. "I was hoping you were with him."

"Lucas?" she asked. Lucas was Skipton's crime scene officer, and also Collins' frequent companion on cheese-based outings.

"Yes – are you alright, Adams? You sound stressed."

"You could say that."

"Holiday going well, then?"

"Sure. What's up?" Because Lucas didn't sound *un*stressed, and that was not a normal state for him.

"I can't get Collins on the phone."

Adams took a breath. "No. Me either."

"Have you seen him?"

"Not for a couple of hours. What's happening, Lucas?"

A pause, just a little too long, then he said quietly, "There's a call out for you."

"What d'you mean?"

"I mean … no one's *saying* anything, but there's mutterings, and someone's set a car outside Maud's cottage to wait for you to get back."

"Maud has?" Adams asked, having to get the words past a tightness in her chest.

"I'm honestly not sure. She doesn't seem happy, but you know she looks out for her team. There's just this … talk …"

"About my mental state?"

"Um. Yes. Then Collins stopped answering, and … well, I

don't know. Something else must've happened for this sort of reaction, but it's not reached me yet."

Adams found she could hardly breathe, was barely aware she could see Rory emerging around the curve of the lane ahead, jogging toward her with something clutched to his chest.

"Have you pinged his phone?" she managed.

"Nothing."

"What about … he asked for a trace on another number earlier."

"Nothing there, either. I'm sorry."

"Right." She grabbed her own phone, ignoring her rolling stomach. "I'm sending you another. Belongs to a Chloe McGill. She was with Collins last time I saw them. Try hers."

"Alright. What's going on, Adams?"

"I don't know yet. But I'm going to figure it out." She hesitated, then said, "Does Maud know you're talking to me?"

"No."

"Can we keep it that way?"

He didn't answer straight away, then just as Rory reached the car Lucas said, "I'll let you know if I get something back on the McGill number. Keep your phone on." Then he hit disconnect, and Adams looked at Rory as he opened the passenger door, his face pale.

"What?" she asked, and he simply offered her what was in his hands.

It was the cat, after all.

"Is he *dead*?" Adams demanded, as Midge jumped over the passenger seat into the back, scattering water everywhere. Adams winced, but the cat was more of an issue than her upholstery, as much as she hated to admit it. Rory clambered in awkwardly, still clutching Thompson. The cat's tabby fur was drenched, making him skinny and unfamiliar, and his eyes were closed.

"No, I got him breathing," Rory said.

"Cat CPR?" she asked dubiously.

"Just cleared his airway and gave him a couple of puffs. You need to learn these things. You've got a dog now."

Adams waved vaguely, indicating the general lack of Dandy. "Somehow I'm not sure normal rules apply." She examined Thompson, sprawled limply on Rory's lap, feeling a strange mix of hot fury at whatever had caused this, and a sneaking horror that if Midge hadn't got out of the window, they'd never have found the damn cat. And he was a mouthy pain, but he was also *Thompson*. She found she couldn't imagine him not hanging around, being difficult about things. "What happened?"

"I don't know. The girls must've smelled him or something. There's a bit of a stream at the bottom of the field there, and by the time I got over the wall Midge was already in it. She grabbed him and brought him to me."

Adams reached into the back and scrubbed Midge's ears. "Good girl."

Midge whined, peering at Thompson.

"We need a vet," Rory said.

Adams took a breath, then said, "You're going to need to take my car."

"What?"

"I just got a call from Lucas. Collins is missing, so presumably Chloe as well. Lucas can't get a ping on his phone, and apparently they're looking for me. I can't risk being caught up in any weird, contrived investigation until I've got *everyone* back." Her parents, her partner, her ... whatever Chloe was, plus her invisible bloody dog and the robot cat, who was not hers, but was definitely her responsibility right at this moment.

"Alright," Rory said, and she gave him a startled look.

"Oh. Good. I expected more argument."

"No, I don't mean *alright, I'll take your car and go to a vet.* First off, if I so much as get some extra mud on the bumper you'll know and never let me live it down, but also we're not splitting up. We're dropping like damn flies."

She could hardly argue that, but she gestured at Thompson. "What about him, though?"

Rory looked at the cat. "Well, he's breathing, and his pulse feels fine, as far as I can tell."

"Yes, but—"

"Tuna," Thompson said, not opening his eyes. His voice was even raspier than his usual rough tones, turning his pack-a-day BBC presenter accent into something that had been dragged through a voice modifier.

Adams gasped a little bubble of laughter, and Midge yapped, peering between the seats with her tail wagging violently.

"That answers that, then," Rory said, rubbing the cat's side gently.

"*Tuuu-naaa.*"

"You sound like a zombie," Adams said.

"Am walking dead," the cat agreed, still not opening his eyes. He coughed, a nasty, wheezy sound. "Tuna would help."

Adams started the car. "What happened?"

"Too weak. Need tuna."

Adams exhaled slowly, changing up through the gears. They needed a place to pull over where they were neither going to be run down by an oncoming 4x4, or spied by any local coppers. "Check the glovebox," she said to Rory.

He opened it, peered inside, and grinned. "Are you carrying cat treats around now?"

"It's not *me*. This woman in Morrisons saw me dithering over the cat food because diddums here is so bloody fussy, and basically *made* me buy them."

Rory ripped open the little box of fish paste sachets, and Thompson's eyes flew wide at the sound. "Oh, that'll work," he said, grabbing for Rory's hand with his front paws, claws out.

"Easy. Let me open the damn thing first."

"*Give it!*"

"I *am!*"

"She did say they go bonkers for them," Adams said, mostly to herself, as Thompson lapped the paste from the end of the sachet with an unseemly degree of pleasure.

By the time she'd found a gate to pull into, squeezing them off the road and under some trees, out of sight, Thompson had gobbled down three sachets and was demanding a fourth at the sort of volume which suggested he hadn't suffered any ill effects from his dip in the stream.

"They're *treats*," Rory was saying. "You'll only throw them all up again if you eat more."

"I almost *died*. Saw all seven lives flash before my eyes."

"I'm not having you throw up on my lap."

"Or in my car," Adams said, switching the engine off. "What happened?"

"I was *traumatised*." Thompson pawed at the glovebox hopefully. "I need to get my strength back."

"Talk first, treats later."

He narrowed his eyes at her. "You can't bribe me."

"Sure?"

They watched each other for a moment, and she found herself having to resist the urge to at least give him a good scratch behind the ears. That would definitely weaken her bargaining position, though.

"*Fine*," Thompson said, and she wondered just how traumatising his experience had been. It seemed unlike him to cave so quickly. Either that, or the treats really were good. "I went looking for Big Man and the witch—"

"Excellent band name," Rory said, then made a carry on gesture when Adams and Thompson both looked at him. "Sorry."

"*As I was saying.* I went looking for those two, but couldn't sniff them out. Usually I'm not bad at tracking – none of that dog stuff, following scents and so on, but people leave signatures on the world. They have a *feel* to them, and as long as I'm familiar with it I can usually latch onto it from the Inbetween and pop out wherever they are. That's how I can always find you," he added to Adams. "You're pretty distinctive."

"How so?"

He shook himself off, scattering water over Rory, then started grooming his flank, mumbling something.

"Less fur, more talk," Rory said, poking him.

"*Ugh.* Can't a cat clean themselves? But fine. You're bright and dark all at once, like the moon behind clouds. It's interesting." He looked at Rory. "And you've got something else going on too. Can't make it out exactly, but you're easy to pick. Anyway, Collins feels like an old tree on a hilltop somewhere, and Chloe is all feathers and hooks. Makes my tail twitch, but not in a bad way. Usually not hard to spot, only I couldn't get a sniff of them anywhere. Nothing. So I thought well, I'll try York, but Ash & Yew's shift-locked up to the nose hairs, of course. Finally managed to get hold of Charles when he popped out to the pub, and he hadn't seen them. They never made it there. Went back to the cottage, and still no Collins or Chloe, but I spotted a couple of what looked like coppers waiting outside."

"What?" Rory said.

"Yeah, Lucas mentioned it," Adams said.

"Wow. They're really coming for you, then."

"Yes, thank you, I had realised this."

"Sorry," he said, and gave her a grin. "Do you want a treat too? Would that help?"

She scowled at him and looked at Thompson. "So then what? How did you end up in the stream?"

"Ah, yeah." He groomed his flank again, rather urgently, until Rory poked him. "Give over! I'm getting there. You lot have no sense of story."

"I have a strong sense we're running out of time." Adams gestured through the windscreen. "It'll be getting dark soon."

Thompson huffed. "Look, it's a bit embarrassing, okay? I nipped through the kitchen window into the cottage, because I never did finish the mackerel, and then ..." He sighed. "And then someone grabbed me by the scruff. No idea if it was Vladimir Dodgyduke, but you don't grab a cat by the scruff unless you know what you're doing. I got hold of their arm and did my thing – and let me tell you, they'll be needing some bandages after that – and they bloody well hefted me into the portal."

"You went *in?*"

"No, they hurled me at it, but I shifted as I went. Only all those damn charms and countercharms have got everything so messed up I couldn't get a grip on things. I spun out entirely, hit a couple of dimensions I do *not* want to go back into, bumped into whoever chucked me in again, bit them a couple of times, rolled straight down what I think was some sort of fae royal banquet table, then your damn mutt picked me up like I was a chicken dinner and threw me at you. I came out of the Inbetween in complete free fall. I suppose I'm lucky I hit the stream and not a rock."

"Did you see my mum and dad? Fergus? Anyone at all?"

"No, just the mutt."

Adams slumped forward, arms on the wheel, thinking. "I

can't worry about him right now. If he helped you, he's obviously okay, right?"

"I mean, he's a devil's dandy dog. *Okay* is a relative term."

She looked at Rory. "We need to get to that farm. If Mum and Dad aren't there, that farmer has to know where they are. And there's no way Collins and Chloe disappearing can be unconnected."

"What farm's this?" Thompson asked.

"Up there," Adams said, nodded into the fields to their right. "Turns out it belongs to Jacob, the farmer from the sheep demo where Mum and Dad vanished."

"And you found this out how?" Thompson asked.

"We tried to get through a stone circle, but got chased out before we could open it. I assume it was the farmer and some workers guarding it. Armed."

Thompson stared at her for a moment, fur standing out in sodden clumps, then said, "How are you still alive with such poor survival instincts?"

She ignored him, looking at the sky. "It'll be dark before long, and we're hidden from the road well enough to stay here for a bit. Rory, have you got enough signal to find the farm on maps?"

Rory pulled his phone out. "Let me try."

Adams stayed where she was, hunched over the wheel as if it could speed the evening. It still wasn't much of a plan, but it was getting closer. She could feel it in the tingling in her fingertips. The farmer, the sheep, the circle, the fae. Yes. They were getting there. And wasn't that a bloody relief?

THEY DIDN'T REALLY HAVE to worry about hiding from traffic. It was late enough in the day that any walkers had already emerged from the fells, collected their cars and gone back to B&Bs or hotels or, more likely, the nearest pub, and barely anyone passed on the road beyond the field. It didn't seem to be particularly well-used, and Adams wondered again if there were charms on the land, turning people away in case they wandered too near the stone circle up on the hill. She asked Thompson, but he seemed disinclined to be helpful, and took himself off to lie in the grass underneath one of the trees while Rory narrowed down the possibilities for where the farm might be. Finally he came and joined her where she was leaning against the wall, watching the last of the light fading.

"Here," he said, showing her the map app on his phone and zooming out slightly. "Got to be this one."

Thompson wandered over, and tried to make the leap to Adams' shoulder. She grabbed him, scowling, and settled him in her arms. "Don't. I've only got a T-shirt on and I don't fancy puncture wounds."

"Excuse *me*. I'm very graceful."

"Even so." They both peered at the map, then Adams said, "Can you find that?"

"Me?" the cat asked, and squinted at the screen. "I don't know. Maybe? Maps are so *human*. They don't have any decent scents on them."

"There's a stream here," Rory said, tracing it with his finger. "Likely the one you fell in—"

"Was *thrown* in."

"—and the fell here is that one there." He pointed across the fields.

Thompson peered into the distance, then huffed. "If you say so. I can't see sod all that far off. But I can try. I suppose you want me to just pop on over and find out if your parents are there?"

"And Collins and Chloe," Adams said. "Let us know what

building they're in, how many people about, dogs, all that sort of thing. Then we know what we're getting into."

"Anything else? Coffee order? Foot massage?"

"You could call some backup in on them," Rory pointed out, ignoring Thompson. "Rather than us going in."

"That too." And that should've been her first thought as well, and it worried her that it wasn't. Only she knew that if she *did* bring the police in, she was never going to get hold of Velmyr, and he'd still be out there, holding the leash of the faery cake and able to pull it any time he wanted. She needed that fixed before she got back to anything like normality.

"You realise I just had a near-death experience?" Thompson asked. "And there is such a thing as too much shifting?"

"Oh? Shift-lag, is it?" Adams asked.

"No. But the Inbetween isn't empty. There's things in there that hunt and wait, and if you're popping in and out too much they start pinpointing where you're coming from. Some say they even catch your scent, and then you can never shake them. They're always following you just on the other side of the world's skin, and their patience is eternal."

Adams and Rory both stared at him, and he looked back with wide green eyes, then said, "Eh. That's mostly stories for kittens, though. Other than the pinpointing bit. They do that."

"So you'll go?" Rory said.

"Sure. But I expect the rest of those treats when I get back." He jumped down from Adams' arms and stalked off, his ragged ears pricked and his coat still rough with damp patches. He leaped the wall and was gone.

Adams went into the boot and rummaged in her bag, coming up with the crisps and the fruitcake. "Dinner?" she offered.

"Can't imagine anything better."

17

UNWELCOME REUNIONS

"Can I use your phone?" Adams asked Rory as she handed him a bottle of water.

"Sure." He passed it over, and she left him fending off the dogs with the help of some biscuits, walking a little further away and taking her own phone from her pocket. She'd taken the SIM out as soon as they'd parked, and now she pulled up Maud's number and tapped it into Rory's phone.

It only rang twice before Maud answered, her voice crisp. "DCI Maud Taylor."

"It's Adams."

There was a pause, and Adams knew she'd be jotting the number down, ready to find its last location as soon as she hung up. Then the DCI said, "I've been trying to get hold of you."

"I thought you might be."

"Where's Collins?"

"I don't know," Adams said. "But I'm going to find him. I'm working on it now. Whoever took him has taken my parents, too."

Another silence, then a slow intake of breath. "What's happened, exactly?"

"It's Toot Hansell stuff," Adams said, and Maud made an irritated noise.

"Toot Hansell stuff has always been weird things happening at bake sales, and women of a certain age making a nuisance of themselves," she said. "Maybe some very unexpected resolutions to investigations. A bit of weirdness, sure, but not vanishing officers. So what's really going on, Adams?"

"There's nothing else I can tell you unless you want me to explain *everything* about Toot Hansell stuff."

"I'm not sure I even believe in Toot Hansell stuff anymore. It just seems to be one disaster after another, following you about."

"That's not fair," Adams said. "I've solved my cases."

"You have," Maud agreed. "But in Leeds the evidence vanished. In Harrogate it was the suspects that disappeared. We lost a copper in York. Then in London, a whole bunch of homeless people went missing. Some people might say your cases have a pattern."

"You can't seriously think—" Adams began.

"It doesn't really matter what I think," Maud said. "I've been doing my best to give you space, to give you a place to settle here, but I'm starting to question my own judgement. That whole thing in Harrogate, with the poisoned beer, was utter carnage. You brought in a bunch of civilians to help, rather than calling in backup, and dragged Collins into it with you. Are you honestly telling me there wasn't a better way to handle that?"

"There wasn't," Adams said, her voice flat. "I'm sure of it. Nobody else had the skills that were needed."

"Well, it's got to stop. You're off your patch more often than you're on it, and now *my* decisions are being called into question, and I'm not having it. So you need to get back here so we can work on this situation together."

"I can't do that," Adams said.

Maud took a deep breath. "I don't think you understand. There are people looking for you, and I can't order them to stand down."

That crawling, anxious feeling which seemed to have taken up residence in Adams' belly bloomed into nausea. "What do you mean?"

"I mean when people are worried that a copper's gone rogue, Adams, it's not always going to be handled in-house, especially when it's a pattern that runs across half the bloody country. So come in now. Better that than them dragging you back."

Adams pressed her free hand against her leg, fingers digging into her jeans, and said, "I'm going after Collins and my parents. Once I have them, I'll come back. Just tell me that if I do that, you'll vouch for me. You *know* I'm not the problem here."

There was silence for a moment, then Maud said, her tones very precise, "I can't promise you anything. Just get yourself back here."

Adams didn't answer. She just hung up carefully, then took the SIM card out of Rory's phone before walking back to sit on the edge of the car's open hatchback next to him.

He took the phone when she handed it to him, and gave her a ragged chunk of fruitcake instead. "Alright?"

"No."

"Was that Maud?"

"Yes."

"Not good, I take it."

"No. Apparently it's not her after me, but someone higher up. IOPC, perhaps. Independent Office for Police Conduct. I don't know how long we've got to find my parents."

Rory looked around. The dusk was coming in heavy now, darkness sneaking across the valleys, and he said, "We can get moving any time, I think."

Adams nodded, picking at the fruitcake. It had glacé cherries in it, and she flicked one into the grass, making a face.

"We'll figure it out," Rory said, bumping her shoulder with his. "You've got this. You always do."

She stared at the cake. "I've lost Collins, Chloe, and my parents. I've no idea where Dandy or Fergus is. Thompson almost got thrown in a faery portal. I don't feel like I've got it."

"Eh," Thompson said, and they looked around to see him perched on the nearest stretch of wall. "I've been thrown in worse things, to be honest."

"Must be your charming personality," Rory said.

Thompson showed him a tooth and said, "Move yourselves, then. Chop chop. Humans to rescue and all that."

"You found them?" Adams asked, her heart suddenly kicking into high gear.

"Nope. But that farm is shift-locked so tight I just about got whiplash bouncing off it. There's something going on in there, for sure. *And* there's faery stink all over the place. If they aren't behind it, they know about it. So move your furless little feet."

They moved.

FIGURING out the best place to park was tricky, since the farm was at the end of its own long track, and while they risked putting the SIM back in Rory's phone for long enough to check a couple of maps, there didn't seem to be any footpaths or parking spots marked anywhere in the area. Finally they agreed they'd just follow the road to roughly the closest point to the farm, and figure something out from there. That necessitated a rapid jaunt through the unlit lanes, Adams winding her way up and down rises and through gullies, around smooth green curves and blind bends, half-expecting a marked car to pull out on her from a gate or junction at any moment, or high beams to come barrelling up behind her. But they saw no one, and other than Rory muttering something about not signing up for a rally driving experience, and the cat complaining when Pinto fell on top of him, the trip was uneventful.

Both phones were now SIM-less, but Rory had the screenshot of a map pulled up on his anyway, following it manually and calling out the turns as they passed various junctions, the miles ticking down on the odometer.

"Anywhere here," Rory said, clinging to the door with one hand and his phone with the other.

Adams slowed, and a moment later a gated track opened to their left. She idled past it, giving them time to read an over-large white sign whose fat red writing declared *Private Property No Trespassing No Thoroughfare No Right of Way*. Next to it another read *Beware of Dogs*, and below that, *No Ramblers!* On the other side of the main sign a fourth one added, *Trespassers will be PROSECUTED!!* and had a picture of what was clearly a bear trap underneath the text, suggesting prosecution was the least of one's worries. Almost as an afterthought, faded white paint declared the gate to belong to *Rawdon Fell Farm*, and there was another of the A4 fliers promoting the sheepdog demos in Hawes.

"Welcoming," Rory said. "Very keen on his privacy for someone cashing in on the tourists."

"I suppose he doesn't want any tourists falling into faery circles."

"Not unless he wants them to, anyway," Thompson said, not particularly helpfully.

A little further on they found a gate on the other side of the road, unmarked and bland. It was padlocked shut, but the bolt cutters in Adams' boot made short work of that. The ground was rutted and churned up but dry enough, and she tucked the car behind the wall, as out of sight of the road and any cruising police cars as she could manage. She cut the engine and they got out, the long, lingering twilight breathing its last around them. Birds called in the dimness, and the heavy shapes of cattle were visible as shadows at the far end of the field. Adams frowned at them, but they seemed to be keeping their distance.

They loaded up, Adams settling her backpack on again, and Rory swore. She looked at him.

"I lost the very big stick," he said. "I must've dropped it on the hill."

"Well, I don't have a spare," she said, doing up the straps over her chest. "You're going to have to do without."

"Aw. I really felt included there for a moment."

She handed him her Maglite, tucking her duck keyring into her jeans pocket. Its light wasn't as powerful – most of the time, anyway – but she preferred it to the torch. "You can hit someone pretty hard with that."

He gave it a couple of swings, and nodded. "That'll do."

"Yes, super helpful in the event of faery attacks," Thompson said. "Who's giving me a lift? I've already done plenty of running around for you lot today, plus, you know, near-death experience."

Rory crouched down and pointed to his shoulder. "Try to keep your claws in."

"Try to walk smoothly, then."

They headed off, two humans, two dogs, and a cat, climbing the wall over the lane and crossing the field beyond as the shadows merged into darkness and stars multiplied across the sky above them, following the lines of the land toward something unknown.

THEY FOLLOWED the general direction of the farm track, keeping a field between them and it wherever they could, and just as the last of the twilight was vanishing and it was starting to become all but impossible to see where they were putting their feet, the farmhouse emerged out of the folds of the land. Light spilled from the doors of one of the outbuildings, a big metal-sided barn two storeys high, turning the parked tractors and assorted equipment in the yard into fantastical, crouching beasts, a tangle of shadows and cables and clutching limbs. As they got closer they could see warm lights on in the house, rendering it oddly idyllic and peaceful, like a painting set amid the empty fells.

They stopped at the final wall, ready to duck out of sight if anyone emerged from the barn's open doors, but no one did. Adams looked up at the slope of the metal roof, and wondered what was happening under it. It'd be a good place to hold captives. There was no one about to hear them shouting for help.

She shifted her attention to the house. No curtains drawn over the windows, and she imagined there was little point up here. Not like there were nosey neighbours about. She spotted what was probably the kitchen, the windowsills cluttered with old bottles, and beyond that she could just make out low wooden beams and a noticeboard on the far wall, cluttered with paper. The only other window she could get a decent view through from here was next to it, the blue light of a TV flickering across walls that held a clutter of framed photos. A couple of sofas and two mismatched chairs crowded the room, fat and well-worn. One of them held Jacob, his head flung back and his mouth open. She couldn't see anyone else from here, or any sign of the dogs, but there were a couple of lit windows upstairs which suggested he might not be alone, plus the lit barn indicated someone was likely still inside, maybe one or more of the motorbike riders. She adjusted her stance, settling in to wait.

They stood there in silence for a good ten minutes before Thompson said, "This is boring."

"*Shh,*" Adams said. "We need to see who else is around."

Thompson gave an exaggerated sigh. "Such a shame you don't have an expert in stealth and infiltration with you."

"I thought you couldn't go in there," Rory said.

"I can't *shift* in there. I can go and have a nose around on paw. And I can already tell you there's no cats here, and that's *super* suspicious, if you ask me. What self-respecting farm doesn't have at least one cat?" He jumped from Rory's shoulder to the top of the wall, vanishing over the other side without waiting for a response. They watched him slink across the yard, his tabby fur blurring into the patchy dirt and gravel. He slipped through the nearest barn door, and a moment later a clamour of excited chicken noises went up. Thompson bolted out, pursued by a sprinting cockerel, and vanished into the depths of some mysterious bit of farm equipment that looked like an overgrown torture device.

"Well, that was effective," Adams muttered, and they watched the cockerel stalking around, chest up and head bobbing proudly. Thompson remerged from the bowels of the machinery, jumped soundlessly to the ground, out of sight of the bird, and prowled toward a different door, ears twitching.

"At least he's persistent," Rory pointed out.

A volley of barking went up from inside, and Thompson appeared again. He wasn't sprinting, just loping at an easy pace which meant the two old border collies in pursuit could keep up without quite catching him. He headed around the barn and along a track that led away from the yard, and Adams and Rory looked at each other.

"Do we give him enough credit to think that was deliberate?" she asked.

Rory started to answer, and just then a large figure with close-cropped hair appeared at the barn door, looking around the yard curiously. With the light behind him it was impossible to make out their features, but they wiped their hands on a rag, shrugged, then turned back inside and shouted in a deep voice, "I'm putting the kettle on, Eric. You almost done?"

An indistinct reply came back from inside, and the figure nodded. "Alright." They stumped off toward the house, wellies thudding dully on the hard ground, and Adams looked at Rory.

"*Eric?*" she whispered. "Like the guy at the pub?"

"When the fae gold appeared," Rory whispered back.

"And they were so damn keen for us to go to the demo after."

Rory nodded, his face set, and they looked back at the barn. It only took a couple of minutes for a second figure – presumably Eric, and they had the build for it – to emerge, switching the lights off as he went. The barn was plunged into darkness, although one security light remained on over the door, illuminating the yard starkly and meaning any approach to the doors was going to be like dancing across a stage. Adams couldn't see any cameras, but anyone watching wouldn't need them. All they'd have to do was look out a window.

"Bollocks," she said quietly, once the kitchen door had swung shut again.

Rory peered at the light, then at the house. "If we go behind that tractor there"—he pointed—"then that front loader, then the trailer, we'll have cover almost all the way, at least from the kitchen. And that's if they're even looking. They hardly seem to be keeping a close eye on things, do they?"

"True," Adams admitted, then checked for Thompson. "Have the dogs come back?"

"Haven't seen them."

"Alright." She headed for the gate. "Let's do this fast."

It felt wildly exposed in the yard, even with the equipment theoretically between them and the house. Anyone looking out of an upstairs window couldn't fail to see them in that cold glare. But they couldn't wait all night. There wasn't time. Every minute that passed was one closer to her dad deciding to try some sort of faery cake because it'd be insulting to their hosts to turn it down.

They made it without hearing any shouts, for what that was worth, and Adams slipped out from behind the trailer and ducked quietly into the barn, Rory close behind her. After the harsh light outside it was suffocatingly dark, and she had to wait a moment for her eyes to adjust. When they did, she discovered a floor mostly given over to a couple of Land Rovers that appeared to be in the middle of being cannibalised for parts, as well as four quad bikes, one of which was tilting sadly sideways on a missing wheel, and some pens that were empty other than a smattering of hay in the bottoms. Chickens clucked and mumbled in the dimness, and the cockerel strutted out to glare at them. Adams had to stop herself from whispering *shhh* at the thing. She was spending far too much time talking to non-humans, and it was evidently becoming a habit.

A set of rough wooden stairs in one corner led upward, and light outlined a door at the top. She glanced at Rory, touching a finger to her lips, and pointed up. He followed her gaze and nodded, then gave her an exaggerated shrug that she guessed meant *What do we do now?*

She pointed at him, then jabbed a finger at the main door. *Keep watch.*

He pointed at her and shrugged again.

She pointed up the stairs and he shook his head violently, then grabbed her arm and pulled her close enough that he could whisper, "There's no cover. If anyone opens the door they'll see you straight away."

"We need to see if anyone's up there," she whispered back. "Watch the house and make sure no one comes out."

"We've not even checked down here properly." He pointed across the length of it, to the far wall. "That's a partition. It's not the outside wall."

She followed his gaze, frowning. He was right. She was missing things because she was in too much of a rush. But they'd been messing around for so bloody long. She looked around, wondering where Thompson was. He'd be the best possible lookout, but he hadn't reappeared, and she supposed she should just be happy he was keeping the dogs away.

"You check it," she whispered to Rory. "I'll take upstairs."

He was close enough that she saw him grimace, but he went, moving quietly around the conglomeration of machinery, Midge and Pinto keeping close to his heels. She turned the other way, picking her way past the cockerel, who eyed her in a belligerent manner, and tried the first step. It seemed solid enough, and she kept close to the wall, bringing her weight to bear on it. It creaked, but only softly, and she took another step, taking her baton from the side pocket of her pack and easing it gently out to full length as she went. She still couldn't hear anything from upstairs, no voices or movement.

She was halfway up when a whine rose from the base of the stairs, and she froze. Another whine, this one threatening to turn into a little bark, and she peered back down the stairs, heart going too fast. The shaggy, two-tone form of a border collie loomed at the bottom, and she had an abrupt stab of disappointment, even though she'd already known it wasn't going to be Dandy.

"*Shhh,*" she whispered, and the dog whined again, a little yap on the end of it. There was just enough light for Adams to make out milky, clouded eyes as Millie put one front paw on the steps, whimpering plaintively. Dammit, *why* did she keep collecting bloody animals? She eased back down toward the dog, digging in her pockets in search of a treat. She was out. "Quiet, girl."

Millie's tail wagged gently, and she had another try at the stairs, then backed up again, giving a slightly louder yap.

"*Shhh.*" Adams hurried down the last two steps to crouch in front of the dog, scuffling her ears. "Good girl. There we go."

Millie backed up a step, gaze fixed on Adams. Earlier she had seemed fully blind, and there was no way she could see much from those milky eyes, but Adams could feel the weight of her gaze anyway.

"What's up?" she whispered.

Another little whine, another step back. Adams looked back at the door above, and Millie yapped, sharp and insistent.

"Okay, okay. I'm coming."

Millie turned, leading her toward the door at a slow, hesitant pace, casting around here and there as she tried to find her way past the bikes and the pens. Adams wanted to grab her and hurry her along, but that wasn't going to speed anything up. Quite the opposite, since she had no idea where the dog was taking her, or why. But Millie had been the first to realise something was wrong at the sheep demo, the only one to face down the faery ring, so maybe she knew something. And right now Adams was willing to take any possible lead she could, no matter how thin.

Millie stopped at the door, her nose lifted to the sky and twitching enthusiastically, then turned and led the way around the barn, staying so close to the wall that her shoulder brushed it with every other step. Adams looked around warily then followed. She was out of cover here, and if anyone looked out of the house windows she was going to be lit up like a beetle in a display case.

Millie didn't stop, though, evidently confident Adams was still following, and before long they ducked around the side of the barn. This side faced the house, but there were no lights flooding the rutted ground and its extensive collection of decrepit farm gear. Weeds grew up around flat tyres and rusted blades, and nothing looked like it had been put to work for a few years at least.

The barn backed onto a drystone wall, and Millie stopped when she reached it, pointing her nose into the gap between the stone and the metal panels. She whined, glanced at Adams, then whined again.

"What's back there, girl?" Adams asked, joining her to peer into the narrow channel. She couldn't see anything, the light not reaching back here, and she wondered if she dared risk using the duck. She glanced over her shoulder at the house, but she couldn't see anyone, so she cupped the little brass keyring in her hand, keeping her fingers closed around it as she squeezed the wings. The narrowest beam of pale light dribbled out, illuminating a veritable thicket of nettles choking every bit of available space. In the middle of it was a hefty stick and she sighed. "That's it? A *stick?*"

Millie growled, stumbling into the nettles to grab one end of the thing, wobbling slightly as she tried to pull it out.

"Careful," Adams said, squinting at it and frowning. It was

long and smooth, more like … more like a staff. "Is that *mine?*"

The old dog dropped the stick and backed up, looking up at her.

"Really?" She looked at the gap and its harvest of nettles. "Is it important?"

Millie yapped, an irritable, impatient sound, and Adams would've shushed her, but the sound was drowned out by an absolute explosion of barking from the other side of the barn, accompanied by a slamming door and a chorus of shouts.

"*I'll bloody have you!*" someone bellowed, and someone else roared, "*Call your damn dogs off!*"

A whistle went up, high and thin, and Adams was sure it was Rory. The barking intensified, and he yelled, "*Leave it! Get in!*"

She hesitated, wanting to help but knowing there was likely nothing she could do, and the barking went up a notch, turning to snarls and then some yelps.

"*Where the hell did that cat come from?*" someone shouted, and Thompson came barrelling around the barn, ears back. He leaped to the top of the gate next to Adams, his ears back. "Run, can't you?" he hissed, then vanished into the field beyond.

He was right. She couldn't get caught as well, otherwise they were *all* done for. She ran for the gate, swinging herself up and over as a shout went up from the front of the barn. She landed easily, already breaking into a sprint despite the fact she could barely see where she was putting her feet, hoping she wasn't going to break an ankle on the rough ground, ignoring Millie's wavering howl of disappointment.

But it wasn't the broken track that stopped her.

It was the shout of, "Dad, *don't!*" followed almost immediately by the sound of a shot, flat and hard and final, and utterly unmistakable.

18

POSH GITS & SOUTHERNERS

ADAMS DIDN'T PAUSE, SIMPLY SPUN BACK TO THE GATE, dropping instinctively into a crouch as she did so. But there was no one in the yard waving a gun at her, no one silhouetted against the farm's light except Millie, who gave a little, disapproving yap.

"Come *on*," Thompson hissed from somewhere in the darkness. "No point both of you getting shot."

Adams had no intentions of *anyone* being shot. She ran back to the gate, scrambled over and dived for the shelter of the barn's wall, barely avoiding being tripped over by Millie, who pattered after her. There were no more gunshots after the first one, but the shouting and barking was even more frenzied than it had been.

"Dad, *put it down!*" someone was yelling. "What're you *doing?*"

"Sodding rich toffs, coming up here trying to steal my land—"

"Shut up! Just *shut up,* you mutts!"

The barking didn't ease one bit, all but drowning out more shouting, and Adams slipped up to the corner of the barn, peering around it warily. Jacob was clutching a shotgun that looked like it had probably been bought new by his own father, if not grandfather, and not maintained much since. In the glare of the barn's outdoor light, the wood stock was cracked and the barrels alarmingly rusty. He waved it vigorously, causing two of the three hefty – and familiar – men in the yard to drop into crouches, alternately waving and trying to cover their heads. Eric was standing next to Jacob, out of the firing line, and he made a grab for the gun.

"*Dad!* Give it to me."

Jacob swung around, and Eric dived sideways, stumbled, and nearly face-planted on the hard ground. "Don't you tell me what to do! Trespassers! We've got *trespassers!*"

"I was just looking for directions," Rory offered, and Adams spotted him crouched on the ground, half-hidden behind a tractor and clinging to Midge and Pinto's collars. "I was out walking and it got dark on me."

"Likely story," Jacob bellowed, swinging the gun back to bear on him. Rory ducked sideways, trying to drag the dogs with him, and they collapsed in a barking, struggling heap, while the farmer's two border collies tried to rush them. The other two men – Mike and Stu, if Adams remembered right, Mike still in a white singlet and Stu looking distinctly sunburnt, and no wonder they'd looked so interchangeable, they had to all be brothers – grabbed for the dogs. Stu missed, and the farm dog darted at Midge, who wrenched herself free and lunged to meet it.

"*Midge!*" Rory shouted.

"Dog fights!" Jacob shouted. "He's trying to steal them for *dog fights!*"

"*Stop!*" Stu yelled, trying to get between the dogs.

"Don't—" Eric started, and Stu gave a shriek, staggering backward.

"It *bit* me!"

"Don't bite my son!" Jacob roared, aiming the gun at Rory again, who rolled away, trying to take cover behind the tractor. Mike let go of the other dog and ran after him, and Adams grimaced, then stepped out, raising her voice to be heard over the chaos.

"Detective Inspector Adams, North Yorkshire Police," she declared, holding her baton at the ready. "Everyone needs to calm the hell down."

Jacob swung the gun toward her. "*You!*"

Adams raised her free hand placatingly. The gun looked in even worse shape from this angle, if that was possible, and the ends of the barrel were horribly dark. She doubted its aim was going to be terribly true, given the state of it, and judging from the way the barrel was waving about the place, Jacob would've had enough trouble even with something brand-new and shiny. But at this range he'd have to try really hard to miss, plus she thought there was a decent chance the whole thing could blow up in his face. She didn't fancy either option.

"Put it down," she said.

"I will not! What the hell are you doing on my land?"

"You know what I'm doing. I'm looking for my parents."

"Well, I don't know anything about that," he said, and they stared at each other.

"Gloria?" Eric asked. "You're looking for Gloria?"

Adams glanced at him. "Do you know where they are?"

"He hasn't seen anything," Jacob said. "None of us have." His aim seemed to have steadied, the gun pointed directly at her.

"You need to put that down," she said. "Unless you want to risk shooting a police officer?"

He snorted. "You're not here on *police business.*"

"That's beside the point."

"Well, there's nothing for you to find here. You should toddle off back where you came from."

"Where I came from?"

"Yeah. Down south. *London* or whatever." He said it with the deep scorn of someone who'd never been past his county's borders.

"Right." She raised her voice. "Rory? You okay?"

"Yeah."

She risked a glance around. He'd emerged from behind the tractor, dragging Pinto with him, and had recaptured Midge at some point. Mike had hold of the two farm dogs, while Stu was sitting in the dirt with the leg of his trousers rolled up, examining the unbroken skin of his calf with something like disappointment. Eric was still next to his dad, and now he tried a hesitant reach for the gun.

"Get off," Jacob snapped, jerking it away.

"Sorry. But she is a copper, Dad."

"So? She's a *trespasser.* Both of them are. And twice in one day! Sodding posh gits and southerners, cluttering up the place, trying to take my land!"

"I don't want your land," Adams said. "We don't do farming down south."

Jacob scowled at her. "I'm not that stupid."

Adams shrugged, tapping her baton against her leg. "I'm from London. I can't even keep a cactus alive. I certainly don't want your farm, and this one's not a farmer either." She tipped her head at Rory. "He's already got one he can't run."

"Harsh," Rory said.

"Yeah, seriously," Mike said. "That was uncalled for."

Adams ignored them. "All I want is my parents."

"Don't know nowt about that." Jacob still had the gun on her.

"I need you to put that down," she said, her voice calm.

"Not till you're off my damn land."

"Dad, come on," Eric said. "She's looking for her mum."

Jacob scowled, taking a step away from his son with the gun still raised, the barrel swaying between Rory and Adams. "You're too soft, lad. You'll see. They come up here with their money and their *ideas*, and want to buy up all our land. Plough the whole lot under and turn it into a bloody housing estate, see if they don't."

"I can't emphasise how much I don't have the money for that," Rory said. "My own house only has half a roof."

"And I've got even less interest in housing estates than I do in farming," Adams said. "So can you put the gun down?"

Jacob shifted his aim from her to Rory. "What were you doing snooping in our garage, then?" he demanded.

"I wasn't. Didn't see any garage," Rory said immediately.

"He wasn't in it when I got out here," Mike said. "He was just in the yard."

Jacob took one hand off the gun and dug in his pocket, pulling out an astonishingly shiny iPhone in a sleek case. He waggled it. "I got him on camera. *Snooping*."

"Well, it was just a garage. Nothing interesting," Rory said.

Eric rubbed the back of his head. "Ah, dammit."

"What?" Adams demanded, thinking of all the *keep out* signs. Evidently they weren't just about the stone circle. "What was it?"

"Nothing," Rory said. "Nothing at all. I didn't see anything."

"Well, I can tell *you're* not police," Jacob said. "Shocking liar."

Adams looked from him to Rory. "Collins' car," she said, and Rory grimaced.

"I mean, no plates, and everyone has a silver Audi, right? So no way of knowing. Couldn't say."

Adams swore, and looked at Eric rather than Jacob. "Where are they?"

He gave her a bewildered look. "Who?"

"Detective Inspector Colin Collins, and Chloe McGill. Their car's in your bloody garage, isn't it?"

"I mean, there's a *car*—"

"Three cars," Rory said. "Bit of a chop shop, I'd say."

"Excuse me, we're artisan automotive refurbishers," Mike said. "*Chop shop* is so demeaning."

"Where are they?" Adams demanded.

"We're not *kidnappers*," Eric said, but he was looking at his dad rather than her.

"Oh? Then what about my parents?" She took a step toward him. "My parents who were drinking with you? Who got chased by *your sheep* before they vanished?"

Eric shook his head. "Look, Gloria's *amazing*. We'd never touch her. And chased by the *sheep*? Really?"

"You seriously don't know farms, do you?" Mike asked.

"You were the one set off my sheep at the demo," Jacob said flatly. "But never mind that. Trespassers are *not* welcome. Don't care who you say you are."

Adams looked at him. "My parents weren't trespassing on your land, and neither were Collins and Chloe. What have you done with them?"

"Do you ever stop with the damn questions?"

"No. What have you done?"

Jacob gave a huff of exasperation. "I'm in my rights to deal with the situation. It's my farm!"

"Dad?" Eric said. "What d'you mean?"

Jacob scowled at him. "I can't tell you everything, can I? Bloody bleeding heart. You almost brought a damn *kitten* back once. Because it was *cute*."

"I was ten!"

"We don't have cats on this land! It's not the way we do things!"

Eric folded his big arms over his chest. "That has nothing

to do with this. Have you got *people* here? *Again?* We had an agreement! And we've only just stopped the damn pagans tromping around the place every solstice!"

"And I told you there was a reason we needed to *let* them, you daft hapeth. Look at us now – doing sheepdog demos for pocket change!"

Eric pressed a palm to his forehead. "Dad, please tell me you didn't bring anyone up here."

There was silence, then Mike coughed and said a little apologetically, "We were told it was a delivery gone wrong, like. That they were meant to be bringing us the Audi, but went rogue on it. So me and Stu brought them in."

Eric pushed his hand against his forehead even harder. "*Who?* Who told you?"

"It was a phone call, like usual."

Adams swung toward Mike. "Who from?"

"I dunno. Not our usual guy, but sometimes he's … indisposed, like."

"Right, well. Do you realise you've abducted a police officer?"

"He didn't say," Stu said, looking at her with wide eyes.

Adams squeezed the bridge of her nose, then looked up to find Eric staring at her, still with his hand pressed to his head, and felt a moment of solidarity with him before remembering he was likely still involved in the vanishing of her parents, if not Collins and Chloe. But one abduction at a time. "Where are they?" she asked again.

"Dealt with them the old way," Jacob said before Eric could answer. "Same way we're going to deal with you."

"*Dad,*" Eric said. "You didn't!"

"It's my farm. I can do what I want."

Adams wondered for a moment if it was worth walking back to the barn just so she could hit her head against something a bit more solid than her own hands, but instead she took a deep breath and said, "Okay. So what's that? Did you feed them to the pigs or something?"

"*No,*" Jacob said.

"Gross," Stu added, and she scowled at him.

Jacob jabbed the gun at her, and she tried to see if his finger was on the trigger. "That's stereotyping, that is."

"Well, excuse my city ignorance. Just what the hell's going on here, then? Chop shops and abductions and *dealing* with people? Would anyone care to clarify *any* of this?"

"I'll tell you what's *not* going on," Jacob said. "*You.* I'm not having this. I'm not having you sneaking about on my land, trespassing and *snooping.* You say you're police? Why don't you come back here with a warrant, then?"

Adams scowled at him. "If I've got reasonable cause to believe someone's in danger, I can make the call to enter a property. And you swinging that bloody blunderbuss about is definitely reasonable cause. But if you really want, you can call my DCI in Skipton, and she'll vouch for me." Maud probably wouldn't, not right now, but it might distract him at least.

"I'm not a fan of the police. Always sticking your noses in, just like cats."

"Dad," Eric tried again. "We all just need to calm down a bit—"

"*I'm calm,*" Jacob bellowed, swinging the gun in his son's direction. Eric ducked with a fluidity which suggested he had some practise at it.

Adams moved fast, bringing the baton up in one smooth movement, and slamming it straight down on Jacob's arm, hoping she didn't break anything, but willing to put up with a little breakage to get out of this ridiculous stand-off.

That was the plan, anyway.

Instead she was just in time to duck as Jacob swung back toward her, and that duck saved her from the worst of the impact as Stu and Mike piled on top of her, flattening her to the ground under a pile of large, vaguely sweaty farmer limbs.

"*Adams!*" Rory shouted, as she fought to get out from under the crushing weight of both men. "Let her go! *Let her go!*"

"Nope," Jacob said. "Into the trailer with them, lads."

The men hauled Adams to her feet, spitting dust and cursing, and Mike wrenched the baton away from her. She scowled at him.

"Dad, this is a *terrible* idea," Eric said, but he didn't move to try to disarm Jacob again, who now had the gun aimed firmly at Rory.

Stu nodded vigorously, although without easing his grip on Adams. "Gloria was really nice, and the copper's only trying to find her, like. Couldn't we—"

"She shouldn't have sodding well lost her mum in the first place, then, should she?" Jacob said. "Bloody careless, if you ask me."

Adams started to say something, but before she could Mike seized both her arms, pulling them tightly up behind her back. "Hey," she started, then tried to twist away as she felt the unmistakable bite of cable ties closing on them. "*Hey! This is assaulting a police officer.* Unlawful detaining of a police officer, too. What the hell d'you think you're doing?"

"We deal with things our own way up here," Jacob said. "Let's go."

⁂

RORY WAS CABLE-TIED TOO, and both of them loaded into a caged trailer that was definitely more built for sheep than it was for humans. Midge and Pinto were left tied up in the yard, howling piteously. Millie sat down next to them, adding her own howls in a show of solidarity. Adams couldn't see Thompson anywhere, and she wasn't sure what he was going to be able to do anyway. Shower them with disdain, most likely.

Eric paused on his way to the quad bike which was attached to the trailer, giving Adams another apologetic look. "I'm really sorry about all this."

She scowled at him, shuffling around on her knees to face him properly. "Great. That helps so much."

He grimaced. "I didn't know about your friends."

"And my mum and dad? What about them?"

He looked away, to where Jacob was trying to start another quad bike without relinquishing his gun. The other two dogs watched, ears back in disapproval. "I'm sorry. I really like your mum."

"Well, I'm sure she'd approve of this," Adams snapped. "Never mind what you've done to *them*."

"We didn't do anything to them."

"Then where are they? Someone did *something*, so who? You can get out of this now, you know," she added, dropping her voice. "Just let us go."

"I can't."

"Why not?"

He shrugged, a helpless little gesture from such a huge man. "He's my dad."

"Your dad is *abducting* people."

"I heard that!" Jacob shouted. "Bloody *hell*, you've got a gobby one there, mate."

"Wow," Rory said, mostly to his chest.

Adams scowled at Jacob, but didn't bother replying, just slumped to the floor of the trailer, leaning back against the cage wall as Eric got the quad bike into gear and they bounced off toward a gate that led up into the fells.

"At least it's not pigs," Rory said.

"I'm not reassured," Adams replied.

The ride was deeply uncomfortable. The trailer had zero suspension, bouncing and clattering wildly, and sending Adams and Rory jostling into each other as they tried to stay relatively upright. Adams hit her head on the cage twice, and Rory smacked his face into it hard enough to split his lip, and eventually they gave up the fight and let themselves be shaken down into the bottom of the trailer, where they were still jolted mercilessly, but at least couldn't fall any further. By the time Eric stopped and cut the bike's engine, Adams was more than willing to be thrown into the nearest pigsty if it would just stop the endless bouncing.

They lay there, Rory wondering aloud if cumulative whiplash was a thing, as Eric unlatched the trailer's door and peered in at them.

"Sorry about the rough ride," he said, as if he were a taxi driver apologising about the traffic.

"Sure," Adams said. "Definitely the worst of my worries right now."

Eric grimaced, and stood back as she wriggled her legs off the end of the trailer and stood up, surveying the land. She wasn't quite sure what she expected – to be delivered to the Gentry, perhaps, or dumped into a portal, or maybe simply rolled into a bog or a tarn, to sink deep beneath the surface and never return. But the stubby reach of the bikes' head-lights revealed nothing more than tussocky grass and scat-tered stones, and beyond that the night was too dark to reveal its secrets.

"Come on," Eric said, as Rory sat on the edge of the trailer looking around.

"Oh sod off," Rory snapped. "I'm getting there."

"Stop faffing," Jacob said, appearing in front of the other bike's headlights in grim silhouette, his gun still clutched to his chest. "I'm going to miss the late news if you don't get a move on."

"Oh, *no*," Adams and Rory said together, and Eric made a sound that was suspiciously like a snort.

"Come on," he said, and turned a torch on – *her* torch, Adams noted, with a certain indignation. He must've captured it off Rory. He shone it across the grass, casting each blade in sharp relief. "This way."

"Have you checked their pockets?" Jacob asked. "And her bag's still on! Why've you left that on?"

"She can't get into it with her hands tied," Eric said. "It's fine, Dad."

"It better be," Jacob muttered.

Adams kept walking, feeling the rub of her keys in her pocket, hooked to the duck and her multi-tool. Her baton was gone, but she still had her duck. That was something.

Even with the torch behind them, Adams couldn't tell where they were walking to. The beam didn't reach far enough, and her own shadow, and that of Rory's ahead of her, made the darkness too deep to be sure of anything. Beyond the light, they could've been walking through the middle of a forest or along the edge of the cliff, for all she could see. She thought they might be going uphill, just from the slight burn in her thighs, but before she could be sure of that she stumbled on a little drop in the land, and then decided they must've been going *down*hill. It was wildly frustrating and disorientating, and she was just about to demand Eric tell them what they were playing at when Rory gave a sudden, astonished yelp. She swung toward him as the yelp turned into a howl of horror and he dropped out of sight, vanishing downward with the same impossible urgency as an insect gulped from the surface of a river by a starving fish.

"*Rory!*" Adams shouted, and tried to stop, but a hard shove between her shoulder blades drove her after him. She stumbled, trying to keep her balance and come to a halt at the same time, and for one staggering moment she thought she'd managed it, then the ground crumbled under her feet, and she was falling. Rory had stopped shouting, and she just had time to wonder if that meant he was dead or if there was a portal down here, then she hit cold water with a flat and undramatic splash, the speed of her fall plunging her deep below the surface.

The water still remembered the winter's ice, and her hands were still tied. She hadn't even had time to take a breath before she hit.

The pigs were sounding pretty good.

19

DOWN IN THE DARK
WITH THE BITEY THINGS

ADAMS' SHOULDER BUMPED INTO ROCK AND SHE PUSHED OFF IT
as well as she could with her bound hands as she tried to
figure out which way was up. She didn't feel like she'd rolled
over in the fall, so up should still be *up*, but it was desperately
dark, nothing to give even the slightest indication of what
was wall or bottom or – *please, no* – the top of a submerged
tunnel. She had the sense she was moving fast, the water
whisking her rapidly along, and she risked kicking, hoping
she was right about the surface being above her head somewhere. She didn't have all that much breath to spare if she
was wrong.

She broke the surface more quickly than she'd expected,
and stole a precious, startled gasp of air, cold and desperately
fresh. She heard a shout, which must mean Rory had
survived the fall as well, but she didn't waste energy answering, just let herself bob low in the water again, working to
reach her keys. It was almost impossible with her hands
bound, but because of the way they'd set up the cable ties she
had a little bit of flexibility. They'd tightened one firmly
down on each wrist, then used a third to link them, which

made it impossible for her to wriggle free, but also meant she could use her hands marginally independently. She quickly found that if she stopped trying to stay afloat and just drifted she could curl herself over her knees and work her fingertips into her hip pocket. She sank as she wriggled and twisted, forcing her arms further around, then gave a little bubbling yelp of victory as she hooked her fingers through the keyring. She straightened, tightening her grip in a sudden horror that she could drop them, and kicked for the surface once more.

She bobbed there, spinning in the current and catching her breath, then swore as she bumped into something softer than the rock. Her mind instantly threw up the idea of the farmer stashing trespassers down here, bloated corpses plugging up the waterway, then Rory gasped, "Adams! Is that you?"

"Rory, bloody hell." He was braced across the tunnel, back against one wall and feet on the other, and she'd washed into him, but the current was threatening to sweep her past. She managed to get her legs around his, anchoring herself in place, and said, "Don't get any ideas."

He laughed, a little breathlessly, and said, "The lengths I go to, to get you alone."

"Don't move," she said. She didn't have the breath or inclination to explain further, all her attention focused both on not being dragged away by the swift-moving water, and not dropping the keys from her chilled fingers. She fumbled with them, her multi-tool stubbornly resisting her attempts to open it. Distantly, she could hear a roar, sounding unpleasantly waterfall-ish or rapid-like. Bumpy and possibly deadly, either way.

She almost dropped the keys a couple of times, but finally persuaded the multi-tool open, quietly thanking Eric for his lack of proper professional criminality. Maybe he hadn't been willing to defy his dad entirely (and, given the shotgun, that was fair enough), but at least he'd left her with her kit. She tried not to rush, even as Rory's precarious position slipped, and he barely managed to catch them again before they were washed toward that ominous roar. It seemed to take forever, but finally she managed to get the knife hooked into the linking cable tie without stabbing herself. She sawed at it as carefully as she could, gouging her wrist more than once but ignoring it, and eventually her hands popped free as the tie parted. She huffed a heavy breath out, stretched her hands a couple of times, then shifted position and hooked an arm around Rory's waist.

"Oh, hello," he said. "Come here often?"

"Shut up or I'll stab you."

"Should I have a safe word?"

"Do you want me to leave you tied up?"

"Is that a trick question?"

She shook her head and ignored him, concentrating on fumbling with his bonds and making sure she wasn't going to stab him accidentally. She wanted to mean it if she did.

It was much easier to get him free than it had been herself, and a moment later he gave a sigh of relief, shifting his position and almost sending them both tumbling back into the current. They had a moment of scuffling around to get braced again, then Adams tried the duck. It wasn't the first time she'd been in the water with it, and it lit up faithfully, painting the sheer walls around them in a pale glow.

Rory looked at her, his face made ghastly by the shadows, and said, "You're a proper Girl Scout, aren't you?"

"I'm a police officer. Being prepared comes with the territory."

He nodded, peering up above them. "Don't suppose you've got some crampons in your pack or anything like that?"

"No," she said, craning her neck as she shone the light around. They were in more of a crevasse than a tunnel, the river running through the base. The walls leaned toward each other until they smashed together, forming a peaked roof overhead, as if two raw slabs of rock had been heaved up by unknown forces, then had dropped back into place and simply stayed there. There was no gap, no sign of sky or a route out. Crampons or not, there was nowhere to climb out here. Maybe if they could work their way back to the gap where they'd fallen in they'd have a chance. She shone the torch upriver, the water plucking and tugging at her.

"Do we try going back?" Rory asked. "Downstream doesn't sound great."

"No," she agreed, listening to the churning water. "How far have we come, though?"

"It can't have been that far?" He sounded doubtful.

She turned the torch the other way, but she couldn't see anything, just the river rattling along at a fierce pace. "Alright. Let's give it a go."

"You lead," Rory said. "I might be able to catch you if you slip."

"Sure, make it my fault," she said, but she was already moving.

She couldn't claw her way along the rock and hold the duck's wings down at the same time, so she let it go out, submerging them in the utter impenetrability of the darkness. It was immediately disorienting, only the rush of water giving any sense of direction. She took the key ring in her teeth, too worried about it falling out of her pocket if she put it back, and began to pull herself along the walls, using both her hands and the toes of her trainers. Rory followed, the water ripping at them like a living thing, mischievous and eager to play.

She slipped once and crashed into him, grabbing a

handful of his shirt as he flattened himself to the rock, almost losing his own grip. They struggled for a moment while she scrabbled to find new handholds, then she was crawling again, working her way steadily along the wall. Every now and then she paused to shine the duck's light above them, trying to see the crevice opening to the world above. But every time there was nothing but solid rock, leaning over the endlessly roaring torrent.

Even given how hard they were working, the water was painfully cold. Adams found herself shivering, fingers cramping and grip weakening, starting to slip on the stone. But she kept going stubbornly, and finally began to think she could feel a little bit of openness above them, a touch more space between their heads and the rock. She was just considering stopping again and trying the torch, to see if there was a way out above, when her tenuous grip on the wall gave. She was mid-reach for the next handhold, clinging on with only one hand, and even though she slammed herself to the wall as well as she could, the grasping stream was too strong. She lost her grip with her other hand as well, feet slipping instantly, and spun free, slamming into Rory. He tried to catch her, but he must've been just as tired and cold as she was, and it was too much to hold both of them against the inexhaustible current. Adams grabbed one hasty breath, then they were tumbling down the torrent together, banging off the rocks to each side and trying desperately not to lose touch with each other.

Adams took the duck in one hand, clutching it tight as she was shoved underwater and back to the surface, pummelled by the current, the roaring ahead building inexorably. She tried to grab onto the walls with her free hand, or to find an outcropping to brace herself against, but each time she was ripped away before she could do more than slow herself slightly. They were swept relentlessly along, bouncing painfully into obstacles and each other, accelerating rapidly as the noise ahead built and built, swallowing everything, until nothing seemed to exist but the absolute thunder of the water.

There was no escaping it, no way out but through. Adams curled herself up, catching one final, deep breath, and covered her head with her hands. The roar was almost as suffocating as the weight of the water, and then she was falling, deeper and further into the earth, helpless as flotsam.

It wasn't a long fall, and rather than splatting onto rocks, as she'd half expected, she splashed down into a deep pool. The water churned wildly, tumbling her one way then the other, and she let herself go with it rather than fighting, until suddenly she was released, the terrible grip of the current fading. She bobbed up, breaching the surface, the air down here so cold that for a moment she wasn't sure if she might still be underwater until she felt hair sticking to her cheek. She gasped a breath and switched the duck on, playing it wildly around a long, low-ceilinged underground chamber, a small lake spreading serenely away from the thunder of the waterfall.

"Rory?" she called. "Rory!"

She paddled in a circle, keeping the light high. Where … *there.* A bobbing object not far from her.

Rory was face down, unmoving, and she swam toward him frantically, grabbing his shoulder and hip to roll him over. He remained motionless, and she shook him wildly, shouting his name. Still no response, and she hooked an arm around his chest, lifting his chin to open his airway, and started towing him toward the nearest shore, swimming hard.

The shallows came up fast, and before long she was stumbling onto a tiny, rocky beach, getting Rory just far enough out of the water that she could kneel next to him and check his airway was still open, working rapidly. She leaned over him, her cheek almost touching his mouth, and thought she could feel a whisper of air, but between the cold and the water she couldn't be sure.

"Rory," she said, tapping his collarbone sharply with her knuckles and shining the torch on his face. "Rory!"

He flinched, opening one eye and squinting against the light. "*Ow.*"

She rocked back on her heels, taking a gasping breath and rubbing her face with her free hand. "Bloody *hell.* You scared me."

He coughed, and rolled heavily onto his side, spitting on the rocky beach. "My house is constantly flooding. Takes more than a bit of water to do me in."

"Who knew being posh was so risky."

"You have to be so posh you're broke," he said, spitting again. He nodded at her bag. "*Gah.* Don't suppose you've got a flask in there?"

"No." She unslung it and dug inside, coming out with a couple of Yorkie bars. "Got these, though."

"Thanks." He took one, and struggled up to sitting, Adams helping him get settled. "Are you part fish?"

"I just float better," she said, opening her own chocolate bar and taking a bite. It was desperately sweet.

They sat there in silence as they ate their Yorkies, the sound of the waterfall filling the chamber. The water at their feet was perfectly clear, only the reflection of the duck's lights on the ripples showing where the air met it. Finally Adams got up and shone the torch over the walls, examining them. There wasn't much of note, no passageways or tunnels that she could see, and she waded into the water a little, trying to see to the shore across the lake. The wall appeared more textured on that side, as if there might be some depth to it, and she looked at Rory.

"We're going to have to swim across, aren't we?" he said.

"You can stay here. I'll shout if I find anything."

"No chance," he said, getting up and following her into the water.

They waded as far as they could, Adams having to start swimming first. The current was gentle this far from the falls, and it didn't take long to cross the little lake, but the whole way across Adams was waiting to bump into something, braced for the bones of a lost sheep, the bobbing corpse of a calf that had tumbled down here and not been able to get out. Or worse.

But they made it across without incident, and as they waded toward the beach Rory said, "That went alright."

"No monsters."

"No corpses."

Adams grimaced. "I was trying not to think about that."

"Me too," he said, and grinned at her, then frowned. "What's that?"

"Don't," she said, not turning to look where he was pointing.

"No, really."

She turned reluctantly, and for a moment didn't see what he was pointing at, hoping for bones but expecting worse. Then she saw something small crumpled at the edge of the water, washed in by the currents. She splashed over to it, her stomach tight, wanting it to be something else, a hide or a sweatshirt (although she didn't want to think how something like that might get down here) or just a lump of tussock. But it wasn't. It was a canvas satchel, and she picked it up to peer inside. A sodden notebook, a flask, and a clutter of pens, all jumbled up with silt and stones.

"Is it Chloe's?" Rory asked, his voice quiet.

"I think so." Adams stared at it, then took the flask out and offered it to Rory.

He made a face. "I don't think I want it now."

"No. Me either."

Rory took the satchel from her and slung it over his shoulder. "Alright. We can give it back to her later."

"Unless she's in there," Adams said, tipping her head at the water.

"We don't know she is. And anyway, you can't drown witches. That's one of the tests, right? The menfolk get upset because some woman's a bit too clever and independent, so they try drowning her and if she dies she's not a witch. So Chloe'll be fine."

Adams gave a half-hearted smile. "What about Collins?"

"I don't know," he said and put a hand out, touching her shoulder lightly, then giving it a quick squeeze. "We'll find out, but not if we hang about here and get hypothermia."

Adams shivered, suddenly aware of the cold again. She turned the light on the walls, which receded away from the beach here more than they had on the other side, although it was impossible to tell if that meant there was a passage to be found or not. "True. Let's go."

She led the way, trainers squelching across the stones, while behind them the waterfall filled the still air with damp petulance at their loss.

Adams fully expected there wouldn't be any way out but further downriver (and who knew how far that would be, or if they'd survive the trip), but one of the rough nooks in the wall revealed a narrow passageway, damp and greasy at its base and looking like old rains had chiselled it out of the stone. She ventured in, having to turn sideways to get past a hefty outcropping that narrowed the channel hungrily, and peered around a corner just beyond. It opened up, still tight but more than passable.

"Here we go," she said, with more confidence than she felt, and Rory ventured in after her. He had to wriggle to get past the pinch point, and Adams tried not to think of Collins. If he and Chloe had ended up in here, he wouldn't have got through this spot. But maybe there was another way out, or they'd decided to drift further downriver and try elsewhere. There was no point worrying about it, anyway. They needed to get out before they could do anything else.

"Hope it doesn't get smaller than this," Rory said, having to stoop to avoid the low roof. "Not loving it so far."

Adams didn't answer. She was also hoping it didn't get any tighter, and was counting how many experiences she wasn't enjoying repeating. Falling in rivers, for one, and being underground, and she didn't like how things had been spiced up with the addition of confined spaces. It felt like a bad direction to be going in. So rather than offering up any sort of reassurance, she just kept working her way forward, waiting to run into a dead end, a rockfall or a pinch point that was too tight to pass through. There was no guarantee there'd be a way out, and up here on the fells, deep in a hidden cave network that extended to who knew where, unmarked, probably unexplored, and slap in the middle of land protected by an unhinged farming dynasty, they could be down here forever and never be found. No one would even know where to look.

She didn't share these thoughts with Rory, and he didn't share any of his own with her. She imagined they were running in the same direction, though. It'd be hard not to.

But they didn't run into any dead ends, at least not at first. The passage meandered along, not feeling like it was climbing, which was a bit concerning, but the way was free from rock falls, and didn't narrow to the point where they couldn't get through, although there was some more wriggling involved, including one spot where Rory had to dive in on his belly, arms over his head, and Adams hauled him out the other side while he kicked feebly with his feet to help himself along. She was briefly concerned he might be stuck there permanently, but between the damp of the cave and the mud, he eventually popped through to the sound of ripping fabric. He clambered out, looking down at himself mournfully.

"I liked this T-shirt," he said.

"At least you have clothes," Adams said. "I'm still living in gym gear and cheap fleeces, since I can't get back inside my own house."

"That sentence started off with such promise."

Adams ignored him, because she'd just been confronted with their first junction (and also she couldn't dignify that with a response. It was hardly the time). The passage fractured ahead of them, and she shone the torch each way. One either curled around a corner just before the light petered out, or came to an end. The other direction …

"Are those *bones*?" Rory asked.

"Yes," Adams said, playing the light over them. There weren't a lot, and she didn't think they were human, but they were broken in unpleasant ways, making her think of creatures hunching over them in the dark, gnawing through to the marrow.

"Other way?" he suggested.

"Definitely." She turned resolutely down the passage, and found that it was indeed a corner, but one which was going to necessitate more wriggling. She sighed, and got down on her knees to duck under the crushingly low ceiling, shining the torch through the gap. It looked like it opened up further on, so she crawled in, having to lie on her belly and pull herself through using her elbows, the keyring clutched in her teeth and the whole place plunged into darkness. She slid free onto rocky ground and put the light on again immediately, wondering for the first time how long the duck's battery might last, if it even had one. It was showing no sign of faltering yet, at least.

"Help," Rory said, waving his hands at her. She grabbed his wrists and pulled him through, having one dodgy moment where she thought his shoulders wouldn't manage it, then he puddled to the floor with a groan. "Are we there yet?"

"No idea," she said, shining the light around.

"Adams," Rory said, his voice strained.

"What?" she asked, already starting toward the next corner.

"Look down."

She did, and had to resist the urge to find a rock to jump onto, like a cartoon woman menaced by a mouse. Underfoot, what she'd thought was a rocky bottom was made up of bones in varying degrees of slow decay, pale and grey and rounded, and broken in that same unsettling manner. She couldn't think of any way it was natural.

"Oh," she said.

"Go back?" Rory suggested. "There were fewer dead things, at least."

Adams considered it. None of the debris looked fresh, no scraps of flesh or stench of decay. Maybe it was from some old sinkhole that had covered over. It didn't *have* to mean someone was wandering around down here, munching on femurs. She started to say just that, but before she could speak an unearthly noise rose from the tunnel behind them, the screech of a banshee or the wail of a lost soul, and Rory grabbed her arm with both hands. She froze, mouth dry, and listened to the sound fade away.

"What the hell was *that?*" Rory whispered.

Adams wasn't sure she wanted to know the answer.

20

A DOG, A DUCK, &
A VERY BIG STICK

When the horrifying cry had faded away, the tunnel was so silent Adams' ears felt stuffed with cottonwool, and she wondered if the creature had rendered her deaf, the better to hunt her in the dark. She swallowed hard, throat clicking, and, against her better judgement, released the duck's wings. Darkness pounced on them, wrapping a swaddling of impenetrable shadow across their tiny slice of the world, and Rory's hands tightened on her arm a little more, the only anchor in the nothingness.

Well, almost the only anchor. She crouched, taking him with her, hearing his breath hitching in his throat, even though he was obviously doing all he could to control it. The bones shifted and scraped under her feet, both reassuring her she wasn't deaf, and also making her wince at the sound. It seemed far too loud, and she stayed where she was, waiting. A moment later the wail went up again, full of woeful fury, and she used its cover to sift frantically through the bones until she found one that felt fairly sturdy.

"Here," she whispered, pushing it into Rory's side. He grabbed it with one hand, still holding onto her with the other, and the scream trailed off again. A muttering filled the space behind it, as if the beast was licking its chops or growling in dissatisfaction, and she very softly passed her hands over the bones, looking for another with some heft to it. She found one that felt suitable, and rested her fingers on it, waiting.

Sure enough, the wail started up again, full-throated and raging, and she grabbed the bone, standing and pulling away from Rory as much as the space would allow even as he hissed, "It's getting closer!"

She didn't answer, because she already knew that, and the bones had made too much noise as she stood. The scream cut off abruptly, and a pounding silence filled the narrow passage. How close had it been? How fast could it move? How *big* was the damn thing? Given the sheer volume of bones in here, it was either substantial or one of many. And wasn't *that* a delightful thought? A pack of shrieking monsters, stalking them down here in the dark?

The silence was long, and no mutterings filled it this time, offering no way to track where the creature was. Adams didn't move, the bone raised in her right hand, the duck in her left, waiting, straining to hear scraping claws on the way through the gap, the passage of a scaled or bristle-haired body passing slick and hungry across stone worn smooth by its endless patrol. Had it – or they – been in the water? Had it been following them the whole time, padding silently and hungrily after them like some persistence predator? Or had it caught their scent only when they entered its warren of tunnels?

It didn't matter. She caught the smallest of clicks, maybe a talon knocking against stone, or a bone shifting under stealthy paws, and the skin-crawling screech flooded the tiny chamber, tearing through the silence and slamming Adams' heart into even higher tempo. She jammed the wings of the duck down, twisting slightly so she was ready to swing the bone at the thing's snout or ears or teeth, whatever looked both handy and painful.

Light exploded around them, the duck apparently as agitated as Adams, and Rory gave a startled cry, shielding his face with one hand and using the other to lash out blindly with his bone. The creature's scream shattered on the edges and dissolved into a stream of colourful cursing that seemed to owe a lot to farm animals and vegetables, and something small and sleek dived between their legs. Adams spun, keeping the light trained on it, looking for the rest of its companions, because surely nothing that small could've made a racket like *that*, and barely stopped herself following through with the bone.

"*Thompson?*"

"Fetid sodding mole people," the cat yowled at them, all wild eyes and dishevelled fur. "I'll tear your useless eyes out and swap them for Brussels sprouts!"

"Thompson! It's *us.*"

The cat squinted against the light. "Adams and Posh Spice?"

"Sodding *hell*," Rory said weakly, sinking to a crouch among the bones. "What was that *sound?*"

"Acoustics," the cat said, tail twitching. "I was trying to scare away anything bitey."

"Are there bitey things down here?" Adams asked.

"You're knee-deep in a graveyard. What do you think?"

Adams looked at her feet. "Knee-deep is a bit of an exaggeration."

"Fine, *I'm* knee-deep. There are *bones*. And it's not like they all pottered down here to die peacefully, is it?"

"I thought it might be an old sinkhole that covered over."

"Your optimism is charming, and likely misplaced. This whole place stinks of fae and their nasty critters, which is why I didn't even get a whiff of you two. I thought my shift had gone completely off course."

"And you couldn't shift out again?" Rory asked.

"Not until I figure out where out is. This is as good as a cage until I can find an opening."

"But you got in."

"Yeah, through an opening *somewhere*. Between the shift locks and the fae charms I was bounced about the place like an addled squirrel, *and* I ended up in the water. *Again*."

Adams rubbed her forehead, and made a face as she realised she still had the bone in her hand. She kept hold of it, though. "Did you come from the passage on the right?"

"The what?"

"That side," she said, waving.

"Yeah. No whiff of fresh air I could catch. My whiskers say there's a current coming from somewhere along here, though." He inclined his head deeper into the tunnel.

"Let's go," Adams said, shifting her grip on the bone and turning into the passageway. "I don't want to meet the bitey things, and your racket's probably got them coming out of the walls."

"Pretty good, right?" the cat said, and led the way into the dark.

THEY WERE WALKING and scrambling and crawling for a good hour before they came to a junction and Adams felt the first, faintest touch of a breeze on her face. She took a deep breath, and Thompson said, "See? Told you I knew what I was doing."

"Sure you did," Rory said. "That's why you had a yowling meltdown back there when something dripped on you."

"I didn't know what it was. It might've been the venom of

some giant underground spider, paralysing me so it could suck me dry."

Adams ignored them both, following the current of fresh air. Her hand hurt from her tight, constant grip on the duck, and she had so many scrapes and bumps she wasn't sure if her knee ached most, where she'd evidently bashed it at some point, or the spot on her spine where a particularly small gap had gouged the skin deeply enough that it wouldn't stop smarting, or her head where Thompson's unexpected meltdown had caused her to jump and bang it on a low ceiling. The cat's route hadn't exactly been gauged on what was most suitable for humans, and there had been more than one point where they'd had to turn around and find another way through.

But now the walls were slowly opening up, the ceiling rising above them until they were in something that was more cavern than tunnel, the air fresher and sweeter with every step. The ground grew mossy, the scent of rich earth and green life rising around them, and finally, *finally* the stars emerged above, just a narrow slice revealed between high walls, but it was actual open sky, familiar and distant all at once. They were in a sinkhole or steep-sided, sunken gully of some sort, and for one awful moment Adams thought they were trapped still, unable to climb up the sheer sides. But the torch beam landed on a jumble of rocks at the far end that formed a precarious stairway to the fells. It wasn't going to be an easy climb, but it certainly wasn't going to stop them at this point.

There was a bit more scrambling after that and a lot of lifting each other up, but eventually Adams hauled Rory up out of the hole, and they collapsed onto the damp grass next to the cat, flopping to their backs to stare up at the stars. Adams felt like she'd gone without seeing them for years. Rory dug into Chloe's satchel and produced the flask of whisky, offering it to Adams. She took it almost reluctantly, wishing she knew where to start looking for the others, and sat up to have a mouthful before handing it back. She was thirsty, making the alcohol feel too harsh, stinging her throat, but it was warming, and she stayed sitting with her arms propped on her knees, surveying the landscape. The fells rolled away in every direction, folded and shadowed and multilayered under the cool glow of a half moon. There were no lights to mark farms or houses, nor any headlights laying a telltale line across a distant road. She wondered briefly if they were even still in the Dales, or if they'd crawled out into Faery.

She looked at Thompson. "Any sign of Collins and Chloe?"

"No." He sounded serious for once, sitting with his tail curled over his toes and his gaze on the distant land. "They could still be at the farm, hidden by the charms, or they could've been dragged through to Faery. They're out of my range, anyway."

"And you didn't find anything, nosing around the farm?"

"I didn't exactly have any time for *nosing around.* I was running interference on the damn dogs, then trying to follow you lot. I had to walk *ages* to get past the worst of the charms, had a near-miss with a fox who thought he'd be clever and give me a nip – he won't be trying *that* again – and then do some bloody fancy shiftwork, if I do say so myself, to track you up here, and we all saw where that got me. I'm tired, and my paws hurt, and I have been in the water far too much for any self-respecting cat. Plus I've been in and out of the Inbetween *way* too often and close together. Something touched my tail last time."

"Ugh," Rory said, with a little shudder, and had another swig of whisky.

"Quite. Any biscuits in that bag?"

Adams unslung her pack, digging inside, and came out with the box of fish paste sachets. The box was a disintegrating mess, but the sachets were fine, so she ripped one open and left the cat licking it hungrily while she got up and stared across the landscape, as if the different angle was going to help orientate her. She still couldn't see any landmarks.

Rory joined her, offering her the flask, and they stood there with the breeze plucking at their damp clothes and soothing their scraped skin, trying to ignore the shivers that were getting deeper and more heartfelt with every moment. Nothing revealed itself as a way forward, but they had to do *something*, because it was bloody cold out here. Adams was about to suggest that they just choose a direction and try it – maybe uphill in the hope that a wider view might reveal something – when movement caught her eye, indistinct in the low moonlight. Something emerged over the nearest rise, scuttling silently toward them, low-slung and multilimbed.

She grabbed Rory's arm. "What the hell is *that?*"

Rory didn't answer straight away, then he said hesitantly, "That's … is it just me, or does that seem like a lot of legs?"

"Yes. And it's a lot of legs *across*," Adams said. "Can you have lots of legs across?"

"What?" Thompson asked, and she picked him up so he could watch the thing approach. "No," he said, leaning back into her as if to put more distance between himself and the creature. "It's all a bit blobby to me, but no. I've not seen anything like that, and I don't want to."

"Should we run?" Rory suggested. "It doesn't seem fast."

As if hearing them, the thing picked up speed, a racing shadow with incomprehensible proportions, impossible to make sense of.

Adams aimed the duck at it. "Stop!" she shouted, putting as much authority into her voice as she could.

The thing kept coming. She squeezed the duck's wings, hoping it would flood the land with light, but the beam fell short, as was to be expected from a little keyring torch, and she wondered if she should be relieved because it meant there was no danger, or worried because it meant the duck was scared. Maybe it was like Dandy, variable depending on its mood.

And while all of this was going through her head, the thing was still running toward them, rippling across the ground, holding such tight formation that it couldn't possibly be different creatures, even though that would make more sense. But surely they'd move around each other then, jostling for position, not be moving with such single-minded precision.

Then suddenly Rory whistled, the sound high and carrying, and a strangled bark went up from the raft of legs, although they didn't split apart. Adams let the light of the duck go out, waiting for her eyes to adjust again as the creature kept coming.

"Midge? Pinto?" Rory called, and this time the reply was more of a joyous whine. Finally they were close enough to see the two dogs, with a third wedged between them, running shoulder to shoulder in admirable lockstep. The moonlight reflected on the pale eyes of the third dog.

"*Millie?*" Adams said.

The old dog whined, and the trio came to a stop, tails wagging, all of them with their teeth clamped firmly around a very large, very familiar stick. Midge and Pinto let go, rushing to Rory and fussing over him, and Millie grumbled as one end of the stick thudded dully to the ground, pulling her head at an angle. She kept hold of it, still looking at Adams with those milky eyes like splinters of the pale moon, and Thompson jumped free with a huff as Adams crouched, reaching out a hand to scuff the old dog gently behind the ears. She whined again, and Adams put a hand on the stick.

On the *staff*. She'd felt it, hadn't she, when she took it from the car, something grown into its grain reacting to the old, deep magic of the land. And she'd used it like some sort of weapon before, when she'd been trying to recapture the sorcerer's necklace. The duck had helped then, too.

Millie released the staff, and Adams lifted it in both hands, bouncing it gently and feeling the weight of it. It wasn't like the necklace, or the book. She couldn't feel any sort of hungry power baking off it, tempting and sly. There was *something*, sure, but it was more like the duck. Dormant and inexplicable, a shadowy sense that it was *different*, but with nothing she could point to in explanation. It wasn't even ornately carved, or inset with stones or gems or shells or anything of interest at all. But she kept hold of it anyway, reassured by its warmth, and patted Millie again.

"Good girl," she said, and stood up, looking at Thompson dubiously. "I suppose this is important?"

"They're dogs. They probably want to play fetch." He sounded unconvinced, though, and padded over to sniff the staff. "I mean, it's *something*. Smells a bit like you."

"It has been living in my car for a year or so."

"That could be it. Where's it from?"

"The sorcerer's house. I, um, *borrowed* it when I went after the book and the necklace. It did stuff."

"Did stuff?" the cat asked, narrowing his eyes at her.

"I don't know. It seemed to work with the duck or some-thing? I was able to push back some of the charms that were being chucked around."

"*Huh.*" Thompson gave it another sniff. "It doesn't smell sorcerer-y, but my nose is so full of water still, who knows."

"Who knows," Adams echoed, adjusting her grip on it.

"Can I suggest you mention things like *Hey, here's a useful staff I took from a sorcerer* before we get tangled up with fae next time? Or, you know, do some research?"

"Do I have to repeat again, I am a *police officer,* and this is not my area of expertise?"

"Do *I* have to repeat, you need to stop telling yourself that?" Thompson asked, and they glared at each other.

"Well, I feel left out, yet again," Rory said, and looked at the dogs. "You couldn't have brought me one, too?" They gave him a reproachful look.

Millie yapped gently, and Adams looked at her. The old dog staggered in an uneven circle, her nose twitching, then suddenly stopped, snout pointing toward the top of the hill as if she could smell something. Adams peered in that direction, but all she could see was the top of the next rise cutting off the night sky.

"What is it?" she asked the dog.

Millie didn't acknowledge her, just started forward, walking stiffly. Adams grimaced. She must be exhausted. She wasn't quite sure how far from the farm they were, but they couldn't see it, so it had to be a long way for an old dog to run. She followed Millie, walking next to her and keeping her gaze on the ground ahead, making sure the collie wasn't going to plunge into another underground abyss. Millie plodded on, unheeding.

"Adams," Rory said, "what are you doing?"

"Millie wants to go this way."

"Oh, the blind dog?" Thompson asked.

"It seems so."

"Great. Perfect guide. Any chance she's going to do a Lassie and lead us home?"

"Kind of seems like we're off uphill," Rory said, following Adams. Midge and Pinto ambled next to him.

Thompson huffed. "Fantastic. *Fantastic.* Well, one of you can give me a lift."

Adams clicked her fingers at him. "Hurry up, then."

"No sense of decorum," Thompson complained, trotting to catch up. "And it smells even worse here than it did at the farm. Stinks of ley lines and fae and sodding sheep dung."

"Well, that seems to indicate we're in the right place, then."

"This is very much the wrong place," Thompson said, stopping to glare around. Midge licked the top of his head as she overtook him, and he slapped her with a paw.

"*Ew.* Honestly, I've never hung out with so many dogs as I have around you lot and I hate it. I hate *every second* of it."

"Yet here you are," Rory said, and picked the cat up.

Thompson hung from his hands, teeth bared and ears back. "This is undignified. Now I'm *glad* there's only dogs here. They know nothing about dignity."

"And us," Adams pointed out.

"You two? You've not exactly conducted yourself in a manner becoming of a cat. Worse than humans, if that was possible."

"Should I put you back down, then?" Rory asked.

"No. But you're holding me wrong. Do better."

"Good thing you're useful," Adams said, and Thompson hissed at her.

Rory rearranged the cat until he stopped complaining, then fell into step with Adams as well as he could, given the rough ground. "Where're we going?"

Adams shrugged, and gestured at Millie, who was keeping up a steady if uneven pace. "She tried to show me the stick – the staff – in the farmyard, but I didn't have time to grab it. She saw the faery ring back in Hawes before even Dandy did, too. So following her seems like *an* option, anyway. We don't have anything else to go on."

"She's seeing stuff we don't, for sure," Thompson said.

"She's blind," Rory pointed out. "As you just said."

"And as she is," the cat retorted. "Don't try to catch me out, Posh. But just because she's blind in this world, doesn't mean she can't see plenty in another. It may well mean she *does*, in fact."

"Faery?" Adams asked.

"No idea. Find out soon enough, I imagine."

"Could it be a trap?" Rory asked uneasily. "We weren't meant to get out of the caves, and now she's taking us somewhere to finish us off?"

They all looked at Millie, still ambling stiffly along and giving no sign of having heard them, then Thompson said, "We'll find that out, too. But she seems to like you, Adams."

"The weird ones always do," Adams said.

"Offence taken," Rory said.

POLICE VS. GENTRY

Millie's pace was slow but unflagging, and while Adams stayed close to the old dog, she barely had to intervene except to guide her around the odd patch of thistles, or redirect her toward a gate. Their progress still felt painful, though. Adams was itching to run ahead, to sprint toward the farm and drag Jacob out by the scruff of the neck, to get answers about where her parents and Collins and Chloe were. Well, maybe not Jacob, as she wasn't sure her conscience would allow her to manhandle someone whose dentures were probably older than she was (and her mum would certainly have something to say about it, even if it was all in the cause of finding her). But Adams felt she could definitely do some manhandling of the sons with zero guilt.

She couldn't do it alone, though, especially not with Dandy still missing. And then there was the fact she'd lost all sense of orientation, and didn't even know which way the farm was. So she just trudged along next to Millie, using the staff like a walking stick and feeling as if she needed a pointy hat to go with her quest.

The first ridge brought them only more stone walls and a

smattering of startled sheep watching them pass, with yet another ridge visible ahead. No buildings, no lights, no lanes. Nothing to give them a pin to hang the world on.

"Shouldn't we be seeing *something* by now?" Adams asked. "There's not this much empty land up here, is there?"

Rory made a dubious noise. "Maybe we're going in circles."

Millie looked over her shoulder and huffed.

"Probably shouldn't cast aspersions on our guide."

"I suppose not," he agreed. "We're definitely still in the Dales, right?"

No one answered, then Adams said, "Thompson?"

"Eh?"

"Are we still in the Dales?"

He didn't answer immediately, then said, "We're definitely in *a* dale."

Adams stopped. "Did we come out of that bloody cave into Faery or something?"

"How should I know? The whole area's a bit porous."

"*Porous?*"

"Yes, ley line intersections, magnetic anomalies, all that stuff. That's why the stone circle. But it means the feel and the scent are all messed up. I'm not sure what part of the spectrum we're on."

"Spectrum?"

"Are you just going to keep repeating words back at me like a pirate?"

Adams blinked. "I think you mean parrot."

"They're pirates."

"Not all of them."

Millie gave a growling yap, and they looked at her. She'd stopped, peering back at them. Her eyes collected the light of the moon more than it seemed they should, rendering them strangely luminous. They started walking again, and she turned away, trotting off into the distance. She seemed to be moving a little more quickly and easily, and Adams had a simmering moment of unreality, when she seemed to be seeing things at two levels, their reality overlayed on something deeper and richer, more *real*.

"What spectrum?" she asked Thompson.

"Reality's not that clear-cut, no matter what you lot like to think. Some places are clearly human, other places are clearly Folk, others blur at the edges. And Faery used to be much more a part of the Folk world. When the Gentry were forced back, because they were worse than sorcerers for messing about with humans and making life difficult for everyone, the borders were reinforced. But in places it still seeps through. It's not so surprising, really. Even individual realities are variable. Everything's a spectrum, except cats. We're a constant."

Reality as a spectrum. Adams sighed deeply and wondered if another shot of whisky would be justified.

The land was rising, the climb getting steeper, and she peered up at the flank of the slope above them. Millie was still marching onward, following little sheep trails that cut back and forth, easing the climb to something more gradual. They fell into single file behind her, and when they crested the ridge Adams wasn't surprised at all to see the flat top of the fell they'd summited earlier that day stretching out ahead of them. The air seemed thinner now, the world she knew far more distant, and under the moon the pale stones of the faery circle glimmered, as if dusted in something crystalline that reflected and refracted the light.

"Oh, hairballs," Thompson said, twisting out of Rory's grip and climbing to his shoulder. "Yeah, more Faery than human up here."

Adams thought that, for once, she could feel what the cat meant. The sky was so cluttered with stars she couldn't make out the usual constellations, giving her an uneasy suspicion she was somehow seeing them from a different angle. The curve of the moon held the shadow of its darkened half, and in the folds of the land beyond the fell lights glimmered here and there, but they were vague, unfixed things, questionable and unreliable, reminding her of that glimpse of a strange world through the portal under the stairs. *Porous* felt about right, the evidence of her eyes not to be trusted.

Millie gave a low yap, and Adams looked at her. She turned her snout toward the faery ring, then checked on Adams.

"Coming," she said.

Rory started forward, and Millie barked, sharp and flat.

"Interesting," Thompson said. "That for you or me?"

Rory tugged the cat off his shoulder and put him on the ground. "Find out, shall we?"

Thompson shook out his paws, and held one up to inspect it. "Ugh. I'm sure I'm getting fae gunk all over my paws."

"Fae *what?*"

Adams ignored both of them, following Millie as she led the way to the edge of the circle. The old dog stopped just short of the stones, nose twitching, and looking from Adams to the staff.

"What?" she asked.

Millie just stared at her, motionless and silent, the moon collecting in her eyes. A new wind picked up, curling across the fell top and diving into the circle, taking little swirls of dust with it.

Rory started forward again, and Millie's head swung immediately in his direction, her worn teeth showing in the beginning of a snarl. Midge and Pinto pressed in front of Rory, and he grabbed their collars.

"Someone's got her whiskers in a knot," Thompson

observed. He hadn't moved, one front paw still raised distastefully.

"Just me?" Adams asked Millie, and the old dog looked up at her, then into the circle, and back again.

"Don't," Rory said.

"Posh is right," Thompson said. "Bad idea."

"Do you know where my parents are?" Adams asked Millie.

The dog looked back with eyes like fallen stars, and Adams thought of the creepy fan-boy descriptions of the fae in the old books, and shivered.

"Thompson," she called. "Can dogs be fae?"

"Sure. Look at your mutt."

Adams frowned at him. "He's not fae. He's a dandy."

"What d'you think that is, then? Probably why he's not here, in fact. Off hanging with his mates in Faery."

Millie huffed in a manner that indicated she'd had enough of theorising, and took the end of the staff in her mouth, tugging on it.

"Stop that," Adams said, tightening her grip. Millie tugged harder, bracing her paws and pulling toward the circle. "Millie! Drop it!"

Millie did not drop it. Millie heaved on the end of the stick with a strength that should have belonged to a much bigger and much younger dog, and Adams, seized by a sudden certainty that she couldn't lose the staff, stumbled forward and into the stone circle.

The wind came up fast. Not just fast, it came in *strong*, sharp-edged and hungry, cutting to the bone and twisting into coils that lifted the thin grass, like miniature tornadoes waiting to be born. Adams shivered again, still trying to reclaim the stick, and behind her Rory shouted, but it was distant and distorted, as if he were shouting into a well.

Millie was still trying to pull her forward, making it hard

to concentrate on what was happening. "Millie, *stop*," Adams snapped, jerking the stick back toward her. Millie paid exactly as little attention as she had previously, tugging Adams further away from the edge of the circle. Adams braced herself, tightening her grip on the staff, not even sure why she was so determined to hold onto it. It had something to do with the feel of it, a strange heat that seemed to rise into her knuckles and curl around the joints of her hands, a sharp contrast to the chill breeze, yet feeling like an answer to its call.

She looked down at the staff, and she couldn't be sure – of course she couldn't, the cat was right, she was *terrible* at this sort of thing – but, just as the rocks glimmered a shade paler than the land around, clear-cut in the night, so too did the staff. There was nothing luminous about it, it hadn't suddenly become a glow stick, but it was more real, more in the world, particularly after the stumble into the circle. She looked up, searching for Rory, and somehow the ring of stones was much further away than it should be, and also *higher*, as if she were standing at the bottom of a full-length swimming pool, staring up through the water at the indistinct images of watchers on the edge.

"Rory?" she said uncertainly, and Millie stopped pulling, although she kept hold of the stick. A rush of warmer breeze washed around them, carrying the scents of honeysuckle and damp earth, and the whole hilltop shivered.

"Hello, Detective Inspector," a silken voice said behind her. "How nice of you to save me the trip."

Millie let the stick go with an air of satisfaction, and Adams turned to face the Gentry, thinking old dogs had plenty of tricks. Nasty ones, too.

IT WAS QUICKLY apparent Velmyr had positioned himself behind her so that when she turned his robes were billowing just so in the wind, and his silken hair rippled delicately back from his brow. His chin was lifted, and the moonlight turned his pale skin to porcelain and rendered his eyes alarmingly luminous, turning him into an uncanny statue and lending rather more credence to Rory's books, other than the thankful lack of sticky lips. The effect, however, was ruined somewhat by Millie wobbling around Adams and sitting down on the hem of the fae's deep red robes.

"*Ew.* Get off," he said, shaking the cloth irritably.

"Do you glow in the dark?" Adams asked, more to keep him distracted than because she really cared.

"What?" He looked up, still trying to dislodge the dog.

"You're all shiny."

"I am *Gentry.*"

"Of course." She planted the base of the staff firmly on the ground, feeling a tremor run up it and into her arm, then tucked her free hand into her pocket, closing it over the duck. "Where are my parents?"

"Your parents?" he said, with a rather poor effort at looking innocent.

"Yes, the ones you threatened on multiple occasions and who are now missing?"

Millie looked up at Velmyr and barked imperiously.

"Silence, mutt."

She barked again.

"Silence!"

"Is she yours, then?" Adams asked, and he made a face.

"We do not associate with animals from your base world."

Millie growled, and took a mouthful of his robes, tugging them.

"She seems to know you."

"Get *off!* Horrible creature!" He tried to swipe at her with a be-ringed hand, and she snapped back with surprising accuracy. He jerked away, clutching both hands to his chest, and tried to step away, but Millie was still on his robes, preventing him moving. She glared up at him with an old dog's single-minded determination, growling unevenly. Adams wondered if Thompson was right, and she was seeing rather a lot from behind those murky eyes, at least in the fae version of the world.

"Help me," Velmyr said, eyes wide as he stared at Millie, then looked frantically at Adams. "Help! The beast is attacking me!"

"She's not attacking you. She just wants something."

"*What?*"

"I don't know. What did you promise her for pulling me in here?"

He narrowed his eyes at Adams. "I don't know what you mean."

"You do." Adams nodded at Millie. "She led me up here and pulled me into the circle. Why?"

"Don't be ridiculous. If I wanted an animal to help me, I'd get a proper fae one, not *this*." He twiddled his fingers at Millie, then snatched them back as she bared her teeth. "*Ugh*. I'll have to burn these robes. Bad enough having human dirt on them, but *dog?* So disgusting."

Millie swung her head toward Adams, and they stared at each other. Adams had an idea she was meant to do something, but what? And if the dog hadn't brought her here under the Gentry's directions, then what were they doing here at all?

"What about Collins and Chloe?" she asked aloud. "What've you done with them?"

He gestured impatiently. "Honestly, I can't keep track of you people. Strange little names, and you all look the same."

Adams wondered if that was speciesism or racism, or

both. She didn't like it, either way. "Well, there's four of them missing, so are they all together? Are they safe?"

He held out a hand. "Book first."

She shook her head. "Proof they're safe first."

"I am Gentry. I—"

"I'm police. You think I'm just going to believe you? I need proof."

"Give me the book." He ripped his robes clear of Millie and stepped forward, suddenly towering over her, no longer softly luminous but alight with threat and fury, a raging beacon in the night. *"Give it to me now!"*

Adams raised the staff without thinking, grabbing it with both hands and holding it across her body, ready to fend him off. The duck dangled from her fingers, the keyring hooked over one. *"Show me my parents!"*

Velmyr laughed, a savage, sharp sound that felt like it tore the air. "You think you can fight me with your little stick? You're on the doorstep of Faery now, woman. By my grace only do you still breathe."

Adams took a deep breath just to prove she could, and said, "Velmyr Duskthorn, you're under arrest for—"

He laughed again, the noise thundering painfully in her ears, and shoved a hand toward her, as if to push her over. She swung the staff, hard and fast, and the duck exploded into light, blazing like a flare. Velmyr cried out, stumbling back, and Millie gave an affronted yelp as he tripped over her. The fae's cry turned into a shriek, indicating the old dog had done more than just yelp, and Adams took a step forward as the duck faded, leaving its afterimage burned in her eyes.

"Where are my parents?"

"This *mutt*—" He tried to make the same palm-out gesture at Millie, and Adams smacked him neatly on the forearm with the staff, setting the duck blazing again. "*Ow!* How *dare* you?"

"She's an old dog. Leave her alone. Now, my parents?"

He glared at her, clutching his injured arm. "How did you even do that? What do you have?"

"A burning desire to arrest you, but if I can't do that I'll settle for some grievous bodily harm. Where are they?"

He narrowed his eyes at the staff, stilling as he did so. "Is that …?"

Adams pointed the staff at him. "Last chance."

"It *is*."

"Is what?"

"*Thief*," he breathed, his eyes not moving from the staff. "How did you get that?"

"It wasn't thieved," she said, which wasn't entirely true. It had been borrowed without permission, but then gifted to her after the fact. Sort of.

Velmyr lunged forward, reaching for the staff, and she jumped backward, trainers slipping on loose stones. She stumbled on the edge of balance, then the Gentry was on her, bearing her to the ground. She hissed as she smacked painfully into the rocky hilltop, although her pack protected her somewhat. She didn't try to get up, just concentrated on keeping hold of the staff as Velmyr attempted to wrench it away. He was undeniably strong, hissing in fury, but there was no way she was letting go.

"Give it to me," he snarled. "*Give it!*"

"Sod *off*," she managed, and slammed the staff toward him without releasing it. He squawked, jerking back to avoid being hit in the face, and she tried to follow through and roll him off. He was more solid than he looked, though, and recovered fast, throwing all his weight behind the staff and forcing it toward her throat.

"Filthy little human," he hissed, sharp teeth flashing. "Putting your horrible paws all over our stuff."

"Your *stuff?* You've got my *parents!*" She tried to jam a knee somewhere delicate, but he had such a tangle of robes going on she couldn't get any force behind the blow. She wasn't even sure if the anatomy was right.

He reversed direction again, trying to wrench the staff away, and Adams almost lost her grip. But she clung on doggedly, letting his momentum pull her to sitting, then slammed the staff forward once more, twisting it sideways at the same time and catching him squarely on one pointy ear. He yowled, but didn't let go, and that was when Millie buried her teeth in his arm. His yowl turned into a full-throated shriek, and Adams shoved him to the side, tearing the staff out of his grip. The night vibrated with his scream, the faery circle trembling and shifting, offering glimpses of other realities and shattered dimensions, and she spotted Rory at the edge, waving frantically. Other shapes loomed beyond him, and she looked back at the fae in time to see him place his hands around Millie's throat, forcing her onto her side on the ground, paws working frantically as she tried to scrabble away.

"Hey!" Adams snapped, and he looked around at her, snarling, all that ethereal beauty fallen to shreds. She drove the base of the staff straight down on one of his fancy silken slippers, and he wailed, releasing Millie and clutching his foot instead.

"You—"

She didn't wait for her species or gender to be insulted again. She lifted the staff and yelled, *"Tell me where they are or I swear I'll ram this duck straight up your—"*

She never got to finish the sentence, because the fae threw both hands out, a fast movement filled with a rage and frustration so intense she could almost taste it. Millie flew up and backward with a howl, and Adams managed to hook the dog around the belly as she went past, the impact jerking Adams sideways and sending them slamming back to the ground together. They were still caught in the wave of power coming off the fae, and it tumbled them over like flotsam caught in surf, both yelping in fright as much as pain. Adams just had time to wonder if they'd roll straight off the edge of the fell, then she hit a larger rock with her shoulder, hard enough to make her cry out in a wordless gasp of pain, and someone grabbed her under the arms, dragging her backward.

The world shuddered, twisting in on itself, then righted, and when it stilled she was sitting on the ground outside the faery circle, still clutching both Millie and the staff.

The circle was empty.

The Gentry was gone.

She said something even worse than her intentions with the duck had been.

22

AN INVITATION TO DANCE

Adams looked up, still swearing, expecting to see Rory. Instead Eric looked down at her, his face drawn in anxious lines.

"You're not going to hit me with that stick, are you?" he asked, and she glanced at the staff, still clutched in her hands.

"No. Well, maybe, actually. What the hell did you just do?"

"Got you out before the circle closed and you were gone forever."

"I couldn't get in," Rory said, leaning over her. "I tried, and it was like getting stuck in jelly. I thought I was going to suffocate."

"But we got here in the nick of time," Eric said cheerfully. "Pulled him out, then you."

"We?"

"Hi," Stu said, joining them. "Oh, look. You've got Millie. Well done. She's such a nightmare for wandering off, trying to get into Faery."

"*What?*" Adams looked at the dog, who was panting heavily and still lying half on top of her. She pushed her gently off and sat up, waving the men away. She was starting to feel like a very displeased Snow White, with them leaning over her like that, despite the fact that the size discrepancies were backward. Millie rested her head on the ground, little shudders working through her, and Stu crouched down, putting a hand on her side and petting her soothingly.

"There you go, old girl. You have to stop. She's not coming back."

"Who?" Adams demanded, then pinched the bridge of her nose. "Hang on. Someone explain to me in very simple words what's going on, because the last I saw of you two, you were throwing us in a *sinkhole*, and now you're dragging me out of faery circles and getting in my damn way. What the hell's going on?"

"Yeah, sorry about all that. The sinkhole's Dad's thing," Eric said. "We keep trying to talk him out of using it, but old habits and all that."

Rory grabbed Adams' arm as she scrambled to her feet. "Possibly don't hit them just yet. They seem to be here to help."

"I'm a police officer. I'm going to bloody well arrest them, not hit them." Although hitting them sounded quite good too. "Are you trying to tell me throwing people in a damn sinkhole's some *family tradition?*"

The brothers looked at each other, then Eric nodded. "For generations. I mean, usually we just pop a sheep down that's dying anyway. It's enough to keep them happy, and that keeps the land happy."

"Them? The sheep? I doubt they're happy."

"Not the sheep. The beasties."

Adams looked from one brother to the other, thinking of the bones in the caves, then nodded. "Alright. I'm coming back to that later, because I have a lot of questions, some of them official. But first, where are my parents? Did you put *them* down the sinkhole?" Her stomach heaved as she said it, nausea climbing up her throat, but she kept her work face on, hard and ungiving.

"*No!*" Eric clutched his chest with one hand. "*Never.* We didn't even realise they'd been taken until you said."

Adams narrowed her eyes at him. "You didn't take them?"

"Cross our hearts," Stu said, doing exactly that in the vague area of his chest. "She's lovely, your mum. I'd fight the faeries for her myself, I would."

Adams gave him a dubious look. "What about the faery coins at the pub?"

"The what?" Eric asked, and Adams remembered the brothers scrabbling for the tokens just as much as everyone else, except her and Rory. They'd been under the same enchantment as her parents.

"It does seem more likely the Gentry took them," Rory said. "Or some fae working with him. Unless this lot have got some chemical agent that knocked me out for half an hour without me even seeing them sneaking up to the car to administer it."

"What about the sheep?"

The brothers looked at each other, and Eric shrugged. "Sheep are pretty easily influenced. Doesn't take much to set them off."

Adams grimaced, but he was right. "Collins and Chloe, then."

"Ah. Yeah." He tucked both hands in his pockets, looking at the faery circle. "We should go before that fae comes back, you know. He seemed right angry."

"We're not going anywhere. Where are they?"

"We lost them," Stu blurted, and Adams turned to look at him.

"You what?"

"We *had* them, but they got away on us somehow."

She considered hitting him with her staff, even though

she'd said she wouldn't. It felt like it might be quite satisfying. "Your dad said they'd been dealt with the old way."

Eric grimaced. "We haven't told him. He's going to be *steaming.*"

"*I'm* steaming," Adams said. "Very much so. *Explain.*"

"Well, me and Mike picked them up," Stu said.

"You *picked them up?* Specifics."

"We didn't hurt them or anything, just took them to the farm. And they were comfortable, like, they weren't tied up or anything, and they had furniture and stuff, and Mike made a cottage pie, he makes really good ones, with peas and gravy and—"

"*What happened?*"

"I … I dunno."

"Adams," Rory said, and she ignored him.

"You don't know? You kidnapped a police officer, lost them, and *you don't know what happened?*"

Stu's words seemed to have failed him, so Eric said, "It's true. I really didn't know before, but after you came to the farm, I went to see them so we could figure out what to do. They were gone."

"And me and Mike didn't do anything," Stu said quickly. "I mean, after catching them, like."

"Adams, I think we have a problem," Rory said.

"I know we do," she snapped. "These absolute … these …"

"Chocolate teapots?" Stu suggested. "Dad says I'm as useful as one of them sometimes."

"Can't imagine why," Rory said, and pointed over the top of the fell. "Lights."

"Aw, *bollocks,*" Eric said. "That'll be Dad and Mike. I hoped we could nip out without being noticed, see if you'd managed to make it out of the caves and give you a hand. Then we saw the circle kicking off." He gave Adams a hopeful look. "I did leave you all your kit, you know."

"Yes, great. Is this the same logic you use to decide that kidnapping people's fine as long as you give them *shepherd's pie?*"

He grimaced. "Sorry. But, um, any chance you could leg it now? Dad's just going to want to chuck you back in again, and probably us as well."

Adams looked at the bouncing headlights climbing toward them, and realised her hands were hot again. She looked down at the staff, and found the duck softly aglow with light. She wasn't even sure how she'd managed to keep hold of it the whole time, but somehow it was still there, in the same hand as the staff, as if the two had quietly bonded and formed some symbiotic relationship, steadily feeding off each other.

"I can't," she said. "I need to get my parents, and they've got to be in there." She pointed the staff at the faery ring, and the wind curled around them again, cold and hungry, stronger than before. Millie set up a wobbling howl of protest, her eyes on the circle. Midge and Pinto joined in, and the wind wailed back on the edge of hearing, setting the world shivering at the edges.

"What's *that?*" Eric asked, looking around with his heavy brows pulled down. "I don't like that."

"There's very little I like about any of this," Adams said. "But if you want to help get my parents back, you can start by getting that gun off your dad before he shoots his own foot off."

"We've got bigger problems," someone said, and they turned to look at Thompson, his paws set wide and his ears back as he stared into the stone circle.

"*Ooh,* a cat," Stu said. "You shouldn't be up here."

"You shouldn't be walking and talking at the same time, yet look at you go," Thompson said, not looking around.

"Eh?" Stu said, looking at Eric for clarification. His brother was watching the circle uneasily.

"Something's coming," Thompson said, looking at Adams. "Velmyr's coming back?"

"More than that. I think he's bringing reinforcements, but I'm not sure what." The wind snarled, as if to underline his point, strong enough to make Rory stagger, and something in the circle *pulsed*, a brightening or a darkening of the night, and Adams couldn't seem to tell which it was.

"We need to go," Eric said, his voice suddenly strained. "We need to get out of here."

"We need to get my parents back. I thought you were worried about Gloria."

"I am, but …" He gestured helplessly at the stones. "This is *bad*. I've never felt this before."

"What sort of beasties?" Rory asked suddenly. "In the caverns? What sort of beasties?"

"Hungry ones," Stu said. "Dad used to say he'd throw us to them when we misbehaved."

"*Super*," Thompson said, and looked at Adams. "Farmer John's right. Something big's coming. We need to go, and come back when things are a bit calmer."

"But …" Adams couldn't even say she didn't feel what he was talking about. There *was* something coming, riding in on a clawing, freezing flood of dread. And if she could feel it, it had to be more than big. It had to be *huge*.

"Whatever we're doing, let's do it fast," Rory said, glancing at the approaching headlights. "Those bikes are almost here."

"We're going to get thrown in," Stu said gloomily, scooping Millie into his arms and standing up. "Dad's going to throw us *all* in the hole. Or chuck us to the fae, more like."

"Come on," Eric said. "Come on, we have to go!"

He and Stu broke into clumsy jogs, running toward the

quad bike that was parked not far away, the trailer still attached to the back.

Rory looked at Adams. "What do you want to do?"

"We need to get out of here," the cat said. "We're going to be fae snacks." His tail had bushed out and his ragged ears were back, pupils huge in the moonlight.

The wind snarled at them again, and this time Adams didn't think it was just the wind. There was something else behind it, something living, grinding and harsh, a clamour of feet or fists or stone. She slammed her own fist into her thigh with a growl of frustration. She didn't know enough to fight this, and she couldn't drag Rory into something they might never get out of, or the two farmers for that matter, useless as they were. "Let's go," she said, and they ran for the quad bike. Stu was already sitting in the trailer, still clutching Millie as if she might protect him from the dark, and Eric waved them on frantically.

"*Come on!*" he shouted. "Hurry!"

The lights of the approaching bikes bore down on them, the beams bouncing violently. They were going too fast on the rough ground, risking overturning if they hit anything wrong, but they weren't slowing. Adams ran for Eric's bike, swinging onto the back as Rory and his dogs piled into the trailer. Thompson flung himself after Adams, diving into the gap between her and the farmer just as Eric jammed the bike into gear, revving the throttle wildly. They bounced in a tight circle, aiming to head back along the top of the fell. It looked to be the only way off for anyone not on foot, but it meant they were going to be running straight at the oncoming bikes.

And they'd been seen, even though Eric didn't have the lights on. The two bikes split apart slightly, as if to give them room to race down the middle, but even as Eric straightened up and aimed for the gap, the bikes turned toward each other again, converging rapidly.

"Keep going," Adams shouted at Eric, and he leaned forward, as if that might make them quicker or slimmer. He didn't ease back on the throttle, and the quad bike was picking up speed, bouncing violently, the engine screaming.

The three bikes were all heading for the same point, all going at the same speed. No one was slowing, no one pulling back, and the wind rose and rose, the shrill whistle of it in Adams' ears taking on a tone that was almost metallic, fevered and hectic.

Eric broke first. He jammed the brakes on, hard enough that Adams slipped and collided into his back, squashing Thompson between them as he gave an outraged squall. The trailer made a horrendous crashing sound, apparently trying to wrench itself free, and only the weight of the men and dogs in the back kept it in place, accompanied by a chorus of alarm from both species. The oncoming bikes stopped just short of them, almost touching their front wheels, fully blocking the way forward. Behind the lights Adams saw Jacob level the shotgun at them, leaning back in his seat.

"Eric," he called. "Get them off there."

"No, Dad. We need to help her. It's her *parents.*"

"It's too late." His voice was calm, holding none of the fury Adams had expected. "Come on, lads. Off the hill, and we'll leave them to it."

"Jacob," Adams started, and Jacob climbed off the bike, the gun worryingly steady and its aim not moving away from her as he walked forward into the spill of the headlights, his face cast in grim lines.

"You want to find your parents? Off you pop into the circle and you'll be right back with them."

"Dad, put it down," Eric said, not moving from the bike.

"I *told* you—"

"*No*," Eric repeated, and Adams slipped off the bike on the far side, keeping her gaze on Jacob.

"Eric, it's fine," she said. "Go with your dad."

"I won't. We need to help you."

"You need to listen to your father," Jacob said. "This isn't our business anymore." He shot an anxious look at the circle, and as if in answer the wind gave a deeper rumble, all metal and menace.

Rory and Stu had climbed out of the trailer, and Rory edged toward Jacob, who swung the gun on him.

"Rory, don't," Adams said sharply, and took a step back. "Give him space."

"But we need to help Gloria," Stu said. He was still holding Millie, the old dog peering over his shoulder in the direction of the circle. "She's nice, Dad. *Really* nice. We can't just let her go."

"It's too late. They're gone already. And if the fae want these ones too, we're going to let them have them."

"But—"

"*We're going to let them have them!*" Jacob bellowed, and turned the gun on Adams again. "In fact, we're going to walk you to the door. Move."

"Dad," Eric tried.

"*No!* You don't know what happens when they don't get what they want. You don't remember." The gun wavered, and Jacob hitched an uneven breath, looking as if he was about to say something more, then shook his head. "No, lads. This is how it has to be. Move it, copper. You too, toff."

"Alright," Adams said. She still had hold of the staff, and she moved toward the circle, taking her time.

Rory joined her and said quietly, "What do we do?"

"Probably whatever the man with the gun says, at least for now."

"Well, that's simple enough."

They walked ahead of Jacob all the way to the edge of the stone circle. Inside, swirling mist shot through with luminous, glittering shades filled the space, reaching to the edge like the liquid in a furiously shaken snow globe, refusing to reveal anything until it settled. Adams stopped at the border, feeling a feverish heat baking off it, and tightened her grip on the staff.

"Keep going," Jacob said. His voice shook, and Adams turned enough that she could see him. His eyes were on the mist rather than on her, the gun's aim drifting, but still keeping too close to her for comfort.

"Who did they take?" she asked. "Was it a child? Your wife?"

"Shut up."

"Why would you help them when they did that?"

He glared at her, his face drawn and tight. "I still have sons. And one day *they* might have sons, or daughters, if they can ever get their acts together."

"The fae are threatening you?"

He laughed, a soft, humourless sound. "The fae *are* threat. They always have been, always will be. Just as we feed the gap to keep the beasties happy, we serve the fae to keep *them* happy. You don't want them unhappy."

"You don't," the silken tones of Velmyr said, and Adams looked around to see him standing just inside the circle. The mist was thick behind him, revealing nothing, and he appeared to have changed his robes for something with an even higher collar, and no rips in the hem. "You do very well, though, Jacob. Good little human."

Jacob made a face, but said, "We brought them back."

Velmyr sniffed. "And the others?"

"In hand."

"Ha," Thompson said, startling them all. Adams looked around to find the cat standing next to her, ears back. Millie had joined him, panting over his ears, which he seemed to be ignoring for the moment. "They're not *in hand.* He's lost them."

"*Ugh,*" Velmyr said. "A *cat.* I knew one had been sniffing around. I could smell your stench."

"Offensive," Thompson said. "Besides, nothing stinks like a fae. All honeysuckle and grossness."

"At least I don't smell like a litter box," Velmyr said, and they bared their teeth at each other for a moment, then the Gentry looked at Jacob. "What does the thing mean, you lost them?"

"Thing yourself," Thompson said, tail twitching. "And he's *lost* them. You know, doesn't have them anymore? Like you lot lost the right to be in this world?"

"Silence, furball, or I'll throw you to the beasties."

"Cats can't enter Faery. Come out here if you want to fight me. Oh, no, *you can't,* because it breaks half a dozen treaties and the Watch'll chuck you back like a rotten herring."

"*The Watch* are worthless scraps of mangey fur with no lineage among them. Filthy *mongrels.* You don't even have a decent coat."

"Unlike the Gentry, who're more inbred than a pedigree poodle, you mean? How's that crumbling gene pool working out for you?"

"Steady on," Rory muttered, but Adams didn't say anything. The cat wasn't goading the fae for no reason, she was sure of it.

Velmyr bared his teeth at Thompson. "Silence! I could crush you like a … a cat."

Thompson looked at Adams. "Not known for their imagination, fae. That's why they're always nicking away with humans. Humans have *imagination.* They've got *ideas.* It's what makes them so bloody dangerous and so … *human.*"

"We have ideas," Velmyr said indignantly. "We're much better than humans. And cats."

"No one's better than cats, and you're doubly not."

"Come here and say that."

"Actually physically can't. You come here."

Velmyr took a step forward, then stopped, narrowing his eyes. "*Ugh. Cats.* You think you can fool me that easily?"

"I wasn't far wrong."

Velmyr looked at Jacob. "The others. The little witch, especially. I want her."

"They … ah …" Jacob looked around. His three sons were having a heated argument by the bikes, which was rapidly devolving into pushing and shoving, and Stu was apparently trying to get Mike in a headlock. "We'll find them."

"You *have* lost them?"

"Told you," Thompson said.

Velmyr hissed, and pointed one long finger at Adams. "Then give me the book. Quickly."

"Show me my parents first. How do I even know you have them?"

"Oh, I have them. And unless you give me the book, they're going to dance in Faery for a thousand, *thousand* years."

She tapped her fingers on the staff. "Hand them back, and I'll give you the book."

He narrowed his eyes at her, and she saw the realisation dawning. "You don't have it?" He sounded almost bewildered, as if he hadn't even imagined her not complying.

"Parents first."

"No. You get *nothing*, little human. But I'll take you instead." He beckoned to her, and she felt the pull of it somewhere in her belly, a hot, fierce desire that made her dig the heels of her sodden trainers harder into the old ground, and cling to the staff a little more tightly, an anchor to the world. "You and that staff, even with your filthy paws all over it."

"I'm not going anywhere," Adams said, hearing the breathlessness in her own voice.

"Oh, you are." Velmyr grinned, toothy and furious, and Adams almost gasped at the weight of *need*, the desperate want that flooded her, to take his hand and dance, dance until the world ended, wild and full of abandon. "You *are*."

He reached forward, his fingers impossibly long and elegant, and she found herself watching them helplessly, wondering how they'd feel on her skin, what honeysuckle would taste like, how easy it would be to just *dance*, and nothing else—

Thompson leaped at her, clawing his way up her back and onto her shoulder, making her cry out as much in shock at the broken connection as in pain. "*Retreat!*" he yowled.

Adams staggered back, just evading the fae's clutching fingers, but Jacob was right behind her, and he shoved her forward again. She swore, stumbling, and managed to get the staff up between her and Velmyr, bypassing his hands and slamming it into his chest while the cat fought for balance on her shoulder. Velmyr snarled, grabbing the front of her workout jacket, and they grappled frantically on the edge of the circle, Adams trying to pull him out and the fae trying to pull her in. Thompson tried to reach the fae, scrambling down her arm, but ran into a barrier where the circle started, hissing in fury as he was bounced back. He lost his grip and tumbled to the ground, leaving her alone with the furious Gentry.

At the edge of her vision, she saw Rory tackle Jacob, the farmer roaring protests and fighting to get his gun free while Rory clung to it grimly, and the sons' shouts rose dimly, as if heard from a vast distance, as they ran to help. She had no idea what side they were going to be on when they got there, and she heaved, trying to throw herself backward onto the ground outside the circle, but Velmyr was stronger than he'd seemed before, or she was more tired. She couldn't get enough purchase to pull him out of the ring, and she was fighting frantically to stop herself going in.

"Just come with me," Velmyr said, his pale gaze fixed on Adams and his voice all silk and promises. "There's no point in fighting this. Maybe you belong here anyway. Maybe this is what you've been looking for all along."

Whatever hold his words had had over her a moment before, it was gone now. She didn't bother answering, just threw herself backward once more, and for one moment she thought she had him, he was stumbling toward her – then something hit her in the lower back, hard and solid, shoving her violently. She cried out, lurching forward, and Velmyr gave a hiss of triumph, pulling her into a tight embrace with the staff crushed between them.

"*Adams!*" Rory shouted, but it was too late. She plunged through the ring and into the murk beyond, the fae clutching her still more tightly as she fought to push him away, and everything smelled of honeysuckle and sweet wine and cloying heat.

23

THE ARMY RISES

PANIC SURGED IN ADAMS' CHEST AND BELLY, VISCERAL AND animal-like, clawing at her reason, and she shoved it down. Sure, Velmyr was Gentry, some sort of terrifyingly powerful fae sorcerer, and sure, she was about to fall into Faery with nothing but a duck and a very big stick, but he was still just one person and she was a *police officer*, and she had had *enough*. Enough uncertainty, enough doubt, and enough magical bloody shenanigans. She'd been in here before, and she'd got out. This was going to be no different. She stopped resisting and drove herself forward instead, letting loose a bellow of rage, sending Velmyr stumbling back, and wrenched the staff away from him as he struggled to keep his balance.

"*Stop this!*" she shouted. "I am *done*."

"You're not," he said. "This is just the beginning." He inclined his head, sweeping an arm out, and the mist cleared around them, revealing row upon row of waiting soldiers. Soldiers with bare knees and helmets and what appeared to be socks and sandals, like old men off to the beach, if old men were armed with shields and studded leather armour and dented helmets. She blinked at them.

"What …"

"Seize her," Velmyr said, waving one hand elegantly. "She holds what you seek."

The soldiers surged forward, and Adams decided she was smart enough to know when running was the best option, because sometimes it really was. She fled for the edge of the ring.

She didn't think she was going to be able to get out. She fully expected to hit some sort of membrane, like Rory and the cat had when they tried to get in. But she raced straight across the divide between the worlds at a flat sprint, emerging into chaos. Rory and Jacob had been joined by the three giant sons, but rather than all of them trying to flatten Rory, Eric had his dad in a bearhug, trapping his arms to his sides and holding him off the ground while he kicked and bellowed in fury. Stu and Mike were still engaged in their wrestling match, just closer to the circle, and Rory was staggering at the edge of the ring with Thompson hanging from his neck and yowling abuse while Midge and Pinto tried to pull them both to the ground.

"Get *off*, you mad bloody feline!" Rory yelled.

"Brains of an *earthworm!*" Thompson snarled. "Don't *touch* it!"

"I have to—"

"Sodding *kittens* with more sense—"

"There's an army," Adams shouted at them, and Rory swung around to see her, abandoning his efforts to dislodge the cat.

"Adams! Are you okay? I was trying to follow, but—"

"Posh Spice is as inbred as the damn fae and wanted to take his amulet off," Thompson spat.

"Never mind that," Adams started, and was interrupted by Jacob.

"What are you *doing?*" the old farmer bellowed, trying to raise the shotgun even as Eric trapped his arms down even more tightly. "How are you out?"

"He's got an army," Adams repeated. "A sodding *Roman army,* by the look of things."

Jacob stopped struggling. "The ghost army? Oh, you utter numpties. You've done it now."

"They looked pretty solid for ghosts," Adams said dubiously.

"*Numpties,*" Jacob repeated.

"Let's move," Adams said, ignoring him as she backed away from the ring, still clutching her staff. From this side the mist remained thick and opaque, offering no clue as to how close the soldiers might be.

"Put her back in," Jacob said. "Put them *both* in. It's the only thing that might save us."

"Dad, we can't," Eric started.

"*Put them in.* You heard her – the ghost army's coming. We have to give them what they want."

Adams grabbed Rory's elbow, pushing him toward the bikes. "Go. Now."

He let himself be pushed, but Mike had extricated himself from Stu's grip and he grabbed Adams' arm. "Stop," he said, and she spun around and smacked him neatly on the ear with the staff. "*Ow!* That's *assault!*"

She pointed the staff from him to the others. "I will arrest every bloody one of you if you so much as breathe at me wrong. We're getting off this hill *now.*"

There was a pause, and into it rose the sound of clanking spears and marching feet, drifting out of the faery circle and filling the night with oncoming threat.

"Oh, dammit," Eric muttered, and put his dad down, giving Adams a regretful look. "You should've gone earlier."

"Run," Adams said to Rory, and they broke into a sprint as the farmer and his sons lunged after them.

The big men were surprisingly fast, Eric taking Rory down with a solid tackle that turned into a scuffle with Midge and Pinto barking hysterically and trying to find someone to bite. Adams turned back to help just in time to take an arm to the chest as Stu hit her so hard her feet went out from under her. She bounced to the ground, jarring her tailbone and biting down on a cry, and Thompson leaped over her and into the man's face, claws and teeth bared. Stu cried out and stumbled away, and somewhere a man shouted, "North Yorkshire Police! Back off *now*, all of you!"

Which would likely not have been enough but, before Adams had even properly registered who was shouting, Mike screamed, and she heard a rather indistinct "*Mmmip!*"

"Is that a *robot?*" Stu shouted. "Have you got police *robots?* Is that legal?"

"*Brrrip!*"

Adams rolled to her feet, her chest suddenly tight and full all at once as Collins and Chloe ran toward them across the top of the fell, Collins hefting a large wrench and Chloe swinging a hammer with far too much relish.

"Stop it!" Jacob shrieked, brandishing the gun. "*Stop!* You have to get in the circle! You *have* to!"

Chloe ducked as the gun swung in her direction, then came up having swapped her hammer for a stone. As Jacob turned to aim at Adams, the young woman hurled the rock, hard, and it smacked into the farmer's cheekbone with a painful-sounding *crack*, making him yelp and stagger. Collins was already halfway to him, and by the time Jacob had recovered from the missile Collins was already wrenching the gun off him.

"That's enough of that," he said, and pushed Jacob firmly back as he tried to reclaim the weapon with frantically scrabbling hands. "Stop that. Behave."

"You can't!" Jacob shrieked. "You'll get us all stolen away!"

"We need to go," Adams said, raising her voice over Jacob's shouts as she pulled Rory to his feet. Fergus was chasing Mike across the rocky ground, the metal cat's ears pricked in delight, while Midge and Pinto held Eric at bay. Not that he was doing much – both he and Stu seemed unsure which way to swing their loyalties now, especially as Thompson was promising some truly graphic punishment if they so much as moved.

"Yeah, it does feel weird up here," Chloe said. "What's happening?"

"We've got the bikes," Eric ventured, pointing at them. "We should all fit—"

"*No!*" Jacob yelled. "No, you don't understand, the fae—"

"Will be taking you *all* now," Velmyr said, and the group turned as one toward the circle. The mist had lifted like a curtain, collecting into a low cloud above the fell top, luminous with moonlight, and the Gentry stood at the edge of the ring, the wind lifting his hair from his cheeks and the mix of headlights from the bikes and the wash of the moon turning him into a gleaming vision. His robes looked as if they'd been arranged by a fashion photographer, and behind him stood the soldiers, row upon row of them, faces indistinct and shadowed. They still seemed substantial, but also not quite *there*. Their spears looked sharp enough, though.

Jacob dropped to his knees in a move Adams suspected was designed to appeal to the Gentry's sense of the dramatic. "No, please," he said. "*Please.* Not my sons."

"But then you'll all be together. You and your sons and your wife. You can dance forever in Faery. Don't you want that?"

"Please don't. We've done what you asked."

"Not very well." He flicked his fingers at Collins and Chloe. "You were meant to bring them to me."

"It was the robot," Stu said. "We didn't expect a robot."

"*Brrrip!*"

Velmyr made a disgusted little moue. "Soulless machines of metal. So *human.*"

"*Brrrip!*"

Velmyr ignored him, clicking his fingers imperiously. "Come on. Over here, all of you. Or do you want me to send my army after you?"

On cue, the soldiers levelled their spears in almost perfect formation, the moonlight glittering on the metal tips. Adams wondered why, given Velmyr's own predilection for shininess and drama, he hadn't found himself a prettier army. The Roman ghosts' aesthetic leaned toward some fairly mismatched gear that pushed the definition of *uniform* to its limits (and included grubby legs, battle-scarred helmets, and the whole socks and sandals thing). Maybe he thought it was more intimidating – or, given the *Kind regards*, maybe he wasn't as powerful as all that, and just had to work with what he could.

Jacob stumbled to his feet, backing up with his arms wide. "Stay back, lads," he said. "I'll not let them take you."

"You make it sound like you have a choice," the fae said, and raised one hand. The army started forward, the sound of their feet and dully thunking armour oddly muted.

"Stop," Adams said, stepping forward. "I'll go."

"What?" Rory demanded.

Velmyr gave her an amused look, but held up one hand, and the soldiers halted. "Why would you do that now?"

"If you let the rest of them go, and bring back my parents, I'll go with you."

"And? It's the book I want."

"I don't have it. But you can take me, and the staff." Because he'd been plenty interested in that just before. She thumped the base of it into the ground, setting up an echo somewhere on the edge of hearing. She frowned, and the soldiers shifted.

"That's hardly a deal when I'm going to take all of you, and the staff will be mine anyway."

Adams tipped her head slightly. "I think you would've already done that by now, if you could."

Velmyr tried for a fearsome scowl, but she'd seen the twist of his mouth, and Thompson hissed in sudden delight. "You're right! He *can't.* Filthy bloody trickster, messing with hexes and using humans and dogs and ghosts instead of just grabbing you. He's not meant to be doing any of this at all. That's why there's been no other fae involved. He's on his own."

"Shut up, furball. I'm a *lord.* I'm not *alone.* I command multitudes." He swept an arm out, indicating the army.

"Bite me, sparkle boy. They're *ghosts.* And every faery and his bloody aunt's a lord. It's what humans called you, is all. It's not *real.* You just can't let it go now you're entirely irrelevant."

"I will gut you like a … a …"

"Aardvark? Artichoke? Come on, you can do it!"

"You should take the deal before I change my mind," Adams said, raising her voice over the cat. "It's as good as you're going to get."

"*Shut up!* What is *wrong* with you all? I am *Gentry!* Who are you to not obey?"

"North Yorkshire Police," Adams and Collins said together.

"Cat," Thompson said.

"Witch," Chloe put in.

Rory sighed. "I need a title."

"*You will obey!*" Velmyr roared, and the air on the top of the fell reverberated with the sound, shaking the night air and setting the stars shivering, as if they'd plunge from the sky with the horror of it. Not even the dogs howled, frozen in place, and Adams wondered if she and Thompson had just misjudged the situation rather drastically. There was a moment of silence as the fae's bellow faded away, and in it Adams spotted a shadow blooming out of the circle. It resolved itself into something large and dreadlocked, and her heart kicked up a notch as Dandy loped easily out of the ring, red eyes gleaming, and stopped next to Adams. He looked up at her, then pawed the bottom of the staff.

"*No,*" Velmyr said, pointing at Dandy. "Traitorous hound."

Dandy pawed the wood again, not looking away from Adams. She took a breath, then raised the staff and slammed the base into the ground again, and that same, bone-deep shudder went through the land, fiercer now, as if feeling her intent. She looked at Velmyr. "Bring out my parents. *Now.*"

"You can't—" Velmyr started, then looked around as the ranks of soldiers shifted uneasily. "Stand still. What're you doing?"

The movement continued, a ripple originating from deeper in the circle and swelling steadily toward them.

"This is *unacceptable!*" the fae bellowed. "*You will obey!*"

"Yeah, you might need a different approach, Tinkerbell," Thompson said, and Velmyr snarled at him, stepping forward with his robes rippling elegantly and his face cast in the sort of angles Adams had only ever seen in magazines, usually accompanied by pore-less skin and worryingly skinny legs.

"I will *crush* you insolent little meat-bags," the fae declared, striding out of the circle with his chin high and both hands out to his sides, his fingertips crackling with static electricity that made Pinto yip when a spark bounced on her nose. "I've had enough of this disrespect. You will bow! You will submit! You will *bring me what I want!*"

"*Disgraceful,*" a new voice said, and Adams spun back to the circle, clutching the staff so tightly she was vaguely startled it didn't crack under her fingers. Gloria walked down an aisle of very upright soldiers in her floral sundress and favourite sandals, frowning at Velmyr. "What a *horrible* little person you are."

Velmyr blinked at her. "I am fae."

"I don't care what you call yourself," Gloria said. "Going around threatening people. I've a good mind to have a word with your mum."

"I don't … I am fae. I am *Gentry.*"

"I'm still going to talk to your mum. Being posh is no excuse for poor behaviour."

"Mum?" Adams said, and Gloria looked at her.

"Jeanette. There you are. I was wondering when you'd get here."

"We ran into a few problems. Got dropped in an underground river."

"Again?"

"The Thames wasn't underground," Adams protested.

"Hello love," Hugh called, following Gloria with his glasses pushed up on his forehead. "Everything alright?"

"Not really, Dad. Can you both get over here? Quickly?"

"They cannot," Velmyr said. "They're my captives."

"We absolutely are not," Gloria snapped, and took Hugh's hand. "Come on, love. We're leaving."

"You cannot cross the circle," Velmyr said, somewhat smugly, and Adams watched as Dandy slipped past him, taking Gloria's free hand delicately in his mouth. She didn't seem to notice, and he walked her toward the border, still hand in hand with Hugh.

"*Stop that!*" Velmyr said, starting toward them. "Release them, you mutt!"

Gloria stopped, one finger already raised to shake in the fae's face, and Adams sprinted forward. But Dandy was faster, taking two lunging leaps to cross the edge of the ring and dragging Gloria with him, Hugh stumbling forward with a startled cry as she towed him along.

"*Hugh!*" Gloria exclaimed. "Why did you push me?"

"I didn't, love—"

"*Get back in the circle!*" Velmyr roared, reaching for Gloria, and Eric lunged past him, making both the fae and Adams' mum cry out in surprise. He grabbed Gloria, hefting her off her feet with some difficulty.

"I've got her!" he shouted, staggering away. "Don't worry Gloria, I've got you!"

"Put me *down*, you silly boy! You'll do yourself a mischief!"

Adams stepped between Eric and Velmyr, the staff raised, intercepting the Gentry as he reached for Hugh, who was trying to get Eric to put his wife down. "Back off," she snapped at the fae, and he flicked his hands at her, setting off a searing whiff of ozone. She ducked, raising the staff instinctively, and the duck, still dangling from the keyring looped over her fingers, flared into wild life. She hadn't touched it, but the worn brass flashed like a lightning strike, the heat searing her hands. She didn't drop it, though, just swung the staff at Velmyr as he stumbled back, eyes wide in astonishment, and Dandy surged in front of her, teeth bared. Velmyr took another step back, eyeing the dandy warily.

"Get them out of here," Adams shouted, not sure who she was directing the order at, just keeping her eyes on the fae as she backed away from him and the circle, her parents behind her.

"You can't get away," Velmyr hissed. "I'll find you again.

I'll find *all* of you, unless you stay. You and the staff and that thing." He nodded at the duck, eyes luminous and greedy.

"Deal's off. You should've agreed earlier."

"You think you can dictate to *me?*" He raised one hand and shouted something, words in a language Adams didn't entirely recognise, and the soldiers surged into motion.

"Oh, bollocks," she hissed, trying to back up faster without falling over anything or anyone, since there seemed to be a lot of squabbling going on among the others. Velmyr didn't move to stop her, simply strode forward with an easy, fluid grace, the press of soldiers following him. The mist still swirled on the fell top, but it had drawn higher, dancing like a misplaced aurora, collecting the moonlight and fracturing it in strange colours to spill over the marching legion below.

"Do it," Thompson said, and she looked down at him, staring up at her with wide green eyes.

"Do what?"

"The staff. Do it again."

"I don't know what it does."

"Neither do I. But otherwise we're getting overrun by a ghost army. *Do it.*"

She hesitated, but she didn't have any better ideas right now, and the army was bearing down on them. They weren't going to be able to outrun ghosts. So she did it, slamming the base of the staff into the ground, bracing herself against whatever was going to come next.

Once, and the duck lit with a warm glimmer. The army paused, a ripple of uncertainty passing through them.

Velmyr glared at her. "Stop that."

Instead, she did it again, the reverberations deeper and wilder, the duck brightening, and the soldiers turned to look at her.

"*Stop.*"

A third time, before the vibrations of the first had even

fully passed away, and the duck blazed with light. One of the soldiers at the head of the troop stepped forward and said something to her in the same unfamiliar language as the fae had used.

"Um, sorry?" Adams said.

He pointed at the staff and said something else, his eyes shadowed below his helmet, the cheeks of it rendering his face difficult to read. He wasn't dressed much differently to the others, but he had some ornate designs worked into the chest plate of his armour, and he carried himself with a hard-worn authority. Adams supposed he was their captain, or commander, something like that. Definitely Romans. That meant …

"Is that Latin?" she asked him.

Velmyr snapped something, and the commander looked at him, then replied in the same language, still pointing at the staff, or the duck. It was hard to say which. Velmyr snarled, stomping one slippered foot on the ground. Instinctively, Adams stomped the staff. Velmyr pointed at her, shouting at the commander, who looked from one of them to the other with his face set in stern lines, his eyes quick and dark.

"*Parlez-vous français?*" Collins called.

"They're *Romans,*" Chloe said.

"It was worth a try."

The commander didn't even look at them. Velmyr was still shouting, his voice rich and commanding, pointing from Adams to her parents, then at himself, his head high and regal. The commander looked at her, then at the staff. She thumped it again, but whatever power had been there had waned, the duck fading. The commander looked back at Velmyr, gave a brisk nod, then raised a hand. The soldiers swept around him, still not quite substantial, and surrounded the little group on the hilltop.

Adams ran to her parents, trying to fend off their attackers, but the army somehow slid around her, keeping clear of the staff, and took hold of everyone. The group fought furiously, shouting and cursing, but their fists and kicks didn't seem to connect, passing though bellies and jaws with barely a hint of resistance. Despite that, the soldiers didn't seem to have any trouble restraining Gloria and Hugh, Collins and Chloe, Rory, and the farmer and his sons, burying them in a suffocating blanket of tunics and shuffling, insubstantial bodies, muffling their shouts. Not even the animals escaped, Thompson swearing and spitting in incandescent fury as he was bundled up in wisps of mist and ghostly hands. Dandy hurled himself into the fray, trying to force the soldiers away from Gloria and Hugh, but there were too many of them, and a shout from Velmyr meant they didn't even try to catch Dandy. They lashed out at him with spears and short swords instead, eyes hidden behind their helmets, and he skittered back, attacking again, then giving a little yelp as a weapon found its mark.

"Dandy!" Adams shouted. "Get out of it! *Get out!*"

He paid her as much attention as he ever did, and she plunged after him, wielding the staff furiously. The soldiers parted around her, avoiding contact with the wood, but reformed again immediately, plucking at her arms and legs, trying to hold her in place as she struggled toward Dandy. She could barely breathe for the ghosts, choking on the stench of old smoke and stale mud, spilled blood and fear and tedium.

"Seize her!" Velmyr shouted, and the soldiers redoubled their efforts. She kept the staff moving, panting, and Dandy yelped again as something hit home.

"*No!*" She fought harder, and then Fergus was there, plunging through the mess to join her with his metal claws flashing and his black eyes wide. A mutter of unease passed through the soldiers, and they pulled back from the guardian, leaving Adams free.

"What's happening?" Velmyr demanded, craning to see into the mass of soldiers and captives. "What are you doing? Get them into the gate, you useless wraiths. Hurry!"

He raised his hand and the army surged back toward the ring, sweeping their captives along with them and washing around Adams and Fergus like an outgoing tide, leaving nothing behind but the barren fell top.

"*Stop!*" Adams shouted, not even sure who she was addressing. "Stop, you *can't!*"

The army didn't stop, and she couldn't see any way to make them, not even with Fergus' help. The soldiers might not want to touch the metal cat, but they simply went around him, fracturing and reforming again, leaving nothing to fight.

"Stop!" she yelled again. "Mum! *Dad!*"

But they were swept toward the portal and there was nothing she could do about it, except follow.

Which she did.

2 4

"QUACK."

Adams sprinted after the army and their captives, and as she did so Hugh abruptly shouted something in Latin. It might not have been exactly the same dialect as the commander and the fae had been using, but it was close enough to Adams' ears. They were almost at the edge of the ring, but his voice was imperious, and the commander held up one arm, his hand in a fist. The troop stopped, and the commander asked Hugh a question, frowning, as Adams hurried toward them, the ghost soldiers parting around her and Fergus like the sea. Dandy was standing in front of Gloria, his teeth bared and his dreadlocks matted darkly on one shoulder, making Adams' heart squeeze painfully.

"What're you doing?" Velmyr demanded, striding to intercept her. "Can't you just *behave?* Accept you're beaten, for fae's sake!"

Fergus stepped in front of him, baring his teeth and letting out a steam kettle whistle, and the fae froze, lifting his hands to his chest. "*Ew.* What is this metal monstrosity?"

Hugh ignored him, talking to the ghost commander haltingly and pointing at Adams.

The commander examined her, then asked Hugh something else.

Hugh replied, hesitated, then shrugged and added, "*Quack.*"

"*Quack?*" the commander said, looking at Adams again.

She looked from him to her dad, who nodded, then she held the duck up, still clasped to the staff, and said, "*Quack.*"

"*Quack,*" the commander agreed, then looked back at Hugh, who started talking again.

"Shut *up,*" Velmyr said in English, trying to get past Fergus, who snapped at him with literal needle teeth. The fae jumped back, then stayed where he was and started talking rapidly in Latin, rather more fluently than Hugh, gesturing at the commander impatiently as he spoke.

Hugh interrupted, talking just as urgently, but stumbling over the words, and Velmyr tried to kick Fergus, who lashed out, tearing the fae's robes. Velmyr shrieked, then rounded on the commander again.

"*Get them!*" he shouted in English, waving furiously. "Useless damn ghosts! Should've left you in your scummy barrow!"

The commander scowled, suggesting he understood the gist if not the words, and looked at Adams as if waiting for something.

Adams hesitated, then banged the end of the staff on the ground again. The duck instantly bloomed with light, and the troop came to attention.

"Dad, what's going on?" Adams asked.

"It's the Roman ghost army," he said. "I told you about them just the other day, remember? Local legend. It's fascinating, actually—"

"*Dad.* History lesson later."

Velmyr tried to sidle sideways into the circle, and Fergus hissed again, the sound shrill and threatening as he slipped between the fae and the border with his teeth flashing. Velmyr staggered backward, snapping his fingers as if trying to raise that trapped lightning again, but he couldn't seem to manage it. Fergus snarled, matching the fae with surprising grace as they darted from one side to the other, Velmyr trying desperately to get past the metal cat and into the safety of the ring.

Hugh glanced at him, then said to Adams, "This gentleman here says they've been guarding the portal since they first discovered it, but it's a sleeping guard. The gateway's not meant to be used, and the troop should never wake other than for their yearly ride out. They can be awoken in an emergency, though, and they answer to the highest ranking fae—" He broke off as the commander turned toward him and said something. Hugh straightened himself up as well as he could, given he was still being held firmly in place by ghostly hands, and said something in a sharp tone. The commander looked at Adams, and she nodded firmly, hoping that was the right answer.

He kept looking at her, so apparently not.

"*Quack*," she offered, raising the staff slightly, and Dandy slipped out of the mess of ghosts to stand next to her with his head down and his teeth showing, eyes on the fae.

"*Quack*." The commander turned away, said something, and the soldiers released Hugh.

"Ah, that's better," he said, rubbing his hands. "I've told him I'm your advisor, because you're a queen. A warrior queen, who doesn't speak the language, because ..." He hesitated. "That doesn't matter. But he wanted to know why you didn't have a wolf on your staff, so I told him the duck was more powerful these days. Only I can't remember the word for it, so ... *quack*. And now he seems to think that means a specific *kind* of very powerful duck, and, well, I think we should just go with it, really."

"*Quack*," the commander said, looking at Adams with his eyebrows raised.

"Ah … *quack?*"

"*Quack* yourself!" Velmyr bellowed. "Stop listening to them! Listen to *me!*" He switched language, his fine hair dishevelled and his crown drooping over one ear, waving furiously, and the commander gave him an unimpressed look, then turned back to Hugh with impatience written in every line of his stance, and rattled something off.

Hugh answered, then looked at Adams. "Right, I've told him you outrank muggins there, which he seems quite willing to believe – I don't think they much like him. There's also something about a dog, but I can't quite get that bit. He wants to know what now?"

"Tell them to let everyone go," Adams said.

Hugh said something to the commander, who frowned and spoke sharply, waving around.

"He said that someone has to answer for waking them."

Adams looked at the staff in her hand, and then at the commander, who lifted his chin, waiting.

"*Them!*" Velmyr yelled. "*They* have to pay— *Ow!*" The *ow* was because Fergus had just nipped his foot, stolen the slipper, and scampered away with it, looking as satisfied as a metal cat could.

Adams lifted her chin back at the commander and pointed the staff at Velmyr. "He was the reason for this," she intoned, trying for warrior queen attitude, and the duck's light flared into something almost blinding.

The commander turned toward Velmyr, who froze, a stone in one hand as he prepared to hurl it at Fergus. "What?" he asked, and the commander said something. "No! She's not a queen! She's just some dirty little human! You can't—"

The commander said something else, his voice flat and hard, and Velmyr straightened up, smoothing his robes as if he was about to come quietly, then abruptly spun and bolted into the dark, away from the circle, head down and pale hair flowing, his robes hiked up in his hands and his skinny legs flashing pale in the night. He threw himself onto one of the quad bikes and kicked it into life.

"Hey!" Eric shouted. "That's ours!" He bolted after the fae with his brothers barely a pace behind him, all of them yelling furiously, and the commander looked at Adams, shaking his head with a certain disapproval.

"I know," she said. "Bloody civilians." Her tone must've mirrored his thoughts, because he gave her a surprisingly warm grin, looking suddenly solid and very human. She lifted the staff and pointed as dramatically as she could. "After the fae!"

The commander nodded, turned around, and roared something to the troops, ending his declaration with a "*Quack!*"

"*Quack!*" the troops roared back, and they sprinted after the fae and the brothers, setting the ground shaking with the thunder of ghostly feet.

They washed past the animals and the humans, pouring down the slope and leaving the fell top suddenly bereft and silent. No one spoke until Jacob said, "Now you've gone and done it. My poor sheep. Bloody ghost Romans running across my land! *Again!*"

"I don't actually care," Adams said, and he gave her a startled look. She ignored it, crouching to hug Dandy, who leaned against her with a heavy sigh and licked her ear.

"I always knew my Latin would come in handy," Hugh said. "*Dead language,* my foot."

Gloria patted his arm. "Well done, dear."

IT TURNED out that Gentry were not expert quad bike riders, and once the brothers had righted the stolen bike from where they found it at the bottom of the fell, it was still running well enough to return to the top.

"Did you see him?" Adams asked Eric. "Velmyr?"

He shook his head. "The army was gone, too."

She sighed. "Dammit. I would've liked to talk to him."

"Well, I'm sure you will at some point," Jacob said. "He was right miffed at you. The fae don't forget, you know."

Adams gave him an uneasy look, and Hugh said, "Well, never mind. All's well that ends well, right?"

Everyone looked at him.

"What? No one's hurt. We're all here. Bit of excitement, is all."

"Dad, have you been drinking?"

He gave her an affronted look. "*No.*"

"He did keep trying," Gloria said. "All those pretty people coming around with wine and cakes and things, and I kept saying we shouldn't, because it had to be enchanted, but *no, it'd be rude not to*. That's what your father kept saying."

"Well, it *was* rude!"

Rory snorted, and Adams said, "You didn't have anything, though, did you?"

"No, every time I tried I kept dropping it, or it kept vanishing," Hugh said. "Made me wonder if it was a dream. It had that quality to it."

"Other than the cat sliding down the table," Gloria said. "That seemed very real."

They all looked at Thompson, who huffed. "Not my choice. I shouldn't even be able to get into Faery, so that was a hell of a portal under the stairs."

Gloria looked at him for a long time, then at Adams, and said, "We're not actually dreaming, are we? The cat talked?"

"You just met a ghost army."

"Yes, but somehow the cat's weirder."

"He is," she agreed, ignoring Thompson's insulted huff, and pointed at the bikes. "Let's get out of the cold."

The trip down to the farm was bouncy and uncomfortable, ten humans, the three old dogs, and one cat crammed onto the three bikes and into the sheep trailer, while Midge, Pinto, and Dandy ran easily along the track ahead of them. Adams didn't glimpse Fergus, but he arrived into the farmyard at the same time as the bikes, so clearly his wings were more than decorative. Jacob grumbled all the way that bringing coppers on a family outing to the farm was just the sort of foolish notion he expected from his gormless sons, but when they arrived he climbed off the bike and stalked toward the house on skinny legs, shouting, "There's no good china, and if anyone starts telling me they want oat milk or some such muck, they can get right off now."

Collins looked at Adams. "Does that mean we're invited in?"

"I suppose so."

"Is that safe?"

She shrugged, and pointed to a large lump on the side of his head. "Is that how they got you?"

"Yeah, sheep all over the road blocking it, and when we stopped they got the jump on us."

"And here I thought you were police," she said, grinning slightly, then nodded at Fergus, who was watching curiously. "He didn't earn his keep, then."

"*Brrrip!*"

"I covered him up," Chloe said. "Threw a blanket over him and told him to stay, in case anyone got sticky fingers, or … well, I figured a sentient metal cat might raise some questions. Which worked out well, because then he broke us out, so it was all good, really."

"Other than my concussion," Collins pointed out.

"Are you coming?" Eric asked. He already had Gloria's arm, guiding her toward the kitchen with Hugh ambling next to them, while Stu hurried ahead, pointing out the potholes.

"Watch out for that one! It's a bit deep. And mind the … the … *mess.*"

"We're coming," Adams said, looking for Rory. He was crouched with Midge and Pinto, fussing over them gently, and looked up at her as she let the others walk ahead. "Alright?" she asked.

"In one piece. You?"

"Mostly."

"Would coffee help?"

"Almost definitely."

They followed their would-be captors into the warm light of the low-ceilinged kitchen, where Jacob and Thompson were already shouting at each other, apparently about the cat trying to stick his nose in the milk.

The china definitely wasn't fancy, but there were plenty of mismatched mugs, most of them not chipped, plus lots of tea, strong coffee, and some own-brand supermarket malt loaf, as well as a box of assorted biscuits, which, Stu confided to Adams, only came out for company. Judging by how stale they were, they didn't get much company up here, and she gave hers to Dandy, letting her hand rest on his head for a moment. She still didn't quite understand his vanishing acts, but he'd been there when it mattered – including stopping her dad falling prey to fae hospitality. He'd evidently taken himself off to find them, and that was the important bit. It wasn't like she could ask him where he'd been before that, anyway.

"Right," she said, once they were settled. "Jacob. You and the fae. Explain."

Everyone looked at the old farmer, who grumbled into his tea. "It's tradition," he said finally, and when Adams just raised her eyebrows, he sighed. "We used to have a right big lot of land, you know? And how it started was, you looked after the land, and it looked after you. So some people went to the stones, to keep the Good Folk happy, and the odd one went into the hole, to keep the beasties happy, and between them they blessed the land, and we had the best sheep in the county, plus no flooding, no landslides, not so much as a sniffle, to be honest. But it got trickier, you know? People started to notice that not everyone who worked on the farm came back, and word spread. The beasties started taking livestock uninvited. The fae took my sister off for a couple of years when I were just a lad, and she went off and became an *accountant* after that." He stared at them. "An accountant!"

"Horrifying," Chloe said.

"It were. She still calls up now and then wanting to see my books, and she's been retired ten years. But anyhow – the wool prices went down, and then the meat, and every bloody solstice the fae would be banging on the doors wanting someone to dance. But me and Dad figured out how to manage it, and I thought I could handle it even after he went. I gave the beasties any sick animals, and took all the footpath signs down, kept everyone away from the hill, other than the odd mad lot who come up to dance around the stones, and honestly, that's on them." He shot Adams a pointed look, and she took a sip of her coffee. It wasn't bad.

"Then one night the fae came, and they said they wanted our Eric," he said, nodding at the big man hunched over his biscuit. He looked faintly startled. "Firstborn and all that nonsense, you know. We had charms all over so they couldn't just walk in, but they said they'd get him one way or another. My wife wanted to move away, but I said no, I could handle it." He scratched his thin hair, and sighed. "Well, one night they took Stu instead. My wife went up the hill with only

Millie for company, and walked into the circle. She sent Millie back with the lad, and that was the last we saw of her."

There was silence around the table, other than Stu sniffling, and Mike patting him absently on the back, then Gloria said, "I'm very sorry, Jacob. That must've been terrible for all of you."

Adams stared at her, "Mum, that doesn't excuse—"

"I didn't say it did. But it's still dreadful."

Adams rocked back in her chair and looked at Millie, then frowned. "How long ago was that?"

"Thirty years, near enough."

"But Millie …"

"Oh, aye." Jacob looked at the old dog, and offered her a biscuit. She took it gently. "She's as much fae as she is dog now. No idea how long she'll live. Maybe forever. Her eyes were like that when she came back, and every now and then she takes off, usually at the solstice, and next thing someone's missing, a rambler or some witchy sort planning on dancing round the circle at the full moon. She was always a right good working dog, so she never seems to have any trouble getting people to go where she wants. I think she still hopes she can trade one of them for our Mae, but no luck. Does cheer the farm up every time, though."

Adams looked at her, thinking of the solid push in her back sending her into the stone circle, and of Dandy holding Millie back from the faery ring in the field. Had he realised she was the one laying traps? Or had he thought he was protecting her? She frowned. "Mum, Dad, what happened in the car, do you know? Rory doesn't remember."

"I'm not quite sure," Hugh said, looking at Gloria, who made a doubtful face and waved away the biscuit tin Eric was offering her. "We got through town just fine, then a whole lot more sheep appeared, so Rory had to stop. There was this *push*—"

"More a pull," Gloria said.

"As you say. Whatever it was, everything *blinked*, like going from underwater to below, then we were in this … I suppose it'd be a glade, wouldn't you say, love?"

"It certainly had glade-like qualities," she agreed. "Pretty lanterns, lovely scents, lots of pretty people, some very odd music—"

"*Ugh*," Thompson said. "*Fae*. Pretty this and pretty that. It's gross."

"It was rather unsettling," Gloria agreed. "But I don't remember how we got there at all."

"Cake," Adams said, and Chloe pushed the malt loaf toward her. "No, the faery cake at the farm shop."

"You ate *faery cake?*" Thompson demanded. "Honestly, did you *want* to be stolen away?"

"The cupcakes?" Hugh asked. "Really?"

"But it was terrible," Gloria said. "Very dry. Over-mixed *and* over-baked, most likely."

"One expects better from faery cake," Hugh agreed.

"I'm seeing the family resemblance now," Thompson said. "You're all very odd."

"Says the talking cat," Gloria said.

"That's not *odd*. It's very normal, you're just too human to realise it. Anyway, your terrible cake gave Verity Dibbleduck a little hook to pull you in on."

"Can he still do it?" Adams asked, frowning.

The cat huffed. "No idea. Better get those amulets, hadn't you?"

Adams sighed, and took another stale biscuit. She supposed she had.

Collins leaned his heavy forearms on the table and scowled at Jacob. "And us? What were you playing at?"

Jacob folded his own arms over his skinny chest.

"Crossed wires, was all. Thought you were stealing an associate's car."

"But why did the fae want them?" Rory asked. "He said you were meant to bring them to him."

"Usually they'd go in the hole," Stu said helpfully. "But I guess he liked the idea of having a police officer and a witch." He gave Chloe a doubtful look. "Are you a witch?"

"Yes."

"You're not very witchy."

"*I am.*" She pointed at her hair. "I even have a snake."

Stu pulled back in his chair as Mabel peered out at them and flicked her tongue irritably.

Adams looked at Jacob. "Did Velmyr tell you why he wanted them?"

"I don't ask questions. Every now and then the fae leave me a note, and I do what they ask. But if they don't want them to dance, they send them back with little hooks in them, like the cat said. That'd be my guess. Only more like Millie, herding up strays."

Adams and Collins looked at each other. That was an unpleasant thought, that people might be out here with *hooks* in them, fae sleeper agents, ready to drag people off into portals. Or push them in, as had happened at the house, and she wondered if that had been a neighbour or a passerby, or someone else entirely.

"More tea?" Eric asked.

Gloria nodded thoughtfully, then said, "I have quite a lot of questions, but first: Can someone explain the talking cat to me?"

"Cats are inexplicable," Chloe said, around a mouthful of malt cake.

Thompson purred. "It's one of our best qualities."

2 5

SEIZING THE CROWN

It was two days later, and Adams was sitting in Maud's office, trying for a position that struck the right balance between relaxed and attentive. She wasn't sure she was managing it, and her stomach was far too heavy with the poached eggs her dad had insisted on making for her. He and her mum were at Rory's house, equipped with amber amulets from Ash & Yew, watched over by Thompson and guarded by Dandy, all while telling her she was making a fuss over nothing. Adams did not consider them being tugged into Faery *nothing*, and she was still uneasy about the lingering threat of the Gentry, even though Eric had called to tell her they'd found one of his slippers where the underground river bubbled up out of the sinkhole. It didn't make her feel any better. She wasn't sure if fae could even die, and she'd have rather seen a death certificate to prove it.

But that wasn't her concern right now. Her concern was Maud, who was leaning back in her own chair, watching Adams with a level gaze. Adams waited, letting the moment spin further into discomfort.

"Collins claims he dropped his phone in a stream and just never thought to check in," Maud said finally.

"Oh?"

"Yes." They were silent again, then Maud said, "More Toot Hansell stuff, then?"

"I told you that at the time." Adams couldn't quite keep the edge out of her voice.

"And I told *you* that it's getting excessive."

"That's not something I can control."

"You can control your response to it."

Adams looked at her levelly. "How? Ignore it? Pretend it's not happening? Let people get away with it?"

Maud grimaced. "Sometimes certain things have to be allowed to slide to keep the overall peace."

Adams looked at the window rather than at her DCI. She knew that. She knew it and hated it. She'd just done it herself on the farm. She'd agreed that, if the brothers shut down their chop shop and guaranteed to keep her appraised of anything fae-related that happened in the area, she wouldn't take it any further. None of them had been responsible for anything but kidnapping Collins and Chloe, and while *that* had been a hard one to let slide, it was pretty clear Velmyr had been the one behind the call pretending to be their contact. Collins was complicit in the decision to make the deal, of course – in fact, it had been his idea – and still she hated it. It made her feel she wasn't just on a slippery slope, but accelerating down it on a well-waxed sled.

Aloud, she said, "I know. But these haven't been little things. They've been *dangerous*."

Maud folded her hands on the desk, regarding Adams with level blue eyes. "Colin vouched for you. Said you were the best DI he's worked with, and anyone questioning your judgement should get *themselves* examined. Lucas backed him up, and even Jules."

"Jules? Really?" Adams had yet to exchange more than a few words with the computer tech, and those were spread over the entire time she'd been here.

"She seems to like the fact you don't waste time talking at her. Anyhow, that was enough to get the IOPC to ease off, at least for now. But this isn't going to go away."

"Why?" Adams asked. "Where's it all coming from?"

"You know I can't tell you that. Any complaints are confidential."

Adams nodded. True, but also convenient. "So what now?"

Maud shrugged. "You go back to work. Keep out of Toot Hansell business. And keep all this bloody nonsense out of my station, can't you?"

Adams nodded. "I can try."

"Good." Maud got up. "Was the cottage comfortable?"

"Yes, great."

"Any problems?"

Adams grimaced.

"Oh, no. What did you do?"

"I'm going to fix it. Just don't go under the stairs for a bit, alright?"

ADAMS TOOK the potholed gravel drive up to Rory's dilapidated country house, the roof on the righthand side looking increasingly threadbare every time she came up here. The weather had reverted back to more typical Yorkshire summer, grey and overcast, and the fields looked rich and luminous, the walls painted a darker shade in the damp air. Everything smelled fresh and vital, engaged in furious growth, deeply real and with no whiff of honeysuckle anywhere, for which she was thankful. She found herself checking for it constantly. That, and mushrooms.

She parked in front of one of the low-slung stone outbuildings and walked around to the back patio, hearing her mum laughing before she reached it.

"And then she tried to turn her brother in to the police for stealing her ice cream," Gloria was saying. "Of course, he deserved it, but I'm not sure he saw it that way."

"Has she arrested him since?" Rory asked. "That seems like a missed opportunity."

"No, and he didn't learn anything, either," Adams said, walking up to the outdoor table with her hands in her pockets. "He's still stealing people's ice creams."

"He is not. He's …" Gloria hesitated, and waved vaguely. "He does finance things. I'm a little unclear on the details."

"So am I," Adams said. "I think I have to be, otherwise I really will have to arrest him."

"Wine or beer?" Hugh asked.

She looked at her watch. "It's only three p.m."

"You're on holiday still," he said.

"Coffee?"

"No," Gloria said firmly. "Honestly, Jeanette. It's not a food group."

Adams sighed and sat down, checking the garden, which was pleasingly ramshackle and overgrown. Dandy stood on the roof of one of the sheds, surveying the fields with his dreadlocks rippling rather dramatically in the wind while Midge and Pinto whined for him to come down. She frowned. "Where's Thompson?"

"He left," Rory said. "I think he was bored."

"I think Hugh asked him too many questions about tele-portation," Gloria said, and Adams snorted.

"Yeah, he's funny about that." She looked at the heavy sky,

clouds fat and low. "Why are we out here? It feels like it's going to rain."

"It's not raining yet, though," Rory said, getting up and heading toward the doors of the kitchen, lying open onto the patio. "Got to make the most of it."

"You see?" she said to Gloria. "*Northerners.*"

Gloria smiled at her, a thoughtful, warm smile that both eased something inside Adams and made her even more anxious at the idea of them leaving. What if Velmyr followed them to London? Or someone else did? Thompson had said he'd get some cats he trusted to keep an eye on them, but what could they do? Really?

"I think the north suits you," Gloria said.

"It does not."

"It does," Hugh agreed. "You have some very interesting people around you."

"I'm going to take that as good interesting, not *we need a word* interesting," Rory said, returning from the kitchen with a beer in each hand and setting one in front of her.

Adams narrowed her eyes at him. "What are *you* drinking beer for? You on holiday too?"

"I'm landed gent— *Ugh.* No I'm not. I'm a jobless landowner. I can drink when I want."

"Definitely good interesting," Hugh said. "Rather less worried about you now, to be honest."

"You never had to worry," Adams said.

"Of course we did," Gloria said. "All you did in London was work, and then there was the bridge incident, and then you were just so *evasive* about everything after you moved up here, and didn't want us to visit, and now … well. Now it's all fine."

Adams stared at her. "You were abducted by *a faery.*"

"A fae," Rory pointed out, and winced when she raised her eyebrows at him. "Sorry, not the point."

"Yes, and it all makes sense now," Hugh said. "Plus it's not like you're dealing with it alone." He looked around vaguely. "I would still like to see your invisible dog, though."

"I rather think that's not the point of an *invisible* dog, dear," Gloria pointed out.

"But it's fascinating. I patted him earlier, and he feels like a sheep. Leaner, of course, so if I had to guess, something like a Komondor?" He looked expectantly at Adams, and she took a deep breath.

They hadn't talked about it, not really. The days after the showdown on the fell they'd just sort of … walked around the subject, and Adams had been too busy trying to figure out how to get rid of the portal under the stairs, and fielding calls from Maud, and getting amulets from Ash & Yew, and convincing Fergus to go back to York, and dealing with large farmers turning up with eggs and offers to take Gloria (and Hugh, although that was rather an afterthought) on outings three times a day. It had been fraught and strange and uncomfortable, and they simply hadn't *talked.*

So now she said, "You're taking the whole fae thing very calmly."

"You have to accept what's in front of you," Hugh said.

"Faeries? Invisible dogs? Talking cats?"

"The cat was a surprise," he admitted.

"Not really," Gloria said. "They always look like they're up to something."

Hugh nodded. "And the invisible dog's a relief, really. Explains all the missing toast and so on."

Adams looked at her beer and took a swig. "Did you know anything about it before? I mean … Mum, your charms and stuff …"

She waved vaguely. "They're superstition, dear. My mum made them, and my gran, and we've just always done it. Now

I think maybe it was rooted in some truth, but I don't know anything else about it."

"And other than your great-aunt, who was convinced she had pixies in the pantry, I've never run into such things," Hugh said. "And honestly, I think her pantry pixies had quite a bit to do with the sherry that was in there, too."

"But you knew not to eat or drink anything in Faery," Adams pointed out.

"Everyone knows *that,*" Gloria said. "It's in all the stories."

"But the stories aren't real! How … you're not making any sense." She scowled at them both. "You can't just be okay with this."

"Of course stories are real," Hugh said. "Not all of them, of course, but there's always *some* truth in the good ones, in the feeling if not in the facts. And when you find yourself in the middle of one, well. You simply have to accept it and carry on." He raised his eyebrows at her. "I didn't see *you* sobbing under a blanket shouting *It's not real!* You just stepped up and commanded a Roman ghost army like it was nothing."

"Yes, but …" She gave up. "It was really dangerous. You could've been stuck there forever." She wanted to add, *and it would've been all my fault,* but that felt childish and needy. She didn't need their reassurance. Just their understanding that this wasn't some holiday jaunt.

"But we weren't," Gloria said. "Really, Jeanette. This isn't like you. Stop *fussing.*"

Adams frowned at her. "I'm not *fussing.*"

"You are," Hugh said.

She looked at Rory. "Tell them. Tell them how serious this is."

He plucked at his beer label. "I think they know."

"And we shall go home, and wear our amulets, and carry

on," Gloria said. "We could be hit by a bus on the way just as easily as stolen off to Faery."

"Much more likely, really," Hugh said cheerfully.

"Thanks for that," Adams said. "I feel so much better."

Gloria patted her arm. "The point is you can't protect us all the time. Also it's very annoying." She got up. "I'm getting another wine, and some nibbles, and then we'll sit here and enjoy our last evening together."

"But—"

"*Jeanette.*"

She sighed. "Yes, Mum."

🦆

ADAMS WOKE TO A SILENT HOUSE, feeling the weight of dread before she even had her eyes open properly. No creaks in the old walls. No sound of her dad snoring in the room next door. She slipped one hand over the side of the bed to find the staff, closing her fingers over the reassuring heft of it, then grabbed her keys from the bedside table, the duck dangling between her fingers as she rolled to her feet and put her back to the wall. The déjà vu was almost suffocating, and she found herself wanting to scream into the night, *enough! Stop it! We're done!*

But she didn't. She checked the room, large and unfamiliar, the wallpaper peeling in places and the sash window letting in a whisper of damp night air where it didn't meet the sill properly. Rory had given her parents his room, since he said it was the only one he could be reasonably sure the ceiling wouldn't fall in on, and Adams was in the room next door. She pulled on her trainers then went to check on them, hearing their even breathing from the threshold. They were still there, even if Dandy had once again vanished, and

Thompson had declined to come back. She headed for the stairs.

They creaked on the way down, but she didn't waste time trying to find the quietest route. Rory was asleep on the sofa in the living room, but the house was big enough he was unlikely to hear her. Also so big that she wasn't going to check it all. Instead, she slipped through the kitchen and let herself out onto the patio, the staff tight in one hand and a slow rage curdling in her belly. If this was Velmyr again she was going to follow through on her threat about the duck.

Dandy stood on the edge of the patio, golden retriever sized. It was raining, a soft drizzle that rendered the night misty and soft-focused, as if seen through a dirty lens, and she could see the droplets beading on his dreadlocks. There were no outside lights on, no streetlights anywhere near, and the only illumination came from the dim outline of the moon, swelling toward full behind the clouds. *Three nights,* Adams thought suddenly. The solstice was tonight, then. She didn't know if that was relevant or not.

She went to join Dandy, placing a hand on his head. He looked up at her, red eyes glittering, then back at the garden. Beyond it would be the fields rolling downhill, green and lush and flourishing in the damp, but she couldn't see that far through the haze of drizzle. The rain was gentle and chilled on her bare arms, and a moment later Thompson padded up to join them, his ears back against the damp. He didn't speak, just sat down on the opposite side of her to Dandy, and she wondered if she was dreaming. She didn't think so. They waited.

It wasn't the fae that turned up. It was the army, and they didn't *arrive,* exactly. They didn't march up the field, or around the side of the house. One moment all was over-grown flowerbeds and the indistinct shapes of old walls, then the cloud simply seemed to bloom into shapes that became soldiers, lined up and silent, staring at the house. She tightened her hand on the staff, and watched the commander step forward. They stared at each other for a long time, neither of them saying anything, then he reached into the folds of his cloak and took something out, presenting it to her with both hands, his head bowed slightly. She looked at it, then nodded.

"Thank you," she said, the words falling heavy into the silence.

It was Velmyr's crown, thin and delicate and intricate, made of some strange metal that felt chilled when she took it from the ghost. He stepped back, stared at Dandy for a long moment, then said something to her.

"Okay," she said, since she wasn't sure what else to say, and she wasn't about to wake her dad to translate.

He smiled suddenly, that warm and oddly disarming smile that crinkled the corners of his dark eyes, touched a hand to his heart then his forehead, and stepped back. The soft rain coalesced into mist around the troop, and when it lifted there was nothing left but the empty garden. Adams stood there for a long time, with the staff in one hand and the crown in the other, until the cat said, "Cool. You've got a ghost army now."

She looked at him. "Really?"

"Well, they didn't bring you Venal Dampsquib's crown for nothing. That's as good as his head. No need to worry about him coming after any of you now."

"Oh." She looked at it. "That's good."

"Yes. And considering his whole kitchen sink approach to recruitment, he was just working with whatever he could. I doubt there's some mass fae movement against you. Happy now?"

Adams thought about it. Velmyr was gone. She still had no idea why he'd wanted the book, or who he might've been working with, or who had set the IOPC on her. But her parents were as safe as they could be, and she was going to make sure they still wore the amulets, Velmyr's crown or not. Thompson and Chloe had de-hexed her house. And on top of that, she'd discovered a new use for her very big stick. She still felt faintly adrift, and supposed she'd been hoping at some level that her parents *had* known about Folk, that there was an answer, some lineage or family tree to explain what the hell was happening, that maybe she came from a long line of witches or magicians and someone had just neglected to tell her, but it was just her.

It was still just her.

Well, and the dandy, the cat, a Fergus, and humans of varying degrees of usefulness.

She tapped the staff lightly on the patio, listening to it echo. Her dad was right. She just had to accept what was in front of her, and that was the fact she was herself. She wasn't magic. She was police, and she was human, and there was no bloody way she was letting any faeries or fae or anyone else mess up her patch.

She had a duck, a dandy, and a very big stick, and she was going to damn well use them.

"Hello?" Thompson said. "I'm getting rain in my ears."

"The horror," she said, but turned and walked back inside, still flanked by the cat and the dandy, and behind her the garden shivered with rain and silence and secrets, and ghost armies flooded across the wild, untamed fells, and blind dogs walked the hills in search of the lost, and old magic shivered in the veins of the land.

And upstairs her parents slept on undisturbed, and Rory was already in the kitchen with the kettle on, his hair rumpled with sleep, Midge and Pinto looking as half-awake as he did as he slid a mug of coffee to her, unquestioning. Adams gave Dandy a biscuit, and opened some mackerel for the cat, and argued with him when he complained about it being in oil, while the warm old walls of the crumbling house held them in a gentle sort of safety, even with the drafts and leaks and gaps in the walls.

And that was enough. Because such small things are the threads that bind the world.

THANK YOU

Lovely people, as ever, thank you so much for joining me for a slightly (Fae-ly?) frantic romp around the Dales. I hope your feet are still dry and your Yorkie and caffeine supplies have held out, and that you're eyeing any mushrooms with great caution, just in case …

Adams certainly will be, but we'll have to wait until 2026 to see if she manages to fend off any rogue sheepdogs (and if her mum manages to fend off besotted young farmers). I can't wait to share the next story with you, lovely people. I appreciate your being here so very much.

In the meantime, though, if you did enjoy this book, I'd very much appreciate you taking the time to pop a review up at your favourite retailer or on Goodreads (or both, if you're feeling particularly generous).

Reviews are better than Faery cakes (much better, actually) to writers. They make us all giddy and excited and inclined to dance on desolate hilltops in the moonlight—wait, no.

That's witches.

Eh. Same thing. *Anyhow,* reviews tickle the retailer's algorithms, and encourage them to show our books to more readers. And more readers mean I get to write more stories, so, yes. They're basically magic, and if you fancy doing one, I would appreciate it very much. :)

And that is all from me. Thank you again so much for reading, lovely people. If you'd like to send me a copy of your review, theories on what exactly *did* happen to Rory's mum, or anything else, drop me a message at <u>kim@kmwatt.com.</u> I'd love to hear from you!

Until next time,

Read on!

Kim

A QUIET NIGHT OUT

It really shouldn't be too much to ask for ...

Collins just wants a quiet night out at the monthly cheese and wine club. An evening of tasting and savouring and civilised conversation, none of which involve Fae or Folk or talking bloody cats.

That was the idea, anyway.

But life in Skipton since Adams arrived has hardly been calm, let alone predictable.

So he really shouldn't have been that surprised when someone mentioned aliens ...

Grab your posh shoes – we're out on the town in this free short story download!

Scan above to grab your free story, or use the link below:
https://readerlinks.com/l/5025951

*The blood moon rises, and in the wilds of the Dales, some-
thing is coming ...*

DI Adams has faced down Folk, fae, and feral geese, but
waking in a ditch on the Yorkshire moors, unarmed and

uncaffeinated, is a new low. Worse still, her duck is missing – and so is Dandy.

Gingerbread villages, Yorkshire alligators, and haunted, statue-riddled woods would be challenge enough. But as the moon rises, the hunt rides out, and behind it something ancient stirs ...

Get Adams' next adventure now!

ACKNOWLEDGMENTS

As Adams is ever so slowly realising, some things we just can't do alone. Or maybe we *could*, but it'd be highly inadvisable and very likely to result in cross-dimensional battles, infuriated cats, and the disapproval of our peers (who may or may not include the infuriated cat).

Luckily, I am ahead of her in this. I realised a long time ago that I cannot do all the things, and many people are much better than me at the things. So this is my very small thank you to all the wonderful people who have done very large things for me. If I have missed you here, know that a) I can only fit so many pages in the book; and b) I love you and appreciate you anyway.

Firstly, to my amazing beta readers, who set me back on the story path when I wander off it into the boggy marsh of my own imagination, and also provide excellent insight into things such as Yorkshire colloquialisms and appropriate naming conventions. My stories would not be half as good without your input, support, and advice.

To my *amazing* Ko-fi members, who remind me again and again just how wonderful people can be. Thank you for your unfaltering support, patience, and good humour. You make me want to write *all* the stories.

To the lovely people of The Toot Hansell Auxiliary, who prove that social media does not have to be a swamp of horror, but can instead be an oasis of kindness. Thank you for being so perfectly, wonderfully, yourselves.

To Lynda, the least scary editor (TM), who is also a

wonderful friend, and the best sort of person to share grammar jokes with. As always, all good grammar praise goes to her, while all mistakes are mine. Find her at <u>www.easyreaderediting.com</u> for fantastic blogs on editing, grammar, and other writer-y stuff.

To my lovely friends, online and off, who might read my stuff and might not, but are always in my corner. I don't know how I got so lucky as to know you all.

And finally in the list, but never in my thoughts, thank *you*, lovely reader. Thank you for reading, for believing, for diving into these strange tales over and over again. Without you there would be no stories, and therefore slightly less magic in the world. You are amazing, and I hope we can keep sharing worlds for a long time yet.

Until next time,

Kim x

ABOUT THE AUTHOR

Hello, lovely person. I'm Kim, and in addition to the DI Adams tales I also write other funny, magical books that offer a little escape from the serious stuff in the world and hopefully leave you a wee bit happier than you were when you started. Because happiness, like friendship, matters.

I write about baking-obsessed reapers setting up baby ghoul petting cafes, and ladies of a certain age joining the Apocalypse on their Vespas. I write about friendship, and loyalty, and lifting each other up, and the importance of tea and cake.

But mostly I write about how wonderful people (of all species) can really be.

If you'd like to find out the latest on new books, learn about giveaways, discover extra reading, and more, jump on over to www.kmwatt.com and check everything out there, or join me on the membership site for monthly short stories and weekly updates.

Read on!

amazon.com/Kim-M-Watt/e/B07JMHRBMC
goodreads.com/kimmwatt
bookbub.com/authors/kim-m-watt
facebook.com/KimMWatt
instagram.com/kimmwatt
youtube.com/@KimMWatt-yd1qb

The Beaufort Scales Series (cozy mysteries with dragons)

"The addition of covert dragons to a cozy mystery is perfect … and the dragons are as quirky and entertaining as the rest of the slightly eccentric residents of Toot Hansell."

– Goodreads reviewer

The Gobbelino London, PI series

"This series is a wonderful combination of humor and suspense that won't let you stop until you've finished the book. Fair warning, don't plan on doing anything else until you're done …"

– Goodreads reviewer

The DI Adams Mysteries

"… will grip you within its story and not let go so be prepared going in with snacks and caffeine because you won't want to put it down."

– Goodreads reviewer

The Hollowbeck Paranormal Cozy Mysteries
(With Amelia Ash)

"It's a no-brainer to recommend this one to anyone who enjoys cozies. Or laughing. Or paranormal stuff. Or sarcastic wit. Or great writing in any form."

– Amazon reviewer

Short Story Collections

Oddly Enough: Tales of the Unordinary, Volume One

"The stories are quirky, charming, hilarious, and some are all of the above without a dud amongst the bunch …"

– Goodreads reviewer

Need more stories?

Join the membership site for monthly, member-exclusive short stories, behind-the scenes content, early access to ebooks, and more!

Free stories!

The Cat Did It

Of course the cat did it. Sneaky, snarky, and up to no good – that's the cats in this feline collection, which you can grab free by signing up to the newsletter. Just remember – if the cat winks, always wink back …

The Tales of Beaufort Scales

Modern dragons are a little different these days. There's the barbecue fixation, for starters … You'll get these tales free once you've signed up for the newsletter!